Kingdom of the Dead

Thank you for being my reader! Without you books are nothing!

Pavel Kornev

An NPC's Path

Book Two

Magic Dome Books

Kingdom of the Dead
An NPC's Path, Book Two
Copyright © Pavel Kornev 2018
Cover Art © Vladimir Manyukhin 2018
English Translation Copyright ©
Irene and Neil P. Woodhead
Published by Magic Dome Books, 2018
All Rights Reserved
ISBN: 978-80-7619-001-6

This book is entirely a work of fiction.
Any correlation with real people or events is coincidental.

Also by Pavel Kornev:

An NPC's Path LitRPG series:

The Dead Rogue
Kingdom of the Dead
Deadman's Retinue
The Guardian of the Dead
The Nemesis of the Living

The Sublime Electricity steampunk series:

The Illustrious
The Heartless
The Fallen
The Dormant

Table of Contents:

Chapter One. The Doldrums.. 125
Chapter Two. The Raid of the Dead.......................... 252
Chapter Three. A Deadman in a Strange Land........ 345
Chapter Four. The Dead Burglar.............................. 427
Chapter Five. The Kingdom of the Dead.................. 494
Epilogue..

Chapter One
The Doldrums

1.

THE TOWER OF DARKNESS was impressive. Overpowering, even.

No amount of advertising could impart the sheer splendor and magnitude of that pitch-black obelisk which towered over the bay. In reality, it looked much more-

In reality?

I cussed and shuddered.

In reality! Dammit! I already considered the

✝ An NPC's Path: Book Two ✝

game a reality! Having said that... that's how it was for me now, wasn't it?

I couldn't press the logout button. I had no hope of ever waking up in my virtual reality capsule . My character's dead body had already become part of the local scenery. It had ensnared me like the Devil's own net and would keep me so until the day I was reborn.

Reborn in the game, that is. Or until I was dead in real life. There was no other way. Sad, but that's how it was.

As soon as I realized it, I felt free from the Tower's suppressive illusion. I didn't feel like looking at it anymore. I even wanted to go back to my cabin. Still, I forced myself to stay on deck. Dammit! I'd been striving to get to the capital now for too long to cower in a dark corner and miss all the interesting bits.

The barge glided down the Azure river whose far banks disappeared into the morning mist. Small islets emerged out of the milky fog that hovered over the water. The river's navigational lights flickered everywhere I looked.

Soon the river bed began to split into a multitude of narrow gullies. The current grew faster. The orc crew lined the decks with long

Kingdom of the Dead

poles in their hands, preparing to guide the boat around any eventual obstacles.

On top of the mast, my undead pet spread his wings and filled the air with a thunderous *Craah!*

Wretched bird! The problem was, the game didn't recognize me as a bona fide player, and therefore I couldn't control my own pet. The bastard did what he wanted.

The orcs raised their heads, scowling at the bird. Still, none of them wanted to be the one to climb the mast. They'd already known from experience that they wouldn't be able to shoo him away for too long.

In any case, soon they had more important things to do: the helmsman couldn't control the current, leaving the other crew members to fend the boat off from the numerous jetties and breakwaters.

According to the latest figures, there were up to half a million players in the city at any given time. Even the sky-high local prices couldn't scare them off. The capital of the dark world had been prudently built on a plethora of small islands which helped to somewhat contain its restless inhabitants. There were even rumors

✝ An NPC's Path: Book Two ✝

circulating about banning entry to the city to all new players below level 25. But this was still in the preparatory stage.

I caught a glimpse of the stone embankments peeking out of the mist. Then the barge surged through into the open. The wind blew away the murky fog. The rising sun's rays glittered on the rippling waters.

Immediately my Perception dropped. I pulled the hood down.

A dark shadow fell from behind me. I turned round. The side of an impossibly high galleon loomed over us. It overtook our boat in seconds as it headed out into the open sea, the players on its upper deck not even trying to conceal their contempt for us.

The orcs hurried to raise the sail which immediately caught the wind, pushing the barge into port. The enormous back of some sea monster flitted amid the waves, then disappeared into the depths.

I loosened my white-knuckled grip on the rail. Some monster that was! What if it had swallowed us whole?

Still, I forgot about the leviathan as soon as I glimpsed a giant golden dragon take off from

† Kingdom of the Dead †

one of the islands. Two gryphons trailed in his wake, blindingly bright sunrays reflecting from their riders' polished armor. And to top it all, a three-masted flying ship appeared from behind the Tower of Darkness.

I picked up my dropped jaw from the floor and shrugged. This was all virtual. It was only a game.

Still, these attempts at self-persuasion didn't help me much. The capital of the Dark Side seemed so boundless that my mind refused to contemplate it. Where was I supposed to go? How? And what for? This was a huge world which didn't give a damn about some deadman's problems.

Stubbornly I ground my teeth. I didn't care! This was no different from any other time I'd had to follow a new map. It always felt incomprehensible. I knew that I'd work it out, given time. I might not even have to, provided Isabella hadn't wasted her time and had managed to approach the right people.

A cold shiver ran down my spine. I had too much at stake to wager all my hopes on a casual acquaintance. I didn't even know how she was going to react to my arrival after such a

✟ An NPC's Path: Book Two ✟

prolonged absence. The priestess had never been known for her patience.

I forced myself to dispel any doubt. The level gap between us wasn't that big anymore. She could no longer smoke me with a single blow from her staff these days.

I chuckled. This time I'd be able to make myself heard. I'd make her see things my way. Everything would be just fine.

I had no doubt I'd see Isabella in the very near future. We were bound by a quest, after all. We could track each other's position on the map. And if her marker was to be believed, she was already waiting for me on the pier. Perfect opportunity to talk things over.

THE PORT TURNED OUT to be absolutely enormous. It was bigger than the entire island that housed Stone Harbor. On one side, it was lined with deep-water quays for sea-going ships; on the other, with jetties for smaller river craft. The harbor was absolutely packed but miraculously, there were no collisions between any of the boats.

Miraculously? Oh no. That was navigational magic at work. The orc helmsman

✝ Kingdom of the Dead ✝

stared almost unblinkingly at the ghostly sorcerous sphere that was his pilot.

Gradually, other passengers came up on deck. There weren't very many of them, though. Few players had managed to coincide their login with their arrival in the capital. They had no need to: the moment the ship moored, their respective respawn points were transferred automatically to the vicinity of one of the local Towers of Power. There was no shortage of them in the capital. Minor places of power were located on every even remotely important island.

Neo had come up on deck, too, and frozen open-mouthed. The other players cast sideways glances at our white monastic habits embroidered with silver phoenixes. Although they knew better than to ask questions, their attention made me cringe.

You had to face it: arriving at the Tower of Darkness wearing the robes of a god of Light wasn't a very good idea. What was the point of going Incognito if every Tom, Dick and Harry regarded me as potential quarry? The sooner I discarded those robes, the better.

A few larger boats which resembled Chinese junks sailed past. Our helmsman let

✝ An NPC's Path: Book Two ✝

them through, then steered our barge into the farthest corner of the port toward a lopsided jetty which was occasionally washed by the wake of other vessels.

Here, the picturesque buildings with their stained-glass windows gave way to squat warehouses, the bustle of the port replaced by silence in its deserted narrow lanes.

Not far from where we were about to moor, some fishing boats were bobbing on the waves. My Night Hunter's refined sense of smell made me cringe from the sharp stench of rotting fish.

The side of our boat collided softly with the wooden trestles of the jetty. I felt a slight jolt. As soon as the sailors had laid down the gangplanks, the fanged captain began screaming at the top of his voice,

"Everyone off! Quick! Move it!"

The passengers hurried across the unstable gangplanks onto the jetty. A loud group of stevedores moved toward the barge past them, adding to the unruly crowd of players who'd already bought tickets for the return voyage.

I struggled out of the heaving mass of people and stood in the middle of the fishscale-covered jetty. I rearranged the swords behind my

🗡 Kingdom of the Dead 🗡

back and looked around, searching for Isabella.

The Elven girl was waiting by the nearest warehouse. Much to my surprise, this time she was clad in a modest cloak, long and shapeless, instead of her usual eye-catching combat armor.

Neo tugged my sleeve, "Auntie Bella!"

"Please keep your voice down," I said as I headed toward her. She'd already stood up straight, staring at us in disbelief.

In disbelief? — you could say that! Her eyes had very nearly popped out of her head!

"What the hell?" she cussed the moment we approached. "What have you done to the boy, Kitten?"

I shrugged. "It just happened."

"It just happened?" she hissed, furious. "*Just happened?*"

Neo hurried to hide behind my back.

"Yeah," I said.

"You can't be left alone for one minute!" she scowled. "Where have you been? Why didn't you reply to my messages?"

"Eh," I faltered. "How about I tell you everything as we get going? Okay?"

She shook her head. The teeth of the skull topping her staff started to chatter. "I don't think

✝ An NPC's Path: Book Two ✝

so! Come on then, out with it!"

A few heads turned to the sounds of our exchange. I tapped a finger on the silver phoenix on my white-robed chest,

"I'm afraid our clothes aren't the best choice here. We'll have to change first."

Isabella sized me up with her glare — but luckily, she must have decided to leave it be for the time being. She pointed at a dark passage between the two windowless walls of the adjacent warehouses. "Screw you, Kitten. We'll see about that... *later*..." she'd managed to inject a lot of meaning into the last word.

I shrugged and led them off the jetty. A long desperate *Craah!* followed in my wake as the undead black phoenix left the boat's mast and took to the sky. His tatty wingbeats didn't strike one as particularly graceful but they kept him aloft. When a curious seagull got too close to him, he gave it an almighty whack with his beak, sending it tumbling straight into the water.

"Get a move on!" Isabella snapped. "Where on earth did you get those stupid clothes from? What happened to the boy? No, belay that! Start from the beginning! Why didn't you use the portal?"

Kingdom of the Dead

"It's a long and sad story…"

Isabella turned round to me, scowling. "You'd better not test my patience, Kitten!"

I replied with an equally malicious smile. Not that she could see it behind my mask.

"Okay," I heaved a sigh, unwilling to strain our relationship any further. "I was late because some bad dude had started hassling me at the worst possible moment. And by the time I'd sorted him out, the portal had already closed."

'But why didn't you reply to my messages?" she demanded, fuming.

"My PM box is glitchy," I lied. "I can read messages but I can't reply to them."

"Very useful!"

"Listen, why should I lie to you? You still have the shard of the Sphere of Souls!"

This last argument calmed her down a bit. "Okay," she grumbled. "So what have you been up to all this time?"

I didn't get the time to reply. The passage between the two walls had led us out onto a wide square so busy with players that our ears rang with all the clamor.

"Cheap power leveling services!" shouted a knight in full armor with a huge halberd slung

☦ An NPC's Path: Book Two ☦

behind his back. "I can rush you from level 25 to 50 in a week!"

"Join us for a raid on the Lights!" one of Isabella's Elven compatriots screamed, theatrically brandishing his longbow. "PM me for details!"

"An island quest!" a blue-skinned pirate with golden earrings hollered. "The Treasure of the Corsair King! Piles of gold just for the taking!"

"WTS full Amber Cross set!"

"A Gray Mountains raid! Dwarven mithril!"

"The sword of the Star Destroyer! Half-price! I need money urgently!"

"Strength runes to order!"

I felt lost in all the cacophony around me. Isabella tugged on my hand, forcing me out of the way of a demonologist who towered above the crowd, pale like death itself. A hell hound on a leash trotted subserviently behind him, its smooth coat oozing black infernal flames.

"Portals to Infernal planes, I'll send you and bring you back, but I don't lay claim to any loot," he murmured occasionally under his breath.

Strangely enough, he seemed to be one of the most popular, constantly hassled by other players who asked him about his fee.

🗡 Kingdom of the Dead 🗡

Humans and elves made up the majority of the crowd but there were enough dwarves and orcs amongst them too. Occasionally my eye chanced on some truly strange creatures. And as for armor and weapons, the choice was mind-boggling. My flamberge sword paled into insignificance next to them.

As we skirted the outside of the crowd, Isabella warned me, "Keep your eyes peeled. The local pickpockets go after noobs like you."

Indeed, the place seemed perfect for thieves of all kinds. Most new players arrived in the capital by sea. Many of them didn't have enough patience to even make it to the shops, spending all their hard-earned cash right here in this impromptu junk market. Some never even got the chance to spend anything.

I stopped gawking around and hurried to check my inventory. The wretched skull was still there. Big sigh of relief.

Isabella swung round to me again. "You Kitten, and you… whatever you are… move your backsides!"

We followed her into a side lane and soon left the noise and clamor of the crowd behind. Isabella led us via some dark deserted alleys until

✝ An NPC's Path: Book Two ✝

finally we rejoined the motley stream of players. After a short while, we found ourselves on the square behind the port's main building.

"Wow," Neo whispered, unable to conceal his delight.

I too slowed the pace, studying the wide square in front of me. Beyond it flowed a canal, with a temple towering on its opposite bank.

Its dome topped with a spire, the majestic building seemed to grow straight out of the water which somehow added to its mystery and charm. A flying carpet floated from behind it. I shook my head, forcing my mind to reject the illusion.

This was only a game. Just a bunch of pixels evoking an image in my brain. Virtual reality made all kinds of things possible.

"Come on, Kitten, move it!" Isabella called.

I followed after her, pulling Neo by the hand. He looked just like any other provincial boy would, stunned by big city life.

The realization of this made me cringe. This boy too was supposed to be a bunch of pixels. A combination of ones and zeroes. Just part of a program code.

I caught up with Isabella. "Where're we going?"

Kingdom of the Dead

"Somewhere away from here," the Elven priestess replied. "You two with your white robes might just as well have targets on your backs."

You couldn't argue with this. I kept receiving new messages about others' interested stares. All sorts of unpleasant whispers followed in our wake. I pretended I didn't hear anything even though some of them made me wish I could sort out some of the jokers with my flamberge.

I'd have loved to but I couldn't. The burly city guards in their black armor wouldn't hesitate to chop any potential troublemaker to pieces. If I made the first move, they'd immediately send me to meet my Maker. And even if they weren't strong enough, I'm sure the city wizards would give them a helping hand. Other players wouldn't just stand aside looking on, either. Anyone would be eager to earn some XP and boost their Reputation by smoking a couple of outcasts.

"Should we hire a gondola?" I suggested as Isabella ignored the rentals wharf and headed for the bridge.

She snorted. "Is your name Rockefeller or something? You don't even know their rates!"

I cussed under my breath.

Immediately an agonizing pain pierced the

✝ An NPC's Path: Book Two ✝

base of my skull. It felt as if I'd been pierced with a red-hot poker.

Or had I been?

I swung round just in time to see my undead phoenix drop into the canal, struck by an arrow. My pet!

A Drow archer brandished his bow victoriously as he issued a long piercing whistle. A few passersby applauded his skill.

A crimson haze filled my eyes.

Firstly, it hurt. Dammit! I couldn't remember the last time I'd experienced pain in the game. Secondly, it had been my pet! Ugly and dead, but mine nevertheless!

The pain just wouldn't subside. A system message appeared at the very edge of my vision, informing me of the attack. The city guards had ignored the shooting entirely. Their protection didn't extend to covering the dead.

Bunch of lowlifes.

A wave of fury surged over me. Still, what remained of my common sense made me pause before launching an all-out attack. Unfortunately for him, the Drow was only level 28. And he was alone.

"Hold this for a moment, Neo," I handed

Kingdom of the Dead

him the black orcish longsword and stealthed up.

"John!" Isabella shrieked. "What do you think you're doing?"

I didn't even listen. The Drow had already slung his longbow behind his back and sashayed toward the rentals wharf, apparently unable to even conceive that someone might try to attack him in full view of the city guards and other players.

So he'd downed a bird, big deal.

The archer appeared slim and lanky. He definitely had good agility numbers. But as for his constitution, he'd most certainly given it a miss. I had every chance of winning in a couple of powerful blows — but had I missed, it could turn into a painful and protracted fight.

Unwilling to drag it out, I attacked him with a well-practiced combo. Downward, from left to right, then sideways!

Scythe of Death combo!

The undulating blade of my flamberge hacked into his right shoulder, slicing through his fine chainmail. It went right through his ribcage with a surprising ease, then exited his left

✝ An NPC's Path: Book Two ✝

flank, sparking on the cobblestones. The momentum swung me round; I managed to keep my balance at the right moment without being dumped on my backside.

I raised my sword again but stopped in full swing. There was no need for another attack.

Player Lucas III is killed!
Experience: +1496 [25 674/28 300]; +1496 [25 718/28 300]
Undead, the level is raised! Rogue, the level is increased!

My single blow had cleft him in two, leaving me standing over his dead body at the center of the busy square covered in blood from head to toe. My own blood was boiling with adrenaline.

And not just mine. The crowd around me bristled with cold steel. Still, seeing as the PK mark never appeared over my head, gradually the players began to calm down.

"Have you got a vendetta going on, you two?" a bearded sorcerer asked me as he reluctantly deactivated a combat spell already flickering between his fingertips.

"Yeah, sort of," I mumbled, stepping back

🗡 Kingdom of the Dead 🗡

from the pool of blood spreading over the cobblestones. Then I swung round and hurried toward the bridge. The other players gave me a wide berth. Now they knew better than to stop me, especially because the city guards had completely ignored the murder.

"Are you freakin' mad?" Isabella hissed.

I shrugged. My headache had finally subsided; the flashing system message in the corner of my eye had now disappeared.

"Listen, Roger," Isabella addressed the skull topping her staff, "don't you think our Kitten is completely off his trolley?"

"Give it a break," I said, retrieving the black sword from Neo. "He killed my pet bird. I just repaid him in kind."

She cussed and dragged me into some dark side alley. "Wait for me here," she said. "If you so much as move, I'll lop your legs off!"

I wanted to tell her where to stuff it but reconsidered just in time. It was pointless trying to aggravate the situation. Instead, I began wiping the Drow blood off my mask and gloves. There was no way I could get it off my white robes.

"Poor bird," Neo sighed. "He was so

✝ An NPC's Path: Book Two ✝

funny..."

I shrugged. I hadn't felt attached to the undead phoenix in the slightest. The only thing he ever did was squawk. He'd only been good at making noise. Completely uncontrollable. And this way, I'd avenged him and had even managed to level up a bit in the process. I was dying to find out what new kind of undead went after a Night Hunter.

Still, I didn't have the time to check my stats before Isabella arrived.

"Get changed," she ordered, hurling a shapeless gray cloak at me.

The boy got an identical one in a smaller size. Still, I was reluctant to discard my white robes. I threw them into my inventory and donned the cloak. "Where to now?"

"To hell," she snapped.

"You seem to be a bit jumpy today," I said. "Is it because your negotiations about the fragment of the Sphere of Souls didn't go through, or what is it?"

"It's got nothing to do with that! Whatever possessed you to pick a fight in full view of everyone? And what if the Drow had dodged your first blow? You'd be still dancing with him now!"

† Kingdom of the Dead †

"I'd love to have seen him dodge it," I smirked as we walked out into the street. "I stabbed him in the back, didn't I? Plus I was stealthed."

"Don't speak too soon! There're amulets for that! And plenty of various Agility skills you don't even know about. Oh dammit! I'd completely forgotten who I was talking to!"

She strode along the street. I hurried after her. "So what about the Sphere?"

"We've reached a preliminary agreement but I decided not to meet the customer without you," she replied, then hurried to add before I could ask her any more questions, "No! Your story first!"

I heaved a doomed sigh.

2.

THE INN WHERE Isabella had taken us was located on the third or fourth island from the port. There was no direct route there. Better-off players would go by boat while all the others had to amble down damp lanes too narrow for two carriages to pass each other. And whenever I'd

✝ An NPC's Path: Book Two ✝

managed to find a shortcut through winding side alleys, I had to elbow my way through the crowd of like-minded players.

We crossed a bridge, then another and yet another, before we finally could take a ferry across a wide canal. When at last we turned back to the embankment, I attempted to protest,

"Wait up! Why are you going around in circles? Couldn't we take a more direct road?"

She stopped and shook her head. "This is Hellspawn Island, private property of the clan."

"Oh really?" I whistled, looking up at a tower dominating the houses, its peaked roof topped with the statue of a dark angel. "The whole island? They must be rolling in it!"

"Shut up and move it!"

THE OLD ARCHER INN occupied the corner building of a busy intersection. We took the back door and climbed the stairs to the third floor. The room wasn't too spacious but it was a double. In the real world, it would have slept at least five people. But here, it was only the means of getting a permanent resurrection point. That worked out cheaper and more convenient than constantly reentering the game next to one of the Towers of

🗡 Kingdom of the Dead 🗡

Power.

Do you want to make this rented accommodation your new login location?

I'd have loved to, but unfortunately, that option was still blocked for me.

"Neo, go get some shut-eye," Isabella motioned the boy toward the other room. When he was gone, she swung round glaring at me. "What's wrong with you, Kitten?"

I deactivated Incognito, removed my mask and flashed her a toothy smile. "Why, what's wrong with me?"

"Oh," she drawled. "My Kitten has turned into a scruffy junk yard cat! My Kitten is a tough nut now!"

"Your *Kitten*," I cringed as I uttered the word, "just wants to get to the Kingdom of the Dead. So what about the Sphere?"

She slumped onto the bed and crossed one leg over the other, making sure one of her shapely thighs was in full view. "Tell me what happened to you two. I want to know everything."

'What's the point? It's a waste of time.'

"Go on!"

✟ An NPC's Path: Book Two ✟

With a shrug, I drew both my swords from behind my back and set them in the corner. I perched myself on the windowsill and looked out into the street. It was already getting dark. The flood of players heading for the port had eased up. They unhurriedly strolled around, gawking at shop signs and checking out various entertainment establishments.

Still, I knew better than to test my Elven friend's patience. I gave her a quick run-down of all my adventures, starting with the necromancer's attack and the defense of Stone Harbor and ending with our restoration of the Temple of the Silver Phoenix.

"So you do have a vendetta," Isabella said pensively as she listened to my story. "That could become a problem."

"That's nothing," I waved her concerns away. "He'll never find me now. I've disabled map tracking."

She shook her head. "Don't be so sure, Kitten. There're plenty of other ways of tracking an enemy."

"Like what?" I asked rather nonchalantly.

She was already standing up. "Don't leave the room. I'm gonna arrange a meeting and come

Kingdom of the Dead

back for you."

"A meeting with whom?" I asked.

The slamming of the closing door was her only reply.

I didn't give a damn. With a shrug, I opened my stats. I really should use this time to distribute the available points. This may be just a game but admittedly I couldn't wait to find out what kind of undead I'd turn into this time.

Unhesitantly I increased both Strength and Perception. But when I was about to invest a skill point into Stealth, I froze open-mouthed.

I didn't just have one point available. Not two, even. I had a whopping twenty-six points!

What was going on?

Could it have been some kind of error?

I decided to check it by increasing Stealth to 15 pt. And just as I was trying to add another one, a new system message flashed up,

Further skill increase will be available after additional training!

Still in disbelief, I increased Dodge to 15. Ignoring a new message, I opened my character profile.

✝ An NPC's Path: Book Two ✝

John Doe, Executioner, Hangman
Undead. Junior Lich. Level: 25./ Human, Rogue. Level: 25
Experience: [25 674/28 300]; [25 718/28 300]

Strength: 28.
Agility: 27.
Constitution: 24.
Intelligence: 5.
Perception: 14.
Life: 1200.
Endurance: 1300.
Internal energy: 475.
Damage: 216—324.
Covert movement: +15.
Dodge: +15.

Critical damage when attacking in stealth mode, backstabbing or attacking a paralyzed target.

Professional skills: "Incognito" (3), "Execution", "Hangman".

Fencer: two-handed weapons (3), weapons in one hand, "Sweeping Strike", "Powerful blow", "Power lunge", "Sudden blow", "Accurate Blow", "Crippling Blow", "Blind Strike", "Rapid Strike".

Creature of the Dark: night sight, penalty for

Kingdom of the Dead

being in sunlight, Lord of the Dead, Almost Alive, Skin of Stone +5.

Neutrality: the undead; subjects of the Lord of the Tower of Decay

Enemies: Order of the Fiery Hand, the Swords of Chaos clan.

Immunity: death magic, poisons, curses, bleeding, sickness, cures and blessings.

Achievements: "Dog Slayer" Grade 3, "Tenacious", "Man of Habit", "Defender of Stone Harbor" Grade 1.

Wait a sec. A Junior Lich?

But a Lich was a dead sorcerer, wasn't it? How could I possibly be a sorcerer with my meager 5 pts. Intellect? And where were my old skills, dammit? Where was my Sprint? And what had happened to my Claws of Darkness?

Suddenly I knew where all the extra skill points had come from. They had been deducted from all the deleted skills.

Bastards! Give them back!

So this latest upgrade of my undead status had only served to bring more disappointment. But what if I was wrong and things weren't as bad as they looked?

✝ An NPC's Path: Book Two ✝

I opened my Magic tab. Pointless. I didn't managed to activate a single spell from the sorcerer's book.

Level-1 spells available to study: 0

Dammit! My penalty to Intellect had left me without any hope of ever using magic. What was the point in making me a Lich, then?

I walked over to a mirror on the wall and stared at my reflection.

Deathly pallid skin clung tightly to my skull. My sunken eyes reflected crimson Infernal flames. Nothing else. The fancy black lines covering my face were now gone, replaced by magic runes and formulas. Admittedly I looked better for it. But as for the rest, it had been a change for the worse.

My teeth were as sharp as before. My nails still resembled claws. But as for my bite, it no longer could syphon my victims' Life and Stamina. Also, I'd lost the ability of stunning an opponent with a single blow. My Night Hunter Sprint was also gone. And what had I gotten in return? A magic which I couldn't even use? Shit!

I perched myself on the windowsill and

Kingdom of the Dead

stared mindlessly out the window. The evening street was bustling with revelers. Many of the players weren't even wearing armor or weapons. They'd come to the world of the Towers of Power intending to have a good time and be merry.

As for me, merry wasn't on the agenda. If the truth were known, I was deep in it.

Having said that, as I continued to level up, theoretically I could level up Intellect to the 10 required pts. I gave it some thought and decided it wasn't a good idea. Magic was all well and good but how was I supposed to know what I'd become at level 60? Did I really want to waste five points only to lose the ability to use magic later? I didn't need that.

In all honesty, my lich didn't stand a chance against real wizards while my level-1 spells were poor protection against a top warrior. The sheer thought was ridiculous.

What a predicament.

I heaved a doomed sigh. I really should stop worrying prematurely. After all, if Isabella managed to secure our participation in the raid on the Kingdom of the Dead, all my leveling mistakes would become irrelevant. And I knew she could do it. You could tell just by looking at

✝ An NPC's Path: Book Two ✝

her she was one pushy lady.

I stopped torturing myself with bouts of regret and concentrated on my professional skills. The memory of how long it had taken me to smoke the immobilized Nest Hunter still smarted. So I increased Execution, bringing my chances of killing a character whose level was equal to mine with one blow to 12%.

But that wasn't all.

Execution II
Your firm hand and sharp eye allow you to strike where your enemy is the most vulnerable!
+4% to your chances of dealing a critical hit
+2% to your chances of dealing a crippling blow

Not bad. Not bad at all. But no more than that.

I breathed a sigh and began studying the Lich's abilities. The Skin of Stone was nothing surprising: all it offered was some additional protection. That wasn't so bad for a newb but didn't sound too serious for a level-50 player. Still, it was better than nothing. It wouldn't make things worse, that's for sure.

Kingdom of the Dead

The Lord of the Dead was also a rather predictable skill which allowed you to control the undead. That sounded quite interesting, the sole problem was that the combined level of the controlled creatures couldn't exceed half of that of the Lich.

However, the last of my new skills — "Almost Alive" — made me scratch my head as I read its description:

"Almost Alive"
You haven't been dead for very long so you haven't yet forgotten what it feels like to be alive. You can fool even the most attentive observer, but remember: the moment the sun rises, its light will render your camouflage useless.

Very interesting. So what did that actually mean? That I didn't need Incognito anymore?

I stood in front of the mirror and activated my new skill.

Immediately my face rounded. I got a bit of color back in my cheeks. My eyes lost their dark fiery glare. That was the extent of it, though, if you didn't count my waning internal energy. Anyone who wished to double-check me could

✞ An NPC's Path: Book Two ✞

still access my profile which still classified me as Undead. But not if I used it in combination with Incognito...

The sight of a mask on their companion's face normally makes people nervous. But this new skill allowed me to look perfectly alive without having to use such blatant disguise.

"Neo?" I called, turning to him. "What do you think?"

The boy yawned sleepily. "You've changed again, Uncle John!" he announced.

I laughed. "You're dead right there!"

"You've changed but you're still the same!"

"What makes you think so?"

"I just feel it."

I frowned. "What is it you can feel?"

The kid faltered in hesitation. "I feel you should be burned at the stake. Sorry, Uncle John."

I snorted, unable to contain my laughter. "That's nice of you!"

I hadn't expected what happened next. Creaking, the wardrobe door opened a crack. I could see darkness swirl amid its empty hangers, blacker and thicker than in the deepest of cellars.

My hand lay on the hilt of my Soul Killer

Kingdom of the Dead

hook. Still, I didn't have to use it. The darkness parted, releasing a bird's scruffy head. My undead phoenix focused his unseeing white gaze on me.

Then he opened his beak. "Craah!"

I cussed in relief. "What a scarecrow!"

The dead phoenix sprang out of the wardrobe and alighted on the cupboard, his powerful talons leaving deep scratches in the polished wood.

"The birdie's back!" Neo exclaimed in excitement.

"That's not a bird. His name is Scarecrow."

The Black Phoenix opened his beak again, preparing to emit another ear-rending squawk. I was getting a bit fed up with it. I threw a protesting hand in the air — and he froze in place.

Lord of the Dead!

I still hadn't sensed any mental connection with my pet. Still, my new skill had somehow kicked in. Being an undead, Scarecrow had fallen under my full control.

"You don't mean it!" I muttered as I forced

✝ An NPC's Path: Book Two ✝

open a creaky window.

The room filled with the noise of the city night. Obeying my order, the undead Phoenix jumped onto the windowsill, emitted another shrill squawk and soared into the air.

Strangely enough, I felt as if I was being pulled into the air after him. The city roofs and the snaking ribbons of the canals flashed through my mental view. My head spun. Exhausted, I collapsed to my knees.

"Uncle John! Are you okay?"

"I'm fine," I said. "Perfectly fine. I'm all right."

I managed to stop myself vomiting. It wasn't that difficult: after all, my stomach had been empty for quite a long time. I dumped myself on the bed and leaned my back against the wall. My first attempt at controlling a flying undead mount had proven not to be too pleasant.

In the meantime, Scarecrow had landed onto a neighboring chimney and had begun sharpening his beak on the blackened firebricks, casting sarcastic glances at me. For some reason, I was absolutely sure I'd be able to bring this cantankerous bird back under my mental control the moment it was necessary. Which in turn

⚔ Kingdom of the Dead ⚔

opened some very interesting avenues...

"Uncle John? I'm hungry!" the boy said.

I looked first at him, then at the door. Reluctantly I scrambled back to my feet. "Come on, then."

I wasn't sure whether I should take the flamberge with me. In the end, I left it in the room because it would have been little use in the narrow corridors of the inn anyway. In case of an attack, I'd be far better off brandishing my bone hook, Soul Killer.

The door key hung on a nail hammered into the doorframe. I took it and walked out first. Neo followed. I locked the door and took the creaky stairs to the bottom floor.

When we'd reached the spacious dining room, empty and badly lit, I was in for another surprise. The innkeeper — a short stocky middle-aged guy who stood there toweling beer mugs — turned out to be a player.

My world was blown apart. Why would anyone pay good money to access virtual reality only to work in a bar, and in such an ungainly body at that?

"Hi," I managed, suppressing my surprise.

"Good evening," the innkeeper replied. He

✝ An NPC's Path: Book Two ✝

noticed Neo and raised a quizzical eyebrow.

"A quest," I explained curtly, as was quickly becoming a habit. "Can you give him something to eat?"

"Not a problem," he chuckled, opening his guest book. "And your names are…"

"We're with Isabella," I offered. "The Dark Elfa."

"That's right. It's full board. Take a seat, please."

I motioned Neo toward one of the tables and stayed by the bar. I was curious to see if my newly-acquired Almost Alive ability could conceal my undead nature.

"Only the boy's eating!" I shouted after him as he disappeared into the kitchen. "I don't need anything!"

He peered out of the kitchen, balancing a loaded tray. "Beer?"

"No, thanks," I replied. "I still have a business meeting to attend."

He gave me a wink. "A business meeting. In the game?"

"Well, it's not as if you're slaying dragons either."

The innkeeper laughed. He set the tray

✟ Kingdom of the Dead ✟

down on the bar and proffered his hand. "Mark."

"John," I replied, prudently keeping my profile closed.

He smiled. "Nice to meet you, John. Get stuck in, boy!"

Neo didn't have to be told twice. He grabbed the tray and carried it to his table.

"I can see you're curious," Mark smiled. "You're probably asking yourself what's in it for me, right?"

I looked over the spacious room with its paneled walls, carved furniture and the cartwheels which served as chandeliers. "Well, it's a nice cozy place."

Mark produced a dusty bottle and filled a shot glass with some acid-green liquid. "Nice joke!" he laughed, then downed the weird drink. He exhaled noisily and added without a trace of merriment, "You're not so far from the truth, you know that? This place is indeed cozy. Not everybody's into raids and stuff. Some of us would rather have a nice meal and a glass of wine without having to suffer from hangovers and high blood pressure afterward. Not to even mention the fact that a night of virtual passion won't end up with a visit to the doctors as it sometimes

An NPC's Path: Book Two

does in the real world. And even if someone slits your throat, well... it's only a game, ain't it?"

I chuckled. It had never occurred to me before that someone might go virtual simply to continue with their boring little lives.

"You'd be surprised how many people come here just to check out our brothels and bars. They're not interested in dragons in the slightest."

"How strange," I murmured. "But still, for you it must be more than just entertainment?"

He nodded and rubbed his nose which was quickly turning red from the drink. "Here, I could finally fulfill my lifelong dream of opening a small drinking establishment. I've invested half of my pension fund into it and I don't regret it one bit. I've already recuperated about 40% of it, so returns are quite decent."

As we spoke, a respectable-looking gentleman in a black cloak and a wide-brimmed hat appeared at the top of the stairs. A long rapier hung from his belt: not a serious weapon really but rather a status item unsuitable for any serious killing.

Mark saluted him. The man nodded, crossed the room and walked outside.

Kingdom of the Dead

"The place is excellent," the innkeeper told me. "Lots of traffic. These days, you just can't buy something like this for a reasonable price."

I allowed myself a quiet chuckle. "It doesn't look as if you have to fend new guests off with a stick."

"Why should I?" he sounded genuinely surprised. "This isn't real life. Money works differently here. Whoever needs a suitable login point for their needs has to rent a room. I pay for the server's capacity and put the difference into my own pocket. It's not my thing to offer strip shows to the public. Don't get me wrong, they do pay very well. But you can go bust in no time, too. The locals have seen everything. Competition is stiff. Each and every one of the local girls is a player. Nobody wants NPCs anymore."

"You don't mean it."

He nodded. "Oh yes I do. So why would I need all the hassle? Everyone should do their own thing."

"Does that mean that all the local establishments have been bought up by players?"

"In large city centers, yes, almost all of them," he assured me. "There're certain quotas, of course. Some places aren't even put up for

✝ An NPC's Path: Book Two ✝

sale. But that's on the Dark side. The Lighties don't approve of private enterprise."

"Why not?"

"There, they concentrate on players' interaction with each other. Things like quests, raids and events. Killing ten orcs, finding fifty golden lotuses, delivering a hundred messages... I'm exaggerating a bit, of course, but I personally find it a bit of a rat race. No opium dens or women of easy virtue for you there. They could lower the age limit to 14 right now if they wanted to and they wouldn't even have to change a thing!"

I flashed him a polite smile, realizing that Mark's unfulfilled real-world dream had also included a grateful listener at the bar. In the course of our conversation, at least ten people had descended into the room and left straight away without saying a word to their innkeeper.

"You want a drink?" he offered again.

"No, thanks. I'll pass."

He refilled his glass and shook his head. "You know, John, these days I'd be too scared to invest so much money into the game."

"Why is that?" I offered the cue he was apparently waiting for.

† Kingdom of the Dead †

He downed his drink and sighed. "Before, I could see how the strategy of this world was working. And I agreed with it. But now something weird is going on. You tell me: how could they have axed the Intuit Project? Eh?"

I'd never heard about it before. I told him as much.

"All these little icons and logos flickering before your eyes," he explained. "I find them so annoying. They only distract you. At some point, they were going to completely abandon them and make the special-ability control entirely intuitive. But somebody in their infinite wisdom must have deemed it too complicated for the average player. They said it would take too long to implement and that the contrast with the competition would be too drastic."

I nodded pensively. He had a point. I hadn't seen any icons in my field of vision for quite a while. How had I managed to activate my special abilities, then? For me, my inventory was just a bag like any other. Had I spent too much time in the game? Possible.

Oblivious of my absent-mindedness, Mark continued to share his reservations with me,

"Sometimes I think that all this

✝ An NPC's Path: Book Two ✝

confrontation between the powers of Light and Dark in the game is only a reflection of the confrontation within its board of directors," he reached for the bottle and reluctantly put it away under the counter.

Now he was completely over the top. Unwilling to listen to any more conspiracy theories, I rose from my stool. "I don't think it's possible."

He waved a dismissive hand. "It may sound crazy if you don't know the shareholders list. Half of the shares belong to the game developers and the other half is owned by a company that holds the patent for players' brain data processing algorithms. They may well disagree on the game's future."

I shrugged. "Possibly."

The innkeeper was about to add something else when the front door swung open, letting in Isabella.

"Good evening, Ms. Ash-Rizt!" the innkeeper piped up.

She gave him a nonchalant nod. "Kitten?" she motioned me toward the stairs. "Need to talk."

"Neo," I turned to the boy. "Finish your food

Kingdom of the Dead

and go back up to your room."

"I've already finished!" he replied, running after us.

I caught up with Isabella on the stairway. "And?"

"We'll talk upstairs," she snapped.

Once we'd got inside and locked the door, she couldn't help but reproach me, "I thought I told you not to leave the room?"

"Oh, give it a break," I waved her concern away as I deactivated both Incognito and Almost Alive.

My illusionary face fell away, revealing the taut skin stretched over my skull. She recoiled.

"What the hell is th-?" she gasped, stopping midword. "A *Lich*?"

"A Junior Lich."

"But how did you-"

"I keep leveling."

"You're full of surprises, Kitten," she drawled in amazement. "A Lich, of all things!"

I shrugged. "So what? A dead necromancer, big deal!"

She shook her head. "Oh no. This is totally different. Don't even try to compare death magic and the magic of the undead."

✝ An NPC's Path: Book Two ✝

A long-suffering sigh escaped my chest. The magic of the undead! I couldn't even dream of ever learning it. Still, I decided against sharing my own problems with her. "So, what about the meeting?"

She beamed, pleased as Punch. "Relax, Kitten. We're expected."

"When?"

"Right now," she flashed me a mysterious smile. "But first we need to get ready."

She removed her shapeless cloak. I couldn't help letting out a low whistle of surprise.

Her armor was trimmed with black patent leather which made her appear extremely sexy. She'd always looked a bit frivolous, playful even — at least until she transformed into a furious harpy — but now she reminded me of one of those women of easy virtue mentioned earlier by Mark.

"Is Kitten into hardcore?" she squinted at me, playing with her cat o' nine tails. "I'd make a good dominatrix, trust me!"

"What kind of sick masquerade is this?"

"That's only part of it," she licked carnivorously her brightly painted lips as she threw me a collar and chain. "Try this on."

Kingdom of the Dead

"What the hell?"

"Come on, Kitten, don't drag it out! We don't have all day!"

"But-"

"Just put it on!"

3.

I WAS LED TO the negotiations on a chain.

Isabella walked in front, seductively swinging her hips. Either she was trying to warm to her role or her impossibly high stilettoes prevented her from walking normally. They definitely weren't made for trotting on cobblestones. Not that I gave a damn. She could break her neck for all I cared. She'd had the audacity to make me wear that collar! The fact that I wasn't wearing the mask worried me much more as, even though my Incognito prevented other players from seeing my status, they could all see the morbid face of a deadman.

Yes, I was supposed to be a zombie on a leash. I wouldn't call it a great career choice. Still, it was for a good cause.

I cussed under my breath and increased

✝ An NPC's Path: Book Two ✝

my pace to slacken off the tautness of the chain. I wasn't very good at keeping up with her while having to impersonate a lethargic zombie at the same time.

"Don't rush!" Isabella hissed out of the corner of her mouth.

I obediently eased up.

The Tower of Darkness was enveloped in thick gloom. Torches and magic lanterns struggled to illuminate the narrow lanes around it. Crowds of tipsy players surrounded the houses of ill repute; the silent shadows of city guards stole along the streets; ladies of the night were beckoning new clients: this was an ordinary city living an ordinary nightlife of clubbing, alcohol and whores.

Although I attracted unfriendly stares, no one had attempted to attack me. Nobody wanted to be sued for damaging somebody else's property. As long as I was on a chain, I was out of harm's way. Humiliating but safe.

As we turned into a deserted lane, I caught up with her again.

"Mind telling me what's with the masquerade?" I whispered furiously.

She swung round and sized me up

☥ Kingdom of the Dead ☥

unkindly. "Firstly, our potential partners can see that you're dead, anyway. And secondly, you're my trump card. Now do me a favor and shut up!"

We turned onto a busy crossroads where a lanky Elf attempted to give her a slap on her backside. Without even changing step, Isabella gave him a tick with her cat o' nine tails as she walked past. I snapped my jaws and bulged my eyes.

The Elf guffawed. At least he had a sense of humor.

"Where are we going?" I asked her once again.

Isabella winced. "You'll see in a moment."

The clanking of cold steel reached us through the darkness. I shouldn't have listened to Isabella. Leaving the flamberge back at the inn maybe hadn't been such a good idea.

We turned a corner and saw two warriors who were fighting desperately right in the middle of the street, surrounded by a thick noisy crowd. None of the onlookers attempted to interfere though.

I peered at the scene. A prompt popped up:

A Duel!

✝ An NPC's Path: Book Two ✝

Someone shrieked. A voice thundered, "Stop thief!"

A young lad lithely sneaked past me and disappeared into the swirls of darkness. A translucent lasso flew after him, unstealthing him, but the thief had already sneaked into a dark side alley. No one dared chase after him any further. His victim's angry shouting continued to trail behind us for a long time.

The street turned toward a narrow and deserted canal embankment. There, I caught up with Isabella again and strode alongside her, doing my best not to step on the chain which clinked over the cobblestones.

"Is there a way of protecting oneself against pickpockets?"

Isabella shrugged. "Everything's possible. Depends on how much you're prepared to pay."

"Could you be a little clearer?"

Seeing as there was no one near, she deigned to reply,

"If you grease the palm of the Lord of the local Tower, he can safeguard your inventory for a while. It's not cheap. Also, his protection is disabled the moment you leave town."

"Aha. And what if you need permanent

🗡 Kingdom of the Dead 🗡

protection for a particular item, regardless of the owner's location?"

She stopped and heaved a sigh. "What do you need that for? What else don't I know about you?"

"Well," I faltered. "The necro I have the vendetta with wants to take a certain artifact from me..."

"That's your problem," ignoring my explanation, she walked on.

I grabbed at the chain and forced her to stop. "I don't think so! This artifact is indispensable for my rebirth. And if it gets stolen-"

I didn't need to explain any further.

"Show me," Isabella said, acceding to my request.

I pulled out the charmed skull and laid it reluctantly in her hand.

She studied it for a while, then looked up at me. "If you're screwing me around-"

"I'm not!"

"I'm gonna wring your balls," she promised. "In order to protect this crappy rock, I had to waste some of my Goddess' Benevolence! Have you any idea what it cost me to get it in the first

✝ An NPC's Path: Book Two ✝

place?"

"I'll make it worth your while."

She chuckled and covered the artifact with her hand. When she removed it, the skull's empty sockets glowed with a crimson flame. "Take it."

I hurried to put it back into my inventory. "So how does it work, then?"

"A thief will lose his fingers."

"Excellent!" I exclaimed.

Suddenly something put me on my guard. "Wait a sec."

We were just approaching yet another bridge when my undead phoenix — who for reasons known only to himself had tagged along with us — began circling the water. I mentally reached out to him, trying to peer into the darkness that reigned over the city from the advantage of the bird's eye view. Nothing aroused my suspicions. Still, something was wrong.

"Can we give this bridge a miss?" I asked Isabella.

"There's no time," she snapped. Then she added, pointing at a couple who'd just walked out of a side street and were headed for the bridge. "Look, everybody else is crossing."

Only they didn't. As soon as the two

Kingdom of the Dead

revelers reached the bridge, they were encircled by shadows. The next moment both seemed to be resting peacefully on the ground. Not asleep though — but bleeding to death.

Four killer rogues expertly frisked their bodies and jumped into a boat bobbing on the waves by the embankment. The next moment, the only thing that still reminded us of them was the quiet creaking of the rowlocks.

"Who'd have thought..." Isabella drawled, looking puzzled. "Come on, Kitten!" she jerked on the chain. "We're almost there."

We hurried past the lifeless bodies and ran onto the bridge. My night vision made out the boat disappearing down the canal. Unfortunately, I couldn't see exactly who was in it.

"Nice quiet city," I snorted.

"Just some underage brats on an adrenaline trip," she said, hastening her step.

I followed reluctantly after her. The phoenix emitted yet another squawk and flitted off into the darkness.

As soon as we crossed the canal, we immediately bumped into a group of players preparing for a raid. A very focused sorcerer was busy chalking the outline of a portal on the

✝ An NPC's Path: Book Two ✝

cobblestones. A priestess was casting some blessings while all the others were checking their equipment and distributing healing potions and mana vials. Their average level wasn't too high but their gear was nothing to sniff at. Even I with my limited knowledge of the game had recognized a few legendary sets.

By the same token, the players had recognized me.

Not literally, of course. They saw a black leather-clad lady with some sort of creature on a chain and had been smart enough to identify it.

"A zombie!" someone shouted. "Anyone for some free XP?"

"Count me in!" a burly seven-foot warrior growled, drawing a fiery sword from its scabbard.

This time Isabella knew better than to threaten them with her whip. She strengthened her grip on her staff. "Just try it!"

Her furious growl made the warrior waver in indecision.

Isabella had partially turned into a Fury. Her face sharpened. Her gaze filled with a grim glow. But even so, we stood no chance against a numerous group like this.

Luckily, we didn't need to.

† Kingdom of the Dead †

"Let them go!" the sorcerer ordered. The warrior obediently returned his sword to its scabbard.

We hurried to turn a corner.

"Nice quiet city," I repeated.

"Those wretched paying players!" Isabella cussed. "I can't stand all those rich daddies' boys!"

I nodded. With levels as low as theirs, amassing such impressive amounts of gorgeous gear must have required some serious cash injections. Still, who was I to say? One man's meat is another man's poison. Some players used real-world money to buy fantasy weapons and armor while others invested it into a virtual catering business. The world economy had long transcended the limits of the real world. Stock speculators habitually hyped up online startup stocks sky high, even when all of the said startups' assets were located on a single server.

Still, all such thoughts of a possible merger of the virtual and real-world economies flew from my head the moment I saw the grim building on the other side of yet another canal and the figure of a dark angel topping the imposing tower looming behind it.

✝ An NPC's Path: Book Two ✝

'Wait," I said in confusion. "This is the residence of the Spawn of Darkness!"

"Of course it is," Isabella replied.

I didn't believe my ears. "Do you want to say that the most powerful Dark clan deigns to deal with us?"

She laughed. "They'd strike a deal with the devil himself provided he helped them to get one over on the Sons of Light. Or do you really think that no one on the Light side is trying to collect the Sphere of Souls?"

I tended to disagree so I simply shrugged but said nothing.

The bridge to the other side was paved with slabs of marble and lined with statues of various fantastical creatures intertwined like struggling snakes. There were no guards posted on it.

"We can't just walk into the clan's territory, surely?" I asked.

"Shut up!" Isabella hissed. "You're a brainless zombie and don't forget it!"

I cussed under my breath but obeyed.

The moment I reached halfway across, a sharp pain pierced the top of my head. It felt like I'd been smashed with a hammer. I very nearly doubled up in agony. A bunch of scorched black

🗡 Kingdom of the Dead 🗡

feathers drifted to earth.

No one seemed to have bothered to add my dead phoenix to the guest list.

"Move it!" Isabella hissed.

I forced myself to stand up straight, spread my shoulders and staggered after her with the faltering gait of a walking dead.

The guards awaited us at the opposite end of the bridge: ten swordsmen, two sorcerers and a dark priest who was the only player among them. He raised his staff whose crystal top began to glow, dispersing the nocturnal shadows.

The control didn't take much time. The priest flagged us through.

"Keep going straight on," he said. "There'll be someone waiting for you."

Immediately after the bridge, we came across an impossibly high wrought-iron gate topped with sharp spikes. But we weren't important enough for them to open up. We only merited entry by the small side gate.

"Follow me," the gatekeeper strode through the square toward the clan's tower rising at its opposite end. Incredibly, the statue of the dark angel stood out clearly in the surrounding gloom.

Still, I didn't get the chance to take a good

✝ An NPC's Path: Book Two ✝

look at it. No one expects to stumble across a sightseeing zombie. We're supposed to walk with our faces in the dirt, just like pigs.

The gates into the order's residence stood wide open. The gatekeeper saw us into a spacious hall and asked us to wait.

Even after he'd left, I continued impersonating an emotionless corpse even though maintaining an impassionate face was quickly becoming a struggle. Minutes passed but nobody called for us. In the real world, there would have been nothing strange or humiliating about this. But here, considering the cost of being in virtual reality, our hosts' behavior promised us nothing good.

After a while, Isabella cussed under her breath. She stood opposite the front door staring grimly at the statue of the dark angel above it: his slender body, his ripped wings and the fiery gaze on his beautiful face. A dark sword thrust aloft by the creature's right hand was matched by his left hand which clutched a flaming whip.

"This is the clan's patron," Isabella said. "They didn't even bother to give him a name. Cheap and cheerful."

Her voice rang with unbridled sarcasm. It

✟ Kingdom of the Dead ✟

was as if she was trying to let the invisible observers know she was pissed about the unexpected delay but not enough to lose it.

Her angry tirade hadn't produced any effect. The doors stayed close.

Gradually other players started to arrive at the reception hall. No one spoke to each other as each kept their own company. I tried not to stare: they were nervous enough as it was, annoyed at the presence of a zombie.

Finally, the doors opened and a valet in a luxuriant livery announced,

"Isabella Ash-Rizt! Please follow me!"

The unkind jealous stares of the multitude of players in the room were all upon her. Ignoring them, she proudly walked down the corridor, head held high.

The passage was lined with four-armed statues. It took me some time to realize that they weren't just any old statues but golem guards. Their swords and armor were fashioned from some metal that looked a lot like mithril, only it had a purple glow.

The audience hall was truly enormous. Its walls and impossibly high ceiling disappeared in the shadows overhead. It was illuminated with an

✝ An NPC's Path: Book Two ✝

eerie light that was focused on three thrones that towered opposite the entrance.

The valet headed toward them. Wherever he walked, the stone tiles began to glow in his wake. We followed him. Immediately the slabs of stone under our feet started emitting a visible reddish radiance as if warning everyone of the approach of an enemy.

"The case of the shard of the Sphere of Souls!" the valet thundered. He then stepped aside, leaving us alone with the clan lords.

An impossibly tall knight in black armor and a closed visor was sitting on the central throne. There was nothing of Light about him. It seemed as if darkness itself enshrouded him, snaking around him in hundreds of ghostly shadows.

Lord High Steward

That was the only prompt I received when I'd focused on him.

A female figure in ice armor was sitting on the left-hand throne, her face concealed by a veil of snowflakes. An enormous white wolf lay at her feet.

⚔ Kingdom of the Dead ⚔

The opposite throne was taken by a player clad in fiery garb. Their names — Lady Blizzard and the Duke of Inferno — said nothing to me.

Isabella lowered a respectful head. I just stood there like a sore thumb, staring impassively at the crowd heaving behind the thrones. All the players here were levels 80 to 90, and they looked the part with their legendary weapons, bespoke armor and unique pets. I'd never even heard of some of their classes and professions.

And there we were, offering them a deal. Yeah right.

The Lord High Steward snapped his fingers. An alchemist stepped forward.

"Allow me to evaluate your artifact," he said.

Isabella produced the shard of the Sphere of Souls but wasn't in a hurry to give it to him, holding it in front of her in her upturned palm.

It didn't become a problem. The alchemist studied the item's cold glow using some clever optical device.

"Three out of a hundred!" he pronounced his verdict.

The Lord High Steward nodded his

✝ An NPC's Path: Book Two ✝

approval. "How much?"

Isabella put the fragment away. "I'm not interested in your money."

Whispers swept around the hall but the Lord High Steward kept his cool. "Explain yourself," he demanded.

"You rub my back and I'll rub yours," Isabella said.

"Are you seeking our protection?" Lady Blizzard suggested.

"Or are you looking to join the clan?" the Duke of Inferno chuckled. "Our waiting list is years long. And you're not a particularly valuable addition to it, Priestess."

Isabella shook her head. "I want to join your raid on the Kingdom of the Dead. And trust me, you might find me quite a valuable addition to it."

The crowd of players behind the thrones spoke all at once, voicing their indignation. I felt like we should make ourselves scarce.

Still, the Lord High Steward remained impassive. "Go on," he said, motioning the crowd to calm down.

"I have neutrality with the subjects of the Lord of the Tower of Decay. I'm the best scout

Kingdom of the Dead

you can ever find."

The black knight shook his head. "This status isn't as unique as you think, Priestess. We don't require your services."

Nonplussed by his aloofness, Isabella shook the chain, attracting everyone's attention to my humble self. "And how many pet zombies do you have, may I ask? Not some brainless dorks but sentient beings? Who can act on their own will and are capable of using the artifacts of the subjects of the Tower of Decay? And who are capable of disabling any magic defenses?"

She swung round to me. "Kitten, *speak*!"

I obediently said in a purposefully slurred voice, "Nice to meet you, ladies and gentlemen!"

The players began talking over each other, discussing the extraordinary proposition.

Once again the Lord High Steward motioned everyone to keep silent. "One moment," he turned to the other two to confer.

Isabella allowed a tiny smile to flutter on her lips which vanished the moment the black knight spoke again, announcing the clan's decision.

"We'll pay you fifty grand for the fragment. And another thirty for your zombie control."

✝ An NPC's Path: Book Two ✝

Isabella seemed shocked by such a shameless proposition. She threw back a proud head. "Well, if that's what you want. Let's go, Kitten. You're worth much more than some stinking thirty grand!"

The Lord High Steward leaned forward slightly. "Let's make it sixty and forty. That's a hundred grand in total. This is our final price."

"I don't need your money. I want to join the raid!"

He shook his head. "Sorry. It means we haven't come to an agreement."

Isabella shrugged indignantly and turned to go. But before she could take a step, one of the players — a certain Prince Julien — stepped forward.

"What the hell?" he demanded. "Are we just gonna let her go? The Fragment is as good as ours!"

Silence fell. I could hear clearly the clinking noises as Isabella's staff began to flex its joints. My teeth began to ache in anticipation of all the shit that was about to hit the fan.

A prince! Who on earth had appointed this scumbag a prince?

This was no problem for Isabella. She

Kingdom of the Dead

would just respawn in the inn, end of story. And me, how was I supposed to get out of here? Or did I stand a better chance of reaching the Kingdom of the Dead if I went with the clan? No way. They'd see right through me straight away.

The pause only lasted a couple of seconds. The Lord High Steward shook his head. "We're not the ones who break the law."

"We're the ones who make it!" the Prince shouted passionately.

I was pretty sure that many of those in the crowd wholeheartedly agreed with him.

This time the decision had already been made. "Go!" the black knight gestured to Isabella to leave.

She hurried to comply. I trudged behind her like a dog on a chain.

Isabella didn't say a word as we forced our way through the crowd of other supplicants still waiting their turn in the reception hall. Only when we'd crossed the bridge, did she finally revert back to her normal self.

"Never mind," she said through clenched teeth. "Two can play at this game."

With those words, she hurried off home.

"Why did they let us go?" I asked as I too

✝ An NPC's Path: Book Two ✝

shed the role of a dumb zombie.

She shrugged. "My guess is as good as yours. They might have thought we were part of a bigger scam. Because trust me, even the Spawn of Darkness can be dealt with if they overstep the line."

"But what if they did try to get rid of us? You didn't think about that, did you?" I was angry and didn't even try to hide it.

The priestess only smiled. "Trust me, Kitten. I knew what I was doing."

She didn't bother herself with any explanations, and I knew better than to hassle her.

A resounding *"Craah!"* came from the darkness above our heads. It looked like my dead phoenix was back in the game.

"So what now?" I asked.

Isabella chuckled ambiguously. "Don't worry. We'll hear from them."

"But we don't have the time!"

"Are you getting edgy, Kitten?"

"Screw you!" I was about to wrestle the chain from her hand when a loud procession appeared from a neighboring street.

Half a dozen mercenaries armed to the

⚔ Kingdom of the Dead ⚔

teeth walked out in front, followed by a level-85 fire mage. A bodilicious Elven girl scurried next to him, while three player bodyguards who closed the procession eyed us with undisguised suspicion.

Strange as it may seem, this was the first high-level character I'd met on the streets of the capital. The clan's residence we'd just left had been teeming with them, but not the city itself. I turned to Isabella for an explanation.

She snorted. "They don't have the time to hang around the city. Those who level up seriously treat the game as their job. It can also be quite dangerous."

I couldn't believe my ears. "Dangerous? Get away with you! They're real killing machines!"

"Anyone can get killed. You just need to try harder or muster more people. Some PKs target high-level players."

"What the hell for?"

"XP. Cool gear. Some clans even put contracts out on them, just to weaken a rival clan."

"Put contracts out?"

"Sure. Can you imagine the size of their black lists? Even you have just made yourself a

✝ An NPC's Path: Book Two ✝

sworn enemy."

I shuddered. "You mean they can really take people out?"

"If they can fork out quick enough," she smirked. "Now listen. My game time's coming to an end. I'll take you to the inn and log out. Tomorrow we'll decide what to do next."

We turned off into a narrow passage between some houses but had barely taken more than ten steps before a portal popped open before us. Immediately another one opened loudly behind.

Before I could even blink, the lane was packed with humans, elves and dwarves pointing their swords and halberds at us. The crowd bristled with magic wands and loaded crossbows. I swung round and saw the same picture.

Now we were deep in it.

Isabella promptly transformed into a Fury. Still, it didn't look as if we were going to win this battle. Our enemy was way too numerous — even though these weren't players but just some hired NPCs.

Prince Julien stepped forward. He was in fact an 89-level Dark Knight. His deep-blue armor sparkled with protection spells; the white

Kingdom of the Dead

hilt of his two-handed sword fashioned out of a demon's bones peeked from behind his shoulder. If you asked me, he had no need of the mercenaries' help. He was perfectly capable of making mincemeat out of us as it was.

"Now it's every man for himself," I warned Isabella, fully intending to stealth up and leg it out of there.

"Stay where you are!" she snapped, then turned to the prince, 'How can I help you, my boy?"

Strangely enough, her sarcastic address seemed to have hit its mark. With a jerk, the prince closed his visor fashioned as a tiger's head baring its teeth and concealed his handsome face and the dimple on his chin.

"Don't screw with me," he said. "Just give me the shard."

"Oh, so we're robbers now, are we?"

"You can get your money from the clan's treasury. You'll be sorry if you don't go along."

She laughed. "So you needed your bodyguards to tell me that? Are we so afraid of women?"

I just couldn't help myself. "He just doesn't know what to do with you!" I offered my two

✝ An NPC's Path: Book Two ✝

cents. "He brought them along as advisors!"

"I didn't want to waste my time chasing after you, that's all," he said through clenched teeth as he reached behind his back, fully intending to make me pay for his own embarrassment.

His sword swished out of its scabbard. I prudently took cover behind Isabella's back.

The prince snorted. "This is your last chance to resolve this peaceably."

His original plan was pretty clear now. By arriving at the head of a large surprise group of mercenaries, he'd expected to intimidate Isabella into surrendering the artifact to him. She had to do so willingly. The chances of him retrieving the item from the priestess' dead body were too slim.

Isabella could see right through his little scheme just as well as I could but didn't want to deprive herself of the pleasure of seriously pissing him off.

"The boy likes to dominate?" she purred. "Bad boy! Very bad boy!"

The prince's sword faltered in his nervous hands, its deep blue blade covered in black runes. I didn't like the sight of it at all. I grabbed at my collar, preparing to rip it off and stealth up

Kingdom of the Dead

when Isabella decided to make him certain concessions.

"You want the fragment, don't you?" she smiled as she reached into her inventory. "Aren't you afraid of invoking the wrath of the Mistress of the Crimson Moon?"

At the sight of the ball of ghostly light the prince shuddered. Still, he didn't let himself be provoked. He knew better than to insult the goddess.

"I don't think she even cares about this piece of junk," he said sarcastically, sticking out a demanding hand. "Give it here!"

Isabella blew on her hand. The white glow disappeared, replaced by an unhealthy-looking crimson. "Take it. Just make sure you don't burn your pretty little fingers."

He snatched his hand back. "You bitch!"

"Come on, take it," Isabella insisted. "You'll need my mistress anyway once the sphere is complete."

Julien averted his stare from the artifact glowing dark red in her hand and even attempted a swing with his sword. Still, reason got the better of his emotions. "Let's get outta here," he said.

✝ An NPC's Path: Book Two ✝

The mercenaries sheathed their weapons and began drifting off down the lane. The prince followed his henchmen.

"We'll see each other again," he dropped.

Once he'd disappeared round a corner, Isabella heaved a sigh of relief and returned the artifact to her inventory.

"What have you done with it?" I demanded.

She began backing off down the lane as if waiting for the prince to return. "It was touched by my mistress' will," she reluctantly explained. "Now no one can use it without my permission. But the moment this miserable excuse for a prince realizes he's had a perfect chance to get one over on his competition…"

The idea that that bunch of armed cutthroats could return at any moment made me reach out mentally to my dead phoenix. Immediately the world around me changed, gaining color, brightness and speed. In fact, it became fast as hell.

My Scarecrow flitted over the city. I could see the whole place through his eyes: all the roofs, the chimneys and the weathercocks of the houses below. Amazingly, this dead bunch of feathers didn't hit anything in mid-flight. It flew

☥ Kingdom of the Dead ☥

toward the canal and perched on one of the lampposts.

The prince was striding along the embankment, heading for the bridge. The mercenaries followed him at some distance. The shadows thickened, disgorging a few figures clad in dark cloaks and hoods. They didn't attack the prince and his men, though. The cloaked figures turned out to be the clan's scouts.

The phoenix's hearing distorted the sounds of human speech a lot, but still I'd managed to make out most of their conversation. I couldn't help laughing.

"What's that?" Isabella jerked on the chain. "Are you out of your mind, Kitten?"

I shook my head, severing the connection. "I've just seen a group of thieves who were hired to steal the fragment from you. And the prince has just upset the applecart."

"Are you serious?" she asked, unable to conceal her surprise. "What makes you think so?"

"I'm a lich, aren't I?" I said with a smug smile. "I can do lots of things you don't know about," I leaned against the wall, waiting for my head to stop spinning.

✝ An NPC's Path: Book Two ✝

She chuckled. "You're full of surprises, Kitten," she tugged at the chain. "Come on now. Let's get outta here before they change their minds."

4.

WE GOT BACK to the inn without any further hassle. The moment we returned to our room, Isabella logged out with a shower of electronic sound effects. I ripped the collar off and hurled it into the furthest corner.

Neo heard the chain rattle and looked out of the other room. "Everything all right?" he asked sleepily.

I waved his question away. "Everything's fine. Go back to bed."

Then I reconsidered and dumped all my trophy amulets onto the bed. "Think you can identify them?"

The boy cheered up. "Of course I can, Uncle John! Let me try!"

He managed to recognize a few simple charms but the bulk of my haul remained unidentified. That upset him no end.

"Uncle John, would you like me to use the

Kingdom of the Dead

phoenix's powers?" he suggested.

I shuddered. "No, please don't. Isabella can do all the rest. Go to sleep now."

Neo sniveled and went back into the other room. I took the Pendant of Enlightenment which offered his owner +2 to Intellect and tried to put it around my neck. I couldn't. I started looking into it and discovered that apparently, the Deadman's Set wasn't compatible with other magic items.

Dammit. If it wasn't one thing it was another.

I lobbed the charm onto the bed, walked over to the window and perched myself on the windowsill, pressing my forehead against the cold glass. The street outside was dark, its gloom occasionally disrupted by bright flashes of magic light. It must have been either some tipsy sorcerers having fun or robbers helping themselves to other people's property. For some, the PK mark only added spice to the game.

Because that's what it was for them. A game. Only a game.

A game is when you can go in and come back out. When you can't come out, it's not a game anymore. It's called life.

✝ An NPC's Path: Book Two ✝

I tapped my forehead against the glass. I might go mad during the night. All this time, I'd had something to look forward to. First to get out of the playpen, then to find the entrance to the Kingdom of the Dead, then to get to the capital... And now I had to wait and I didn't even know what for. It was unbearable.

Should I go out and have a little fun too, maybe? Like smoke a couple of players? Good idea but how long was the PK mark supposed to last? Not to even mention the fact that I might get killed too which threatened me with more complications I really didn't need. Oh no, sir, thank you very much. I should really get in some practice with my Soulkiller.

I'd already drawn the bone hook from under my belt when I heard hoarse crowing coming from the street.

I laughed and reached out mentally to my undead pet. Let's fly, buddy!

ISABELLA LOGGED BACK IN in the early afternoon of the next day. By that time, I didn't know what to think anymore. I circled the room not knowing what to do with myself. I didn't want to go anywhere near the window for fear of the sunrays

✟ Kingdom of the Dead ✟

pouring into the room. The bright light irritated my eyes; my last-night's outing over the city in the body of my dead phoenix had resulted in bouts of vertigo and nausea. I couldn't think straight; my temples and the back of my head were in agony.

For no particular reason, I remembered the conversation I'd had with Mark the innkeeper. That got me thinking who was really in control of the dark side of this world. Was it the game designers or the technical team?

I walked downstairs to get some food for Neo, hoping to see Mark and talk to him. Still, the bar was manned by some other guy. Mark was apparently offline.

The bartender listened to my order and headed for the kitchen. I leaned over the bar and took the first bottle I came across, secreting it under my cape. Was I a thief or just a pretty face? Yes, yes, I knew that stealing was bad. But at the end of the day, food and refreshments were included in the price of the room anyway.

The successful theft had earned me 10 pt. XP. I went back upstairs very pleased with myself.

But the moment I took a swig of whiskey, I

✝ An NPC's Path: Book Two ✝

was crippled by the mother of all convulsions. I dropped onto the bed waiting for my muscles to relax and for my throat to stop burning. Apparently, alcohol and zombies wasn't a good mix.

It took about five minutes for my eyes to stop watering. And that's when the soft popping sound of a portal announced Isabella's return.

"You really know how to drop yourself in it, Kitten!" she said without further ado.

Now why would she say that? I cast a glance at the bottle on the table but no, she'd ignored it totally.

"What now?" I groaned.

"Open the video tab," she commanded. A deep furrow had formed between her eyebrows. She now resembled a vet who was trying to decide whether to euthanize a cat or let it suffer some more.

A video tab? I'd spent so much time in the game that virtual reality had become my natural habitat. I'd already begun to forget about the existence of things like forums and other in-game services.

Her eyes squinted threateningly.

"Yes, yes, I've opened it!" I hurried to say.

† Kingdom of the Dead †

"What now?"

"Look for the top viewed in the last twenty-four hours. You're one of the 'most watched'!"

"Me? Are you sure? It doesn't make sense!"

Unfortunately, she was right. Amongst the "most watched" was a video featuring humble me. A quarter of a million views and third place in the rankings.

The video footage included the moment when the Drow archer shot down my undead phoenix, as well as my return blow. The success of such a normally mundane episode owed a lot to its flashy title. *A Light Player Punishing a Darkie by the Tower of Gloom* was how the uploader had called it.

A monk of the Order of the Silver Phoenix kills the Dark player with one blow and leaves unhindered — in the direct vicinity of the Tower of Gloom of all places!

Just my luck. Still, only when I skimmed through the comments did I realize the entire gravity of the situation. I wasn't interested in either the Dark players' threats or the Lighties' words of support. What worried me much more was their discussion over my flamberge. Even though my Deadman's set didn't tie in with my

✝ An NPC's Path: Book Two ✝

Light player's garb, one of the weapon connoisseurs had promptly identified it and even published its official Wiki image.

Dammit! If Garth happened to see this wretched video, he'd know straight away where to look for me.

A quarter of a million views. Shiiiiiit...

"What's this *'37,000'* next to the screen?" I asked Isabella. "Are they donations to the maker?"

"Oh no, Kitten," she gave me a saccharine smile. "These are donations to take *you* out. Whoever kills you first gets 50%. The one who kills you next gets 50% of the rest. It can be done up to five times."

I shuddered. "Is that legal?"

"The admins will approve of anything that adds an edge to the game."

"Bastards!" I spat. "So much for unrecognizable me! So much for my Incognito! *'Hello stranger! What's this Silver Phoenix on your chest?'*"

Isabella giggled. She must have recognized the song I'd so cleverly reworded. But before it had even registered in my mind, she became serious again.

🗡 Kingdom of the Dead 🗡

"I'm afraid your sword is a bit of an eyesore, Kitten. You're too easily identifiable."

I waved her words away. "I don't care. You'd better tell me what we're gonna do about the shard of the Sphere of Souls. I don't give a damn about the money but I'm desperate to get into the Kingdom of the Dead. Really desperate."

"Relax, Kitten," she smirked as she began to rip the leather trimming off her armor. "While you were snoring away in your comfy little bed, I made the Spawn of Darkness another offer. One they couldn't refuse."

"No way?" I said in disbelief. "Does that mean they're taking us on the raid?"

"No."

I cussed in disappointment. "Why are you so buoyant, then? What kind of agreement do you have with them?"

She reached out to give me a pat on the cheek but met my grim stare and reconsidered. "Firstly, no one's gonna hassle us anymore. Pointless. The fragment has been put somewhere safe. Secondly, the clan has drawn up an agreement that if ever we decide to sell it, they get first option. They're first in line."

"But we're not planning on selling it!"

✟ An NPC's Path: Book Two ✟

She snickered. "Of course we're not. Sooner or later, we'll make them agree to our terms."

I frowned. "So why did you need all this first-option thing?"

"You don't seem to be able to think straight in the morning, Kitten! Aren't you awake yet?" she snapped, not even trying to conceal the annoyance in her glare. Still, she deigned to explain, "The Spawn are sure that none of the experienced players will take us on the raid. Which means that sooner or later we'll be obliged to auction the Shard. And now they have an official guarantee that the fragment won't go somewhere else. Provided we don't manage to talk somebody else into it."

"We won't," I prophesized grimly. "The Sons of Light won't even listen to us."

"They won't," she agreed. "They don't need a lich and a dark priestess hanging with them. But everything's gonna change once the race reaches the final stage, trust me. Once the Spawn of Darkness collect 97% of the Sphere, then they'll remember us, I assure you."

"Does that mean that nobody else on the Dark side collects the Sphere?"

She shook her head. "The Swords of Chaos

Kingdom of the Dead

had their chance but they're out of it now. All the others are just middlemen and profiteers."

When I heard her mention the Swords — the second Dark clan in the rankings — I remembered I was now on their black list. I produced the silver disk I'd picked up from Karl Lightning's body in Stone Harbor.

"Talking about the Swords of Chaos," I offered it to the priestess. "You think you could identify this?"

She gingerly took it from me with two fingers, gave it a long studying look and threw it on the table. "I don't understand your obsession with collecting all sorts of crap," she winced, wiping her fingers on the bedspread. "Where did you get this from? No idea what kind of spell is cast on it but I can tell you that for sure it's deadly."

I put her in the picture, omitting all of the details that she didn't need to know.

Isabella frowned. "Did they blacklist you because of just one murder?" she shook her head in bewilderment. "That doesn't make sense! That's not how you do it! Provided you hadn't messed up any of their plans."

I shrugged. "Apparently, I had." I poured all

An NPC's Path: Book Two

of the amulets I'd found in the sarcophagus onto the bed. "This is my loot from the Dungeon of the Dead. Do we split it?"

She grinned. "Good idea! The Spawn of Darkness paid us ten grand. Of which four is yours."

"Only four?"

"I had to pay a thousand for the storage," she explained. "And another five hundred is for your skull's protection. I don't do charity."

"Never mind," I said, unwilling to nickel and dime it. "I suggest you check the amulets. If you manage to sort them out, we won't have to shell out on their ID-ing."

"Sure," she sniffed and began studying them.

I lay down on the other bed and just stared at the ceiling.

The raid on the Kingdom of the Dead seemed to have been postponed for an undetermined period of time. I couldn't say I was too happy about it.

☦ Kingdom of the Dead ☦

5.

OUT OF ALL THE BUNCH of amulets, Isabella had only failed to identify three: an emerald pendant, a heavy ring with a large star sapphire and a sculpted bracelet of some unknown gray metal. All the rest had turned out to be low-level stuff. But even so, according to her, we could earn six or seven thousand gold from it.

"If we're lucky, these three might cost the same," she suggested, putting around her neck a chain with a bonus to Reputation with NPCs. "I'll take it as part of my cut," she explained.

I nodded.

Sadly, there was nothing useful for me in the whole lot. The Deadman's Set prevented me from wearing both the Star Ring and the Bracelet of True Fire. The former offered a small improvement to all main characteristics while the latter gave +30% to protection from burns. Shame. I could have used both.

"Are we gonna auction them?" I asked.

"No," she stood in front of the mirror, admiring her reflection. "We'll sell it on to a trader. At auction, this junk will take forever to

✝ An NPC's Path: Book Two ✝

sell. Not to mention their rip-off commissions."

She rearranged the chain and cast me a curious look. "What's a Lich's blood circulation like?"

"It's not."

"You useless-" she cut herself short and shrugged. "Never mind. I'll go and get rid of the amulets. You coming?"

I couldn't possibly stand it in the inn any longer. Also, I needed some gear. I scrambled off the bed and reached for the flamberge leaning against the wall. "Sure. Coming."

She frowned. "No, Kitten. You'd better leave this rusty piece of steel here. You'll be recognized in two seconds with that. Have you already forgotten the footage?"

Hesitantly I decided to follow her advice. Instead, I slung the black orcish longsword behind my back.

"If I understand it rightly, size does matter to you?" she quipped.

I waved her sarcasm away. "That's for sale."

She smirked, then donned a short cloak which made her skimpy armor appear less flaunty. Having said that, if anything it made her look even more seductive adding some sort of

Kingdom of the Dead

understatement.

I opened the door and showed her into the corridor. "Neo? We're off!"

The boy peeked out of the other room. "Can I come with you?"

"Not this time," I shut the door and ran down the stairs after Isabella.

CAUTIOUSLY I left the inn. I have to admit I was scared. Who wouldn't have been? The wretched video made me feel as if the passersby would start pointing their fingers at me at any moment. As long as it was only fingers and not swords! Dying now would be very untimely.

Only a game, you say? Yeah right.

Without the flamberge, I felt naked. The black sword was somewhat longer and tangibly heavier. To add insult to injury, it was absolutely useless in a fight. Had things come a head, I had only my bone hook to count on. And admittedly, the Soulkiller was a very capricious weapon. I still hadn't got the hang of it.

Still, we'd reached one crossroads, then another, and nothing had happened. Nobody seemed to be paying any attention to us. There were enough players passing us by in the narrow

✝ An NPC's Path: Book Two ✝

streets but not one of them tried to attack us with shouts of "There he is!" Their glances seemed to just slide off me. My investing into Incognito had completely paid off. Excellent skill, I couldn't praise it enough.

Isabella who walked first seemed to know all the local alleys like a stray cat. Soon she took me out to a bridge. There I had to pull my hood further down, trying to protect my dead eyes from the blinding sunrays.

"Is it far still?" I asked.

"We're almost there," she replied, heading across a square toward a small crowd of about twenty players which heaved on its far side.

I tensed up a little. Still, the players had more important things to worry about. They were engaged in a heated discussion about an upcoming raid, casting impatient glances at a tower with a golden clock face. Its long hands pointed at five to one.

We turned off into a side lane. Immediately my Watchful Stare skill gave me the feeling of a knife between my shoulder blades.

I swung round with the Soulkiller extended but missed. The unstealthed thief froze in mid-step, so the sharpened bone sliced the air in front

Kingdom of the Dead

of his face. The next moment he miraculously dodged my second blow and disappeared down a dark alley. Just like that.

I mentally reached out to my phoenix who was circling the sky above the roofs. He hurried to give chase above the streets but the thief was long gone.

"Clever bastard," I muttered. Personally, I couldn't pull off tricks like that.

Isabella frowned. "What the hell was that? Did someone recognize you?"

"I don't think so," I shook my head as I lodged the hook in my belt. "He had nothing in his hands."

"Must have been a pickpocket," she decided. "Shit happens. Let's go."

I gave the street a wary once-over, turned round and hurried after her.

"By the way," I snapped my fingers as I caught up with her, "my skills are stuck at level 15. What can be done about it?"

"At fifteen?" she gave me a look of superiority. "You need to get some training. Then you'll have access to the next ten levels."

"What kind of training?"

"Are you into Stealth?" she said, second-

† An NPC's Path: Book Two †

guessing me. "There're several schools. The Stealthers, for instance."

"Is there no other way?"

She shook her head. "You can only get trained by Masters and Apprentices. I guess it's a problem for you?"

I nodded. Problem wasn't the word. No one was going to train a deadman. No amount of Incognito was going to help me in this case. A student with a closed profile was a contradiction in terms.

Shit! I had so many points that still required distribution! I wasn't going to invest them into any unnecessary skills.

We left the dark passage and turned into a busy street. There, Isabella headed through an open gate into a shady garden. A shop sign said,

We Buy and Sell Weapons, Armor & Amulets

When she swung the front door open, the vendor behind the counter startled and shook his head. "Ms. Ash-Rizt! Unfortunately, none of your bids on the Crown of Chaos has worked out yet."

The priestess screwed her face up in

Kingdom of the Dead

disappointment. "Is the old man here?"

The vendor hesitated. "Yes, Mr. Lloyd is here," he said after a tangible pause. "You can go through."

"Excellent," Isabella cheered up and pushed an inside door without knocking.

Mr. Lloyd turned out to be an alchemist. He wasn't old at all, just gray. Also, he wasn't human. Neither did he belong to any other game race known to me.

His receding hairline exposed a pair of short horns on his forehead. His eyes glowed with an amber flame.

A demon? Whatever. I wasn't there to sell my soul to him, anyway.

Upon our arrival, the alchemist looked up from his engraving table and winced in annoyance. "What now, Isabella?" he sighed, readjusting his plain overalls. "I told you you couldn't just buy the Crown of Chaos! And you didn't even bother to offer me a realistic price."

"Well, sometimes miracles do happen," she muttered.

The alchemist rose up, insulted.

She motioned him to sit down again. "Please don't start. That's not why I'm here,

✝ An NPC's Path: Book Two ✝

anyway. I just want to give you some stuff."

"What's up with Ulrich, then?" he sniffed, apparently referring to the vendor, and looked at me through the colored lens of an alchemist. "Is your gear so hot that you need a bodyguard?"

"This is a friend," Isabella corrected him. "And no, my gear's not hot. It's just that I can't identify a few things."

"Very well, dearie, lay it out!" he demanded, scooping all of the trinkets crowding the table into its top drawer. "Time is money!"

With a crunching sound, the skull topping the priestess' staff swung around, its teeth chattering.

The shop owner pointed his gnarly finger at him, "Shut your trap, Roger!"

The old man turned out to be a player too. After my conversation with Mark, that didn't surprise me anymore. If the truth were known, playing the part of a fence was admittedly cooler than that of an innkeeper. It must have paid better, too.

Isabella leaned her staff against the wall and laid the three items on the table: the emerald pendant, the sapphire ring and the gray sculpted bracelet.

☦ Kingdom of the Dead ☦

In disgust, Lloyd brushed the pendant onto the floor. "Take that revolting thing away!"

"What's with you now?" Isabella demanded indignantly.

Wincing, he set his lens aside and rubbed his temples. "Have you ever heard about the curse of the Night Druid?" he asked, visibly annoyed. "It kills you slowly but surely. And even once you're resurrected, you'll have to pay a whack of gold to have the curse lifted."

"Are you sure?"

"I've seen its description in a couple of catalogs. Consider yourself lucky you didn't try it on."

Isabella sniffed. "Do I look that stupid?"

"It's just that you all seem to have a penchant for flashy baubles," he sighed, then turned his attention to the ring. "That's a nice item," he gave a nod of approval, turning it in his fingers. "The Ring of Intuition. Unfortunately, only Elemental mages can use it."

"How much would you give for it?"

"Ask Ulrich," the old man said dismissively. "He's the one with a calculator in his head. He'll work it out."

The alchemist laid the bracelet down and

fell silent, studying the metalwork through his magnifying glass.

Isabella slumped into a rickety chair. I leaned a shoulder against the door frame and gave the room a good looking-over. It was lined with bookcases stuffed with dusty old volumes. A magic crystal hanging from the ceiling lit the place up. I didn't see any chests or goods up for sale. No windows, either.

"Very interesting," the old man drawled, puzzled. He poured some kind of magic chemical onto the bracelet. The metal hissed and began to emit a faint white smoke.

"Do you mind?" Isabella voiced her concern.

The old man sniffed as he wiped the artifact clean with a piece of cloth. The acid seemed to have had no effect on the intricate metalwork whatsoever.

"Dwarven silver," Lloyd told us. "The item's ready for rune casting. As it bears no magic, it's unfinished. It might fetch a grand to a grand and a half at auction. Take it to Ulrich."

Isabella scooped both the ring and the bracelet up from the table. I handed her the meager loot I'd farmed while playing solo — the

Kingdom of the Dead

gold ingots and a few precious stones — but decided not to show them either the mithril pauldron nor the fragment of Nest Hunter's bone. I very much doubted they were worth anything. And I certainly didn't want them to laugh at me.

"Tally this up apart for me," I told the priestess.

"And take that dreadful thing away," the alchemist added.

Isabella looked down on the floor and kicked the wretched pendant out of the room. "Good job I didn't try it on. I very nearly did," she muttered as she left the room.

Mr. Lloyd looked up at me. "How can I help you, my mysterious stranger? I don't have all day."

I perched myself onto the chair vacated by Isabella. "I'm interested in the Deadman's Set."

He eyed me with undisguised interest. "Your sword isn't part of the set," he said nonchalantly.

"I'm selling it," I said. "But that can wait. How about the Deadman's Set?"

He gave me a pensive nod, rose from the table and reached into the nearest bookcase, producing a fat leather-bound tome framed in

✟ An NPC's Path: Book Two ✟

steel. "This is what we have or what can be delivered within twenty-four hours," he told me, chucking the book onto the table in front of me. "All the items here haven't yet been listed for auction. Everything is from private vendors."

I opened the book.

"The section you need is somewhere near the middle," he said as he began replacing the items from the drawer onto the table.

The book turned out to be a bona fide catalog. As soon as I concentrated on a picture, it would come into focus, gaining depth and dimension. Prices were listed next to the items. Once I got rid of the loot, that would allow me to maybe buy one or two things. Unfortunately, the prices in the section I needed turned out to be three or even four times more than I'd seen elsewhere.

The Steel Crown of the Deadman went for twelve grand. The Bone Ring cost thirteen and a half and the Ice Gauntlets, all of seventeen grand! This was daylight robbery! I didn't have anywhere near that kind of money. Some of the items in the catalog were even more expensive; and as for unique ones, their prices were sky high.

After a while, my gaze chanced upon an

Kingdom of the Dead

unassuming gray smock complete with a hood and a short cloak. I just couldn't take my eyes off it. The price was fourteen grand.

Shadow of Death
You're surrounded by shadows even when you're standing in plain sunlight, making you inconspicuous for all the others and helping you to avoid enemy blows.
+3% to Stealth
+1% to Dodge

Wow. An ordinary necro wouldn't gain much from wearing it. But a Lich... a Lich would happily sell his soul again to lay his dead hands on it. And a Rogue Lich? That goes without saying. Those bonuses!

But fourteen grand?

"Ahem," I cleared my throat. "Your prices aren't very friendly, are they? Other sets are considerably cheaper."

"Other sets!" he took a peek into the catalog and chuckled. "That's for the sets that can be broken up. But the Deadman's Set can't."

"Does it make such a difference?"

He heaved a long-suffering sigh and ruffled

✝ An NPC's Path: Book Two ✝

his gray hair. "Other sets can be altered at any moment. Non-separables can't. But the chances of a player losing it when he dies are also quite slim."

"This I know."

"That's why the parts of a separable set cost what they cost. But if an item is part of a non-separable set, the buyer pays extra for its not being burdened with something else. Do I make it clear? Are you following me?"

"Not really," I admitted.

"Well," he smiled, "if you don't mind me saying, your boots will let down the price of your complete set by about 20%."

"Why, what's wrong with them?"

"These are Boots of Silence, aren't they? But the Deadman's Set only interests necromancers. Who are either death mages or death knights, and therefore have less need for them than for a chocolate teapot," he allowed himself a light smirk. "You understand now, don't you? If you mix and match items in such an eclectic way, no one will buy the resulting set for neither love nor money. Now a well-balanced set can cost any amount of money you care to ask for."

🗡 Kingdom of the Dead 🗡

I winced. "Interesting. So do you want to say that it would be a waste of time looking for affordable auction options?"

"What sort of money are you thinking about?"

I pointed a meaningful finger at the door through which Isabella had just left.

"I see," he sighed. "In that case, let's wait for her. In the meantime, if you don't mind, let's go back to your sword," he extended a hand. "May I?"

I drew the black longsword from behind my back and laid it gently on the table. "Be my guest."

The old man swept his hand just above the length of the blade, then took his time studying the hallmark through his magnifying glass. Only then did he closed his hand round the hilt. Predictably, his fingers slipped.

He laughed, looking pleased. "To you, the Longsword of the Autumnal Equinox is absolutely useless but the item itself is extremely, extraordinarily rare. I've only heard about one of those and it wasn't for sale."

"How much do you think it might cost?"

Mr. Lloyd gave it some thought. "At

✟ An NPC's Path: Book Two ✟

auction, you mean? I should ask thirty or even forty thousand. But you need to understand that finding a buyer won't be quick. Realistically, you're unlikely to unload an item like this in less than six months."

"Are you sure?" I frowned, suspecting foul play.

A smirk curved his lips. "I know for sure. Rare items are my specialty."

Dammit!

Forty grand! That would be enough to buy the Shadow of Death and there would be some left for the Hell's Pauldrons or even the Helmet of Dark Glory. But...

I sighed and asked him point blank, "How much would you give for it? Here and now?"

He pushed the sword away and shook his head. "Nothing at all. I only know of one player who'd be interested and he's broke at the moment."

"Only one?" I sniffed. "Why is that?"

Mr. Lloyd heaved another sigh. "Orcs are even worse racists than Elves and Dwarves. It applies to not only other races but anyone who's different. There's no such a thing as Light Orcs but their affiliation with the Dark is also quite

Kingdom of the Dead

peculiar, with a distinct leaning toward Chaos. An orc who worships the Equilibrium? I know one. How many do you know?"

I didn't know any such individuals at all. Still, I knew better than to admit to the validity of his arguments, so I changed the subject. "The Swords of Chaos, is it an orcish clan?"

"Not at all. Orcs make up a considerable part of the clan members but far from all of them. The Chaosites believe their religious identification to be above their racial one," he tapped a finger on the table. "So coming back to the sword…"

The door swung open, letting in Isabella who hurled a heavy moneybag into my lap. Gold pieces clinked inside.

"How much did it go for?" I asked quickly.

She shrugged. "Look yourself," she turned to the dusty mirror and began rearranging her hair. "Haven't you finished yet?"

I poured the gold into my inventory. Even though my cut turned out to be quite impressive, I was still almost five grand short of buying the smock.

"Is this together with the option?" I asked.

She gave me a meaningful look and smiled smugly. "Yes, Kitten. That's all of it."

✝ An NPC's Path: Book Two ✝

The alchemist, however, seemed to come alive on hearing it. "Did you say option? Isabella dearie, I hope you haven't got involved in anything serious."

"Ah," she gave him a theatrical sigh. "Don't even go there. It's broken me."

I hurried to rectify my faux pas. "Will you take it off my hands for five grand?" I slapped the sword in front of me.

The old man shook his head. "It's not about the money," he stroked his beard and explained further, "No good you trying to haggle. This has more of an ethical nature."

Isabella drew her attention away from the mirror. "A conflict of interests?" she said with an understanding smile.

The alchemist nodded. "I could give your coordinates to my client and you can negotiate directly. But let me warn you straight away: he has no money."

Isabella snorted. "You have a client who can't pay? Pull the other one!"

"He had to take out a loan to buy the suit of armor of the Autumnal Equinox and he hasn't even started to pay it off yet."

"Shit!" I swore. "Isabella, do me a favor.

Kingdom of the Dead

Lend me five grand."

"I don't think so, Kitten! I've already invested my share into raising my bid."

"Ah, the Crown of Chaos," the old man remembered. "It's a rare and expensive thing. But you can't become the High Priestess without collecting the full set."

Isabella winced. "Don't beat about the bush."

I frowned. "Why do we need that guy if he can't even pay?"

The alchemist shrugged. "He's collected the entire Autumnal Equinox set. The only thing that's missing is a suitable weapon. You might come to some agreement. Does the word *'barter'* ring any bells?"

Isabella gave it some thought. "Tell him to come to the Old Archer Inn," she decided for me. "It's on-"

"On Granite Island. I know it," Mr. Lloyd said.

Isabella nodded and turned to me. "Come on, Kitten!"

"Wait, all of you!" I exploded. "I have almost nine grand in my pocket and you want me to leave without buying anything?"

✝ An NPC's Path: Book Two ✝

The alchemist pushed the book across the table toward me. "Choose something affordable."

"Even better, stop splashing your money around and buy something decent but cheap until you've saved enough to buy the item you need," she advised.

Pensively I stroked the catalog's leather cover.

"Just as a suggestion, you could check the auctions for any bad builds."

"What do you mean?"

"Some people buy everything they can lay their hands on. And a single badly chosen article can seriously depreciate a non-separable set."

I resolutely rose from the table. "Why would I need badly chosen items?"

Mr. Lloyd shrugged, squinting his inhuman eyes. "I simply wanted to be helpful. Also, the items themselves can be quite decent. It's just that some of them are sought after by necros and others, like death knights, but when put together-"

I slumped back into the chair. "Are they really so much cheaper?"

"Let's take a look."

He pulled the book toward himself and

＃ Kingdom of the Dead ＃

began leafing through it.

Isabella gave a theatrical snicker. "I'll go see Ulrich then."

"Please do, dearie," the alchemist said as he turned the book toward me. "Here're some sets which contain only two or three items. Ten grand might do it."

I thanked him and began studying the offers. Still, the sets fell into two categories: very expensive and very stupid. Don't get me wrong: I still could buy something cheap that could considerably improve my other items. But why would I need a set containing an amulet with a bonus to spell-casting rate, a protection necklace against death magic and a bone bow? Or a ring that doubled the number of raised zombies, a two-handed Skull Crusher mace and an amulet with bleed protection. Or an Elemental Shield, a Staff of Death and a runic cuirass?

And so on and so forth. All kinds of junk.

When I'd already despaired of finding anything useful and decided to check two-item sets, I finally discovered the combination of Left Sleeve of Power and Belt of Memory.

The bracer, forged from some kind of dull metal, protected the arm from the wrist to the shoulder. The elbow was covered by some kind of hinged articulation. The steel pauldron sported a single spike.

Left Sleeve of Power (Deadman's Set: 2 out of 13)
Armor: 14
Strength: +2

Seven points Armor for each item in the set? That was actually quite decent, even though the object only protected my arm. With a bit of training, I could parry blows with my arm just as well as I could with my shield.

The wide belt covered with metallic plaques looked just as impressive. But that wasn't what made it so valuable to me.

The Belt of Memory (Deadman's Set: 2 out of 13)
Armor: 1
Adds one extra spell level 1 to 5.

The belt came with spells! Which in turn gave my half-baked Lich access to magic! It wasn't as if I really needed it — but the more I

Kingdom of the Dead

looked at the set, the more it appealed to me. Especially because the owner seemed to have lost all hope of ever getting rid of it so he'd dropped the price to seven and a half grand.

"I'll take it off you," I said to the alchemist, returning his book.

He chuckled skeptically. "There're better ways of pissing money into the wind."

I didn't want to hear. "I want you to close the deal," I demanded.

The old man shrugged. "If you say so. It'll be eight thousand two hundred fifty gold."

"Excuse me?"

He sighed. "And who's gonna pay the auction commission and urgent delivery?"

I gave up and shelled out the money.

"The deal is pending approval," he said. "The stuff will be available in an hour or two. Would you like it to be sent to your inn or would you rather collect it yourself?"

"Send it to the inn," I decided, unwilling to drag it out any longer. A game is an unpredictable thing. One never knew when I might need my new items.

"Would there be anything else?" he asked.

"Oh yes," I chuckled. "I need a few other

things too..."

6.

I LEFT THE SHOP with empty pockets. I'd splurged every gold piece I'd had on gear and wasn't in the least upset about it. Money isn't a goal but the means to achieving it, especially virtual money. What was I supposed to do, bury it? But without proper equipment I couldn't get any further.

The first thing I'd bought was two sets of rogue's clothes, a pair of sturdy gloves with metal studs and molded leather greaves complete with wrought-iron poleynes. Unfortunately, I couldn't use any other protection for my legs because both chainmail and armor plate hindered my Agility and came with a penalty to Dodge. The only piece of armor plate I'd bought was a right-arm bracer. As for a cuirass, the alchemist had suggested I left it until I got myself a Deadman's Pauldron. I'd also bought myself a very simple helmet made of hardened leather. It didn't offer much in terms of protection but at least it didn't prevent me from donning the hood.

But the bulk of my money had gone on the

Kingdom of the Dead

mask. The one Isabella had given me was on its last legs, and walking around the city with an open face wasn't really a good idea — at least not in daylight when my Almost Alive skill didn't work.

The old man laid another thick tome in front of me listing all available offers. But the moment I began leafing through it, Isabella rolled her eyes with a long-suffering sigh.

"Just tell him what you need and he'll have it made for you!" he said impatiently.

I looked up at the alchemist. "Can you do that?" I asked in surprise.

Mr. Lloyd smiled. "That's how we make our money. Normally, our clients come with more complicated orders but I can make an exception for you. Here, draw it," he offered me a sheet of paper.

I somehow drew an oval mask with slits for eyes and a few small holes in the place of a mouth.

"Would you like it to be anatomical?" he asked.

"Yes, please."

"Made out of what?"

"Does it really matter?"

✝ An NPC's Path: Book Two ✝

"Of course!"

"So what would you suggest?"

The alchemist shook his head. "It's only a question of what you can afford."

I opened my purse strings but reconsidered. I was a fool, wasn't I?

I reached into my inventory instead. "Will this do?" I asked, laying the bone golem's deformed pauldron onto the table.

The old man whistled in astonishment. "Black mithril? I would think so!"

Isabella hurried to check it and flashed me an unkind smile. "I can see you didn't leave that dungeon empty-handed, Kitten!"

I turned round and held her stare. "It's a different dungeon. The one in Stone Harbor."

"Really?"

"Yes, really."

The alchemist slapped his hand on the table, stopping our argument. "Sort out your differences in the street!"

He leaned over the crumpled piece of metal, studying it, then sighed. "I'd hate to waste black mithril on some half-cocked bodge job."

I got the hint and replied with an equally heavy sigh.

Kingdom of the Dead

We continued haggling for another quarter of an hour. As a result of which, I'd parted with the rest of my gold while the old man took it upon himself to make me a mask fitted with holders for three magic runes. It was pricey but definitely worth it.

WE PARTED perfectly happy with each other. On the way back, Isabella kept moaning about the time she'd wasted. I just laughed under my breath. As we approached the inn, I couldn't help it any longer.

"You're so mad because you couldn't get the Crown of Chaos, that's all."

I knew I'd touched upon a sore point when she started grinding her teeth in silent fury. I should really shut my mouth and not elaborate upon it any further.

"What kind of crown is that?" I asked, trying to appease her.

She sized me up and down with her piercing glare but replied nevertheless, "It's the last part of the Priest's Set of Chaos. I have all the rest."

I nodded. Suddenly I realized that I'd seen something which matched its description to a T.

✝ An NPC's Path: Book Two ✝

The golems' captain back in the dungeon seemed to have something very similar.

Still, I didn't tell her about it. My preservation instinct prevented me from doing so. Also, what was the point of giving her false hope?

ISABELLA TOOK ME back to the inn, then left on some business of her own. I walked upstairs to my room. I wasn't tired but I did need to restore my internal energy.

The moment I set the orcish longsword in the corner and collapsed onto the bed, Neo peeked from the other room. "Congratulations on your purchases, Uncle John."

Dammit! I should have thought of buying something for him too. I'd completely forgotten. So stupid of me. I wasn't used to caring about somebody else, let alone an NPC. What a shame.

"Have you already eaten?" I asked him simply to break the uneasy silence.

He nodded. "I have. Can I go out and take a look at the city?"

I shook my head. "I don't think that'd be a good idea."

"Why?" he sounded surprised. "I'm gonna take Scarecrow with me!"

✟ Kingdom of the Dead ✟

He opened the shutters. Immediately the black phoenix dove down from above and landed on the windowsill. His powerful talons left deep grooves in the wood.

"*Craaah!*" he yelled at the top of his lungs.

I winced, hesitating, then waved the boy away. "Okay, you can take him and go. But don't leave the island!"

"I promise!" Neo ran out the door, happy.

Scarecrow gave me a sideways look with his cloudy dead eyes, squawked again and took off into the open.

I was doubtful a dead phoenix could be of any tangible help to the boy — but what could happen to him in broad daylight? It wasn't a reason for me to keep him under lock and key!

I bolted the door and returned to the bed. But immediately I had to spring back to my feet. Someone was knocking demandingly at the door.

I grabbed at my flamberge still lying on the table but reconsidered and drew the bone hook from my belt instead. It seemed to be custom-made for close combat in small rooms like the one I was staying in.

There was another knock.

"Who is it?" I asked.

✝ An NPC's Path: Book Two ✝

"Your order," someone replied from the corridor.

I stood behind the door and withdrew the bolt. "Come in."

Me paranoid? I don't think so. Not when you have a crowdfunded reward of seventy grand on your head. Definitely not when you're blacklisted by the third most influential clan or when your arch enemy is hell-bent on finding and killing you.

The door swung open, letting in the alchemist's assistant who looked in bewilderment around himself, looking for me.

Finally, he saw me. "That's where you are, John!"

"What have you got there, Ulrich?"

"Just your auction stuff. Your mask isn't ready yet," he handed me a heavy bundle.

As soon as I'd locked the door behind him, I hurried to rip the packaging apart. The Belt of Memory turned out to be unexpectedly heavy. I put it on over my chainmail, then reached into the box for the Left Sleeve of Power.

It fitted me like a glove. It also came complete with a right-arm bracer albeit devoid of any magic properties. Had I known earlier, I

✟ Kingdom of the Dead ✟

could have saved myself some money.

Deadman's Set: Altered
Deadman's Set: Saved

I stood in front of the mirror and moved my arm around, admiring my reflection. The armor made of some dull metal or other looked incredibly serious. The elbow joint was very smooth with no creaking or play in it. Now I was pretty sure that was why my chainmail was missing the left sleeve.

I opened the item's stats.

The Left Sleeve of Power (Deadman's Set: 7 out of 13)
Armor: 49
Strength: +7

Excellent. Now I could parry blows with my left arm. But only if...

I frowned, realizing I couldn't see the promised bonus to Strength in the stats anywhere. I still had 28 pt. like before. What was that now?

Still, everything fell into place the moment I

✝ An NPC's Path: Book Two ✝

equipped my flamberge. Yes! I had it!

I put the sword down and took the bone hook in my left hand. The bonus was still there. Logical, really.

I started studying the rest of the stuff from the set, trying to find out whether their stats had improved too. The results quickly cheered me up. Even though the chainmail hadn't exceeded 25 pt., the Silver Deadman's Amulet could now restore 7% Health, Stamina and internal energy every 10 minutes.

Now I could use both Incognito and Almost Alive for as long as I wished without risking burning all my mana because the silver amulet could generate it one and a half times faster.

But my flamberge was admittedly the star of the show. The rusty spots on the blade filled with a blood-red glow, revealing black runes. The last remaining chips and dents had disappeared from its point. Its hilt began vibrating slightly in my hand, impatient for a new victim.

Bloody Flamberge (Deadman's Set: 7 out of 13)

Damage: 16-22
Accuracy: +15%

Kingdom of the Dead

Chance of causing critical damage: +15%
Chance of causing bleeding damage: 11% for each wave of the blade used in the strike

Five hundred damage with every successful blow! And what if it were a crit? And if I attacked a triple stationary target? Just think about it!

A bad build? Depends on who's using it!

Then I remembered the Belt of Memory. Had its bonus also worked?

Oh yes it had. My magic tab flashed with a new message suggesting I selected one of the level-1 spells.

That's when my head truly went round. If, at the time of my creating my char, I'd spent several days perusing the forums in search for the best leveling strategy for my rogue, magic still remained unchartered waters for me.

So how was I supposed to work it out?

It went without saying that I didn't even have to check zombie summoning. The undead raised by me would only scare a total newb. Attack spells weren't an option, either. Their damage would be laughable. And as for defense spells, they'd be breached by a single confident blow. I had my flamberge for attack and my

✝ An NPC's Path: Book Two ✝

Dodge for defense. What I needed was some spells capable of improving either of the two. I needed to come up with something to spice it up.

I spent some time collecting all available spells in a single window and began sorting through them, starting with those whose effectiveness depended on the sorcerer's Perception and not his Intellect. I removed death magic and soul magic from the list and started looking through the spells available exclusively to liches. That was something my enemy wouldn't expect.

How's that for spicing it up?

As a result, I opted for Touch of Death, Sphere of Dead Fire and the Leap. The first was an improved version of the Deathgrip already known to me. The second one exploded, decreasing the victim's Perception. And the third one could transport the sorcerer — a bit like a miniport, really, within a limited vicinity. It also was unable to transport him through any obstruction. In my case, 3 inches per Perception point resulted in a Leap of 3 feet. It may sound like nothing but an instant jump like that is precious for a swordsman, even if only for a couple of feet.

Kingdom of the Dead

That's it, then. I selected the spell and immediately tried it by leaping from the mirror back to the table.

It happened in an instant. I didn't even notice it. Just like I didn't notice the 100 pt. internal energy disappear in a flash.

That meant I'd be running on empty after just four Leaps. Still, all other spells burned considerably more mana. And in combination with the ability to detect the stares of others and the ability to hit invisible targets, Leap could become an unpleasant surprise for any rogue.

A deadly surprise.

I nodded to my own thoughts and sheathed the flamberge behind my back, about to leave the room. After some hesitation, I also picked up the black longsword. It would be stupid to have to run back to my room to for it if the orc buyer turned up.

WHEN I WENT DOWNSTAIRS, Mark gave me a nonchalant nod and took a sip of his strong aromatic coffee.

"Help yourself," he nodded at the coffee pot next to him.

"No, thanks," I leaned the black sword

against the bar and sat down on a creaky chair. "Listen, Mark. What you were saying about the Light and the Dark... what do you think? Who is who?"

The innkeeper sniffed. "What's that for a question? That's elementary!"

He didn't have the time to share his conjectures with me though. The front door swung noisily open. An enormous orc in black armor stepped into the inn. He held his horned helmet under his arm, allowing everyone to admire his grayish green skin, bloodshot eyes and the fangs protruding from under his upper lip.

Goar the Autumnal Thunder, Paladin of the Equilibrium

He wasn't just burly but also incredibly tall. He had to stoop when entering the inn, otherwise his head would have hit the doorframe.

Oh wow. I dreaded to even think how much money he'd thrown at his character building in order to circumvent the orcs' racial restrictions. It looked like an awful lot.

He looked around the dining hall, saw the

Kingdom of the Dead

longsword and beelined for me. I stepped toward him with a calm smile.

"John?" the orc boomed.

"That's me," I said, heading to the far corner. "Did Lloyd send you?"

He nodded and followed me. I really didn't have to ask. My sword and his black armor looked as if they definitely came from the same set. No doubt about it.

I set the sword against the wall and sat down, shielding it from the orc. I just didn't like the intent gaze with which he was eyeing his coveted weapon.

Nothing could be easier. All he'd have to do would be to reach out and take it. I was unlikely to stop a level-74 Paladin.

Goar the Autumnal Thunder forced his gaze from the sword and slumped on the opposite chair with a heavy sigh. The chair creaked its protest.

I couldn't help thinking about the guard of the lake. A cold shiver ran down my spine.

"How much are you prepared to pay for the sword?" I moved straight to the point. I'd already decided that the money I'd get for it should be enough to buy me that smock at least.

✝ An NPC's Path: Book Two ✝

Goar frowned and exhaled noisily. "Didn't Lloyd tell you I was broke?"

I smiled. "There's a big difference between broke and destitute."

"That's exactly what I am," he said.

I winced. "Too bad. Come back when you've made some more money."

He cast a quick glance behind my back.

"Not a good idea," I warned him.

That didn't stop him. He was already rising from the table when Isabella appeared out of nowhere.

"I don't think Lloyd will be happy to find out about this," she whispered in his ear.

The orc's goofy grin faded. He slumped back into the chair which creaked in protest under his weight. He appeared visibly shaken by Isabella's warning. An undisguised fear flashed in his eyes, if only for a split second.

I made a mental note. This Mr. Lloyd seemed to be a power to be reckoned with.

"I have no money," Goar said darkly, his hands clasped in front of him.

Isabella pulled up a stool from a neighboring table, sat down on it and gave him a smile. "So what do you suggest?"

⚔ Kingdom of the Dead ⚔

"I could work it off," he didn't sound too sure. "Or I could pay you back later."

I was just about to say that I needed the money now when I noticed Isabella's pensive stare. So I didn't say anything.

"You could work it off?" she said slowly. "How then?"

The orc shrugged. "I could kill someone. Or I could help you level up."

Isabella snapped her fingers. "We need a bodyguard!" she turned to me. "What do you think, Kitten? Should we hire old goofy for a month?"

I nodded. I liked her idea.

The orc, however, didn't seem too excited about it. I'll tell you more: his entire countenance turned into a grimace of disgust.

"Hanging around here doing nothing all month?" his broad nostrils flared. "Yeah right!"

Isabella rolled her eyes. "You, my dear friend, should use your head for a change instead of just stuffing it with food. Do you really think we would have needed a bodyguard had we been going to stay in the inn day in day out? This black piece of steel which for some reason is so dear to you, where do you think it came from?"

✝ An NPC's Path: Book Two ✝

    Goar pensively scratched his cheek with his gauntleted hand. "I want an equal share of the loot."

    Isabella and I exchanged glances. She shook her head. "You don't want much, do you?"

    He frowned at us. "I need to pay my bills. I'll be broke in a month."

    Isabella winced but decided to meet him halfway. "Twenty percent of the loot once it's sold."

    The orc nodded. "Deal."

    He reached out for the sword but I was still shielding it from him. "Aren't we going to sign something?"

    He gave me an evil eye, rose and said solemnly, "I swear by the Equilibrium to serve as a bodyguard to John... what's your name?"

    "John Doe."

    "... as a bodyguard to John Doe for a month."

    Tongues of ghostly flame flittered across his black armor. I handed him the sword.

    He very nearly jumped for joy but forced himself to remain calm. He stepped aside and began turning the sword in his hands as if he couldn't believe his own luck.

Kingdom of the Dead

Watching him, Isabella said with a sour look, "At least some good has come out of that stupid piece of metal."

"I'd have rather taken the money."

"Well, life isn't perfect. One always has to compromise."

I just sighed. You couldn't very well argue with that.

The front door swung open, letting in Ulrich. This time the box in his hands was quite small.

"Your order," he announced, setting the box on the table in front of me.

I swung the lid open and took out a black metal mask from its straw packing.

A Mask of Black Mithril.
Armor: 5
Runes: 0/3

"Everything's okay?" Ulrich asked.

"Perfect," I said, putting it on. It fitted the outlines of my face like a glove.

The alchemist's assistant bade his farewell to Isabella. When the door behind him closed, she said with a sarcastic smile, "You, Kitten, are

† An NPC's Path: Book Two †

now the man in the iron mask!"

"It's actually mithril," I corrected her.

I heard a knock on the door and turned to the sound. Still, no one entered.

"What did you say?" she laughed. "Speak up! I can't hear you!"

In fact, although admittedly dull, my voice sounded quite clear. I was just taking in a lungful of air intending to scream that much in her ear, when I stopped mid-word and gasped instead, "We've got visitors."

A cold unkind gaze prickled my back.

Chapter Two
The Raid of the Dead

1.

Watchful Stare! Leap!

I DODGED to the side. A blurred shadow flashed through the air just where I'd been standing a moment ago. Promptly forewarned, Isabella swung her staff, aiming its steel-topped skull at the attacker and sending him tumbling across the room. The assassin somersaulted lithely through the air, slid under the table and disappeared without a trace.

✝ An NPC's Path: Book Two ✝

I was already otherwise occupied. With a double-handed grip on my flamberge, I spun in place, activating both Sweeping Strike and Blind Strike.

The combo had proven to be the right choice. The undulating blade whooshed through the air. Its tip hit something invisible, faltered and then cut through it, cleaving the table in two.

The invisible wounded attacker recoiled, disappearing into the gloom of the hall. I stepped after him, looking intently for any claret splashes on the floor and walls. No such luck. For some reason, my flamberge had failed to draw blood.

I glanced at the logs and cussed,

Damage dealt: 214

Was that it now? No mention of bleeding wounds at all! That was crazy!

I backed toward Isabella. Immediately something slammed into me, knocking me off my feet. A curved scimitar fell from above, very nearly taking half of my head off; I'd managed to dodge it just in time. I then parried a double-ended weapon with my left bracer — but that was the extent of my success. Before I managed to

🗡 Kingdom of the Dead 🗡

duck out of their way, a thin sharp weapon pierced my side. Was it a bayonet? Or a rapier?

Irrelevant. Its thin blade slashed through my chainmail with ease, passing through my body and pinning me to the floorboards. Immediately another blow sliced through my leather leg protectors. The serrated blade ripped through my dead flesh and shattered the bone, stripping me of any hope of escaping the invisible assassins who were now attacking from all sides. And if I revealed myself to them, they would smoke me without hesitation.

So I decided to keep my Incognito. I was showered with blows. My wrought-iron pauldron had deflected some of them; a few were averted by my chainmail but some of its links were already broken. Another blow split my right pauldron.

My health plummeted. System messages began flashing, reporting the crits received.

Goar's black sword ripped through the air like dark lightning. Our assailants recoiled. Isabella's staff projected a long tongue of colorless flame which followed after the attackers. It may have been colorless but it was hot all the same: the fire flew above our heads but even so,

✝ An NPC's Path: Book Two ✝

our clothes began to smolder.

The attackers, however, didn't seem to be affected by it.

"Get up!" Isabella shouted, transforming into a fury.

What did she mean, "get up"? I grabbed at the sword blade pinning me to the floor with both hands and pulled it out, then rolled onto all fours and grabbed at the edge of the table.

Too slow! Way too slow!

Goar who by then had already slammed his black helmet onto his head, kicked the smoldering chair aside and began swishing his sword over his head, covering me from the assassins. They weren't ghostly shadows anymore as their invisibility had started to wear off. Now I could clearly see two tall silhouettes next to an unusually short one which constantly blurred in and out of focus.

Mark the innkeeper pulled a crossbow from under the bar. He fired at the attackers but missed, wasting the bolt which got stuck in the wall. The shot resounded across the room like a gong, forcing the assassins to charge at us again. Two of them lunged at Goar while the third one hurried to finish me off.

Kingdom of the Dead

As if!

Goar emitted a low growl. The air in front of him thickened. The attackers' movements became sluggish while his own black sword struck out at them with astonishing speed. A severed hand flew through the air; the shadows recoiled.

I awkwardly struck out at my assailant with the flamberge I'd picked up from the floor but twisted my ankle and staggered, very nearly losing my balance. Isabella backed me up by casting a bolt of lightning. The assassin convulsed; another crossbow bolt struck his side, forcing him to forget all about me and take cover behind an upended table.

I heard a crashing noise behind my back. The door of the storeroom swung open. Two golems in plain steel armor barged into the hall, carrying spiked maces on chains. They went for the assassins who by then had completely unstealthed and didn't resemble phantoms anymore. Their gear betrayed them as rogues but you couldn't be too sure because their profiles were inaccessible.

"Push them toward the exit!" Mark commanded.

✝ An NPC's Path: Book Two ✝

The problem was, our attackers showed no intention of retreating.

One of them waved his hands in the air. A thick cloud enshrouded him, swirling and spreading around the hall. It enveloped everything in its impenetrable veil, its burning cold paralyzing us and — more importantly — concealing our enemy.

The cloud tried to freeze me solid and syphon the life out of me. That trick didn't work with a deadman, though. With all her might, Isabella stuck her staff in the floor. The skull's empty eye sockets began casting a blinding light which quickly burned away the gray mist.

"Come to me!" she shouted. Goar and I backed off toward her. The brainless golems, however, perished within the cloud.

I glimpsed a blurred movement beside me and hurried to swing the flamberge. Its undulating blade sliced fruitlessly through the cloudy illusion. This time the assassins targeted Isabella but Goar saved the day again. Imperceptibly he stepped forward and shielded her with his body, then repeated his slowing trick, forcing the attackers to retreat into the mist.

Kingdom of the Dead

I stood with my back to Isabella's staff, its eyes still raging, and began tracing figures of eight with my sword, trying to create a steel barrier between us and the assassins lurking in their frosty cloud.

Goar was covering Isabella. Me, I was only protected by my blade. I wasn't afraid of dying but I really didn't feel like it. I'd much rather chop those scumbags to bits.

Oh the adrenaline!

The short guy went for my legs. I intercepted him, just grazing him with the very tip of my sword which ripped through his leather armor. The wounded midget tumbled out of my reach without completing the attack.

His partner, however, was more experienced — or simply luckier, I suppose. He reemerged just out of my field of vision and swung his serrated blade at me. My right arm hung listlessly.

I gave him a whack in the mouth with the sword hilt. Immediately the stubborn midget jumped on my back and sank his teeth into my neck. I was forced to let go of the sword, grab the bastard by the scruff of his neck and rip him off me, flinging him through the air. The tiny

✝ An NPC's Path: Book Two ✝

assassin rolled aside and began puking black blood and gunk all over the floor. What a dork.

My body swung round on its own accord, dodging a rapier that was pointing at my chest. I parried the serried blade with my bracer. Goar materialized behind the assassin's back, taking a swing with his black sword. Still, his blow didn't find its target as the rogue seemed to have somehow sensed the danger and had disappeared into the mist.

I stepped back into the circle of light cast by Roger the skull. Goar followed me. With a clattering of steel, two assassins threw themselves on him from both sides. Roger's light became much brighter. The gray mist filling the room began to fade and disperse. The frozen golems started to thaw out.

Isabella laughed a laugh that promised nothing good and pulled her staff out of the floor. Resisting the enemy spells hadn't been easy for her. She craved revenge.

The rogues retreated to the exit. But before we could launch a counter attack, the front door shuddered with blows.

"Open up! City guard!"

Mark stopped loading his crossbow and

Kingdom of the Dead

smiled carnivorously. "You scum! You're finished! You'll weep blood now!"

The assassins looked at each other. The one who'd cast the mist stepped forward. "Truce!"

We couldn't believe their cheek.

"Boys, have you gone nuts?" Isabella said sarcastically, waving her hand to Mark. "Come on, let them in now!"

"Wait!" the rogue demanded. "We're gonna tell everyone that this guy," he pointed his finger at me, "is the one from the silver phoenix video. They're gonna crucify you!"

I cussed.

"Mark, wait," the priestess hurried to say. "Let them go. This is personal. We'll sort it out ourselves."

"And who's gonna pay for the damages?" the innkeeper grumbled.

'We will," I hurried to add.

Mark shrugged. Immediately the knocking stopped. The golems staggered back into the storeroom with the broken gait of puppets on a string.

"What kind of shit is this?" Goar snorted, taking a better grip on his new sword. "All right. At least I won't have to share the XP."

✝ An NPC's Path: Book Two ✝

"Not here!" Mark snapped. "You'll never be able to pay for the furniture!"

"Calm down, goofy," Isabella said, then turned to the rogues' leader. "Let's talk."

He cast her a lopsided grin and sheathed his scimitars. After a moment of hesitation, his sidekicks did the same.

I laid the flamberge on a nearby table, making sure it was within reach of my left hand. I couldn't yet use my right one.

The orc balanced his sword on his shoulder without removing his helmet. Isabella, however, carelessly flung her staff behind her back, sat at one of the surviving tables and gestured to the assassins' leader to join her.

She appeared perfectly calm. Me, I didn't like the situation at all and I liked our opponents even less. Something about them wasn't right but I couldn't put my finger on what exactly it was.

All three looked like brothers: pale and thin, their faces gaunt, their eyes sunken, their lips bloodless. And they weren't even a night race. They were human, for crissakes. Even the midget covered in my dead blood was a human too.

"Call me Count," the leader said,

🗡 Kingdom of the Dead 🗡

apparently not in a hurry to open his profile.

Isabella chuckled and got straight down to business. "What do you want, Count?"

"Money," he cast an unkind glance at Goar. "Your goon has upset our applecart so we're prepared to offer you a discount. We can forget the whole thing for twenty grand."

"I just love your self-confidence," Isabella flashed them a sweet smile. "Did you really think that no one was going to recognize the Mist of Oblivion?"

The Count winced. "I didn't think it would have to come to that," he admitted. "It's irrelevant, anyway," he waved her objections away. "That doesn't change anything!"

Didn't it really? That remained to be seen.

The majority of players didn't know the difference between vampires and the undead. Attacking the vampires didn't entail any punishment; also, some alchemy chemicals could only be farmed from their bodies which were dead and alive at the same time.

Goar grunted in excitement, calculating all the achievements he might receive for smoking three vampires. Still the Count didn't seem to be alarmed by the news.

✝ An NPC's Path: Book Two ✝

"We'll simply disappear," he said. "Not the first time. Exposing us won't get you anywhere. We're outlaws as it is."

But even though the vampire leader remained calm, his younger sidekicks seemed to have tensed up. The tall one laid his hands on his weapons: both the rapier and the serrated broadsword. The midget took the hilt of his dagger with his good hand.

"We can also disappear," Isabella parried.

"Just for killing him the first time," the Count pointed at me, "we could get up to forty grand. With a bit of a tip-off, bounty hunters will always find you, even at the bottom of the sea. I'm not even talking about those who hunt for hunting's sake."

"Go stuff yourself," I said. "We're not paying you twenty grand!"

The orc nodded his approval.

"Also, we're a bit strapped for cash, goofy," Isabella smiled. "What we can do is go and rip someone's head off."

"With whose army?" Count snapped.

You could cut the air with a knife when Mark finally joined in the conversation. "So who's gonna pay for the damaged furniture?" he asked,

⚔ Kingdom of the Dead ⚔

laying a new crossbow bolt onto the bar.

The midget sniggered. "Certainly not us! Your so-called furniture isn't worth it."

"Look out the window," the innkeeper told him with a lopsided grin. "You're worse than children, really."

The rogue ran over to the window and cussed. "There're guards everywhere!"

"You won't get out of this place alive," Isabella said. "If you don't want to lose your XP, you'll have to come to terms with us."

The Count leaned back in his chair and shook his head. "You aren't going to believe our word anyway, are you?"

Isabella shook her head. "No, we aren't. What we can do is come to a mutually beneficial agreement."

The Count smiled skeptically, momentarily baring his sharp white fangs. "Speak up, my lovely!"

Hanging behind Isabella's back, Roger the skull turned with another crunching sound. His eyes glared with a vicious flame. Still, the vampire remained indifferent to this blatant demonstration of her power.

She gave him an appraising look. "The

✝ An NPC's Path: Book Two ✝

reward on Kitten's head, we're gonna share it."

'What?" I began.

Isabella waved my protest away, her eyes firmly fixed on the vampire's pale face.

The Count seemed to have been taken aback by her sudden proposal just as much as I had been. Still, he quickly got a hold of himself. "How interesting."

"What the hell?" I growled, theatrically this time.

Isabella's idea seemed to be a perfect way out of this stalemate. Not only did it allow us to half the reward on my head but it could also earn us twenty thousand gold. And I had no intention of sharing it with anyone.

"Fifty percent between three people isn't a lot," the Count finally managed.

"There're also three of us," Isabella reminded him. "Not counting the guards."

The Count winced. After a pause, he nodded and proffered her his hand. "Deal!"

He and the priestess shook on it.

"Don't you need to ask my consent?" I snapped.

Isabella heaved a sigh. "Why, are you so against it?"

🗡 Kingdom of the Dead 🗡

"No, but-"

"Excellent," she said nonchalantly. "Very well. Time is an issue, gentlemen. As a friend of mine likes to say, time is money."

2.

THEY DECIDED to kill me in Purple Hills, a large settlement on the road leading from the Tower of Darkness to the Southern Port. Apart from other considerations, Isabella had thought it prudent to throw other bounty hunters off our track. I didn't object.

The priestess opened a direct portal just for the three of us while the vampires had to use their own means of transport. We had to wait for them in a small park next to the stagecoach station. I had my white monastic robes ready without actually putting them on.

"You sure they're gonna share?" I asked Isabella, casting wary looks around. "What if they rip us off?"

She shook her head. "They won't. This is an official deal. Our fifty percent will be automatically transferred to my account."

✝ An NPC's Path: Book Two ✝

"And you'll forward it on to me," I said pointedly.

"I will."

"And what about my cut?" Goar reminded us.

Isabella curved a surprised eyebrow. "Are you really gonna claim a reward for your employer's murder? You can't be serious!"

He frowned. "Had it not been for me, they would have made mincemeat of you!"

I chuckled. "And without us, you would have never laid your hands on that sword," I pointed at a stage coach drawn by eight horses. "There they are."

The orc let out a noisy sigh but refrained from further financial aspirations.

"Don't worry, goofy, " Isabella said placatingly. "We can be grateful. You'll get your chance to become stinking rich. Kitten, don't forget: we'll meet up by the local Tower of Power."

"I'll be there."

I donned my white cloak of the Order of the Silver Phoenix and replaced my new mask with the old black-and green one, then hurried toward the station.

We had to make it appear perfectly

Kingdom of the Dead

accidental. Just a chance meeting, no more. All would go well provided we didn't come across any of the locals.

I stepped into a narrow street leading away from the park and cast a wary glance around before hurrying past the rows of shuttered houses. The sound of a bell reached me from the station. Immediately a rider on a black stallion appeared from around the bend, followed by a huge dog, its eyes aglow with ghostly flames.

The dark knight studied my disguise and even reined in his horse but didn't reach for his lance and finally rode past.

I cussed and hurried on. Soon I came across three vagabonds in dusty clothes and wide-brimmed hats. I had to step back to the wall in order to let them pass. They didn't even look at me. But the moment they passed my back...

Watchful Stare!

I received the skill's warning a split second before the attack. Although it left me plenty of time to dodge it and draw the flamberge, I ignored it. The outcome had already been predetermined, so what was the point revealing my strong sides

✝ An NPC's Path: Book Two ✝

to the enemy?

The scimitar sliced sideways through my chainmail. I felt weak. The world around me accelerated to the point where I couldn't keep up with it.

Freeze: 30%.

The vampire's magic had slowed me down. Still, I had no intention of playing their game. I doubled up and swung round as I yanked the two-handed sword from behind my back. The Count's second scimitar clanged, deflected by my wrought-iron pauldron.

The midget went for my legs, receiving my steel-clad knee in his face for his trouble. His teeth went flying.

Without a moment's hesitation, I attacked the third vampire with my Rapid Strike. The blade of my flamberge thrust forward with a speed my enemy couldn't have ever anticipated.

One. Two. Three.

He tried to parry the blow with his rapier but lingered just a moment too long. My sword's blade sliced through his arm; my next lunge easily pierced his light chainmail. I pulled the

† Kingdom of the Dead †

sword out of his ripped-open belly and pointed it down, chopping through his knee. My well-aimed blow sliced his meniscus in two.

Still, instead of dropping to the ground, the vampire hopped on one leg as he attacked me with his broadsword. I'd barely managed to parry its serrated blade with the flamberge's guard.

The next moment the Count was already upon me, swinging his scimitars. It felt like standing in the path of an airplane propeller. He sliced through my chainmail as if it were paper.

My health already in the red, I backed off along the wall. The midget, however, jumped on my legs, clutching them and forcing me onto my back. I didn't even try to get up from the pavement; instead, I gave him a solid whack across the back with my flamberge. The midget shuddered but didn't slacken his grip. I turned the sword in my hand, trying to get to the Count...

A flash.

Darkness.

DIRT. GRASS. BUSHES. An overcast sky.

I was back.

I tore the sods of turf apart and climbed

✝ An NPC's Path: Book Two ✝

out of the shallow grave. I put the magic skull back into my bag and slumped onto the ground. Immediately my ears began to ring with the memory of my agony which receded as soon as I tried to turn my head on its side.

Never mind. It's only a game. Besides, I'd already resurrected, hadn't I?

I had indeed. Still, the longer I stayed in the world of the Towers of Power, the clearer and more tangible it became. One day I might believe that it was real. Then my death would become real, too.

And that would be the end of me.

I shrugged the cold off and scrambled to my feet. I had to check my gear. My leather helmet seemed to be the only thing missing. The rest was all there. Not bad. The main thing was, my white cloak had survived. I might have a use for it later.

I picked up the flamberge from the ground, balanced it on my shoulder and headed for the Tower of Power looming over the city roofs, dark and threatening. One look at it made the already miserable day even more somber and foreboding. Or was it just a bad premonition?

I heard the clatter of hooves on the

Kingdom of the Dead

cobblestones and dove into the bushes to avoid a cavalcade of players galloping along. The hunting dogs which dashed after the horses began barking at me but they didn't go into the park and continued to follow their masters.

I cussed, still tense, and forced myself to slacken my white-knuckled grip on the sword.

What the hell? Did that mean that my Dog Slayer achievement, on top of the damage and crit bonuses, also gave me the desire to make mincemeat out of every pooch I came across? That really was the last straw! The game was slowly going to my head. And it really didn't please me — if anything, it scared me a lot. Once I was brought out of my coma, the physical rehabilitation might be the least of my problems. I'd better start thinking about how to keep my brains in gear.

I shrugged and peeked out of the bushes. All clear.

I scrambled to my feet and hurried away from the park. I didn't meet many of the locals on my way, and all of them were busy doing their own thing. No one seemed to be too worried about the recent fight. The number of guards in the streets stayed the same — and as for the

✝ An NPC's Path: Book Two ✝

players, I met none at all other than the earlier cavalcade.

I walked past a small street market with a few customers ambling up and down its stalls and found myself on the town square. There, the Tower of Power which previously hadn't seemed too high from behind all the houses, took on a whole new height, losing its spire in the clouds. It gave me goosebumps.

And not only goosebumps. A fiery whirlwind enveloped me, lifting me off the ground and throwing me into the air, then hurling me back down and rolling me along the pavement.

Dammit!

Fury of a Goddess: defense failed!
Perception penalty: 75%.
Agility penalty: 25%.

My white cloak burst into flames as if it was soaked in kerosene. The mask caught fire too. My whole world turned into a big white blob. I couldn't see anything. I sort of somersaulted over one shoulder, dodging the attack, jumped back to my feet and blindly slashed away with my flamberge, keeping it parallel with the ground.

☦ Kingdom of the Dead ☦

Got you!

Isabella was about to deal me a coup de grace when she ran onto my sword. Her breastplate couldn't withstand the blow from its undulated blade

With a scream, she hit me over the head with the skull topping her priestly staff. Her movement was so lightning-fast I simply hadn't noticed it.

I saw stars. The priestess hurried to step back, increasing the distance between us and leaving a bloody trail on the cobblestones. I'd finally got her!

The fire enveloping me continued to deal damage. I raised the flamberge above my head and went for her — but Isabella dodged my blow with a surprising ease and hurled a fireball at me.

The explosion stunned me. Immediately I received another blow with the skull. But this time, even though I'd missed it, I'd managed to grab at her staff with my right hand while hitting her in the face with the hilt in my left.

Isabella staggered. I grabbed at her, allowing the burning flames to spread to her priestly robes. No way. I burned away much faster than she did.

Which was exactly what we'd counted on.

3.

GOAR AND I WERE OBLIGED to return to the capital on our own as Isabella had to shake off the guards chasing her. In any case, the vicinity of the Tower of Darkness wasn't the best place for a player sporting a PK mark. The logout time wasn't included in the penalty's duration which was why even in the best-case scenario Isabella couldn't make it back to the inn before tomorrow. Having said that, the future reward for my murder more than paid for all the possible inconveniences.

Twenty grand for a stage fight divided by two is still a lot of money.

Really, had players lost XP in the case of death, I'd have thought twice whether or not it was worth it. But the way it was now — why not? Apart from the fact that I'd earned a nice grand total of thirty thousand gold, the reward on my head had accordingly been slashed to a quarter. That was bound to put a lid on all the hoo-hah,

Kingdom of the Dead

forcing the professional bounty hunters to lessen their zeal.

MY WHITE MONASTIC ROBES had been burned to a crisp, so I was forced to put on my rogue's duds. Even though my black-and green mask had survived, I discarded it without hesitation and put on my new mithril one instead. After my fight with the vampires, it now sported three long furrows, adding the word «Scratched" to its original description. Still, it didn't seem to have affected its stats.

"Hurry up," Goar said when I finally found him in the park. "My game time is nearly up."

"OK, let's go," I said.

An unfolding portal ripped through the air. I stepped into its square mouth.

Bang!

There we were back in the inn's dining hall.

The orc rushed upstairs, armor clattering.

Neo ran toward me. "Uncle John! Why didn't you take me with you? I'm so bored!"

I tousled his hair. "Next time," I promised.

"Honest?"

"Honest," I lied. "Have you eaten?"

"Yes."

✝ An NPC's Path: Book Two ✝

"Then go to your room, then."

"And you?" he asked, smelling a rat.

"I'm coming in a moment. I just need to speak to Uncle Mark."

The boy nodded and obediently headed for the stairs. Scarecrow stopped glaring at me with his cloudy dead eyes and, in one powerful wingbeat, sprang from the cupboard onto the boy's shoulder. Neo staggered, his shoulders lopsided under the phoenix's weight.

Seeing me coming, Mark put a bottle of whisky on the table.

I shook my head and said, pointing behind my back, "Have you already cleaned the place up?"

He grinned. "As you can see."

They'd already replaced all the broken furniture, given the floor a lick of paint and covered the burn marks on the walls with some drapes. You wouldn't have believed that only a few hours ago, the places had been such a shambles.

Mark downed a shot of whiskey. "How's things?"

I sighed. "Okay, I suppose."

Suddenly I sensed somebody's presence.

🗡 Kingdom of the Dead 🗡

The bone hook's handle jumped into my hand as if of its own accord.

Still, it turned out to be a false alarm. The shadows thickened, disgorging the Count. The aura of the PK mark still hovered clearly around him, even if dull and fading already.

"Gentlemen!" the vampire flashed us a pearly smile as he lobbed a heavy money purse onto the bar. "My humble contribution to the repair works."

Mark dragged it toward him, looked inside and visibly relaxed. You could see that he was happy with the compensation.

"Problem solved?" the Count asked.

"It is," Mark said. "Still, you'd better go now. Nothing personal. It's just that if one of my guests comes down and sees a PK here, I'm afraid we'll have to renovate the place again."

The vampire grinned. "That's exactly what I wanted to talk to you about," he leaned forward over the bar. "Nobody likes an assassin. We need a place to sit it out. You think you could rent us out your basement?"

"The basement's already taken," he snapped. Then he paused, thinking. "How about in the attic?"

✝ An NPC's Path: Book Two ✝

"Is it dark there?"

The innkeeper took a long key off a bunch and chucked it to the vampire. "Go and take a look."

The Count hurried toward the stairs. The shadows in the dark corner stirred, following him like two ghostly wisps of smoke.

"Aren't you afraid of giving shelter to vampires?" I asked. "Won't you have problems if they're discovered?"

Mark shrugged. "Attics! If you leave them unattended long enough, all sorts of things breed in them," he grinned and began polishing beer mugs with a towel.

Suddenly I realized that the Count had said nothing about the reward on my head. I jumped off my stool and followed the vampires.

The attic was submerged in gloom. Still it can't have been enough for the vampires. The Count's sidekicks were now busy stopping up the cracks in the shutters with rags. The room was rapidly becoming pitch black.

The Count chuckled. "Isn't it too dark for you, John?"

"Not really," I said, removing my mask. "It's okay."

🗡 Kingdom of the Dead 🗡

Now that they weren't afraid of meeting other guests anymore, the vampires stopped pretending to be human. In fact, there was very little humanity left in their appearances now. They looked more like the walking dead with their pallid faces, bloodless lips and taut skin pulled over their skulls. Basically, that's what they were: just another version of the undead.

At level 77, the Count was the most advanced amongst them. The lanky Marquis was twenty levels below him and the little Baron, all of twenty-five.

"I like it here!" the vampire leader announced. "I think we're gonna stay here for a while!" he looked at me and added with a smile, "You can't even imagine how difficult it is to find a sympathetic landlord."

"Yes, I can," I said with a crooked smile. "Is it very difficult to play as a vampire?"

His eyes flickered blue in the dark. He perched himself onto a dusty chest and yawned. "Nothing is easy in this game until you get yourself properly leveled," he finally said. "Why, you wanna become one? If you're level fifty, I could convert you, I suppose. But you'll have to start playing from scratch. You won't be able to preserve any of your old abilities."

I snickered. "Are there many players who agree to be converted?"

The Count smiled. "Not really. Only the most stubborn ones."

The Marquis walked over to us. He threw his rapier and broadsword onto a painter's scaffold and added, "And then you spend the next twenty-five levels hiding away from the sun. It burns you even through your clothes."

"And until you reach level fifty, your magic won't work during daytime."

The Baron laughed. "Shit! I haven't even started living yet!"

I could clearly see the blue notches of magic tattoos glowing on his skin in the dark. From time to time, he scratched them as if they physically inconvenienced him.

"Okay, John," the Count slapped his bony hand on a nearby vat. "Did you want something from me? If it's about you wishing to convert, you need to do a three-month quest first. In any case, we don't need a newb. And you won't be able to survive on your own."

I shook an impatient head. "No, it's not about that. What about the reward? Have you

🗡 Kingdom of the Dead 🗡

received it?"

"Forty grand, every penny of it!" the midget grinned, poking a wooden partition with his dagger.

"We've already transferred twenty grand to your girlfriend," the Count said. "Anything else?"

I could see his patience with me was wearing thin. Still, I decided to use the occasion and discover everything that was still unclear to me. "How did you find me?"

The Count shrugged. "We followed you."

His answer surprised me so much I even left the safety of the wall. "Why the hell? You couldn't have possibly known there'd be a reward on my head!"

For a moment, the Baron stopped poking the wall and snickered. "We just needed a Light Disciple!"

The Marquis tried to hush him up.

"Why?" the Baron turned to him. "What did I say?"

"You needed a Light Disciple?" I repeated after him. "Why? Is their blood any different?"

"Their blood is no different from anybody else's," the Count replied nonchalantly. He pulled out a flask and drank from it, then used the back of his hand to wipe the dark red from his lips. "What difference does it make to you? You're not a Lightie, are you? I can feel it. You smell sort of dark."

"If you need a Light God's disciple, I can find one for you."

The Count stood up and gave me a sharp intense look, apparently thinking of what I'd just said. I didn't want to hurry him.

"Can we trust him?" he finally asked. "Won't he blab?"

"No, he won't," I said. "The only question is, what you need him for."

"We need to get something," he began pensively, then stopped, waving my question away. "Not now. I need to give it some thought."

But it looked like the little Baron had already decided. "This is a very good offer!" he said simple-heartedly. "What's there to think about? It's a no-brainer!"

"You'd better shut your mouth," the Marquis advised him. "You've got a loose tongue, you."

The Baron gave him the finger. "Up yours!"

"You're asking for trouble!"

"Quiet, you two!" the Count shouted, then

Kingdom of the Dead

added with a sigh. "John, how about you make yourself scarce?"

There was no warmth at all left in his voice which now rang with sepulchral cold. Still, we deadmen have thick skins. His irritation didn't get to me at all. I gave him a carefree smile, saluted everyone and left.

I was already walking down the stairs when the Count appeared in the doorway.

"You know what, John," he said pensively, "I just can't work you out. You're not quick enough for a rogue; and for a warrior, you've got a glass jaw. Who are you?"

"Executioner," I said, looking at him expectantly.

"I see," he slammed the door shut.

So much for our conversation.

I winced and cussed under my breath. Not quick enough? A glass jaw? Dammit! He was dead right there! If only I could level up Dodge or at least buy myself a decent cuirass! The problem was, no one was gonna train a deadman — and as for any armor, I just couldn't afford it at the moment.

Having said that, why not? I was about to receive a nice lump sum of money...

✝ An NPC's Path: Book Two ✝

4.

THE NEXT DAY Isabella arrived at the inn with a burned face and singed hair, her clothes covered in blood. Her PK mark had by then already faded.

""Don't ask!" she demanded the moment she walked in. She stepped aside to give way to an enormous bathtub brought in by the servants. The moment the door had closed on them, she unabashedly peeled her clothes off and climbed into the hot water.

Neo had his breakfast downstairs, which was why I decided not to get het up about her lack of propriety and just slumped back onto the bed.

"Can you scrub my back?" Isabella asked.

"No," I said, unwilling to get my hands wet.

"Yeah right," she laughed, soaping her shoulders. "As if I don't remember the fiery embrace you gave me yesterday!"

I chuckled. "Where have you been?"

"First the guards were after me. Then some scumbags decided they wanted to hunt me. I barely threw them off."

"And the money?" I moved to the point.

⸸ Kingdom of the Dead ⸸

"The Count said they'd transferred my cut already last night."

She sighed. "Kitten, you're so mercenary!"

Still, she decided not to test my patience any further. She reached out of the bath and pulled a taught money purse from her clothes. "Take it!"

The heavy purse very nearly hit me in the face. I caught it just in time, opened its laces and grinned.

Thirty-one thousand seven hundred gold!

I was rich. Not for very long though.

"Where do you think you're going?" Isabella asked anxiously when I got off the bed.

"I'm gonna see Lloyd about more items from that set."

"Wait up," she stopped me. "I'm coming with you. I'm gonna raise my bid on the Crown of Chaos."

"Why, aren't you going to heal your burns first?" I asked, pointing my finger at my face.

"They'll heal themselves," she said nonchalantly as she began to rinse the lather off herself.

But before she could climb out of the bath, there was a knock at the door.

✝ An NPC's Path: Book Two ✝

The priestess got back into the water. I sprang toward the table and grabbed my flamberge.

Neo wouldn't have bothered to knock. In which case, who the hell could it be?

"It's open!" I shouted aloud, ready to use my sword at a moment's notice.

The door swung open, letting in the Count.

He stopped in his tracks. "Oh!"

"Close the door," Isabella demanded. "It's drafty in here."

The vampire did as she said. He cast me a sideways glance and winced. "I hope I'm not intruding..."

"Not at all," Isabella gave him a charming smile and ran her slender fingers along the ash-gray skin of her shoulder. "On the contrary."

"I don't think so," the Count snapped. He may have looked like a sinewy middle-aged man but he was actually as dead as a doornail. Just like me.

"Blood circulation," I reminded Isabella. "I told you, didn't I? Without blood circulation, one is useless."

The Count gave me a long look and pensively scratched his neck.

☦ Kingdom of the Dead ☦

I smiled. "No offence meant. Nothing personal. Pure fact."

The vampire nodded and moved on to business. "I'd like to talk to you about yesterday's conversation. We might need a Light Disciple's assistance in a — in an enterprise, sort of. If you think you can arrange it, just name your price."

Isabella squinted but didn't betray her surprise in any other way. She remained silent, permitting me to run the negotiations.

"What kind of enterprise?" I asked. "We need at least some information."

The Count must have come prepared. "We need to get something from a place which is only accessible to a Light player," he replied without hesitation. "And not just any player but one who is consecrated to one of the gods of Light. We'll take care of his or her transport and safety."

I gave a pensive chuckle. "Are you so desperate you're prepared to enlist help from someone you don't even know?"

The vampire bared his small sharp teeth in an unkind smile. "We're in the capital of the Dark world. There aren't many Light players here," he said, then added sarcastically, "I wonder why!"

Isabella plunged her head under water,

then resurfaced, caught her breath and asked, "What is it? Where is it?"

"That's irrelevant!" the Count snapped. "I just want you to introduce me to such a player."

"The Light guy we know only works with us," Isabella said, combing her wet hair. "And he is, how can I put it, one-time use. So everything has to be done the first time. There'll be no second takes."

The vampire turned a chair's back toward the bathtub and sat down on it, leaning his chest on the back of the chair. "Please explain," he demanded.

"It's an NPC," I offered.

"Yeah right!" he sniffed. "Pull the other one!"

"Did you see a boy with me the last time? Or weren't you paying attention?"

"A boy?" he drawled, looking confused. He screwed his neck in his collar like a boxer. "I can't say I remember him very well. But if you two vouch for him…"

"We want more details," Isabella demanded.

The vampire gave her a hesitant look. After a pause, he must have made up his mind.

"There's this deserted monastery that has a

Kingdom of the Dead

very powerful protection at its very lowest level. It won't let anyone through apart from Light Disciples. And there's no other way of getting to the treasury. All we need is one particular artifact. The rest we'll split in equal shares."

I chuckled skeptically. "What makes you so generous?"

He didn't play hard to get. "I'm not sure we can tackle the dungeon's guard on our own," he cast me a doubting glance. "I'm not sure about you, John, but we sure could use a hand from the priestess and her orc friend."

Isabella accepted the compliment with a deadpan face. "Where's the monastery?"

"That's irrelevant."

"Is it on land the Darks took from the Lights?"

"That's irrelevant too."

"If it's on the Lights' territory, we're not getting involved."

The Count paused. "Do I look crazy enough to trespass on their turf?"

"In that case, count us in," Isabella said without even consulting me.

The Count nodded. The priestess sat up in the tub and proffered her hand to him.

✝ An NPC's Path: Book Two ✝

He shook her wet fingers. "We might need a day or two to prepare everything," he warned her. "But first I need to see your Light Disciple. I didn't get a good look at him the last time."

"Could you please wait outside," I said.

Once he'd left the room, I lowered my voice, "You sure it's a good idea?"

She laughed. "It's only a game! You aren't seriously going to mope around the inn waiting for the Spawn of Darkness to finally make up their minds?"

I gave her words some thought. "No, I'm not."

Still, I had a bad feeling about it. I'd hate to take Neo on a dangerous raid like this. One single mistake, and that would be it.

Part of a program code? I beg to differ.

WHEN I WALKED out into the corridor, the Count was waiting for me on the stairs. Together we went down to the dining room. By then, Neo had already finished his breakfast and was fooling around throwing bits of bread to Scarecrow. The dead phoenix caught them with his formidable beak in mid-flight.

The Count heaved a disappointed sigh.

† Kingdom of the Dead †

Neo turned to us. The vampire winced. "Oh."

"Uncle John? Are we going anywhere today?"

"A bit later," I replied, then turned to the Count. "How did you find the monastery?"

He gave me a crooked smile. "We were searching for a fortress for my future clan."

"Your clan?"

"I'm quite ambitious, you know."

We started back upstairs. "What kind of guard is there?"

"A dead dragon," he said quite openly. "Vicious bastard. He can see the invisible. A mouse couldn't creep past him. Even I with my high Stealth couldn't do it, not to even mention the others. They still have a lot to learn."

"Learn what?" I asked curiously. "Stealth?"

The vampire nodded.

"Are you teaching them?" I asked.

"I'm a Master of the school of Shadow Walkers," he said with pride. Then he smiled, apparently realizing the source of my interest. "It's a vampire school. Living beings can't join."

"And what if I could?"

"No, you couldn't," he snapped as he

✝ An NPC's Path: Book Two ✝

swung the attic door open.

I followed him. Once inside, I took my mask off and deactivated my Almost Alive ability.

The Count recoiled. In the blink of an eye, he had the scimitars in both hands. The Marquis dropped from his hammock, jumped to his feet and pointed his rapier at me. The Baron grabbed his daggers.

"A Lich..." the Count drawled. "What a surprise."

I could have used my mental control to force them into it. Instead, I just spread my arms wide. "So how about me joining your school?"

The Count calmed down a little. "You're a player, aren't you?" he asked, sheathing his scimitars.

"I am."

"But you're also dead?"

"It's not as if you're completely alive yourselves."

"That's different."

"I'm a participant in closed beta testing of a new update," I offered him the most believable of explanations. At least now they stopped staring at me as if I was a monster with two heads. Now they had a more serious reason to be anxious.

🗡 Kingdom of the Dead 🗡

"Bummer!" the Baron cussed. "What an idea! Now we'll have hundreds of dead players roaming around. I took a tiny bite of this one and I couldn't stop puking! And what if-"

"Then you shouldn't bite everything that moves, should you?" the Marquis quipped.

The Count gave me a long look. "Do you have 15 pt. Stealth already?"

"I do."

"A Lich leveling Stealth?" the Baron whistled in surprise. ""Where's this world going?"

The Marquis gave him a slap on the side of the head. The two went for each other and locked in a desperate clinch.

Ignoring their scuffle, the Count announced the price of his tuition, "Ten grand. Half upfront. If anything goes wrong, the advance is non-refundable."

I tried to haggle for a bit but he must have realized my interest in this so he didn't budge an inch. I had to agree to his terms with the risk of losing five thousand and getting nothing in return. But what could I do? I was desperate to level up Stealth.

I heaved a forlorn sigh. "Here, take it," I counted out the right amount and handed him

✝ An NPC's Path: Book Two ✝

the gold.

The Count wasn't in a hurry to accept it, eyeing me with hesitation.

"What now?" I said. "You'll get the rest once you've done it. You know I have the money, don't you?"

He winced unhappily but scooped up the coins, then made a complex gesture with his right hand.

"I'm starting the initiation," he warned me. "Be ready."

A quivering gray haze formed between us, repeating my mentor's silhouette, a bit like a shadow which had gained freedom.

"Come on!" he hissed. "Step in, quick!"

I took a step forward, entering the shadow. Immediately I began shuddering all over.

I'd gained new knowledge! Yes! That's what it was!

"Did it work?" the Count asked me, wiping sweat from his brow.

Ignoring his question, I handed him the remaining fee, then began studying my character's new stats.

Student of the School of Shadow Walkers.

Kingdom of the Dead

Maximum Stealth level: 25
Stealth in combat: 1 sec per each 10 skill points
Half-stealth in combat: 1 sec per each 2 skill points

Yippee! Not only could I level it up now but I could also remain invisible for at least two seconds after the initiation of combat. And then I had another twelve seconds of half-stealth!

I used my available points to bring the skill to 25, then asked the Count, "What next? Can you make me an Apprentice?"

The vampire's eyes widened in surprise. "What, just like that?"

"And where am I supposed to look for you afterwards? This way we can do it and part company."

He shook his head. "You need a Senior Master to do that. And trust me, that has a totally different price tag."

"You'll have to shell out fifty grand or more," the Baron informed me. "And waste another couple of weeks on a quest. But no one's gonna work with you anyway. You're a Lich, not a vampire. If you ask me, it wasn't a great idea

✝ An NPC's Path: Book Two ✝

accepting you as a stu-"

"Shut your mouth!" the Count barked.

The midget promptly shut up. He must have said something I wasn't supposed to hear. I hurried to bid my goodbyes and went back downstairs.

I felt good. No wonder! Two seconds were enough for me to crit anyone, anywhere. My flamberge was no comparison to their daggers or even scimitars.

But the moment I stepped back into the dining hall, my good mood disappeared. I stealthed up and drew the sword from behind my back.

Immediately I reconsidered. I shouldn't jump the gun, so I simply stepped back into the corridor.

It was Prince Julien who'd just arrived at the inn, as large as life and twice as ugly. This time he seemed to be having a friendly conversation with Isabella which gave me some hope for a peaceful outcome of this visit. Could it be that the Spawn of Darkness had finally made up their minds? If so, then very soon I might find myself in the Kingdom of the Dead.

I shuddered. Still, it looked like I'd

Kingdom of the Dead

celebrated too early. The Prince sprang up angrily from the table, snapping at Isabella. It didn't look as if the negotiations were going well. At least the Prince hadn't drawn his sword.

I couldn't help it any longer. I unstealthed and walked out into the hall.

On seeing me, Julien froze open-mouthed. His chiseled face turned to stone. A deep line furrowed his brow.

"So, you didn't talk her into showing you her tits?" I asked, using his moment of hesitation. "Once a sucker, always a sucker. I don't even need to ask her."

He started heavily toward me but stopped half-way. "I'll deal with you some other time," he promised, then left the inn, slamming the door behind him.

"You shouldn't have made him angry," Isabella reproached me, spreading her aroma of essential oils.

"What did he want?" I asked, ignoring her scolding.

She shrugged. "He offered to double the price for the fragment of the Sphere of Souls," she said somewhat pensively.

"Are they so desperate?"

✟ An NPC's Path: Book Two ✟

"*He* is," she corrected me. "Prince Julien. Or so I think. He seems eager to show his worth — but unfortunately, he has more money than sense. He thinks that money can buy anyone."

"Money's worth nothing," I said. "So are they going to accept our conditions?"

"The Spawn of Darkness?" she laughed. "Of course they will. The auctions are in turmoil. The profiteers are milking it for every cent."

I grinned. It would have been strange if people had ignored such an excellent opportunity to make money.

Isabella rose from the table. "Are you coming?" she asked, pointing at the door.

I nodded. "Where's Goar?"

"He's busy IRL," she said. "He promised to log in later."

At that moment, Neo appeared out of nowhere. "What about me?" he screamed. "Are you taking me with you? I'm booooored! Uncle John, you promised!"

"Come on, then!" I waved.

Isabella gave me a meaningful look. I pointed at the ceiling, reminding her of our deal with the vampires. "Did you forget? Let's take him with us, just to be on the safe side."

✟ Kingdom of the Dead ✟

The priestess rolled her eyes and succumbed. "Let's go already!"

5.

OUR NEXT VISIT to the demonic alchemist's shop was a bit of a disappointment. No, not really. I'd received what I'd planned to get but nothing more. Even though my hopes of getting more hadn't been exactly ungrounded. Twenty-one thousand gold is quite a bit of money, after all. But unfortunately, it hadn't quite worked out like that.

The Count's words about me being unable to take a blow gave me the idea of spending the money on some armor but unfortunately, cuirasses turned out to be the rarest and the most expensive parts of the Deadman's set. And considering the fact that the set itself wasn't exactly popular, the owners of the parts of armor I needed demanded exorbitant prices.

How about checking bad builds? I went through the catalogs with a fine-toothed comb but found nothing suitable. Either they offered something I needed paired with some useless

✝ An NPC's Path: Book Two ✝

weapon or other, or the cuirasses themselves interfered with my ability to dissolve into the shadows and cost much more than the remaining money I had.

Watching me struggling, Mr. Lloyd was laughing up his sleeve. "That's how people become obsessed," he chuckled.

"This is outrageous!" I exclaimed.

"Not everything can be bought," he said, hiding his strange amber eyes behind a pair of dark alchemist's glasses. "That's the whole point of the game. If you need something in particular, you should rummage through manuscripts, call up a support group and go on a raid. Alternatively, you can join a clan. What you can get at auction is only what clan armorers don't want."

"Bummer!" grinding my teeth, I pushed the heavy book away from me. "Never mind. I'm gonna take the Shadow of Death. Fourteen thousand, wasn't it?"

"Fifteen thousand four hundred," he said, smiling.

I cussed again but accepted. Having said that, what was I mad about? Only a while ago, I would have counted myself fortunate to have laid

Kingdom of the Dead

my hands on an item like that.

While Mr. Lloyd submitted a transaction confirmation and an urgent delivery request, I began leafing through catalogs again. But my remaining five and a half grand didn't even come close to buying me anything decent — and the bad builds offered for this kind of money were blatantly useless.

I had to get a grip. I bought myself a leather helmet to replace the one that I'd lost and also got some simple gear for Neo. He couldn't go on wandering around in homemade sandals.

Finally, I removed my mask. "How about the runes?"

The old man pushed his alchemist's glasses onto his forehead, hooking them over his tiny horns, and ran his long slender fingers over the scratches in the black mithril. "Let's take a look."

He laid a small flat coffer onto the table, swung its lid open and began rummaging through the runes. "How about a bonus to some of your stats, would you like that?"

"Good idea."

"What would it be? Perception, Intellect, Agility?"

"All of them, please."

✝ An NPC's Path: Book Two ✝

He chuckled as he set a rune into its holder on the mask and handed it back to me. But the moment I tried to put it on, a bright spark flashed between the mithril and my face.

I cussed. "What the hell?"

Mr. Lloyd shrugged. "I'm afraid it's not compatible with the Deadman's set. Let's try another one."

He spent at least another half-hour trying to find a rune that was compatible with my set, but all in vain. Finally, he leaned back in his chair looking very puzzled. Then he snapped his fingers. "Of course!"

"What is it?" I asked in surprise.

"The Deadman's set! Death! We need bone runes! And I've only got either stone or metal ones!"

I took the mask back from him. "So where do you think I can get them?"

"I might try to order a set for you," he promised. "I'll let you know when it arrives. And now we can experiment with the eye covers."

He expertly inserted two thick glass lenses into the eyeslits and handed me the mask. Gingerly I tried it on. This time, nothing happened.

Kingdom of the Dead

The alchemist beamed. "Five hundred gold."

"What's that for? Just for two pieces of ordinary glass?"

"This isn't just ordinary glass," he said meaningfully. "They filter illusions. They won't help you against a Master but will allow you to detect most protection amulets. Or do you want me to remove them?"

I shook my head and reached for the money.

The door swung open. Isabella peeked into the room, "You gonna be long, boys?"

I looked askance at the old man. He opened one of the catalogs and told me, "Your order has been delivered. Go and see Ulrich about it."

"Thanks. See you!"

"When the runes come, I'll let you know."

Isabella and I walked out into the corridor.

"How's your crown?" I asked.

Roger the skull cast me a grim glance, chattering his teeth.

The priestess winced. "Don't ask!"

Better not to rub salt into her wounds. I walked over to the counter where Ulrich had laid out my smock.

✝ An NPC's Path: Book Two ✝

He pointed at the wall, "The mirror's over there."

"I probably won't need it."

The Shadow of Death was much more impressive in the flesh than in a catalog picture. Its gray fabric flowed, iridescent with blues and greens. It even appeared black in the shop's dark corner.

A smock. A hood. A short cloak. Drawstring sleeves. Everything was made for convenience.

But its magic properties were its best feature.

Shadow of Death (Deadman's Set: 8 out of 13).

Stealth: +24%.

Dodge: +8%.

And the shadows, look! They surrounded me but didn't fade away when I went outside. How cool was that? No more Perception penalties! Now I could keep the Almost Alive skill on permanently! I didn't need the mask anymore!

Still, thinking about it, I decided to keep the mask for the time being. Magic illusions were all well and good but they weren't a 100%

🗡 Kingdom of the Dead 🗡

guarantee against some astute individuals who could see right through my undead nature. Not a good idea.

I went back into the shop. "Where's Neo?"

Isabella motioned me to follow her. She brought me to the back yard where Neo was busy playing with Scarecrow. The boy would throw a stick and the dead phoenix would catch it in mid-flight either in his beak or in his formidable talons.

"Neo!" I called him. "Time to go back!"

"Thanks for the clothes you bought me, Uncle John!" the boy shouted back.

Now he didn't at all resemble the smutty urchin from a God-forsaken village. He was wearing a pair of leather boots, a good strong jacket and pants, and on his belt the dagger I'd found on the Nest Hunter's body.

He hopped and skipped until he'd caught up with us and walked alongside us. Scarecrow soared into the air and flew high above the rooftops, clearly wary of attracting any stray arrows.

In daytime, we mainly came across the local NPC inhabitants in the narrow streets of the capital. Those of the players who were online

✝ An NPC's Path: Book Two ✝

were either prowling around the unchartered territories or battling Light players in the borderlands. We'd only come across one lanky player on one of the bridges: an Elf carrying the bone flute of a spirit summoner, his entire body covered with the fancy flourishes of ritual tattoos.

The Outcasts clan, I thought mechanically. No idea where I'd heard the name before. It was irrelevant, anyway.

Still, the Elf seemed to have taken interest in us. He jumped off the bridge's stone parapet and asked all of a sudden,

"How much do you want for the boy?"

"What kind of question is that?" Isabella frowned and stopped, hands on her hips.

Her cold tone hadn't seemed to baffle her fellow Elven kinsman. "How much do you want for the boy?" he repeated. "Name your price!"

I stepped forward. "Begone!" I growled.

He made himself scarce double quick. There must have been something macabre in my voice.

Isabella watched him scramble away as if she had him in her sights. "Wretched pervert," she spat.

I shrugged and headed across the bridge.

Kingdom of the Dead

"We shouldn't have taken him with us," Isabella said heatedly. "He's only a child!"

"No, I'm not!" Neo butted in.

"That's irrelevant," I told them both, then lowered my voice. "Don't forget we signed a contract to indenture him. What's the logic in that?"

She sighed and changed her tone, "He can't stay indoors all the time."

"Then tell Mark to hire him to clean the floors," I suggested.

"I don't think the vampires will appreciate it. Also, their information is solid. There's no way they can reconsider."

"We'll talk about it later."

"Okay," she said. "I'll talk to Mark, anyway."

I nodded and turned off into a dark narrow lane which led directly to the inn. There, there were fewer chances of coming across any unwanted passersby. For some reason, I wasn't looking forward to meeting other players anymore.

Still, as is often the way, the shortest way isn't always the easiest. The moment I stepped into the deep shadows, a strange stare prickled

✝ An NPC's Path: Book Two ✝

my back. Someone snatched at the strap of my bag which hung on my shoulder.

A bright flash of light blinded me. Through my watering eyes I caught sight of a man recoiling, his hand ablaze.

The cursed skull fell out of his crooked fingers and rolled toward the wall. The thief tried to pick it up but a swing from the priestess' staff forced him to back off. The thief stealthed up to escape Isabella's fireball which splattered the wall next to him with orange flames.

I grabbed the skull and darted after him.

"Watch out, Uncle John!" Neo shouted.

Too late. His tracks had already gone cold. Or had they? Somehow I doubted that our expert thief had paid enough attention to leveling Stealth, otherwise he wouldn't have had to lie in wait in this dark alley.

I reached out mentally to Scarecrow and forced him to fold his wings and nosedive between the houses. Just as he was about to hit the ground, the phoenix leveled his flight and darted along the street. Everything flickered before my eyes, the shadows blurring into a large dark spot. I felt queasy.

At that moment, my pet must have decided

Kingdom of the Dead

to take the initiative — or should I say demonstrate his nasty character? No idea how, but he must have sensed the stealthed-up thief, spread his talons and buried them in the villain's back, pulling him out of the shadows.

The thief brandished his dagger in vain, trying to get rid of the bird that was clawing him alive. Black feathers flew everywhere. With an indignant croak, Scarecrow hit the man hard on the head with his powerful beak.

Struggling to keep the flamberge in my two hands like a spear, I took a running lunge, fully intending to run him through, then turn the sword inside to cut through his intestines with its undulated blade. Luckily for him, the thief managed to dodge it. The flamberge brushed his ribs, dealing him a wound that bled but failed to kill him. Tormented by the phoenix, the thief swung around dagger in hand.

I laughed, raising the sword for a new strike.

Then the sun shone from behind my back. Instinct told me to duck, dodging the clump of white fire that shot past me. The ghostly spear hit the thief, stunning and immobilizing him without actually dealing him any damage.

✝ An NPC's Path: Book Two ✝

The phoenix wasn't so lucky. He'd been literally shredded, his black feathery remains fading fast, consumed in colorless smokeless flames.

The Light magic had hardly singed me — but even so, my exposed skin smoldered. My vision swam. The ground seemed to fall away beneath my feet. It took all of my effort to pull myself together. Still, I had no choice. The thief was about to come round, and Scarecrow wasn't here anymore to prevent him from dissolving into the shadows.

I forced myself to step forward and swung my flamberge, attacking him with a series of Quick Strikes with a buff to Accuracy which instantly stripped me of 700 pt. Stamina. Still, it had been worth it. I'd hit the exact spot that I'd wanted to hit. I poked him in the neck, pricked him under the arm, then slashed him across the thigh.

Lethal Whirlwind of Steel Combo!
Critical Damage: x3

My sword broke his spine, sliced through his ribs and cut his leg clean off. My blows had

✟ Kingdom of the Dead ✟

merged into one, producing some incredible damage total. The thief dropped to the ground. He convulsed once, then froze in the middle of a spreading pool of blood.

Sadly, the XP I'd received for killing him wasn't quite enough to bring me up to the next level — courtesy of Neo who'd so inopportunely interfered, biting off a considerable chunk of my pie.

I bent down to pick up the thief's dagger and crouched, my head spinning. Whew. It looked like I'd overdone it.

Neo suddenly appeared next to me. He was no longer level 19 anymore — but level 21.

"I'm very sorry, Uncle John!" the boy sobbed. "I didn't mean it! I wanted to help you!"

"You'd better apologize to Scarecrow," I winced, rising to my feet.

Isabella gave the boy a hearty whack around the head. "Now clear off!" she growled at him, then glared at me, her eyes bloodshot. "That goes for you too! Run! The Light magic has alerted half the island!"

Dammit! Staggering, I hurried toward the inn. We'd barely reached the back door when several mounted knights galloped past us along

✝ An NPC's Path: Book Two ✝

the street. A dark wizard's flying carpet whooshed overhead. The guards appeared next.

"Shit!" Isabella cussed the moment we'd finally taken cover in the inn. "The boy's magic makes my head go boom!" she closed her eyes and massaged them. "Kitten, this wasn't an accident, was it? Did they follow you again?"

"Well, what do you think?" furiously I buried the trophy dagger in the wall. "I had five grand in my wallet and that scumbag chose to grab the stone skull! Of course they followed me!"

She nodded. "I'm afraid you'll have to shell out for some new protection."

I just cussed repeatedly, not bothering to keep my language civil. The game had once again thrown up a nasty surprise and there was nothing I could now do about it.

6.

WE'D SET OFF for the raid at night. The vampires had made sure we could get everything done while it was still dark when their supernatural abilities were at their highest. I'd had nothing against this choice. I'd just been happy to flee the

Kingdom of the Dead

inn before Garth could play another dirty trick on me.

What kind of trick? I just didn't know, and that's what was driving me up the wall.

I doubted that he'd send another thief or mount a direct attack. This was Garth: with him, you didn't need to expect the expected.

"John?" the Count called me. "Are you ready?"

I nodded and stepped away from the wall.

The door creaked, letting in Goar, my reluctant bodyguard. "Who? Where? Why?" he demanded, then deigned to expand on his ambiguous questions, "Where are we going? Why? Who are we gonna kill?"

Isabella smiled. "Don't get your knickers in a twist, goofy. You've got a cut in this, don't forget."

"That's only the answer to my 'Why?'," he parried, his wide nostrils flaring, as he watched the Count draw a complex portal figure on the attic's floorboards.

Isabella heaved a sigh. "That leaves 'Where' and 'Who?', I suppose," she said. "I think they're gonna tell us in a moment. Won't you, Count?"

The vampire leader had finished his

✝ An NPC's Path: Book Two ✝

elaborate diagram, drew a circle around it and rose to his feet. Judging by the drawing's hue and faint smell, it must have been done with someone's blood.

"Your job," he said softly, "is to deliver the boy. The rest we'll manage."

"And what about the dungeon's guard?" I reminded him. "What's with him?"

"We'll discuss it on the way," the Count said as he raised a ritual knife and sliced through the palm of his hand.

A single drop of viscous black blood fell from the deep wound onto the floor, its magic restructuring the game's spatial plane to open up a passage into the unknown.

The Marquis and the Baron were the first to enter the portal. Neo was about to dash after them when I grabbed his hand. "Don't move away from me! You understand?"

The boy nodded obediently. Scarecrow on his shoulder cast me an unkind look with his murky blind eyes. He spread his wings wide and emitted a thunderous crow.

"Shut up!" I ordered. "Goar, move it!"

The orc cringed but followed the two vampires, unwilling to disobey our agreement.

Kingdom of the Dead

Isabella ported next.

"Your turn," the Count said. "I'll bring up the rear."

Without letting go of Neo's hand, I stepped into the portal.

Immediately I felt queasy and vertiginous, unable to tell up from down. The air around me shuddered. As its trembling subsided, we found ourselves at the center of a gloomy forest glade overshadowed by towering oaks.

Scarecrow soared into the air and perched himself on one of the gnarled branches. He seemed to like the place. He was the only one that did.

Goar hurried to slam his helmet onto his head and began casting wary looks around him, his black word at the ready. Isabella raised her staff. Roger's empty eye sockets lit up, illuminating the skulls hanging off the branches. All sorts of skulls: human, Elven and orcish.

"What's this?" Neo asked, alarmed.

"This is a place of power," Isabella answered. "Here, everything's soaked in blood."

Her stare said clearly that we shouldn't have taken the boy with us. Still, I didn't accept the blame. If anything, her reaction had

✝ An NPC's Path: Book Two ✝

surprised me. It had been our joint decision. No good pinning everything on me. Or was it her maternal instinct which had suddenly woken up?

A gray figure materialized in the air. The Count softly alighted on the well-trodden ground and blew a noisy sigh. "It hasn't been easy staking a claim on this place. Further ahead lie uncharted lands. Keep your eyes peeled. And put all the lights out!"

Isabella extinguished her staff and stepped toward me. "Neo is your responsibility," she warned me. "Don't let him out of your sight."

A rustling of wings came from above. Scarecrow took off, sank his talons into a bat almost as big as himself and carried his prey into the darkness.

A brief system message informed me of XP gained; still, it was gray and appeared inactive as the XP had been transferred to my pet.

"Hah!" the Baron laughed. "That's one cool birdie!"

"Quiet," the Marquis snapped at him, baring his rapier. "Keep your voice down! Is that clear?"

"Go forward," the Count ordered, then turned to us, "Don't lag behind!"

Kingdom of the Dead

Like two shadows, the Marquis and the Baron disappeared into the darkness. I balanced the flamberge on my shoulder and followed them. Neo scampered after me, his silvery dagger at the ready. Isabella and Goar trailed behind us. If the priestess could move virtually noiselessly, the orc's strained breathing and the clattering of his black armor echoed through the night forest, mocking our attempts at staying unnoticed.

Still, the forest appeared dead, with only the occasional swift shadow of a bat darting overhead. From time to time, our avant-garde reported suspicious holes in the ground and spiders' webs spun between tree trunks. The Marquis and the Baron only relaxed a little when we'd come across an uneven cobbled road. Lined by thick bushes, it looked deserted, grass growing between the stones.

For a while, the Count studied the area warily. Finally he climbed out of the undergrowth. "Almost there," he announced.

We heard desperate squeaking. The Count nearly jumped. "Dammit!"

Scarecrow ignored his protest entirely. He landed on a tree branch holding yet another bat and began ripping its still convulsing body apart.

✝ An NPC's Path: Book Two ✝

No idea whether a dead phoenix could level up but he seemed to constantly receive enviable amounts of XP for smoking little forest critters.

"Right," the Count chuckled. "Let's move it!"

We started off down the road. Soon we started coming across stone obelisks dug into the roadside, covered all over in carved runes. They seemed to be a cross between border markers and protection charms.

Goar slowed up and walked next to the Count. "What kind of guard is it? What's his level?" he kept showering him with questions. "What abilities does he have?"

The Count seemed to be quite puzzled by his questions. He couldn't tell him anything definite. "There's a dead dragon locked in the dungeon's third level. He doesn't cast spells but he's extremely quick and has very high resistance to magic. Plus he can see the invisible," the Count told him everything he seemed to know. "You think you could slow him down like you did to us at the inn?"

"I can try," the orc grumbled. He reached into his bag and produced a fat notebook bound in worn leather. "His size? Color? Wingspan?"

Kingdom of the Dead

He approached the matter with a thoroughness remarkable in a creature as scatty as an orc. Even Isabella stopped casting wary glances around and took a peek into his notebook.

"His scales are black or dark brown," the Count said after a pause.

The restless Baron couldn't help but add his two cents, "They're sort of rotten."

"Keep your eyes on the bushes!" the Count snapped, then continued to describe the dungeon guard, "He's at least fifty feet long, with four legs and clipped wings."

Goar leafed through his book until he found the entry he'd been looking for. "This one?"

"No. He's really not Chinese. And his wings aren't entirely clipped. There's bits of bone still showing through like spikes. His eyes don't glow, either. They're dead."

"He stinks of decay," the Baron added. "His scales have come off in places. But still he's fast as hell."

The orc pensively bit his lower lip. "Did you say decay? That's weird."

"We'll smoke him, anyway," the Baron shrugged it off. "Last time we very nearly did it."

✝ An NPC's Path: Book Two ✝

"Move it," the Marquis shut him up. "Come on, put your ass in gear!"

The Baron cussed and went off to mount the guard.

For a while, Goar walked in silence looking something up online. Finally he shook his head, "There's nothing in the bestiary that seems to fit. It must be something from the latest update."

I sighed. "We'll sort it out."

Obeying a sudden impulse of my Dodge skill, I ducked aside. A bunch of bloodied flesh dropped from the sky, splattering Goar's black armor. He cussed. The phoenix crowed happily in the dark.

There's that dead bastard again!

"Did he do it on purpose?" Goar growled.

"Leave the birdie alone," I said.

"He's right. Leave him to me," Isabella flashed an unkind smile as she wiped drops of blood from her face.

I almost choked on my own laughter but decided not to provoke her any further. I quickened my step to catch up with the Count. "What kind of place is that? Can you tell us now?"

This time he was more forthcoming. "These

Kingdom of the Dead

are the borderlands which we took from the Lights. But the main fighting is further on. Practically nobody comes here. We came across the monastery by pure accident and decided to sit it out there."

"Sit what out?" I asked.

"The contract that was put out on us," the Baron butted in again. "We smoked the wrong guy so they put out a hit on us. We had to lie low for a while. But finding someone in the capital is dead easy so we found this hole..."

The Count rolled his eyes but let his loose-lipped henchman carry on.

"Finding someone in the capital is dead easy?" I repeated. "How do you do that?"

"You leave them a note and they'll work it out for you. It's a whole business," the Count grinned. "You have any idea how many blacklists players have? Some are looking for an enemy while others just can't tackle their foes on their own."

"So they have to pay someone to do it for them!" the Baron chuckled. "We sometimes accept orders too."

I gave a pensive nod. "Is it possible to find out if there's a contract out on you?"

✝ An NPC's Path: Book Two ✝

"You can even buy them off," the Count informed me, then leapt aside. "Watch out!"

He quickly retreated into the shadows. A swarm of flickering green fireflies emerged from the bushes, illuminating the path as bright as daylight. With it came a hail of arrows.

"You bastards!" I gasped, pulling Neo toward me and covering him from the ambushing archers. I wished I could dissolve into the shadows but unfortunately, I couldn't—

Dammit! Two arrows hit my back. One of them bounced off my chainmail while the other pierced its links and lodged between my shoulder blades.

The damage was slight. I scooped the boy up and dashed into the woods with him. Still, the fireflies followed us, preventing us from disappearing into the darkness. An arrow flashed past; immediately, another thudded into a nearby tree. The archers then switched over to Goar and Isabella but the priestess covered herself with a magic shield while the orc's strong armor protected him from the attack.

Almost at once I heard shouting and sounds of a scuffle coming from the bushes. The shooting had stopped. Goar fully intended to

Kingdom of the Dead

hurry to the vampires' aid but Isabella stopped him,

"What if this is a ruse?"

Her reasoning made sense. We stood back to back but no attack followed, only the fireflies continued to flutter uselessly over our heads.

Scarecrow dashed from one of them to another, ripping them apart with his talons and hitting them with his beak. He was covered all over in glittering goo and seemed to be thoroughly enjoying himself. I, however, felt very uneasy; a dull pain was brewing in my back.

What was that now? I couldn't remember the last time I experienced real pain.

Damage taken: 10

What the hell? Deadmen don't bleed! What was going on?

I tried to reach the arrow which was stuck between my shoulder blades but couldn't.

"Goar?" I asked. "Can you pull this wretched thing out of me?"

He pulled at the shaft. My back exploded in pain but he couldn't free the arrowhead from my dead flesh.

✝ An NPC's Path: Book Two ✝

"What's wrong with it?" I growled. "Is it the barbs?"

"No," Goar said in a strangely changed voice. "It has druid magic on it."

He stepped away from me and shouted, "Druids worship the Equilibrium! I won't fight them!"

Isabella squinted at him. "Did you forget about the contract?" her voice promised nothing good.

The orc's face fell. At that moment, the vampires re-emerged from the darkness, covered in blood.

"What Equilibrium are you talking about?" the Baron cussed under his breath. "We weren't walking through the forest! They ambushed us on the road! This is neutral territory!"

"They're scumbags, that's all," the Marquis agreed with him for the first time.

Goar didn't say anything. But I had a lot to say. Something had taken hold between my shoulder blades, growing and gradually syphoning my health. And it would be stupid to die when the raid had barely gotten started.

"Can someone help me get rid of this?" I demanded again.

Kingdom of the Dead

The Count got hold of the arrow shaft and breathed a quiet word. A whiff of death magic touched me; then the pain was gone and the arrowhead slid out of my body.

The vampire flung the arrow aside. "We can't go back on the road. We might come across more pickets. We'll have to go straight across."

Nobody argued with him. You only argue when you have other options. We didn't have any.

We had to go straight across.

7.

WE HEARD THE HOWLING of wolves about forty minutes later when we'd finally left the huge oaks behind.

Here, the tall pine trees reached for the sky. The forest had grown lighter. We had to make a detour but the wolves had already gotten our scent and wouldn't be shaken off. To add to that, the mist started rising, its white nothingness confusing and disorienting us.

"These are druids' lands!" Goar pointed at the mysterious symbols covering a large pine trunk. They didn't appear to have been carved;

✝ An NPC's Path: Book Two ✝

they seemed to have formed naturally on the rough bark.

"To hell with druids!" the Baron cussed.

At the very edge of my field of vision I could make out the dark figures of our pursuers. I just couldn't work out whether they were animals or human beings. There was something in their outlines that was *wrong*.

"We can't shake them off," Isabella finally said. "We need to scare them away."

"First we need to find a suitable place to do that," the Count said. "Losing your boy is the last thing we want!"

You couldn't argue with that. The first bite could cost Neo his life.

Isabella swung round and launched a fireball into the mist which simply disappeared into the milky void. Unwilling to waste her time and energy, she hurried after the others.

After about five minutes, we came to a steep ravine with a fast-flowing stream running along its bottom. We followed its course until we could make out a hill with a deforested summit looming in the distance.

The Count suggested we made a stand against the wolves there, then continue safely on

🗡 Kingdom of the Dead 🗡

our way.

By the time we climbed to the top, my Stamina had dropped quite a bit. Neo was so much out of breath I had to drag him behind me. The orc in his cumbersome armor was breathing heavily but kept up with us all the same. Only Isabella had it easier than all of us. Well, what could you expect from an Elfa?

Midway up the hill, the vampires retreated into the shadows to wait for the wolves while we continued our unhurried ascent. We seemed to have left the howling behind. A tidal wave of peace and calm enveloped us.

Crowing hoarsely, Scarecrow soared into the dark sky.

Immediately Isabella startled and stopped. "Something's wrong here," she said in a low voice.

There was nowhere on the top where we could take cover. At its very center towered the remains of a mighty oak which had been struck by lightning. Still, I took Isabella's warning seriously and began backing off, pulling Neo after me.

The deformed oak stirred, turning into a monstrous creature: a tall hunter with a deer antler crown, a bow and a spear. His inhuman

✝ An NPC's Path: Book Two ✝

gaze took in our group and stopped on me, pinning me down with an unbearable weight. His lips didn't move but his words resounded through my head like a tolling bell,

"Join my retinue if you want to become truly great, man! An incredible power awaits you if you join in the Wild Hunt!"

Would you like to become a follower of the Antlered God?
[Yes/No]

It didn't take me long to reject his offer. I just didn't know anything about the relationship between the Antlered God and the Lord of the Tower of Decay. I didn't want to risk my neutrality with the latter. Also, what was I supposed to do with a new lord's quests?

The creature's eyes lit up with a threatening fire but at least he didn't attack the cheeky bastard who'd insulted him by rejecting his offer. Instead, he disintegrated in a flurry of oak leaves.

Immediately the wolves went for us from behind the hill. Wolves? Oh no. They were half-human, half-animal.

🗡 Kingdom of the Dead 🗡

Goar exhaled loudly behind my back and took a two-handed grip on his black sword. I slid into the shadows, then darted forward and met the attacking beasts with a simple but powerful swing of my flamberge.

Scythe of Death!

The undulated blade swiped three werewolves at the same time. Blood gushed; their guts hung out. I followed with two crippling blows, lopping off the claws of one of them while slicing through the knee of the other one. Immediately I stepped back, covering Neo.

Goar stood at my side and used his signature trick, slowing down the attackers and finishing them off with his heavy sword. Using her staff, Isabella drew a long line in the ground, shielding herself with a wall of fire. The monsters didn't dare leap through the flames but at least two of them went for me.

My Stamina was dwindling. My hands began to shake. Still, I had no choice: I had to hurry up, investing the last of my strength in a series of rapid blows.

One! Two! Three!

✝ An NPC's Path: Book Two ✝

My first strike chopped off the head of one of the gutted ones. The other, however, proved to be a tough cookie. He dodged the first blow with remarkable speed, then parried the flamberge with his claws.

Immediately he went flying back as the skull topping the priestess' staff hit him so hard that it broke his breastbone and crushed his ribs. Before the monster could climb back to his feet, I used the sorcerous Leap to port almost upon him. I raised the sword over my head and invested all of my remaining strength into a slashing blow. My trusty blade didn't let me down, cleaving my victim in two.

Yes! That's how you do it!

Having finished the monster off, I hurried toward my companions. Still, they had little need for me as the vampires had already emerged from the shadows and went for the werewolves, slicing their throats, chopping off their legs and piercing their hearts. Blood flowed like a river. To my surprise, the little Baron held his own. His puny build belayed his speed; his daggers dealt crippling blows, slicing through veins and tendons and leaving his victims for the Marquis and the Count to deliver their coups de grace.

Kingdom of the Dead

I didn't join in the melee. No point overdoing it. As it was, my both incarnations had already grown in levels. If only I could find enough time to distribute my available characteristic and skill points!

The werewolves' mangled remains still convulsed, moving and attempting to reconstitute into a single being: a nauseating Cadaver. I sensed the presence of hostile magic; it must have been the Antlered God that supported life within the carrion. In the end, Isabella had to scorch the dismembered body parts with her fire spells.

"We need to get out of here," I hurried to others, wincing from the unbearable stench of burnt flesh.

The vampires stopped sharing the fangs they'd ripped out of the werewolves' jaws. The Count pointed to somewhere below, "Over there!"

With the death of the wolves, the mist quickly dispersed from the woods, enough for me to make out an opening amid the trees and the ruins of a monastery on it.

Isabella stopped incinerating the monsters' remains, cast a few protection symbols on the glade and announced, "We can go!"

✝ An NPC's Path: Book Two ✝

As soon as we started down the hill, she asked, "Was it my imagination or did that antlered son of a bitch make you an offer?"

"He invited me to join his pack," I admitted. "All of you are already in bondage with some god or other. The Mistress of the Crimson Moon, the Silver Phoenix, even that nonsensical Equilibrium..."

She looked at me as if she wanted to kick me but overcame herself and continued walking in silence. Then Neo started up,

"Uncle John, Uncle John! I could help you with magic! The power of the Silver Phoenix..."

"Stop now!" I cut him short. "Any magic can only be used with my permission! Understood?"

"Yeah," he replied unenthusiastically.

At that point, the trail took a sharp turn and came to an abrupt halt in front of a blackthorn thicket.

"Shit!" the Baron gasped. "Where to now?"

Behind the thicket's rustling prickly branches, the keepers of the local woods awaited us. A gray-bearded high druid with an ash staff and a sickle behind his belt stood with his legs akimbo; behind him towered several lower-

✝ Kingdom of the Dead ✝

ranking casters, all of them players. Predictably, I could also discern the shadows of Elven archers flitting through the undergrowth.

"What's this, some kind of party?" the Marquis grinned, baring his rapier, its blade glowing blue with magic script. "Free XP on the house!"

"Elven blood gives me indigestion," the Baron complained.

The Marquis smiled, baring his needle-sharp fangs, and tentatively swung his broadsword. The Count, however, wasn't in a hurry to attack; instead, he kept sniffing the air and taking in the scene.

I mentally reached out to Scarecrow. Obediently he flew over the treetops, searching for any archers. Still, I lost control of him almost straight away as he nosedived after yet another bat, grabbed it with his talons and soared back into the sky with his prey.

"At least ten archers," I said.

"We can do it," the Count decided.

Goar put his hand on the vampire's shoulder, keeping him in place, then calmly stepped forward.

Immediately the druid raised his staff

✝ An NPC's Path: Book Two ✝

above his head. "Get out of our forest," he demanded, "or Nature's retribution will be terrible!"

Goar stopped, buried the point of his sword in the ground and spread his shoulders, appearing even taller and more impressive. "Let us through and we'll leave."

"You're not welcome here! These paths aren't for you!"

"Equilibrium is a fragile thing. If you tip one side of the scales, both sides will continue rocking for a long time."

"You're not the right one to talk about Equilibrium, orc!" the gray-bearded caster snapped. "Nature's harmony-"

"Nature's harmony will cease to exist once we burn everything here," the orc interrupted him. "And that wouldn't be us upsetting the Equilibrium: we'd be simply responding to your act of hostility. Let us through!"

The caster fell silent for a long time as if the game's mechanisms were trying to calculate how convincing the orc's words had been. Then the druids disappeared into the woods.

"Don't come back!" the old druid announced before escaping into the night.

☦ Kingdom of the Dead ☦

We heaved a sigh of relief. Even though we'd had the upper hand — or so I thought — still, the druids being on their own turf, they could bring us some very unpleasant surprises.

WE'D REACHED the ruins of the monastery without further ado. As we'd wended our way along the crooked forest trail, we'd expected to be attacked at any moment. Still, the High Druid had kept his word. No more arrows had been fired at us. And once we'd left the trees behind, I was surprised to discover that the stone underfoot was in fact earth baked into rock by an incredible heat. This can't have been magic napalm even but something much much hotter.

We felt extremely uncomfortable staying in the open, so we hurried to shelter amid the scorched ruins of the monastery. The fire that once had raged there had failed to melt the ancient stonework but even so, not a single building had been left standing. I got the impression that something had exploded within the monastery walls, demolishing the buildings and bringing down the fortifications.

"Does anyone still live here?" Goar asked warily as he followed the vampires past the heaps

An NPC's Path: Book Two

of fire-licked masonry which used to be the gatehouse.

"Not at ground level, no," the Count said confidently. "Plenty of critters in the basements though, mainly magic ones."

We spent some more time ambling among the ruins until we turned off into the main square where the ruins of a temple still stood. There was virtually nothing left from the once-majestic edifice, its heavy foundations the only reminder of its existence.

"Are you sure the basement hasn't been looted yet?" I asked.

The Count shook his head. "These are the druids' lands. Normally, the Lights give places like this a wide berth. And the Darks are no competition to us because they don't give a damn about the Equilibrium."

Isabella had finally found a spot free from any rubble. "Boys, I need some time to set up a raid shrine."

The Count looked up at the sky, doubtful. Still, sunrise would be a while yet, so he agreed to stop for a breather as we weren't immune to stupid death, especially seeing as the priestess' magic allowed us to resurrect right here and now

⚔ Kingdom of the Dead ⚔

instead of having to trudge all the way back from the Tower of Power. A second chance never hurt anybody.

The vampires split in different directions to guard the place against any unwanted visitors. I left Isabella in Goar's care and went to inspect the ruins of the temple, accompanied by Neo. Did I say inspect? Not really, more like take a quick peek at it.

There wasn't much to look at. The explosion had blown away the walls and inner partitions. A deep jagged hole gaped at the center of the prayer hall.

"Wait here," I told the boy. Warily I approached the hole and stood at its very edge.

I managed to make out two more stories underneath, their several-foot thick floors sporting the same breach at the center. It looked like something incredibly heavy had once dropped here from the sky.

And I had a funny feeling I knew what it had been.

You couldn't make a descent here unless you had either Levitation or some climbing equipment, so I stepped back. Immediately Scarecrow landed on top of one of the few

✝ An NPC's Path: Book Two ✝

surviving columns and began sharpening his beak on the sooty marble. He'd grown a lot; his beak had acquired a distinctive obsidian glint.

"Who's a pretty boy, then?" I shook my head, then turned to Neo. "Let's go!"

We went back to the square where Isabella had just finished setting up the raid shrine as the respawn point for the vampires. Threads of energy reached out from her in every direction, gradually dissolving into the air. For a brief moment, I thought I saw the blood-red glimmer of the Crimson Moon high in the sky.

I looked again but it was gone. Had it been my imagination playing up? I wasn't too sure. You could never be sure with magic. I didn't give a damn, anyway. I'd better sort out my stats while I had the chance.

I improved my Agility and brought up Stamina to the 15 pt. Still, I'd decided against distributing my available skill points. I just wasn't interested in either Pickpocketing or Trap Detecting. What about professional skills? As for learning new combat skills, I decided to leave it till later and improved Execution instead, bringing it to level 3.

The result didn't make me jump for joy but

Kingdom of the Dead

by the same token it hadn't disappointed me, either. Apart from a better chance of killing an immobilized opponent, it also offered much more useful improvements.

> *Execution III*
> You're an expert in anatomy and always hit your opponent's most vulnerable spot — but only when he or she is tied to a torture rack and can't react to your blow.
> Whenever your victim can't see the blow coming, he or she receives critical damage which doubles the chances of your dealing them an injury.
> +6% to your chances of dealing a critical hit
> +3% to your chances of dealing a crippling blow

Not bad, don't you think? But as for magic, things weren't as rosy. Even though my charmed belt gave me access to level-2 spells, they didn't offer anything particularly interesting. I'd had to settle on the Veil of Death which protected a Lich from magic, its mana consumption depending on the power of the attack deflected.

The sky flashed crimson. Isabella heaved a

☦ An NPC's Path: Book Two ☦

sigh of relief,

"We can go now!"

"Follow me!" the Count snapped his fingers and headed for the ruins of the temple. Ignoring the fire-polished steps of the main entrance, he skirted around the building. "There's loads of fire ghosts on the first underground level," he began instructing us as we walked. "No traps — or at least we haven't come across any. Plenty of them on the second level though."

"Traps are your specialty, Kitten, aren't they?" Isabella said with a nasty smile.

I really didn't feel like leading the way and I told her as much, adding a couple of stronger words to make sure she got the message.

"Also," the Count continued, "there're plenty of deadmen on the second level. They aren't very strong but they're scorched so fire magic doesn't affect them. You'd best keep that in mind," the vampire crouched by a surviving section of the wall and pointed at a basement window below. "Here."

The Baron was the first to slide through the dark opening. "It's all right!" he shouted almost straight away.

The Marquis followed his partner.

✟ Kingdom of the Dead ✟

"And what's below apart from the dragon?" I asked the Count. "Are they any other creatures before it?"

"No, only the dragon," he said. "He blocks the only access to the sanctuary. There's no way past him. Come on, Fang, climb in!"

Goar eyed the window cautiously. "Fang?" he chuckled. "You're one to talk!"

Unexpectedly for such a clumsy creature, he squeezed himself through the opening with a remarkable ease.

"Take the kid!" I shouted to him.

"I'm not a little boy anymore!" Neo protested.

I ignored his pleas. "Come on now, get in quick!"

The boy frowned but didn't make a scene and followed obediently after the orc.

"It's okay!" Goar shouted from below.

Still, something seemed to have imperceptibly changed in the world around us. The air trembled as if resonating with an invisible bass string. The droning sound had disappeared before I could work out what it was I'd been feeling. Both Isabella and the Count seemed to have detected some sort of irregularity they too

✝ An NPC's Path: Book Two ✝

appeared unable to explain.

"Is it some kind of signal?" Isabella suggested.

"Or can it be the reaction to the arrival of a Light Disciple?" the Count offered his own version.

"Are you all asleep or something?" the Baron's voice came from below.

"Shut up, we're coming!" the Count replied. "Let's go!"

I let Isabella go in front, grabbed at the fire-licked stone windowsill, dropped down and hung from it, then released my grip. It wasn't very high. I stood up and stepped aside, making place for the Count.

Burned bones crunched underfoot, their recognizable snapping reminding me of the stinky cave where it had all started. I only prayed that my player's journey wasn't going to come to an end in this particular dungeon.

Was it just a bad premonition? I shouldn't be too sure.

🗡 Kingdom of the Dead 🗡

8.

THE BARON WAS TOLD to do point duty. Goar was posted as a rearguard: he still had to contain the dragon.

Can't say the Baron was happy with the task. "Invisibility isn't an advantage against ghosts," he grumbled.

"Just go," the Count said. "You can detect traps better than any of us."

"There were no traps here last time?"

"And what if there are now? Last time there were three of us. And now we have this Light boy with us."

The Baron cussed and forlornly headed down the dark corridor.

"Right, left, left, right, left," the Marquis recited, remembering. "Is that correct?" he asked the Count.

"It is."

We set off on our way. The vampires had no problem finding their way in the darkness of the dungeon. Isabella and I had our night vision, but Neo had to be led by the hand. I didn't enjoy chaperoning him but if I'd let him go, the lad

✝ An NPC's Path: Book Two ✝

would have quickly stumbled into a wall or even dropped down one of the gaping holes in the floor. We'd already come across quite a few of them.

Goar wheezed noisily behind my back. The eyeslit of his closed visor glinted with the magic he was using to help himself see in the dark. An active spell like that could attract ghosts but none of us dared tell him about it: without the spell, he would have been pretty useless.

"Don't go near those bones!" the Baron warned us as we approached two corridors crossing. "It could be a trap."

The Count flashed a smug grin. "What did I tell you?"

We kept walking. After another couple of turns, the gloom began to lift as if dispersed by the torches burning up ahead.

"Make sure you don't fall down. The dragon will have you for breakfast," the Baron whispered, pressing his back to the wall as he shuffled past another gaping hole in the floor. The cracked stone tiles crumbled under his feet but didn't budge an inch.

I looked up and caught a glimpse of the dawn through the hole above my head. A black

Kingdom of the Dead

dot flashed overhead; I heard the echo of cawing. It was Scarecrow hunting bats.

"Wait," Isabella stopped the vampires once we'd cleared the dangerous spot. "These ghosts here, do they only use fire?"

"Yep. It looks like all of them were burned alive."

Indeed, we'd met nothing in the basement: neither human remains nor any furniture, only ash, soot and shapeless blobs of molten metal.

Isabella nodded and spread her arms wide. A translucent veil formed in front of her. Very soon it began to disperse; still, the priestess managed to consolidate and widen it with a few confident handwaves until it blocked almost all of the passage.

"What's that?" the Marquis asked.

"Fire protection," Isabella said, motioning with her hand. The veil moved slightly forward, passed right through the Baron and flew on further.

"Don't bust a gut," the Count said, doubtful.

Isabella just smirked.

The first ghost appeared after the next bend. Still, the fire which escaped the empty

✝ An NPC's Path: Book Two ✝

sleeves of his robe barely licked the Elven protection veil, powerless against it. As soon as the flames died away, the Baron stepped through the magic veil and slashed the monk with his charmed daggers.

From then on, it was plain sailing. Not that the Count seemed happy about it.

"There're too few ghosts here," he frowned. "And logically, there should be more."

"All the better for us," the Baron nonchalantly dismissed his concern. The Marquis, however, nodded and said nothing. He wasn't a big talker, anyway.

After a while, the corridor took another turn and brought us to a spacious hall, its cracked vaulted ceiling supported by powerful columns. Miraculously, the ceiling hadn't collapsed, only had shed a few huge stones. Three more corridors opened into it.

The Count pointed confidently at one of them. "Over there!"

But the moment we started across the hall, we heard a metallic click. Frames of steel bars fell from the ceiling, blocking all the exits.

"Oops," the Baron said as the ghosts of the monks began pouring out of the corridors. The

Kingdom of the Dead

bars were no obstacle for them. In less than a moment, searing tongues of flame licked toward us from every direction.

The Marquis was the first in their path. He went up like a match and rolled over the floor trying to extinguish the flames. He was soon surrounded by the ghosts' black cassocks and couldn't get back to his feet any longer.

The Baron had been luckier. Isabella's magic veil had protected him. The Count had simply disappeared into thin air, turning into an incorporeal whiff of mist which sped into a far corner.

I pressed Neo to myself and activated the Veil of Death. The spell worked sluggishly; my hands felt leaden; but still its murky mist spread through the air around me, consuming the oncoming flames.

Internal energy: –240 [280/520]

Holy shit! It felt as if I'd been rammed by a fast train. I'd been lucky to stay on my feet. And I only had a moment to spare.

"Go for it!" Isabella snapped. She jerked Neo toward her and swung the staff above her

✝ An NPC's Path: Book Two ✝

head.

The purple mist curled, enveloping them from all sides. The now-defenseless Baron was forced to go on the attack. The re-materialized Count assaulted the ghosts from behind. The orc, however, seemed to be struggling. His black armor had withstood the onslaught of the flames — but when he'd attacked a monk with his sword it turned out that its metal couldn't hurt immaterial beings.

Unwilling to repeat his mistake, I drew the bone hook from behind my belt and lunged forward, striking the nearest ghoul.

Phew! It disappeared without a trace!

With my next swing, I disembodied another monk before fire started to pour toward us again.

Leap!

The spell threw me a couple of feet, sending me sprawling onto another ghost. With a quiet ripping sound, the bone hook sliced through his entrails.

Another leap. Another blow. Having dealt with yet another monk, I turned around and saw that the melee was already over.

🗡 Kingdom of the Dead 🗡

The marquis had been burned to a crisp. His friends' clothes were singed and smoking. Isabella and Neo had remained intact. Goar hadn't suffered much from the flames, either, but he swore louder than everybody else because his black sword had failed to slay any of the immaterial beings. He looked daggers at me as if it had been my fault and not that of the game developers.

"You okay?" I asked Neo.

The boy sheathed his dagger. "Why can't I ever use magic?"

"Because your magic isn't good for any of us," I explained.

"But-"

"I said, no."

Isabella crouched in front of Neo and looked him in the eye. "I want you to get something for us," her voice rang with feeling. "It's very important. And if you get tired prematurely, our raid will be for nothing. You're grown up now and you should be able to tell the difference between fun and work."

Neo frowned, thinking, then nodded.

"We aren't waiting for the Marquis," the Count announced. "And watch your step!

✟ An NPC's Path: Book Two ✟

There're traps around here, after all!"

"You don't mean it," I grumbled, then pointed at a blocked passage. "What's with the bars?"

Luckily, between all of us we'd managed to lift them. After some persuasion, the lock snapped, succumbing to our efforts. The bars began to rise until they came to a halt halfway up.

After that, the corridor carried on straight ahead until it brought us to some steps leading down. The dungeon's second level hadn't been subjected to fire. It was lined with tapestries and torch holders. By the same token, its walls were badly fissured.

"Come on, get in front, green one!" the Count ordered once we'd gone down to the next level. "We need a bit of a break."

Indeed, the vampires looked quite a bit worse for wear. Their burns still hadn't healed, even despite the fact that they'd each drunk a vial of thick black blood. The regeneration process was taking way too long. Fire and vampires weren't made for each other, that's for sure.

The orc shrugged but didn't question the

Kingdom of the Dead

order and went first into the corridor. It wasn't as dark here as it had been on the upper level; the walls and ceiling emitted a faint glow which seemed to be coming from the many cracks and fissures. It felt like we were walking through the insides of a volcano.

"What's that further up?" Goar asked, peering intently into the gloom.

"Turn right, then left, then there'll be a big hall," the Count said, remembering the way. "Last time we had no problem getting there. Having said that, we didn't come across any ghostly ambushers last time, either."

The orc nodded and went to have a look. Once we'd cleared the first bend, the tunnel grew considerably wider. And after the second one, it appeared more like a long room.

"We're almost there," the Count warned us. "Baron, check the hall."

Before the Baron could have even gotten a chance to stealth up, tongues of fire illuminated the tunnel. Two figures rushed toward us, engulfed in flames.

Goar stepped toward them, meeting them with a powerful swing of his sword. As soon as its blade met its target, a powerful explosion

✝ An NPC's Path: Book Two ✝

shuddered the tunnel, sending the orc flying through the air.

A wave of unbearable heat seared my face. Still, the fire died out quickly without really hurting any of us.

Dead guards poured out of the hall armed with spears, their bodies charred. I stepped toward them. Crouching, I took a swing with my flamberge, aiming at the blackened spear shafts. I managed to lop off several spearheads; the Baron jumped onto my back and dove into the breach formed by my attack. Like a gray shadow, the Count joined the resulting melee.

I slashed the nearest guard across the legs and stepped back, readying myself to stop a potential attempt at a breakthrough. A fireball came flying from behind the guards' heads and hit me in the chest, exploding and throwing me back several feet.

The flames had failed to set my rogue's smock on fire. Isabella managed to repel the next fireball.

"Kill the wizard!" she shouted, upping the protection.

I couldn't see Goar anywhere. The vampires were busy fighting the guards and a few knights

† Kingdom of the Dead †

who'd arrived to their aid. I dove into stealth and dashed across the corridor ringing with the clamor of steel toward the next hall. My Dodge allowed me to avoid any clashes but only just, so in the end I was forced to use up whatever was left of my mana on a Leap, miniporting behind the guards' unwavering ranks.

Another fireball whizzed over my head. This one was much bigger and brighter than the ones before it. I made a beeline for the abbot. Unlike his ghostly brethren, he turned out to be perfectly incarnate. His burned hands protruded from the wide sleeves of his gilded cassock; his charred eye sockets emitted an infernal flame. His hovering figure exuded an enormous might.

Throwing caution to the wind, I slashed at him with my flamberge, throwing him against the wall. His magic staff split and flew out of his hand, bursting into cascades of smokeless fire.

The shadows which harbored me quivered, about to disperse. While Stealth still worked, I dealt him three more blows: two to both sides of his collarbone, then one to his neck.

The abbot turned out to be immune to critical hits. But even so, his movements became sluggish. Before he could scorch me with his

✝ An NPC's Path: Book Two ✝

magic, I took another swing and in one precise blow took his charred skull off his shoulders. The moment the sword's undulating blade sliced through his vertebrae, the skeleton crumbled to dust. His empty clothes fell in a heap to the floor.

The Torched Abbot is killed!
Experience: +1500 [30 929/32 500]; +1500 [30 973/32 500]

Without wasting my time, I turned round and darted back into the corridor. I lashed out at the guards' backs with my flamberge to scatter them, then lowered my sword onto a knight's helmet. Isabella cast another spell, dispersing the surviving guards who were trying to fight us off by standing back to back and allowing me and the vampires to hack them to pieces without much trouble.

How about Goar? Surprisingly, he'd managed to survive the melee simply because he'd passed out. He couldn't even move so he just leaned his back against the wall and kept downing vialfuls of potions. The vampires didn't look much better. The Baron had barely avoided being decapitated; a sword blow had glanced off

Kingdom of the Dead

his skull, taking a piece of scalp and his left ear with it. On top of that, the Baron sported a gaping hole which had been seared in his side. The Count had his arm almost cut off; half his face had been scorched; he also had a leg wound so deep we could see the bone.

"You see, my boy?" Isabella waved her finger at Neo. "It's a good job you didn't join the fight."

"But Uncle John isn't hurt!" the boy objected.

"Uncle John has been flippin' lucky," the Baron grumbled as he downed a vial of bright scarlet blood.

A shadow flitted across the far end of the corridor. It was the Marquis who'd just logged back in and hurried to rejoin us.

"I can see you're having fun!" he said in amazement, studying the scattered remains of the guards and the miserable state of his companions.

"Collect the loot," the Count ordered as he gulped from a flask. The burnt skin on his face started to turn pale and smooth. Still, he didn't want to overexert his wounded leg and slumped to the floor.

✝ An NPC's Path: Book Two ✝

The Marquis started checking the guards one by one, collecting the trophies, then moved on into the hall toward the slain abbot. He picked up an amber rosary but immediately flung it down, shaking his hand. His burned fingers hissed and smoked.

"You bastard!" he cussed as he hopped about in pain. "Bella! Come have a look!"

Isabella walked over to him and spent some time studying the amber beads, each marked with the symbol of the true flame branded into it. Calmly she picked up the rosary and put it away in her inventory.

"Funny thing," she smiled nonchalantly. However, I got the impression that she'd taken a fancy to the rosary.

The Marquis swore again.

"Does it hurt?" Neo asked him.

"It'll go in a minute," the vampire replied, then turned to his companions, "Will you be long?"

By then, the hole in the Baron's side had completely closed. The Count too had already scrambled back to his feet and didn't appear to limp too badly. The orc too got back to his feet but staggered about, swearing.

⚔ Kingdom of the Dead ⚔

'Hey, greenie, what about your internal energy and what have you?" the Baron teased him. "Come on, show us the power of the Equilibrium!"

"I'm saving it for the dragon," Goar grumbled as he limped toward us. "Where to now?"

The Count looked around and confidently headed for the tunnel at the far end. Both its floor and ceiling had collapsed; only a side staircase had miraculously survived.

"Isabella!" I snapped my fingers as an idea struck me. "And what if you cast your Rain of Fire?"

"The dragon is almost immune to magic," the Count reminded me. "We've tried everything, trust me."

"So what if we just jump on top of him?" I suggested jokingly, approaching a jagged hole in the floor.

"You're gonna break your neck."

I looked cautiously down and shrank back. He'd been right. The monastery's lower level resembled a deep well, its precipitous stone walls exuding a chill from beyond the grave.

My head began to throb: a dull, insistent

✟ An NPC's Path: Book Two ✟

pain. I nearly jumped, then breathed a sigh of relief. It was only Scarecrow who seemed to have finally bitten off more than he could chew, literally.

The Baron was the first to descend. The Count followed.

"The stairs lead directly into the dragon's den," he warned him. "So we'll have to get ready during the last flight of steps. You!" the vampire poked Neo's chest. "You go straight across to the sanctuary. The dragon's protection can't stop you. Still, I'd rather you didn't touch anything there. Just take the artifact that's in the adjacent room."

"What sort of artifact is it?" the boy tousled his red mop. "How do I know it's the right one?"

"It's the only one there. You can't go wrong," the Count replied. "Enough! Let's get moving!"

There were no traps on the stairs. Soon we crowded together on a tiny and very cramped landing.

"Neo, stick behind me," Isabella warned the boy, then began chanting a prayer to her Goddess, asking her to grant her some power.

Goar was mumbling under his breath,

Kingdom of the Dead

mentioning the Equilibrium. The air around his black figure thickened, as if soaking up the surrounding gloom. The vampires simply drank more blood — not out of flasks this time but out of crystal vials. Their movements began to speed up, becoming sharp and jerky.

"What a bouquet!" the Baron blew noisily when he'd finished a third vial. "Honestly, Count, from whom did you make it?"

"Lots of people," the Count replied evasively. His eyes had turned black; a silvery crust of frost began forming on his clothes.

A crimson glow formed above Isabella's head. She began casting blessings, generously sharing the power she'd just received from the Goddess. Predictably I couldn't receive any, thanks to my immunity as an undead. I didn't give a damn, anyway. I could do without it.

A wave of impetuosity flooded over me. I couldn't wait much longer. A blue haze of a regeneration spell enveloped Goar who stepped from the stairs into the dead dragon's den. We followed.

"Neo, get back!" Isabella hissed at the boy.

Grudgingly he obeyed.

"Hey greenie, the stage is yours!" the Count

✝ An NPC's Path: Book Two ✝

said. The three vampires split in order to outflank the dragon and box him in.

I lagged behind looking for the dragon guard but he wasn't there, the granite walls of the well still bearing the terrible claw marks as if the creature had dropped from the sky and tried to break its fall.

"Where is he, then?" the orc asked, slowing his pace.

A bluish black scaly monster immediately dashed toward us from a dark gaping hole in the far wall. His eyes lit up with a malicious flame; his jaws opened, revealing terrible teeth.

Then the paladin orc poured out his power toward the dead dragon, bending reality and entrapping the creature. The captured dragon's claws grated on the rocks. But the magic of Equilibrium had proved to be stronger, slowing the dungeon guard down until he could barely move as if in slow motion.

Goar raised his black sword, aiming a well-calculated blow, but the Baron beat him to it. His swift shadow darted around the dragon, aiming at his flank. Almost imperceptibly, the dead monster contorted his body, grabbed the vampire and impaled him on the sharp stump of his wing,

Kingdom of the Dead

then flung him aside. One blow and he was dead! Just like that!

"Holy shit," I gasped. It was a good job deadmen don't sweat, otherwise the hilt of my flamberge would have slid out of my grip.

Everybody froze.

"The show must go on!" the Count snapped. "Let's get on with it!"

The distorted reality burst at the seams as the dragon escaped his trap. Like a live torpedo it rammed the orc, hurling him against the wall. Still, all his buffs and blessings had allowed Goar to keep his footing.

The two remaining vampires split. All of a sudden I saw the dragon's monstrous head within spitting distance. He was only a few feet away from me. I raised my sword.

"Let me do it!" a kid's voice rang out.

Apparently, Isabella had failed to keep Neo in check. He stepped toward the dragon, raising his right arm as if about to hurl an invisible spear. A blinding light enveloped him.

"Fire in the hole!" I yelled, dropping to the ground and covering my head with my hands.

A moment later, a wave of unbearable heat singed me. A flash of silver light blinded me even

✟ An NPC's Path: Book Two ✟

through my closed eyelids. The light spear had hit the dragon. He began to radiate white beams of light which escaped through the gaps in his rotting scales. The dungeon became as light as day.

A thin glittering thread of energy reached out from Neo to the dragon.

Still, the attack had failed to disembody the beast, only paralyzing him. Once the boy's power was depleted, the monster would come round and then...

I couldn't count on the vampires who'd been stunned by the aftershocks of the Light magic. Goar was still trying to prize himself off the wall. I had to act on my own. The protection that had come with the sorcerous smock was barely holding up but at least the Shadow of Death shielded me from the unbearable light.

I picked up the flamberge and...

And then Goar lunged at the dragon and brought his own sword down onto his muscular neck. The heavy blade crunched its way through the scales already weakened by decay.

And again! And one more for luck!

The dragon's severed head dropped onto the floor. His body spread over the rocks in a

✟ Kingdom of the Dead ✟

heap of rotting flesh.

The shining light expired. Neo staggered; he would have collapsed had Isabella not grabbed him.

"What's up with him?" she asked anxiously.

I remembered the earlier incident in the Temple. "He'll be all right in a moment," I told her.

The two vampires started to come round. Goar kicked the dragon's head. "It's all been too easy," he said, puzzled.

He seemed unable to grasp the fact that he'd just single-handedly beheaded a monster like that. I understood him perfectly. Had Neo not come to our aid, the Baron wouldn't have been the only one going back to his respawn point.

"The sanctuary!" the Count shouted, wiping his teary eyes. "We need to take the artifact!"

"And where's the XP for the dragon?" Goar asked anxiously. "I haven't received anything!"

"Wait a sec," I said. "It's not over yet."

The dragon's hide swelled up and burst. A creature covered in rotting flesh broke the ribs of the carcass and climbed out. It shook itself like a wet dog and stood up.

An NPC's Path: Book Two

"I'm free!" it thundered.

Soul Eater. A Circle-5 demon

The mind boggles.

The incredibly tall demon noticed us and threw his arms open wide. "Come to me, my children," he boomed. Even though his skinless half-digested flesh and bony spikes protruding out of his muscles weren't exactly welcoming, the infernal creature's otherworldly charm attempted to enter our minds and submit us to its will.

All in vain. Deadmen were immune to his magic.

But only deadmen.

Goar staggered and very nearly fell but managed to keep his balance and began droning a monotonous prayer. Isabella hurried to draw her Mistress' symbol in the air, then stared intently down at her feet, waiting for the mental attack to subside.

And Neo? Neo was lying unconscious. He was little help to us now. By the same token, he couldn't create any more problems, either.

"Well, whatever," the Soul Eater grumbled, burying both his hands in the dragon's guts.

Kingdom of the Dead

When he finally straightened up, he was holding a sword, its blade consumed by a purple flame.

"Attack!" the Count shouted, then went for him.

The vampires disappeared in the shadows. I too hurried to stealth up, leaving Goar alone to face the demon's attack. The Soul Eater flung a handful of dragon's flesh at the orc, then took a swing with his sword. Goar parried it with his own but lost his footing and missed the demon's next strike, fast and treacherous. The purple blade sliced through Goar's heavy armor as if it were paper.

A blue glow enveloped the paladin, restoring his health. Isabella flung another fireball at the demon but failed to deal him much damage, so she began pumping her energy into Goar's protection instead.

The vampires materialized behind the demon's back and struck all together. The Marquis' charmed rapier sank deep into the creature's flesh but the Count's scimitars failed to deal him any damage. Ditto for my flamberge which I'd used to slice across his legs — then barely dodged the tip of the demon's sword aimed at my head.

✝ An NPC's Path: Book Two ✝

Goar jumped at his chance and cut through the demon's collarbone. His black sword of Equilibrium grated across the bone spikes, leaving a shallow wound. The Soul Eater struck back, slashing and drawing his victim. The paladin staggered and stepped back.

I let go of the flamberge and drew the bone hook, then slid behind the demon's back. He must have sensed my maneuver because he elbowed me away. The sharp spike had very nearly pierced the top of my head, grazed my skull and went into my shoulder.

I shrank back while lashing out at him with the hook. Its tip easily ripped through his skinless flesh. The demon span on the spot, howling his fury. His purple blade traced a blurred arc through the air, throwing Goar back. The Marquis received a blow to his arm and recoiled. The Count, however, managed to turn into a misty cloud so the sword couldn't harm him.

Luckily for us, Goar was able to rejoin the battle straight away. The Marquis and myself began circling the demon, hitting his back and promptly retreating out of sword's reach. The Count kept a safe distance, incessantly casting a

Kingdom of the Dead

freezing fog.

Finally, the demon's movements began to slow down but even so Goar had his work cut out for him. His black armor was dented and covered in gaping holes. Isabella struggled to pump his shields with energy.

Still, the demon's health was gradually slipping into the red; all we had to do now was exhaust him.

Suddenly he got a second wind. Accelerating, he swept Goar aside and threw a magic lasso around the Count, pulling him toward himself.

The Marquis hurried to his aid but fell foul of the demon's sword and collapsed with a broken leg. The Count tried to struggle himself free but to no avail.

The demon's clawed fist punched through his ribcage with ease, ripped his heart out and clenched it hard. Blood splattered everywhere. A gray haze enveloped the demon, instantly restoring 25% of his health that we'd worked so hard to diminish.

What a bummer! He's gonna shred us now!

The Count saved the day. Without his heart, he rapidly began to shrivel but kept his

✟ An NPC's Path: Book Two ✟

wits about him, investing the last of his strength into one last magic blow. A wave of fierce cold froze the demon to the floor, turning him into an immobilized statue albeit for a split second.

I jumped at my chance and ducked behind his back, burying the bone hook into the demon's ugly hump, then pulled its blade down, deepening and lengthening the wound.

The hook sliced through his skinless flesh from the nape of his neck all the way down to the small of his back.

Execution! The Soul Eater has been killed!
Experience: +4500 [36 179/37 400]; +4500 [36 223/37 400]
Undead, the level is raised! Rogue, the level is increased!

As soon as the freezing spell expired, the demon's grotesque figure melted to the stone floor in a pool of fetid pus. The purple blade clattered onto the floor.

The Count roared with malicious laughter, then crumbled to dust as if the bout of laughter had stripped him of the last of his strength.

Goar peeled the helmet off and greedily

Kingdom of the Dead

gulped the air. The healing aura around him had long expired, leaving him on his last legs.

"I hate demons," he grumbled, unclasping his gauntlet. Blood poured onto the floor. "Shit..."

A gaunt Isabella flung him a health elixir. "This green bastard has completely drained me," she complained.

Indeed, she looked as if she'd lost a good fifty pounds. Her gray face was drawn and pallid.

Much to my surprise, the Marquis wasn't too bad for wear. He emptied three vialfuls of blood, then rolled over on his side and was mustering his strength to scramble back to his feet.

"He hasn't kicked the bucket, your kid, has he?" he asked, licking his bloodied lips.

"He's okay," Isabella replied, squeamishly kicking the demon's purple sword out of the pool of fetid goo. "Here, take this and put it away. It isn't a cheap trinket."

I really didn't feel like touching the demonic weapon. I looked at the Marquis. "You want it?"

He pulled the sword toward himself and chuckled. "The Claymore of the Cursed Flame? It might fetch ten grand at auction."

I can't say the amount was mind-boggling

✝ An NPC's Path: Book Two ✝

but every little bit counts. We'd already amassed quite a lot of loot.

Neo stirred on the floor. Isabella crouched next to him. The vampire shook his head and made for the dragon's den. I followed.

"The sanctuary's there, remember?" I asked, catching up with him.

"I don't need to go that far," the Marquis croaked.

He dropped to his knees by the entrance to the cave and began rummaging through a pile of junk. Whenever he came across something valuable, he'd set it aside. Suddenly he whooped with joy and began kissing the curved blade of a daga. "My preciousss!"

"Wait a sec, goofy," Isabella said anxiously when the vampire had slid the daga into his belt. "The loot is shared between everyone!"

"This is mine!" the Marquis snapped. "I lost it here the last time. The Count's scimitars should be here somewhere too."

"That wasn't in the agreement!" Isabella said indignantly, but promptly reconsidered and wrapped the amber rosary around her wrist. "Kitten, do you mind?"

I shook my head.

Kingdom of the Dead

She turned to Goar. "And you?"

"I'll take my share in coin," he wheezed, spitting blood.

The Marquis continued his search and quickly found the Count's matching scimitars. Technically they were two items and not one but I chose not to squabble over it. Pointless.

"Is Neo okay?" I asked Isabella.

Much to my relief, the boy replied,

"I'm fine, only my head's spinning. I'd rather lay down a while."

"It's okay," Isabella reassured him, threatening me with her fist.

Goar could barely move. The Marquis was busy sorting through the recovered weapons and artifacts. So I just shrugged and walked over to the dragon's carcass.

It looked disgusting and stank even worse. His scales weren't worth the trouble of processing them. Still, I remembered how the demon had fished out his magic sword from within the creature's insides. Overcoming disgust, I started groveling through his rotting guts. If the dragon had indeed swallowed the demon whole, you never knew what else you might find in his belly.

Unfortunately, my fingers only found slimy

✝ An NPC's Path: Book Two ✝

gizzards. I would have long abandoned this sickening task had it not been for Isabella's snickering. I absolutely had to find something if only just to shut her up.

My fingers closed around something that felt like steel. Straining myself, I struggled to pull it out of the dragon's torn guts.

The item was covered in shreds of rotting flesh. It turned out to be a cuirass. When I slammed it on the floor to clean it from all the gunk, I couldn't believe my eyes. The fancy patterns embossed into the metal looked vaguely familiar. For some reason or other, they reminded me of my own tattoos.

"Finders keepers," I hurried to say, then proceeded to put on the fetid cuirass under my companions' astonished stares.

Deadman's Set: Altered
Deadman's Set: Saved

Ghostly Cuirass (Deadman's Set: 9 out of 13).
Armor: 90.
Doesn't impede spell casting or moving in stealth

🗡 Kingdom of the Dead 🗡

Yes! Yes! I'm the best!

The moment I put the cuirass on, it became weightless and translucent, embracing my torso like a shadowy haze. It didn't hinder my movements at all. I tried to stealth up just to check it. It worked without a glitch.

"You've got some cheek!" the Marquis drawled in surprise.

"It's all your fault. You've let the genie out of the bottle," Isabella quipped.

The Vampire ignored her comment. He only seemed to be interested in his precious daga. And... probably the mysterious artifact too, sort of.

"How about we get down to business?" Goar reminded him.

Neo stirred. "I'm ready!"

"One moment! One moment!" the Marquis hurried to finish sorting the loot.

"Give me five minutes," Isabella said. "I'll set up a portal upstairs. I'm sick and tired of being underground."

She drank some kind of potion and began building the portal's energy frame.

I took a wary peek into the dragon's den. The entrance to the sanctuary in its far wall

† An NPC's Path: Book Two †

emitted a blinding light too painfully bright for my dead eyes, allowing me only to make out the outlines of the objects inside.

The Marquis joined me. He could see slightly better, enough to notice a magic staff and the bones of a forearm covered in decayed flesh which lay behind the entrance to the sanctuary.

He whistled in astonishment. "Someone's already been here!"

I stepped closer to the entrance but immediately recoiled as the mask on my face heated up as if it had been thrown into a furnace. Neo, however, walked inside unhindered.

"Should I take the staff?" he asked, looking around.

"Yes! Of course! Take it!" the Marquis shouted as he shrank back, covering his tearful eyes with his hand. "But the artifact is what's important! Is it still there?»

Neo stepped forward and disappeared, consumed by the unbearable light.

"I got it!" we heard him shout.

The vampire breathed a sigh of relief. Immediately the dungeon shuddered, showering us with dust and stone rubble.

"Let's get outta here!" the Marquis yelled

Kingdom of the Dead

and turned tail.

The walls around us wavered, threatening to collapse and bury me forever under a layer of granite many feet thick. Still, I waited for Neo to reemerge, threw him over my back and dashed out of the dragon's den.

The only thought that throbbed in my head was, *Game developers never send players into a situation which they can't get out of.*

When I finally reached the first hall, Goar had already disappeared through the gaping portal. A moment later, the Marquis followed him.

"Quick!" Isabella shouted.

The walls of the well began cracking as the slabs of granite started to collapse and tumble down. I made one final effort but tripped up and barely stayed on my feet, barging into Isabella. Together we tumbled into the portal.

Now!

The blue sky opened above us, its eastern edge highlighted by the rising sun. The ground began to shake under our feet.

The monastery's roof collapsed.

The Count and the Baron were already hurrying toward us from the raid sanctuary.

"Did you do it?" the Count shouted as he

✝ An NPC's Path: Book Two ✝

ran.

"You bet!" the Marquis laughed, handing him the scimitars he'd retrieved from the dragon's den.

The Count took them, replacing his rather mediocre old ones, then headed toward us. "Where's the artifact?"

I let Neo down from my back. The boy pulled out the staff which appeared to have been made from one single piece of diamond and handed it to the vampire.

"No," the Count disregarded it. "That's not it!"

Neo reached into his shirt and produced a blob of deathly white light.

Both Isabella and I stared at it open-mouthed.

A shard of the Sphere of Souls! And it was only marginally smaller than our own!

Neo handed the glittering artifact to the Count.

I hurriedly snapped my fingers. "Wait a sec!"

That was the last thing I did. A fleeting shadow flashed across the sky, followed by a wall of fire which instantly incinerated both Neo and

🗡 Kingdom of the Dead 🗡

the Count. I took cover behind the Shroud, so the elemental attack hadn't burned me alive but only flung me over the stone parapet.

A sea of fire raged around me. I felt I was burning alive — but before I could crumble to ashes, a tall knight in red-hot armor stepped out of the flames and lowered both his enormous swords down on me.

Was it a coup de grace?

Possible.

Chapter Three
A Deadman in a Strange Land

1.

STONE. STONE ALL AROUND. Nothing but smooth stone. And darkness. This kind of darkness only exists in tombs.

I stirred, feeling around me. My fingers chanced upon something rough. I leaned my weight against it, and the crumbling slag gave under the pressure, revealing a way out. I wriggled my way out of the shallow grave.

The midday sun assaulted my eyes.

Kingdom of the Dead

It was already daytime. Where was everybody? What the hell had just happened? The wall of fire, the knight in red-hot armor, his sword blow...

Isabella's raid altar looked as if it had exploded from within. A crater now gaped where it had once been.

Neo!

I cussed. The boy could never resurrect, neither here nor anywhere else. He was only an NPC. A piece of program code.

As if!

A wave of desperate fury flooded over me. My head spun with the desire to find those who'd trampled us into the ground. I would rip them apart with my bare hands!

I opened the logs and frowned. The situation hadn't become any clearer.

You've been killed by a Fire Ifrit!

An *Ifrit*? A demon from Arabic mythology? Whoever could have summoned him to our world and pitted him against us?

I heard hoarse squawking overhead and looked up to see the black dot of Scarecrow high

✝ An NPC's Path: Book Two ✝

in the sky. I mentally reached out to him, studying the area from his height, but saw nothing... no one.

The sunrays were harsh on my raised face. To make matters even worse, I realized I didn't have my mithril mask on. Just to please! Our entire group would resurrect by the Tower of Darkness while I'd have to walk all the way there. And my magic disguise wasn't going to fool very many people.

Could it still be lying somewhere amid the blackened debris?

I started circling my grave, searching for it. Soon I'd indeed spotted a glint of mithril molten into the granite. It took me some time to prize the mask out of the rock. To my great relief, it was almost intact apart from one of the burnt rune mountings. But now it also offered +10% to Fire Protection.

A Charred Mask of Black Mithril, yeah right.

Never mind. Two runes were plenty. I wasn't even sure that Lloyd would be able to get something suitable. Actually... I already had that demonic bone, didn't I? Could I use it instead, maybe?

Wait up! That's not what I should be

Kingdom of the Dead

thinking of!

Another wave of violent fury flooded over me. I forced myself to calm down, otherwise I would have exploded like an overheated boiler.

I'm so sorry, Neo. We shouldn't have gotten you into all this.

I shook my head and opened the stat window, fully intending to improve some of my characteristics. The rest could wait. I brought both Strength and Agility to 20 and habitually left 1 skill point in reserve. I then chose Lightning Reflexes which was next on my professional skills list after Quick Strike. It was used to parry enemy blows and could be very useful in a swordfight.

Okay, so what about magic? As it turned out, apart from the level-3 spell I was entitled to, the game developers had been generous enough to offer one additional spell of the most basic sort. Apparently, my char wasn't a complete idiot although not far off.

I skimmed through the level-3 spells list and came to the familiar conclusion that in order to use any magic practices, I was lamentably short on both Intellect and internal energy. Still, it didn't take me long to choose. I simply

✝ An NPC's Path: Book Two ✝

remembered the ease with which the demon had lassoed the Count, and that's what I decided to learn. It might come in quite handy one day.

And what about a level 1 spell? I chose the Touch of Death. In order to activate it, you had to touch the victim with your hand. Although it didn't deal much damage, it could paralyze your opponent, and my Executioner profession just loved immobilized targets. How much mana did it take? Well, that entirely depended on the caster who could invest their entire energy in the blow if they really wanted to risk their last dime. I might actually find it useful one day.

I heaved a doomed sigh and opened the map, intending to find my whereabouts. That's when I noticed the new icon of an incoming message from Isabella. Just as I'd thought, both she and Goar had been resurrected by the Tower of Darkness. The three vampires, however, had respawned at the local place of power. I still had an hour to join them and port to the capital together with them.

An hour? Easy. Plenty of time.

Kingdom of the Dead

2.

PLENTY OF TIME? I shouldn't have spoken too soon. I hadn't dared take the forest road for fear of coming across any of the locals and was forced to give the Antlered God's hill a wide berth, too. Because of that, I soon got lost in the woods. Finally I came across a trail which led me in a totally different direction. I had to disregard any safety precautions and take the route I already knew. As a result, I'd wasted half of my precious time.

I had to run like mad along overgrown cobblestones, hurrying to our meeting point, then I turned off and took a shortcut through the woods. Bad idea. Don't ask me how I didn't notice a druid meditating in a forest clearing (probably because his clothing merged with the young green foliage) but the fact remains I didn't see him until I was only ten paces away.

The level-39 Forest Keeper turned out to be a player who belonged to the High Druid's retinue. No idea whether he remembered me or just wanted to teach an intruder a lesson but the high grass grasped at my boots, entangling them

✝ An NPC's Path: Book Two ✝

and winding around my legs.

Stealth? Not available.

"I was just passing by," I mumbled, still harboring a vague hope to resolve this peacefully.

With a wave of his hand, the Forest Keeper sent a gust of wind my way, covering me with a cloud of pollen. I was obliged to use the Veil of Death, incinerating the pollen. I then roped my opponent with a Lasso pulling him toward myself, and used the Leap to throw myself toward him.

One! The spell ported me behind the druid's back.

Two! I swung round and raised my flamberge, adding a boost to the already powerful blow.

Three! The undulating blade swept his blond head clean off his shoulders, sending it flying into the bushes and splattering the foliage red. The druid froze momentarily, then collapsed onto the grass.

Another one bites the dust.

Well done! Who's a clever bastard, then? I'd smoked a druid with my very first blow in open combat! And I'd received quite a bit of XP to go with it.

Still, my good mood had been soured

Kingdom of the Dead

somewhat when the bloodied foliage began to blacken and dry. Wherever the druid's blood had fallen, the grass wilted. The tree tops began to rustle.

The forest craved revenge. No idea how I knew: I just did.

I had to run.

I darted off. Nature itself seemed to be against my presence. The grass entwined my feet; tree branches lashed out at my face; sharp twigs tried to scratch my eyes out. A dead pine tree collapsed, barely missing me; an enormous moose flashed past, very nearly trampling me.

Then wolves began to howl.

Ah, dammit! I ran with all my might.

Immediately an Elven arrow whistled over my head and disappeared in the undergrowth. An echo of strange magic rippled through the air. And I still had far to run...

I could already see the circle of moss-covered menhirs and the bushes around them hung with skulls when a gray shadow tripped me. I somersaulted out of its path, swung round and slashed the creature with my sword.

My strike had been successful. The giant wolf dropped to the ground, howling and

✝ An NPC's Path: Book Two ✝

convulsing, while I continued on my way toward the portal. Toward safety! Provided the vampires hadn't lost their patience and left without waiting for me as promised.

An arrow struck my back — but the arrowhead just glanced off my now-materialized cuirass. Two more wolves tried to block my way and were apprehended by a ghostly shadow brandishing two gray scimitars.

The slain wolves collapsed to the ground.

"Move it!" the Count shouted, unstealthing. He swung his scimitars above his head, parrying the incoming arrows with ease, then stepped back into the safety of the menhirs. A moment later, I too rushed inside.

"To the portal!" the Count ordered.

A cloud of midges suddenly enveloped us. Not that it mattered anymore. I dove into the portal.

A new system message reporting the wolf's death from loss of blood came as a cherry on the cake,

Achievement received: Dog Slayer Grade 2!

There!

🗡 Kingdom of the Dead 🗡

The next moment I found myself standing inside the inn's loft. Not just standing there — but surrounded by all the vampires who were staring at me in a most unfriendly way, weapons in hand.

I pointedly sheathed the flamberge, removed the mask and smiled. "What's wrong with you?"

"What's going on?" the Baron demanded. "What kind of dirty trick is this?"

"Please explain," I said without losing my cool. "Can't be that difficult for a deadman."

The vampires exchanged glances.

"Someone's walked off with our artifact!" the Marquis joined the conversation. "We were the only ones who knew about it!"

"Whoever that was, they didn't just walk off with it! They murdered my boy as well!" I reminded them, gnashing my teeth with anger. "They killed him for real! For good! And yes, we were the only ones who knew about the item!"

It looked like they hadn't expected this turn of events.

"Seeing as we haven't gotten the artifact," the Count joined in the conversation, "we're gonna keep all the loot."

✝ An NPC's Path: Book Two ✝

If he'd expected me to voice my protest or even lift a hand against him, he'd been mistaken. "Go ahead, then," I shrugged. "The agreement was with Isabella, not me."

"I don't give a rat's ass who it was with!" the Baron exploded. "The money is ours!"

"Whatever you say," I threw my hands in the air. "But I really should think twice before breaking the word you gave to the Mistress of the Crimson Moon!"

The vampires exchanged grim stares.

"We'll think about it," the Count said through clenched teeth.

"You'd better," I nodded and left the attic.

Just as I began to go down the stairs, the attic door swung open.

"We'll find those scumbags!" the Baron shouted after me. "Then we'll talk!"

I gave him the finger as I turned the corner, knowing that he couldn't see it.

I returned to our room. Isabella wasn't there. I wanted to call Neo, then realized that the boy wouldn't be coming.

This was for real. I'd never get him back.

I heard a screeching from behind the window and hurried to swing it open. Scarecrow

Kingdom of the Dead

— who'd grown considerably — sprang into the room and began rotating his head, looking around. With an uncertain crow, he turned and flitted back out.

Was he missing Neo? Probably. I might be missing him too.

This thought must have become some sort of trigger. A blinding light filled the air, singeing me with a wave of incredible holiness and forcing me to step back. Dammit!

Since our last meeting, the ghost of the Grand Master of the Order of the Silver Phoenix had become considerably stronger. A deadman like myself felt very uncomfortable standing next to him.

"You're guilty of a Light Disciple's death!" the ghost pronounced in a ghoulish voice. "But not everything is lost! You can still bring him back to life!"

I shielded my eyes with my hand. "Can't you just resurrect him?"

The Grand Master didn't play hard to get. "My only temple doesn't provide me with enough energy. You need to cleanse yet another deserted sanctuary! And you need to do it before Neo's soul vacates this world! Once he crosses over to

✝ An NPC's Path: Book Two ✝

the other side, you can't bring him back!"

Bang! The numbers of a countdown began flashing at the very edge of my vision even though I hadn't yet clicked *Accept*. The ghost had given me nine days to *Restore the Mountain Temple*.

"What the hell?" I demanded. "Where am I supposed to get you another temple? I'm dead, don't forget! I can't consecrate it!"

With a metallic clatter, a silver chalice rolled at my feet.

"The place you seek is located in the lands recently reclaimed from the powers of the Dark!" the ghost announced. "Go and fetch some living water from the Temple of the Sun. That's all you need for the ritual!"

Reclaimed lands? The Temple of the Sun? Where was it, anyway?

The knowledge entered my head like the blow of an icepick. An agonizing pain passed right through me. The world around me shuddered.

When I came round, the ghost was already gone, leaving behind the chalice, the countdown and new markers on the maps.

And a headache. Dammit! Not surprisingly: both the Temple of the Sun and the deserted

☦ Kingdom of the Dead ☦

sanctuary I was supposed to restore were situated on the other side of the border, in the vicinity of the Marble Fortress. And if the ruins of the Silver Phoenix sanctuary were located far from any inhabited areas, the source of the living water would be right at the center of the city, in the direct vicinity of the local residence of the Order of the Fiery Hand.

Paladins could sniff out the dead from anywhere, couldn't they? And in the Temple of the Sun, a Lich's illusion would be dispelled in a flash.

Nine days to do it all? Nine days! That's a bastard!

Should I just forget it? The thought brought me a momentary relief even though there was no way I was going to decline the quest. It was just that... just what, exactly?

Why was I moaning about it? I'd just received a unique quest. What was there not to like? It wasn't as if I had too many things to do. Had there been a portal to the Kingdom of the Dead already open, I might have thought about it, but it wasn't as if anything was coming from that department. And I could use some extra XP and new allies.

✟ An NPC's Path: Book Two ✟

Also, Neo needed rescuing. There's such a thing as responsibility in case you didn't know.

But *nine days*?

I cussed under my breath, left the room and went downstairs. The dining hall was busy for a change. A tall samurai armed with a katana and a wakizashi was drinking whiskey with Mark at the bar. At the far-corner table, two Drow swordsmen were lazily sipping their wine in the company of a spooky gladiator covered in scars and hung with weapons like a Christmas tree. Yet another Dark Elf was sitting by the window, this one a Shaman. By capital city standards, all of them were higher than average players: some of them level 60 and above, others just bubbling under.

"Has Isabella shown up today?" I asked Mark.

"She'll be here soon," the innkeeper replied, then returned to his conversation with his new guest.

I took a clean glass, poured myself a shot from the whiskey bottle next to Mark and took it to a free table. I was dying to get sloshed. Still, even the alcohol couldn't help my headache nor my bad mood. My deadman's body just didn't

Kingdom of the Dead

accept it.

I pushed the glass aside and stared darkly out the window. The sound of rolling dice came from the far corner; the shaman was lighting up a pipe of God knows what; Mark was telling whoppers to the samurai.

For all of them, this was just a game. But not for me. It just drove me nuts.

And now this wretched countdown! Where the hell was Isabella now?

The moment I thought about her, she peered into the dining hall. Noticing me, she slid in, perched herself on a chair opposite and demonstratively rearranged her translucent cloak.

As if on cue, the Drow swordsmen stared at their kinswoman — or rather, at her revealing breastplate — but very quickly returned to their own business.

Isabella chose not to provoke them any further by striking any seductive poses.

"The vampires tried to screw around with me but I've sorted them out," she said before I could open my mouth. "They're gonna sell the loot and transfer us our cut tomorrow at the latest."

✝ An NPC's Path: Book Two ✝

I shrugged. "Neo's dead."

She stared at me incredulously. "I know," she said softly. "I'm very sorry it turned out like that. But it's only a game..."

Her words cut me to the quick. I winced, motioning her to stop. "I've received a quest to resurrect him. Neo, I mean."

"That's great!" she sounded sincerely happy. "That'll sort it out, no?"

I shook my head. "It will, but it means I might have to go to the Marble Fortress."

"What?" her eyes widened. She leaned back in her chair and crossed her arms across her chest. "Without me, then!"

"I could use your help."

"Are you nuts, Kitten?" she asked out loud, making heads turn. "The Marble Fortress is the Lighties' territory! You couldn't drag me there even at gunpoint!"

"Why not?" I asked. "It's not as if we're starting a war!"

"The war is already on, Kitten! In case you don't know, the Darks are trying to regain those lands. And we're on the Fiery Hand Order's black list! It's all right for you, but they're going to burn me at the stake! Oh no, for me a raid on the

Kingdom of the Dead

Marble Fortress is a non-starter!"

I frowned but said nothing. While Incognito might have camouflaged my earlier escapades, Isabella could have her head ripped off for killing the Order's Paladin.

"Just put it out of your head," she said. "Don't stick your neck out. Just forget it!"

"Cool it, will ya?" I said but there was no stopping her.

"Forget it! You're staying here! Understood?"

"Oh really? Did you decide that?"

"Yes! I decided!" she glared at me.

I replied in kind. For the first time she was the first to avert her gaze.

"Stupid risk," she shuddered. "And don't you even think of taking Goar with you. He's a Paladin of the Autumnal Equinox, a Darkie. And an orc. He certainly won't be welcome there."

I nodded. "How about the vampires? You think I could ask them to help? What would you say to such a backup group?"

"They're going to find those who scorched us last night. And I'd like to help them. Did you see what it was that Neo took from the dungeon?"

I sighed. "A shard of the Sphere of Souls. It

✝ An NPC's Path: Book Two ✝

was a little bit smaller them ours, I thought."

"If we get a second fragment, the Spawn of Darkness will have to accept us."

"But the vampires? It's their item, isn't it?"

Isabella shrugged and said with a nasty smile, "It was. Not anymore. They lost it. Whatever happens next is very ambiguous from the moral point of view. Also, do you really think the vampires would decline an invitation to be among the first to get to the Kingdom of the Dead?"

What she'd just said made sense. "Very well. Help them. In the meantime, I'll nip over to the Marble Fortress. You think you could port me there?"

"You're nuts, that's what you are!"

"You can or you can't?"

She fell silent, apparently performing some complex calculations. "Thirty-five hundred," she finally said.

"Thirty five hundred what?"

"The portal will cost you thirty-fine hundred," she glared at me. "Not a penny less!"

"But-"

"No, everything upfront."

"Oh, choke on it!" I spat, then began

Kingdom of the Dead

counting out the required sum.

I could only hope that I might lay my hands on something salable in the Marble Fortress. Having said that, it wasn't as if I was giving her my last cents.

The front door slammed. The samurai guffawed at Mark's last joke, then pulled him close. "You're a funny guy!" he said.

In an almost imperceptible motion, the samurai pierced Mark's neck with a long tantō.

The innkeeper collapsed to the floor. The samurai turned away from the bar and drew his swords. "Everybody ready?" he asked.

"Exactly," a familiar voice replied from the doorway.

Garth Deathblade! The bastard!

The gladiators sprang to their feet, overturning their chairs. The smoke from the shaman's pipe filled the hall with some sort of gray mist, blocking my Stealth.

Isabella hurled a combat spell at the Drow but it didn't reach its target, its glittering strip stopping in mid-air.

The next moment the two swordsmen attacked her. The gladiator cast a net impregnated with magic, aiming at me. I used the

✝ An NPC's Path: Book Two ✝

Leap just in time to avoid its gaping mouth. The burly gladiator who hadn't expected such a turn of events opened up to my sword blow but managed to dodge it at the very last moment. The tip of my flamberge just skimmed him, leaving a long bleeding wound in his side which unfortunately wasn't lethal.

I took another swing with my sword but failed to deal him another blow as the samurai had joined in the action. He showered me with a series of swift blows which I could only escape thanks to my lightning-fast reflexes. By a sheer miracle, my Flamberge parried his first three blows, then his wakizashi hit me in the chest but failed to pierce my ghostly cuirass, rebounding off it with a clang.

Immediately his katana flashed toward me. I parried the blow with my left bracer which too had proven too tough for the enemy's weapon.

Take that, you bastard!

A blinding flash exploded in the room as Isabella's magic dispersed the smoke. Even while cornered by the Drow swordsmen, she'd given me the chance to stealth up and escape my pursuers.

"Run!" she screamed.

✝ Kingdom of the Dead ✝

Before I could activate stealth, the samurai crouched in a low lunge, his short sword ripping through my right leg while he slashed out at the left one.

Thigh injury! Agility Penalty: 40%.

Ouch! My wounded leg buckled under me; I collapsed onto my back. I tried to fend off his attack with the flamberge but to no avail: both the wakizashi and the katana struck me, aiming at my knees this time.

"Don't just stand there like an idiot!" Garth hollered from the doorway. "Throw the net!"

With a seriously cunning move, the samurai knocked the flamberge from my hand and stepped onto my chest. I slithered out and rolled under the table to escape the gladiator's net.

They hurried to upturn the table.

"The net, quick!" Garth shouted, keeping a safe distance. He chose not to join in the skirmish, just stood there playing with some sort of fabric pouch. "Make sure you don't kill him! Hey, Johnny! My new master loves having his way with dead bodies!"

✝ An NPC's Path: Book Two ✝

A new line added to his Necromancer status:

Worshipper of the Bone Lord

That promised nothing good.

The samurai took well-calculated aim — then disintegrated in a cascade of blood as if hit by a turbo prop. It was the Count — who'd just unstealthed, raining a torrent of blows down on the samurai's back. His shadow scimitars pierced the fighter's lacquered armor with ease. The samurai began to turn round but the vampire had already slid toward the gladiator, replaced by both the Baron and the Marquis who'd got the samurai in their grip and made mincemeat out of him.

Garth stepped toward me, feverishly ripping at the pouch's strings. I tackled him with my flamberge, turning the blade in the already-bleeding wound. Garth staggered, stumbling over the gladiator's dead body and exposing himself to the Marquis who'd approached and attacked him from behind. Still, Garth managed to stay on his feet and threw a handful of gray dust in the Baron's face.

🗡 Kingdom of the Dead 🗡

The Baron's flesh was instantaneously scorched to the bone. He dropped to the floor, convulsing. Scared by the sight, the Marquis recoiled from the dust still hanging in the air and froze in hesitation, holding his rapier and daga in front of him.

Garth didn't attack him; instead, he pressed his hand to his gashed belly and hurried to the front door.

I dashed after him but lost my footing and collapsed face down onto the table. Even though my steel poleynes had protected my knees from the samurai's swords, my wounds had proven too serious. I couldn't even stand up properly, let alone chase after Garth.

Dammit!

The Baron rolled on the floor, howling. The Marquis joined the Count against the Drow swordsmen. Isabella couldn't join in my chase, either, her path blocked by the shaman as if on purpose. Gritting his teeth from the strain, he was casting a powerful circle of spirits around himself as he backed up toward the door.

I had no choice. I activated the Veil of Death and stepped toward him but the shaman's ghostly protection easily threw me back, stripping

✝ An NPC's Path: Book Two ✝

me of a large chunk of my health.

"You're dead!" I shouted, furious. Using the sorcerous Lasso, I picked up a massive chair from the opposite wall and pulled it toward myself, tripping the shaman.

He collapsed onto his back, momentarily losing control of his spirits. Isabella jumped at the chance and threw herself at him, pummeling him with her staff.

Bummer! What about Garth?

I limped toward the front door and tumbled out onto the porch, catching a glimpse of Garth's dark cloak at the end of the street. There was no way I could catch up with him nor could I hope that the bleeding would kill him. He was getting away, I just knew it!

Or not?

I mentally reached out to Scarecrow, my dead Phoenix. He dove after Garth like a well-aimed spear. I was so weak I was struggling to control him, but even without my guidance he knew very well whom to attack.

Scarecrow invested all his might into a powerful peck at the necromancer's back, knocking him off his feet. Garth went head first rolling over the pavement.

🗡 Kingdom of the Dead 🗡

But Scarecrow... he exploded. Not just exploded but he took Garth with him too, tearing his body from inside.

Garth's mangled frame froze on the cobblestones amid a flurry of blotches of darkness which flowed toward each other and began joining up, forming a black bird. The resurrected phoenix emitted a triumphant crow and soared back up in the sky to the amazement of all.

I cracked a crooked grin and barged back into the inn. By then, the vampires had already finished off the swordsmen and were tending to the Baron's bone dust burns, giving him vialfuls of blood to drink.

The shaman had long been dead. Not that it had stopped Isabella who was still cudgeling his lifeless body with her staff. Blood and bits of brain flew everywhere. Talk about running amuck...

I mustered the last of my strength to scramble to the nearest table and collapsed onto a bench.

"John, you hear me?" the Count shouted defiantly. "All the loot is ours! Got it?"

I waved him off. I was sick of it all as it

✟ An NPC's Path: Book Two ✟

was.

Indeed, our victory seemed hollow. We may have won this round but Garth was bound to be back. And the next time no amount of vampires would save me. I had nothing to show for this: no loot, no XP, only injuries. And now I also had to flee the comfort of this place which I almost considered home.

3.

ISABELLA OPENED a portal to the Marble Fortress the same afternoon. That gave me enough time to sneak into the city before dark, do a bit of recon and show up at the Temple of the Sun under the cover of darkness.

"Stupid idea," the priestess murmured under her breath as she chalked the complex portal scheme on the cobblestones of a small backyard and sprinkled the drawing with colored chemicals. "They'll make quick work of you, remember my words!"

I just smiled. "You're forgetting the Incognito. They won't even realize I'm dead."

She raised her head from her drawing. "The

⚔ Kingdom of the Dead ⚔

mercs heard our conversation. They know about the Marble Fortress."

Admittedly, this fact made me quite nervous too. I shuddered, shaking off any bad premonitions. "They're Dark too, just like Garth himself," I pointed out. "They won't last five minutes!"

Isabella winced but chose not to argue. I looked up at a patch of blue sky overhead. "Why do you need to bother? Couldn't you just buy an ordinary teleportation scroll? Would have been cheaper, too."

She laughed. "Kitten, you're not going on a picnic. Those are contested lands! You're going right into the Lighties' den. An ordinary scroll would port you to some farmer's field. Or even worse, it can be set up at some portal point watched by the frontier guards. In this scenario, your survival chances are dangerously close to zero."

"And where are you going to set up your portal?" I asked.

"Have you made up your mind, then?"

"I have."

Her angry stare almost bored a hole in me. Then she shrugged. "Lloyd sent me the

✝ An NPC's Path: Book Two ✝

coordinates of one of the abandoned places of power. According to him, it's still safe."

"Well, if he says so..."

"If you get ambushed, we'll demand our money back," Isabella didn't even try to conceal her sarcasm.

"That's a relief, then," I replied in the same vein.

"You can still reconsider!"

"Come on, let's get this show on the road."

She hissed a string of curses and slashed her own wrist with the ritual knife. Blood dripped on the cobblestones, spreading a soft glow over them. The lines of the magic drawing started to blaze.

"You didn't forget the return portal activation phrase, did you?" she asked me.

"No, I didn't."

"Off you go, then!"

I stepped into the portal and sank to my knees in molten rock. Or so it felt. Then I sensed being drawn down, deep underground, possibly straight to hell.

I must have screamed. I'm sure I did. I just don't remember doing so.

🗡 Kingdom of the Dead 🗡

I MATERIALIZED in the air under the vaulted roof of a dark cave. I hovered there for another split second, then collapsed to the ground from a height of seven feet. My armor clattered. I heard something snap. The floor under me quivered — but luckily, it didn't cause any rockfalls.

Cussing with relief, I gingerly got up and discovered I was standing on a slab of granite covered in fancy carvings. It looked rather like a tombstone. The carvings must have been gilded once but now all that remained were grains of gold at the bottom of deep scratches in the stone. Apparently, someone had been zealous enough to remove most of the precious metal from the granite.

The symbols looked eerily familiar. I'd definitely seen something like them before. In any case, it was irrelevant at the moment.

I turned round looking for an exit and froze, pinned to the spot by the contemptuous glare of an Angel of Darkness. A stone angel, I mean, who looked much the worse for wear. His black wings lay on the floor in a heap of rubble; his powerful chest was covered in deep scars. The statue's chiseled face had once been deformed by the blows of a heavy hammer: someone had

✟ An NPC's Path: Book Two ✟

taken the trouble of breaking off his lips, ears, and the tip of his nose.

I looked down at my feet and snapped my fingers. Of course! No wonder the pattern had seemed familiar! Exactly such a motif had decorated the residence of the Spawn of Darkness clan.

What a crazy coincidence.

I stepped off the unstable slab, climbed up one of the fragments of the wing and patted the statue on the cheek. Cheer up, Angel!

If the mythical patron of the Spawn of Darkness had been offended by such familiarity, he hadn't shown it. No wonder: I couldn't sense any presence of magic whatsoever in this dungeon. This was a statue. Just a statue.

Then I noticed the soft glow of sunrays permeating the far corner of the cave. I drew the flamberge from behind my back and headed to the exit. I managed to scramble over the heaped remains of vandalized wall carvings, then lay on my stomach and crawled toward a hole overgrown with tree roots and wilted grass.

The setting sun was shining straight into my eyes. For that reason, it took me some time to gingerly climb out of the abandoned sanctuary. I

Kingdom of the Dead

sheathed the flamberge and cut through the roots with the bone hook. I'd almost completely climbed out into the light of day when a giant shadow flashed behind the trees. Fire flared up. I heard a thudding noise and the howling of combat spells.

Oh, great. Here we go again. I clung to the ground, happy I hadn't yet left the hole.

The exit from the dungeon was located on a hill slope. The tall lithe pine trees which grew below didn't hinder the view at all.

Now I could clearly see three giant dragons circling high above. From time to time, one of them would dive and shower one of the many oak groves with fire. Their opponent on the ground replied with blinding flashes of combat spells — but the trees were going up like matchsticks while a thick cordon of Light frontier guards cut the daring players off from any escape routes.

I cussed. How's that for bad timing?

The frontier guards decided to advance only when night had almost fallen and most of the trespassers had already perished in the dragons' fire. The ensuing massacre didn't take long. Finally, the flying monsters sped off, followed by the knights and footmen.

✝ An NPC's Path: Book Two ✝

I prepared to leave my shelter but reconsidered and stayed put instead.

If I climbed out now, what would I do? It wouldn't be a problem to get to the city under the cover of darkness but what was I supposed to do there? The city gates would already be closed and even if they weren't, a lone night traveler might attract the guards' most scrupulous attention. Should I hover in the vicinity of the Marble Fortress at the risk of running into a particularly zealous patrol? I don't think so.

So I stayed where I was.

It felt like such a terrible shame to waste precious time — but very soon I realized I'd made the right decision. As soon as the sun had set, the valley below turned into a scene of short-lived but desperate skirmishes. Flashes of light and the strobing of combat spells illuminated the night. Dragons were soaring; the frontier cavalry was pursuing trespassers while groups of Light players laid in wait to ambush more intruders.

That didn't seem to baffle the Darks in the slightest. Some of them were trying to penetrate the inhabited lands while the others sought to cross swords with the frontier guards, retreating to their own territory whenever the resistance

Kingdom of the Dead

proved too stubborn. It was neither an invasion nor the players' attempts to reclaim the lands they'd already lost. They were driven by the desire to pillage, plunder and murder, all the while leveling up and improving their reputation and social status. Just like it was in real life, the only difference being that here your death in battle meant only loss of XP, nothing more.

AFTER SOME TIME, I'd even begun to regret ever getting involved in this escapade. Still, by sunrise the skirmishes had died down, replaced by a brief lull. I waited for another half-hour just in case, then crawled out of my hole and ran down the slope, threading my way amid the pine trees. The morning mist concealed me better than any Stealth ever could.

I wasn't at all afraid of being discovered — and because of that, I'd brought a heap of trouble upon myself. After some time, I heard dogs barking behind my back. I tried to change direction but the pack stayed on my trail, howling their excitement. Shit!

Scarecrow let out a hoarse squawk overhead. I mentally reached out to him and studied the valley from a bird's view. Things

✝ An NPC's Path: Book Two ✝

weren't looking rosy but by the same token, this wasn't a catastrophe yet: the dogs were still a good two or three hundred yards behind. Their handlers weren't in a hurry to unleash them, allowing the riders who were chasing me in an extended line to outflank me.

As if! I swung round and darted toward the ravine, rolling down its slope, then ran knee-deep in the cold water downstream until I came to a quiet little river, its banks overgrown with bulrushes. That's where I took cover.

The dogs lost my scent by the stream. My pursuers split up: the dog handlers headed for the river while the riders crossed to the other side and began searching the mist-covered field.

I spent the next quarter of an hour sitting up to my neck in water, using Scarecrow to watch my puzzled pursuers. Then I continued along the bank deep inside the frontier lands.

It got light and warmed up quickly; when the mist had finally dispersed, I had to take cover in the roadside bushes, waiting for my clothes to dry out.

Then I was plain lucky. I was already considering trotting off down the road toward the city when I saw a procession of pilgrims. My

Kingdom of the Dead

smock didn't differ that much from the cloaks of sun worshippers, so I followed closely behind, getting as close to the monks as possible whenever we came across a frontier patrol.

Thus we kept moseying on down for another hour. By the time we started coming across farms and fortified settlements, my dusty clothes had taken on the same inconspicuous gray hue as the monks' habits.

The city wasn't that big but the bridge across the stream which followed its walls was packed with noisy crowds which jostled, elbowing their way through. I alone wasn't in a hurry to join them, using my chance to enter the city together with the monks.

The rest was a piece of cake. My Incognito hadn't let me down. Neither the city guards nor the townspeople paid any attention to me. Their gazes seemed to glance off me, diverted. As long as I didn't force my way through or step on anybody's toes, I was safe.

I had already cleared the gates and entered the city when I finally sensed a gaze so intent that it made the top of my head hurt. I stole an inconspicuous look around but couldn't work out who it was that would be so interested in a

✝ An NPC's Path: Book Two ✝

humble pilgrim. None of the players nearby seemed to be staring at me.

The guards' corporal stood in the doorway of the guardhouse. A sneaky-looking Elf crouched in the shadows of the city wall. A Disciple of the Temple of the Sun hovered nearby. A Paladin in reddish orange armor sat astride a most amazing eight-legged horse.

The guard was probably a local warrior put on punishment duty . The thieving Elf must have been on the lookout for the thickest money bag. The young Disciple was there to meet the pilgrims while the Paladin looked as if he was about to join a raid on the frontier territories. His level 99 was almost unthinkable for this backwater, but then again, some of the Dark players were similarly tough cookies.

In any case, players of this caliber never acted alone. They were always surrounded by a numerous entourage so I didn't think that Barth Firefist had arrived here looking for little old me.

But the thief... It looked like his choice had alighted on *my* money bag.

I was right. The Elf slid after the pilgrims like an eel. I laid my hand on the bag slung across my shoulder. In my gamer's mind, the bag

† Kingdom of the Dead †

was firmly associated with my inventory. The thief was smart enough not to get involved with another player, so he promptly emptied the pockets of a few gullible bystanders and sneaked into a dark alley before they could discover the loss of their money and start a hullabaloo.

The Disciple led the pilgrims along the narrow streets of the Marble Fortress. I kept up with them, moving in their rear. I didn't see any more of the Elf; other players hadn't followed us, either, which was good news.

The road kept moving uphill. We took a shortcut toward the Temple of the Sun which towered on top of the hill. Its snow-white building was the highest in the city, surpassing even the Gothic residence of the Order of the Fiery Hand.

It was unfenced. Anyone could enter. I chuckled but stayed close to the pilgrims. You never know: what if I managed to get some living water just like that, without having to kill anyone or break any locks? Crazy, I know. But what if it worked?

It was almost midday — the time of day sacred for all Sun worshippers. Townsfolk began pouring toward the temple. All of them gave way to the Disciple accompanying us, regardless of

✝ An NPC's Path: Book Two ✝

their ranks or titles. Unhindered, we crossed a square tiled with a mosaic of the large sphere of the Sun, then walked through some impossibly high gates.

It was very light inside despite a complete absence of windows. A sole opening in the ceiling let in a focused ray of sunshine which fell on a fountain bubbling in a stone font. Refracted, the sunrays cascaded in all directions in a flurry of colorful spots, reflecting off all the gilded surfaces inside and hurting the eyes, driving you mad with their unbearable glare.

An ordinary human being could have easily survive the Solar blessing. For the undead, however, it was plain lethal. I'd realized it the moment I'd stepped inside.

I felt like I was being roasted from inside like a piece of meat in a microwave. My health plummeted. I smelled something bitter and burning.

I would have caught fire and burned away like a matchstick had it not been for an unnatural cold that began to spread over my body. It hadn't brought any relief; if anything, it had made matters worse. Now I felt as if I were being spit-roasted, first brought close to the fire

✟ Kingdom of the Dead ✟

and then dunked into liquid nitrogen.

Dammit!

I swung round and walked past the townsfolk standing behind me, then darted out of the temple, catching quite a few surprised stares. I decided against fleeing this place for fear of attracting any more unwanted attention. Unhurriedly I walked over to the wall of a nearby building and stood there in the shadow of a fabric awning.

What the hell was going on? Being burned by the holiness of the Sun I could understand, but the cold?

In search for the source of the anomaly I looked inside my bag. The silver chalice I'd received from the ghost was crusted with ice. So!

The Moon Grail
Property: absorbs holiness

I let go of the chalice and loosened my numb fingers, brushing off a layer of frost rapidly spreading over my leather glove.

What an interesting artifact. I wish I could keep it, then I could ignore the biggest part of divine magic. Yeah right. There's no harm in

✝ An NPC's Path: Book Two ✝

dreaming...

A heavy sigh escaped my chest. I winced and looked around. Everywhere I turned, taverns and street vendors began setting up their tables. The air smelled of cooking. More townspeople kept approaching the temple.

Now I noticed that all men were armed with short swords and daggers. Doubtful they'd be of much help if the city's old masters would try to reclaim it, but the weapons added a lot to the uneasy atmosphere of the frontier lands.

As if completing the picture of a besieged outpost, the local militia of armored footmen came up the hill, followed by a Fiery Hand patrol. None of them had paid any attention to me so I stayed put, waiting for the temple service to end. I just pulled my dusty hood over my face.

Very soon the sun would travel further and stop penetrating the temple. Then my time would come. In the half-darkness of the stone walls nothing would prevent me from filling my flask with the living water I so badly needed. Easy peasy.

Indeed, very soon the townspeople began leaving the temple, heading for the local taverns. But the moment I headed for the main entrance,

Kingdom of the Dead

the temple acolytes locked the gates with tall steel bars as thick as my wrist. I could see the fountain and hear its bubbling but there was no way I could get to it. Even Stealth wouldn't have helped.

A wave of fury surged over me. Still, I got a grip, swung round and walked away. Never mind. I'd pay this place another visit at night and it would go very differently then.

I came across another Fiery Hand patrol, on foot this time, so I turned off into a nearby street. Their Paladin gave me a long look but didn't stop me. Immediately the sleepy atmosphere of a small border town felt intense, foreboding even.

A lull before the storm? Maybe. Or it could have been my nerves playing up. In any case, it wasn't a good idea to constantly be in full view of the local guards.

I went down the hill and set off in search of an inn, walking past the stone tower of an abandoned arsenal. After a couple more turns, I found myself by the city wall, right opposite the Midday Light Inn.

I heard the clatter of hooves behind me. Without waiting for more riders to arrive, I

✝ An NPC's Path: Book Two ✝

walked around the tethering pole and sneaked into the inn. As I entered, I looked around the dining hall and breathed a sigh of relief: the only patrons in the room were locals plus a handful of traveling salesmen and pilgrims, all of them NPCs. Not a player in sight. Great timing.

The innkeeper, a short overweight middle-aged man was vegetating behind the bar, occasionally sipping his red wine. I decided not to upset them with the sight of my mithril mask and took it off, using my Almost Alive skill instead. It worked like a dream, so after a bit of haggling I managed to rent an attic room for silly money by capital city standards.

Having gone upstairs to my room, I locked the door and hurried to draw the curtains. From a deadman's point of view, the Marble Fortress was way too sunny and hot. I might wait until the heat had died down a bit, and then...

And then a bell began to toll right behind the window, And another one. And yet another. Was it some kind of ritual? Yeah, right. Stupid question. A peal of bells in a border town could only mean one thing: an alarm.

Still, this didn't look like the right moment for the Darks to strike. Which could only mean

† Kingdom of the Dead †

one thing: this bell was tolling for me. The townsfolk had found out they had a deadman in their city!

But why? How had they done it? Had someone in the temple noticed my suspicious behavior? I shook my head. Impossible. Had it been so, they would have apprehended me there and then. This was something different. Could it be that this uproar was about someone else?

The street rapidly emptied. I decided not to linger in my room and walked out into the back yard, stealing a pilgrim's cloak from the washing line. No idea what I might do with it but I had a funny feeling it might come in handy.

I asked the innkeeper for a beer and took it to one of the far tables by a window that looked onto the street. The other patrons seemed not to be alarmed by the bells. They went on with their eating and drinking so I began to wonder if all my worrying had been for nothing. They might have been trying to catch a thief or attempting to break up a knife fight.

More hooves clattered in the street. I looked out the window. Dammit! A squad of riders in orange cloaks trimmed with black — the uniform of the Order of the Fiery Hand — reined in their

✝ An NPC's Path: Book Two ✝

horses by the inn. Five swordsmen, two monks, a Paladin and his shield-bearer.

It didn't look as if they were trying to catch a thief. I didn't really trust my Incognito, so I surreptitiously got up and moved toward the back door. The moment I walked out into the corridor, the front door slammed, letting in the clatter of armor and the stomping of heavy boots.

"This is a routine control, gentlemen," a deep powerful voice announced. "A dangerous criminal has sneaked into the town..."

I didn't listen any further. I put the mask back on and ran along the corridor. Just as I turned a corner, I bumped right into a monk whose fingers were already emitting the merciless blessing of a cleansing flame.

He was ten feet away: way out of my reach. The moment I drew my sword, he'd roast me and I wasn't even sure that the Veil of Death would be of any help. And in any case, the rest of their bunch would hear the noise and come running.

"Take your mask off!" the monk demanded.

I obeyed. Pointless trying to prolong the agony.

The monk seemed to be pacified by my complaisance. "Come here, my son," he asked in

Kingdom of the Dead

a much softer tone.

Very well... Daddy.

Unhurriedly I stepped toward the monk. As he raised his hand for a fiery blessing, I performed a well-calculated combo.

Leap! Sudden Blow! Power Lunge! Touch of Death!

I attacked him unarmed — but my nails which still resembled claws easily pierced both the glove and the monk's habit. With a powerful swing, I buried my entire hand in his belly, squeezing the slimy guts, and attacked him with a paralyzing spell.

Stun! 00:00:16... 00:00:15...

He froze, his mouth open in a silent scream, unable to either cast a spell nor call for help. I pulled my hand out, disemboweling him and dealing additional damage, then drew the bone hook from my belt and buried it in my victim's neck.

Execution! The monk of the Order of the

✟ An NPC's Path: Book Two ✟

Fiery Hand has been killed!
Experience: +350 [37 529/43 000]; +350 [37 573/43 000]
Undead, the level is raised! Rogue, the level is increased!

Marble Fortress: status has changed!
Current status: enemy

The monk dropped to the floor dead as a doornail while I rushed out into the backyard and vaulted over the fence, heaving my body over into a blind alley. I didn't run but walked unhurriedly away. When I was about to walk out into the street, I finally heard frantic hollering behind me.

Tough luck, guys! Too late!

I didn't even care I'd just become their sworn enemy. This wasn't a PK mark. Incognito would cover it up. Incognito was a power to be reckoned with!

4.

I TURNED A CORNER and opened the game menu as I walked. No idea what awaited me so I really had to improve my stats first of all. Especially

✟ Kingdom of the Dead ✟

because it was a no-brainer, really, just adding 1 pt. to both Strength and Agility and bringing Incognito to level 4, seeing as I now had this possibility.

Why not Execution, might you ask? Because at the moment, I considered Stealth much more important.

The entire world was about to wage war against me, yeah right.

Incognito IV
It's not that easy to hide from a furious wizard — but executioners know how to conceal themselves from search spells.
-25% to your chances of being discovered with the help of magic.
+20% to Stealth.

Excellent. This way all those monks and Fiery Hand Paladins might find the task of locating me slightly more difficult. And I still had to hide from those Sun-worshipping priests today. Oh no, I had no intention of leaving the place without visiting the Temple first. All this effort for nothing? I didn't think so!

I forced myself to calm down and began

✝ An NPC's Path: Book Two ✝

studying level-4 spells. I wasn't particularly spoiled for choice, so it didn't take me long to choose. Why should it, if I now had Haste at my disposal? This was a spell that gave a considerable boost to the Lich's speed for the duration of a few seconds — a real boon for my rogue with his two-handed sword. I'm gonna dice and cube you all!

The alleyway had taken me to a wide boulevard which ran parallel to the city walls. I cast a cautious look around and turned to the left, fully intending to climb the hill and lie low in the vicinity of the temple until darkness fell. The bells tolled non-stop, so I decided to resort to an air recon, seeing as the dead phoenix, alarmed by all the noise, was circling the sky above the city, not daring to land on the roofs.

The bird's eye view of the city didn't bring any relief. The streets were now empty and swarming with patrols. Pickets were being posted at all the crossroads; new squads of Paladins kept leaving the Fiery Hand residence; I even caught a glimpse of the white armor of some unidentified knights. The few remaining players began bustling about: they must have received a quest to find the monk's mysterious killer.

Kingdom of the Dead

Until now, I'd been walking in the open but very soon I might have to either stealth up or try to sneak my way through people's back yards. And unfortunately, Stealth wasn't a cure-all.

As I walked along the rows of houses with ground-floor shops racking my brain for a way to get to the Temple, I heard the clatter of hooves behind my back. My mind seemed to be split; even though I didn't turn round, I could still see through Scarecrow's eyes. A paladin in reddish orange armor which appeared to be made of solidified fire was flying around the corner toward me on his eight-legged horse.

Dammit! It was Barth Firefist, the level 99 player.

Somehow I didn't think he was just riding past. I dashed off toward a gaping hole in a stone wall of one of the nearby houses, followed by triumphant whistling. They were hunting me like a wild beast!

Sorry, guys. Don't hold your breath.

I dove into a narrow side lane, vaulted over the fence that blocked it, then darted away. Catch me if you can!

Still, the paladin's monstrous horse simply rammed through the fence and galloped on.

✝ An NPC's Path: Book Two ✝

What a bastard! I turned off into a small backyard, passed under an arch into the adjacent lane, then hurried to stealth up.

Pointless. The horse was immediately back on my trail like a police dog. It caught up with me in no time and very nearly bit half my head off. Its jaws were packed with sharp wolf-like teeth; its eyes were ablaze with an infernal flame.

I had to dodge, then tried to escape a powerful kick from its hooves. My Stealth had worn off. The Paladin rose in the saddle, swinging a chain mace over his head, its fiery ball studded with a great many dreadful spikes.

I somersaulted out of a sure death. The terrible weapon sailed above my head, hitting the corner of a house and sending a couple of bricks flying through the air in a cascade of masonry. The eight-legged monster's momentum carried it further while I dove back under the arch, kicked a door open, ran through a house and into a neighboring street — directly into the city guards' hands!

I hadn't even slowed down, just taken a swing with my flamberge, aiming at their legs. All three guards went rolling onto the pavement but the Paladin had already ridden around the block

✟ Kingdom of the Dead ✟

and was catching up with me. I had to dive into the nearest gateway. My Stamina kept dwindling and I couldn't do a thing about it. If I failed to shake them off, they'd kill me. Hopefully, only once.

I crossed another backyard and ducked out into a narrow street. A cart loaded with large barrels trundled unhurriedly toward me. There was no way a mounted rider could negotiate it. Just to be sure, I sent the driver sprawling with a backhander.

Unfortunately, this trick failed to stop the Paladin. In one graceful leap, his monstrous horse jumped over the cart and galloped further on, its hooves striking up sparks from the cobblestones.

I just couldn't make it, could I? Everywhere I turned, more Fiery Hand knights were massing. Very soon they'd either corner me or shoot me with their crossbows. And once I respawned in one of the neighboring alleys, they were sure as hell to find me and smoke me for a second time. And again. And yet again...

Dammit! If only I had wings like Scarecrow who was now soaring above the roofs!

The hell stallion's hooves behind my back

✝ An NPC's Path: Book Two ✝

grew louder with every passing moment. Here, the street was a mere three feet wide. When it had taken me to the old arsenal, I abandoned all attempts to escape and ducked into its smashed gates. The Paladin kept close behind, so I had to take a staircase which lined the arsenal's walls.

The monstrous horse leapt after me but recoiled, unable to climb the steep stairs. Not that that baffled the Paladin. He leapt from his saddle and dashed after me, swinging his fiery mace in the air as he ran. The faster it rotated, the brighter it shone.

Our level gap left me no hope of ever defeating him in combat so I just kept running up the stairs non-stop without even trying to fight back. The Paladin was already on my heels, swinging his terrible mace but missing every time, his dreadful weapon leaving deep gaping holes in the thick stone walls.

He would kill me with a single blow! He'd swat me like a fly!

I rammed into some rusty bars blocking my way, broke them out and ran out onto the roof.

A sea of tiled roofs lay below. The houses here weren't adjacent to the arsenal though, leaving me no chance of jumping over to them.

Kingdom of the Dead

My only hope lay on the roof's opposite side but the Paladin had already climbed out too and was bound to hit me with his mace as I prepared to leap. Bummer!

Barth Firefist looked around himself and said with a theatrical shake of his head,

"So, John? You can't run any further, can you?"

My jaw dropped. Incognito was still working! How did he know my name?

You could play chase on this square roof forever. I began flanking my enemy, trying to buy time to run to the other side.

"You thought you were smart, didn't you?" he growled, throwing his hands above his head. "O Holy Flame!" he exclaimed.

Immediately a column of blinding fire fell from the sky.

The blessing was supposed to singe and stun a deadman. Instead, I sensed a bitter cold. The Moon Grail! Its sepulchral chill would have surely killed me had I not been dead already.

I walked out of the flames and cracked a sarcastic smile, desperately trying to stop my teeth from chattering. "Something's wrong, Iron Head?" I said, walking around him. If only I could

✝ An NPC's Path: Book Two ✝

make it to the opposite side of the roof!

Barth Firefist cussed and raised his hand again, launching a wave of intense fire at me. This one had nothing holy about it, only pure unadulterated combat magic.

I promptly activated the Veil of Death which softened the blow somewhat. But even so his spell had thrown me onto the far corner of the roof, very nearly sending me flying to my death on the pavement below.

"Did you really think I only had one char?" the Paladin began to blabber. He just didn't make sense. "Hah!" he guffawed. "You didn't understand anything, did you? That's *me*! Your old friend Garth! Didn't you recognize me?"

Two chars?

The mind boggles! A necro for sale and a level-99 Paladin as his main char? What a bastard!

Then it dawned on me. "So it was you who sold me to the order?" I mentally called Scarecrow while keeping my eyes on the swinging fiery mace.

"Brilliant idea, don't you think?" he laughed, utterly pleased with himself. "Now you're their enemy. No one's gonna say a word

Kingdom of the Dead

when I make mincemeat of you. Because I'm going to. And not just once. You're gonna get your comeuppance, trust me."

"Do you need the skull?" I produced the carved rock out of my inventory. "You can forget it!"

He choked on his laughter. "So what're you gonna do with that, then? Are you gonna chuck it? Come on, go ahead then! You can't throw it very far. And you won't have the time to pick it up! Somehow I don't think you can fly!"

Barth was perfectly confident. He had every reason to be. Even if I managed to throw the artifact onto a neighboring roof, he'd kill me and recover it before I could respawn.

He had all the aces. I had no choice but to activate Joker. I took a swing, investing all of my deathly strength into throwing the skull high in the sky.

A shadow flashed above. Scarecrow caught the artifact in his terrible talons and flapped his wings, gaining height.

The order I'd given him was perfectly simple: he had to take the skull to a safe place. The only such location I could think of was the dungeon with the desecrated statue of the Angel

✝ An NPC's Path: Book Two ✝

of Darkness. That's where he now headed.

Wailing, Barth threw his hand in the air, trying to reach Scarecrow with his magic. I jumped at my chance and went for him.

Haste! Quick Strike!

Three blows merged in one. The Paladin had no chance of avoiding the flamberge's undulating blade — but he didn't even try to do so. Thrice my sword hit the reddish orange armor without leaving as much as a scratch, let alone a dent.

Still, the attack hadn't been completely unsuccessful. I rammed all my weight against him causing Barth's hand to quaver and the fiery beam to miss Scarecrow by a hair's breadth. The phoenix dove down and disappeared behind the city wall.

"You bastard!" Barth gasped, throwing me aside.

He raised his mace, its fiery ball coming down on me. However, Haste was still active, allowing me to roll aside just in time.

The mace's spikes pierced the roof. The Paladin jerked it free and assaulted me again.

⚔ Kingdom of the Dead ⚔

That's when my well-leveled Dodge came in handy. Miraculously I avoided the blow, jumped over the connecting chain and darted off.

I had to get to the roof's other edge!

Garth hissed a curse after me. A fiery wind picked me up and carried me away, roasting me in the process. It hadn't killed me though, only taking two-thirds of my Health. Barely alive, I collapsed off the roof, kicking myself away at the last moment.

"I'm not finished with you yet!" the Paladin shouted after me.

The cobbled pavement came up to meet me. I squirmed, investing the last of my mana into a magic Lasso. Its energy coil got caught up on the drainpipe of the house opposite, pulling itself taut and jerking me aside. I launched myself through an open window, knocked over a table, sprawled across the room and stumbled down a staircase.

A fireball crashed in after me. A powerful explosion set the furniture and the curtains ablaze. Immediately fire took hold, roaring and filling everything with thick acrid smoke.

I didn't panic nor did I follow the petrified lodgers down the stairs. Instead, I ran up to the

✝ An NPC's Path: Book Two ✝

attic. Downstairs promised me nothing good, only more problems: a fearsome eight-legged horse with a remarkable nose for stealthed-up quarry, more guards flooding the city and a furious paladin...

To hell with them all! I didn't care! I wasn't going to choke, I just had to make sure I didn't roast. Which was a good possibility.

The top floors were completely engulfed in flames. The fire was spreading along the wooden superstructure with incredible speed. Enveloped in smoke, I climbed onto the roof and barely managed to jump over to the neighboring house when the roof caught fire and collapsed.

Under the double cover of Stealth and the smoke I walked over to the edge and looked below. Barth had just run out of the abandoned arsenal. The guards tried to stop him but he swept them aside and sprang into the saddle. But before he could dash off, he was encircled by some Fiery Hand knights.

A level-99 Paladin was quite capable of razing a couple of city blocks to the ground. Still, the game's balance wasn't just a pretty word. You can't win a battle with the entire world. Once you were outlawed, bounty hunters would be lining

Kingdom of the Dead

up for your scalp, greedy for their tiny share of XP and fame.

I just hoped that Barth would lose it, forcing them to either kill or at least banish him. Still, I decided not to wait until the end of the show and hurried away, leaping from one roof to the next.

I was reeking of burnt flesh. It looked like I was deep in it.

5.

I DIDN'T RISK acting out the chimneysweep for much longer. As soon as I'd vacated the cordoned-off area, I climbed down into a blind alley, put on the cloak I'd stolen at the inn and walked on, prepared to stealth up at a moment's notice.

I was desperate for my air recon but I'd lost all communication with Scarecrow as soon as he'd left the city limits. I could only pray that he'd delivered my skull to the dungeon of the Angel of Darkness instead of dropping it into the first marsh he saw.

Should I maybe commit suicide just to

✝ An NPC's Path: Book Two ✝

check it? Oh no. I still had things to do here.

I began weaving around the city. At first, everything went fine. The Fiery Hand paladins had stopped combing through the side alleys in search of the elusive assassin. Gradually, the townsfolk filled the streets again; I'd managed to avoid the few remaining guards still picketing the area. The only thing required of me was to remain inconspicuous.

As long as I stayed in the crowd, I was one of many. My Incognito turned me into a veritable invisible man who nobody gave a damn about. The passersby's gazes seemed to be averted away, glancing off me. And Barth? Much to my joy, the scumbag was nowhere to be seen.

I wanted to believe that I'd gotten completely away with it. Still, as it grew dark and townspeople began vacating the streets, I risked attracting the attention of some overly beady-eyed observer.

Others could go drinking in taverns or simply go home to sleep, but for me, neither was an option. I would have pretended to be a beggar, I suppose, but as the night fell, the square in front of the Sun Temple had become deserted.

Having considered all the pros and cons, I

✝ Kingdom of the Dead ✝

climbed the roof of one of the houses on the hillside and lay low on its slope, hoping that I wasn't too conspicuous against the backdrop of the dusty faded roof tiles.

This choice proved to be a decent observation point, offering an excellent view of at least a third of the city. I could see the militia patrols as well as the cavalcades of paladins and an occasional sighting of the mysterious knights in white armor. They definitely reminded me of someone but I couldn't for the life of me remember who it was. One thing I was sure of: they weren't just prowling around the city, they were looking for me. It was a good job they hadn't yet turned up at the Sun Temple.

AS SOON AS darkness fell, I immediately headed for the temple. At first, I'd been planning to wait at least until midnight but the darker the city became, the closer the white knights approached along the hill slopes, apparently bent on continuing their search for the assassin. I was simply afraid of dragging it out any longer.

This time I wasn't going to neglect Stealth. Like an ethereal shadow I crossed the square and stole toward the temple gates. The bars were still there, blocked. There was no way I could lift them.

Unwilling to succumb to the sin of apathy, I moved around the temple but noticed just in time the surges of orange flame ripping through the night. I dove behind a stone bench, then crawled toward a manicured acacia bush.

My anxiety hadn't been for nothing. Soon a few night guards stomped past my makeshift shelter: two warriors and a Disciple. Their torches were suspiciously bright as if they were lit not just by oil and hemp but also by a fraction of the Solar blessing. What if it could reveal a stealthed-up intruder? I'd have to kill them, wouldn't I?

Still, they hadn't noticed me behind the bush so I didn't have to smoke them, after all.

I decided against checking the guardhouse next to the temple. I could always do it later, so I gave it a wide berth for the time being. As if to please, I could see no other doors except from the main entrance.

I was just about to try my luck in the guardhouse when I heard a soft splashing sound. Something was streaming somewhere — probably, underground.

✝ Kingdom of the Dead ✝

I immediately thought of the fountain and started waking away from the temple, trying to work out where the extra water was being diverted to. I passed a neighboring house and walked down the hill until I climbed into a clump of thick dry grass where I finally discovered the mouth of a stone sewage pipe. The effluent which came out of it definitely originated in the temple even though there was nothing holy about it anymore.

I climbed into the pipe. I didn't have to crawl on all fours: I managed to scurry along half-crouched. At some point, I came across some bars but they proved to be entirely rusted through so it didn't take much effort to bust through them. Doubtful anyone could hear the clanking; I was much more worried about any potential traps. But even if there'd been any, they must have rotted away a long time ago.

Trying not to make a noise, I slowly advanced up the pipe, straining to catch the slightest glimpse of light. The pipe was dark as... as the devil's backside.

I suddenly stubbed my fingers on some brickwork through which tiny streams of cold water were escaping. There was nothing holy

✟ An NPC's Path: Book Two ✟

about them, either.

You bastards! What was I supposed to do now, break through the wretched wall? I had neither pick nor hammer on me! And I couldn't make a noise, anyway. Having said that... there must have been a reason for those bars at the entrance. And what if...

I backed up toward the exit, groping at the ceiling above my head. Very soon my fingers closed around thin air, then chanced upon the slimy rung of a steel ladder. Yes!

I jumped up and began climbing until I got to a wooden hatch. Effortlessly and noiselessly I wrenched the rusty bolt away and climbed out into a dark broom cupboard cluttered with mops, empty buckets and dirty rags. I froze, listening, then stealthed up just in case.

The door wasn't locked. I passed through a short corridor, turned right, then left. The sanctuary was on the left, so that's where I headed, then froze immediately, pressing my back to the wall.

Someone was in the temple. Shadows flitted along the walls, chased away by the flashes of fire which dispelled the darkness.

Hearing unhurried steps, I shrank back,

⚔ Kingdom of the Dead ⚔

readying the bone hook, but this proved to be a false alarm. The night watchman walked past and disappeared in the neighboring corridor, probably heading for the guardhouse.

The holy spring bubbled away at the very center of the temple. I could have easily run over to it, filled the chalice and escaped through the sewage pipe. Still, I decided not to rush it and lingered in the dark, counting the passing seconds.

Exactly three minutes later, the light of another torch dispelled the darkness. I wasn't entirely sure it was the same watchman, so I decided to wait some more. Still, the timing of these visits didn't change: exactly every three minutes, the watchman made his rounds. I wouldn't even have to rush.

Should I just smoke everybody here, maybe? I shook my head, dispelling the prickly thought. There was no need for it. Was I a thief or just a pretty face? I had to do it all on the sly. You never knew what sort of surprises the temple guards could throw at me if I made a noise. Also, the residence of the Fiery Hand clan was a stone's throw away.

When the torchlight had disappeared

✝ An NPC's Path: Book Two ✝

again, I ran out of the corridor, pulling the silver chalice from my bag.

Immediately a flicker of daylight flitted across the wall, jumped to the floor and dashed toward me. Luckily, I managed to catch it in my Moon Grail and turned the chalice face down on the tiled floor, trapping the sun phantom. The silver chalice began to heat up until it burned my hands through the leather gloves. I cussed under my breath as I counted the seconds remaining until the watchman's arrival. What a predicament!

Finally, I couldn't take it any longer and began sliding the chalice along the floor toward the fountain on its pedestal. The silver began to cool down. Even though I wasn't entirely sure it had managed to disembody the phantom, I decided to take my chances. I grabbed the chalice by the stalk and turned it round, preparing to hurl it aside if necessary.

It was empty. Not a trace of any light, only the matt white glow of polished silver. A dream item! What a shame I had to part with it.

I stepped close to the fountain and froze. Only a moment ago, the temple had been pitch black. And now I was surrounded by a ghostly

Kingdom of the Dead

shimmer. What the hell?

I looked up. To my amazement, a full moon was peeking into the temple through the hole in the roof. How was it possible? The starry sky outside was perfectly dark and moonless.

A logical chain started to form in my head: *'The moon — the silver — the phoenix'* but I ignored it and held out the chalice under one of the fountain jets. The metal immediately began to freeze, forming icy patterns on the silver. My fingers turned numb and senseless.

The Moon Grail
Property: bestows the Moon's blessing upon you

All done!

Before shoving the chalice back into the bag, I took a peek into it. I wasn't even surprised when I saw that there was no trace of water inside and that the chalice was filled with a ghostly glow as if it were filled with moonlight.

A torchlight glimmered in the distance. I darted off, desperate to take cover in the adjacent corridors before the watchman could re-enter the temple. I made it to the utility room just in time,

✝ An NPC's Path: Book Two ✝

unhurriedly climbed down into the sewage pipe and started out for the exit.

Uncertainty overcame me just when I was about to climb out. Everything had gone too smoothly; I couldn't be sure that the paladins couldn't be laying in wait somewhere nearby. Still, I forced the thought out of my head and slid out of the pipe. Between Stealth and the darkness of the night, I was safely hidden especially because I had no one to hide from. There was not a soul around.

Having emerged out of the thick grass, I walked down the hill slope into a street and hurried away. I'd done everything I needed to do; now I had to make myself scarce ASAP. And somehow I didn't think I could leave through the city gates. I shouldn't underestimate Garth's stubbornness: he may be unable to constantly keep an eye on the city exits but he could afford to hire mercenaries to do it for him. Dark or Light, didn't matter; the only thing a mercenary cares about is getting paid on time. Which moral are you talking about? What's good or bad got to do with it? Somewhere else maybe, but definitely not in a game.

I noticed a brook running down the hill and

☦ Kingdom of the Dead ☦

followed it. Still, almost immediately the torches of the night guards flashed below, so I had to turn off into a nearby lane. As a result, it had taken me quite some wandering around the dark sleepy streets before I finally reached the little river that flowed through the city. On top of some guards and militiamen, I'd come across a few white knights and as I had no idea who they were and what to expect from them, I gave them a wide berth.

Still, I'd made it, and that was all that mattered.

Unfortunately, my hopes for an easy escape from the Marble Fortress weren't meant to happen. The arch through which the nameless river flowed out of the city had been closed off with bars as thick as my arm. I couldn't leave that way.

Without losing heart, I headed for the nearest watchtower. Its ground-floor room was lit; from time to time, the garrison soldiers ran out into the street for a smoke or to take a leak.

None of them bothered to lock the door behind them. I waited for the right moment and snuck inside, climbed a spiral staircase and found myself on the parapet of the city wall. It

✝ An NPC's Path: Book Two ✝

was crawling with sentries — but some one them dosed off while others stared watchfully into the darkness outside with little interest in whatever happened behind their backs. I slid past them like a ghostly shadow looking for a suitable place to jump. Having found it, I climbed over the parapet and stepped from the wall, plunging straight into the river.

6.

EVEN IF THE SOUND of splashing water had alerted the guards, they didn't seem too bothered. A few arrows sank to the bottom, surrounded by bubbles of air, together with a heavy boulder — that was the extent of the garrison's reaction to the suspicious noise.

The river's silty bottom was a much bigger problem. I'd gotten stuck in it so badly that I very nearly didn't make it to the bank.

Regardless of the dirt, my escape was clean. There was no one chasing me.

Only once did I notice strange flashes of white light by the city wall but no matter how many times I stopped and peered into the night, I

✟ Kingdom of the Dead ✟

didn't see anything suspicious. So I just stopped looking back. I had more pressing problems other than keeping an eye on any hypothetical pursuit. The night valley wasn't as deserted as it had appeared from the city wall. I had to shake off prowling predators from my trail quite a few times; and at a certain point, only my well-leveled Stealth had helped me to avoid a scuffle with a loud and boisterous group of gamekeepers.

Luckily, the abandoned temple was further from the border than the city so as I moved away from the Marble Fortress, I encountered fewer patrols. Here, the grasslands gave way to sunbaked rocky foothills.

A fast-flowing brook raced between the rocks. I checked the map and began scrambling over the wet and slimy stones. That was it! The only way was up!

STRANGELY ENOUGH, I managed to get to the mountain temple without any further unpleasant surprises. Here and there, the crevice was blocked by rockfalls, causing the stream to spread and form treacherous whirlpools. Gradually I began to realize why the abandoned temple hadn't yet been discovered by any of the players. Had it not been for the ghost's help, I would have never found any of the secret trails and steps cut into the rock and would have turned back long ago.

On top of everything else, the temple was situated in a cave whose mouth was concealed by a waterfall cascading from the cliff above. At first, I felt perplexed until Scarecrow sighted a rocky trail running along a deep whirlpool. Then everything fell into place.

Oh yes, my dead phoenix was back — without the charmed skull. I shuddered. It felt like running your tongue along your teeth and discovering a gap. Something was missing. I sort of felt uncomfortable — unpleasantly so.

You'd think that now the artifact was safe — and still my heart was restless. The sooner I sorted that quest out and retrieved the skull, the better. Garth might have tracked Scarecrow down, you never knew. What if he had the skull now?

I forced myself not to panic and edged toward the waterfall, casting wary glances at the dark outlines of some rusty armor on the bottom. Immediately the spirits of the drowned warriors started casting curses on me. Not that I cared. I

Kingdom of the Dead

was dead and immune to them.

I stepped through the wall of water, stealthed up and kept quiet. The place was silent. No screeching or clanking noises; the otherworldly howling of ghosts had died away too. The abandoned temple looked deserted.

The problem was, supernatural creatures loved to make their home in places like these. Which was why I kept on my guard, ready to dodge any potential threat.

At first, I couldn't hear anything over the noise of the falling water but as I climbed the steps cut into the rock, its rumbling became duller until it became perfectly quiet. Here, a complex pattern of symbols covered the walls; as I walked, I started coming across some empty niches. The place was perfectly devoid of both the living and the dead.

A staircase lined with a stone balustrade took me to a round room on the top level. The altar lay shattered under its domed ceiling; a dark figure holding a book froze at the center.

A monotonous chant echoed through the temple. I couldn't make out a single word he was saying. Not that it mattered.

The warlock stood with his back to me. I

† An NPC's Path: Book Two †

took a few silent steps toward him, then took an almighty swing at him with my sword. The undulating blade went right through the dark figure as if it were woven from smoke.

The warlock swung round, unharmed, and uttered a brief word of power, throwing me against the wall. I pulled the bone hook from my belt, suddenly realizing that my opponent wasn't human:

The Curse of the Mountain Temple

I darted aside, dodging his attack. The otherworldly creature missed, turning a complex wall carving into a heap of rubble, then materializing next to me again. By then, I'd already overcome my initial stupor and met his attack with a counter-blow from my Moon Grail.

Bang! The silver chalice emitted a bright light which burned holes in the ghost's incorporeal figure. The embodied curse collapsed on the floor and tried to scramble back to his feet. I whacked him over the head with the chalice and he dropped back down.

Now you're gonna get it! I dropped down onto him and began thrashing him with the

🗡 Kingdom of the Dead 🗡

chalice, each blow stripping the ghostly curse of some of its power. One! Two! Three!

The figure disintegrated into a shapeless cloud which flickered with a silvery flame, then dispersed. Still holding the chalice by its stem, I stood up and took a look around.

So what was I supposed to bless here?

"Uncle John," a quiet voice whispered.

I swung round. Neo's translucent form floated out of the heap of stones which had once been the altar. Suspecting an illusion, I raised the chalice and splashed some of the white light on him but all it did was add a degree of corporality to the spirit. It looked like this was Neo all right.

"What do I do?" I asked Neo's ghost.

"Give it to me," he demanded. "I must do it myself!"

An invisible force pulled the Moon Grail from my hand. The boy's soul floated to the ceiling. The temple filled with an unbearable light.

One of the many sparks had dropped onto my shoulder, burning a hole through my flesh. I ouched. "Wait! You're gonna scorch me!"

The light stopped getting brighter but didn't

✝ An NPC's Path: Book Two ✝

cease its intensity, either.

"Uncle John, run!" the boy's voice rustled. "I can't control this force!"

I scampered down the stairs and dashed away from the temple. I didn't so much fear my own death — if push came to shove, I could always respawn by the skull hidden in the place of power — but I dreaded the possibility of having to come back here again in order to resurrect Neo.

With one swift leap, I sprang back through the waterfall. Surprisingly, it was bright as day outside. The whirlpool was frozen solid.

"Here we meet again, strange creature," the white witch said.

Her clothes were white and so was her skin, hair and even her eyes. A white glow spread around her. Her retinue knights were clad in white armor.

Dammit! If it wasn't this lady who'd tried to exorcise me in the Stone Haven.

Leap! Sudden Strike! Sweeping Strike!

The Soul Killer slid into my hand. I microported toward the witch and took a swing,

Kingdom of the Dead

aiming for her throat. No sorcerer would have been able to promptly react to my attack — but still she parried the bone hook with her open hand. The Soul Killer split in two like a piece of rotten wood.

I swung round and darted back into the temple. I'd rather burn alive!

A gust of icy wind hit me in the back, lifting me from the ground and throwing me into the waterfall. The freezing cold assaulted me and everything around, turning me into an ice statue. I couldn't move a limb.

Unhurriedly she walked over to me and patted me on the cheek. Immediately my face turned numb as if she'd given me a Novocain shot.

Like black lightning, Scarecrow came down from the sky but a nonchalant sweep of the white hand disembodied him, turning him into scattered whiffs of darkness which the freezing wind swept away.

"The Darkness has no power over this place anymore," the witch smiled. "No one can prevent me from finding out what you really are."

Once again her long, thin fingers ran across my face. The witch frowned. "This is a

✝ An NPC's Path: Book Two ✝

mistake. This is all wrong!"

Her pale-blue nails reached into my eye socket, extracting my eye.

For the first time in ages I felt pain. Not the fake virtual pain but the real-world stuff, real and uncompromising, the kind which can make you pass out, the kind which can make you go nuts.

Still, madness is a luxury a deadman can't afford. I screamed my head off but just couldn't lose my mind. The pain just wouldn't stop. Black blood poured out of my eye socket, freezing on my face. The white bitch watched me curiously, undeterred, as if I was some sort of exotic animal.

The Restore the Mountain Temple quest is complete!
Experience: +5000 [42 529/43 000]; +5000 [42 573/43 000]

The system message assaulted me with another paroxysm of pain. My ice fetters prevented me from convulsing. My mind faded.

The witch gave me another pat on the cheek. "A prohibited merge of two entities," she said softly. "Requires an immediate intervention."

She raised her hand.

Kingdom of the Dead

Neo ran out of the cave. He seemed to have grown a few years. His modest *Disciple* status had given place to a much more serious *Knight* tag. He was level 28, no less.

The white witch's bodyguards moved toward him, then stopped.

"A creature of Light," the witch identified the boy.

Losing all interest in him, she once again dug her fingers into my mutilated eye socket. Blood went everywhere.

"Uncle John!" Neo gasped. "What are they doing to you?"

Straining my numb tongue, I whispered, "Bless me..."

The boy startled. "Uncle John? What did you say?"

"Bless me!"

"Yes but-"

"Do it!" I rasped, feeling something cold and alien trying to reach into my brain.

Neo threw caution to the wind and spread his arms wide, summoning his heavenly patron.

A blinding silver light went right through the white knights without hurting them. Ditto for the witch. My dead flesh, however, hissed as it

✝ An NPC's Path: Book Two ✝

took fire like a piece of roast on a barbecue.

"Again!" I screamed in a masochistic vigor.

Neo didn't let me down. A fiery whirlwind scooped me up whole, burning me and scattering my ashes. Killing me.

Which was exactly what I needed: death.

7.

ROCK. DARKNESS. Blood.

Scarecrow had been a good boy. He'd taken my charmed skull to the abandoned sanctuary of the Angel of Darkness. Still, something wasn't right. Something was different. Not as it should have been.

Blood! It was pouring down my face, trickling onto the flagstones and accumulating in tiny swirls and motifs, its dark crimson flooding the damaged symbols.

What the hell? I was dead! I couldn't bleed!

But that wasn't all. I was clutching the stone skull in my right hand while my left was holding something round, something that burned my palm with its unnatural icy cold.

A frozen eyeball?

✝ Kingdom of the Dead ✝

My eyesight seemed to have split. I could see things from two different angles, and my mind had a hard time trying to come to grips with it.

I couldn't think straight. Bouts of nausea flooded over me.

What the hell? When you respawned, all the previous injuries were annulled!

Still, I was holding my own eye in my hand. Blood continued to gush out of my eye socket. I was dying — dying from blood loss!

Straining every muscle, I sprang to my feet. The flagstones underfoot cracked, collapsing.

I came round in pitch blackness which was much more than just absence of light. Darkness enveloped me, supporting and holding me in its gravity-defiant embrace. The dungeon had expanded; now it was enormous, both its floor and ceiling disappearing out of sight as if the tile which had given way under my feet had opened a portal to a different universe.

"I thank thee who shared your power and blood with me!"

The voice sounded out of nowhere, scaring the hell out of me. The darkness thickened even further, releasing a clot of such impossible

✝ An NPC's Path: Book Two ✝

blackness it could turn the brightest day into the darkest night.

Somehow I managed to recognize it. This blob of darkness was in fact the disfigured vandalized angel whose statue had caught my attention during my first trip to the dungeon.

The Angel of Darkness stared at me, then said without even trying to conceal his disgust,

"A deadman!"

I coughed up blood, then smirked in a reckless bout of defiance, "It's not as if you're very much alive either, is it?"

The dungeon boss began to grow, making me feel like a tiny grain of sand he could grind into the finest dust. Having said that, could he really? Seeing as he seemed to have taken a liking to my dead blood?

Indeed, I heard a doomed sigh.

"Very well, deadman," the Angel of Darkness uttered. "What is it you want? Tell me."

He assumed his former shape and reclined on his throne which floated in the sea of pitch blackness. I stood cap in hand in front of the otherworldly patron angel of the Spawn of Darkness clan (or was it just one of his incarnations?).

✟ Kingdom of the Dead ✟

Still, we weren't proud, were we? We knew exactly what to ask him for.

"My eye!" I croaked. "Some white bitch has taken my eye out!"

I hear a chuckle. The Angel leaned down, brought his disfigured face close to mine and blew into my bleeding eye socket.

A dark fiery tornado ravaged through my head, throwing me down onto my back and twirling me in its grip. It didn't last very long though. Soon the swirling had subsided; the bleeding had stopped.

But I was still clutching my frozen eye in my hand.

A Sacred Gift of the Darkness
Perception: -5
Intellect: +5

I felt my scarred eye socket. "What the hell? I wanted you to put my flippin' eye back in!"

The Angel laughed. "Sorry, deadman," he admitted calmly. "I can't. If I spend more power on healing your injury, I might have to deny my help to someone infinitely more worthy. Or I might inadvertently offer the Lights an advantage they don't deserve. It's all about the balance. Nothing personal, sorry."

I growled with fury and disappointment. Suppressing a bout of cussing, I decided to appeal to his logic. "Balance-wise it's a bit shitty, don't you think? You might have exerted some power but you haven't put my eye back in! I can't keep holding it in my hand all the time, can I?"

"Put it around your neck," the Angel said without concealing a smirk.

"How do you want me to fight without it?"

The Angel of Darkness stared at me. His gaze penetrated the deepest corners of my digital soul, ruffling through my memories and sorting through my most secret thoughts and desires.

"Well, maybe if we consider this an advance," he said pensively.

"Whatever!" my voice broke half-word. "What is it you want?" I added unenthusiastically.

"I want a shard of the Sphere of Souls," the Angel announced.

I didn't ask how he, the patron of the Spawn of Darkness clan, could have found out about my artifact. My reply was curt and precise,

"Eat shit!"

🗡 Kingdom of the Dead 🗡

The Angel shook what was left of his index finger at me. "Your shard should never, under no circumstances, fall into the Lights' hands. Deal?"

I paused, thinking, then nodded. "Deal."

It wasn't as if I was going to enter into any kinds of negotiations with clans of Light. I wasn't interested in selling the fragment, anyway; all I cared for was getting access to the Kingdom of the Dead.

The Angel took the frozen eyeball and winced as if it physically hurt him to hold something still bearing the imprint of the Light witch's will. I even thought he might discard it. Instead, in one imperceptible twist of his hand, the Angel drew the flamberge from behind my back and slammed the eye onto its steel pommel.

"What the hell?" I demanded, watching in dismay as the sword's rusty blade began to cover in a fine flurry of the whitest frost. "What do you think you're doing?"

"I'm relieving you of the necessity of carrying your own eye in your pocket," the Angel replied calmly.

This was a good lesson. You should be doubly careful with your words when you strike deals with supernatural creatures.

✝ An NPC's Path: Book Two ✝

The Gaze of Frost (Deadman's Set: 9 out of 13)

Damage: 20-26

Accuracy: +17%

+17% to your chances of dealing critical damage

+13% to your chances of freezing your opponent to death to each undulation of the blade used in the blow.

Cold damage: temporary paralysis or 9 pt. health per sec for the duration of 9 sec.

+9 to Perception in combat

Status: unique

I weighed the transformed flamberge in my hand. I knew better than trying to attack the Angel with it (even if this *was* one of his weakest incarnations).

"The Lights will never get the shard of the Sphere of Souls," I said meaningfully. "The question is whether the Spawn of Darkness can get it?"

Now that the blood had stopped gushing from my eye socket and I didn't need to constantly hold my eye in my hand anymore, I felt much more confident.

🗡 Kingdom of the Dead 🗡

The Angel seemed quite amused. "I suggest we make a deal," he said good-naturedly. "You give the shard to my servants when they ask for it. And instead, I'll bestow a fraction of my own power on you."

His words rang with sarcasm laced with curiosity. He seemed to be toying with me, offering me a bait on a sharp hook. If I swallowed it, I'd never set myself free. My every consequent deal would become another tiny step toward hell.

A fraction of his power? I don't think so! I wasn't going to sell myself so cheaply. If the truth were known, I wasn't going to sell myself at all.

"Your servants must let me go to the Kingdom of the Dead. Otherwise there'll be no deal," I quipped, not intending to horse-trade.

The Angel pensively rubbed his mangled face with the stumps of his fingers as if running through all the possible scenarios, then leaned back on his throne and shook his head. "They ain't gonna do it," he said, then raised his hand, motioning me to remain silent. "But! The clan has considerable difficulty trying to collect the Sphere of Souls. And if you could offer them, say, two fragments instead of one..."

"Where do you want me to get it from?" I

✝ An NPC's Path: Book Two ✝

demanded, indignant.

"I think you know the answer to that," the Angel replied with all the guile of the serpent in the garden of Eden. "I suggest you give it some thought before you reject my offer."

He seemed to be reading me like an open book.

The blinding light in Neo's hand, the fiery tornado, the knight in red-hot armor...

He was right. I should give it some thought. If the other fragment hadn't been sold yet... and if we managed to find our attackers and repay them in kind...

If, if, if! This was all academic. By the same token, it could solve so many things. This was the question of my own life.

"The fragment you lost hasn't yet turned up at either the Light nor the Dark camp," the Angel said, exhibiting remarkable knowledge of these things. "Find it, and you'll be granted passage to the Kingdom of the Dead. I'll make sure you do."

"And what if I fail?"

"Then you'll have to give up your own fragment unconditionally," the Angel announced. "And you will beg the Spawn of Darkness to kindly take you along."

✟ Kingdom of the Dead ✟

"This is crazy!" I said, unable to restrain myself. "What kind of cannibalistic terms are these? And what's with that fraction of your power?"

He gave me a meaningful smile. "Have you heard of the Dance of the Darkness school of combat? Its disciples are the best fighters in this Universe. They're unslayable. I could teach it to you, deadman."

I opened my mouth, then closed it again. An advanced dodge! Admittedly, the cheese in his mousetrap smelled delicious.

This was all or nothing.

Really, what was I risking? The Spawn of Darkness's leaders had made it perfectly clear that they weren't prepared to take us on their Kingdom of the Dead raid. The Angel had just confirmed it. Had he lied to me? Possibly. But if I took him at his word and managed to procure another fragment... that would make things so dramatically easier!

All or nothing. This was cheese in a mousetrap. I was playing against an expert cardsharp.

I shook my head. "The fragment doesn't belong to me alone. The will of the Mistress of the

✝ An NPC's Path: Book Two ✝

Crimson Moon..."

The Angel snapped his fingers impatiently. "Leave that to me! Do you accept it or not? Decide quickly! We're running out of time!"

Anxious, I looked around myself. The inky-black darkness surrounding us had begun to dispel, shrinking, pierced by beams of bright light.

'Yes or no?" the Angel asked point blank.

"Will I be the first to enter the portal to the Kingdom of the Dead?" I asked, unwilling to leave this to chance. "No one will enter it before me?"

"Yes, you'll be the first. The absolute first."

"I accept!" I exclaimed.

We shook on it.

The broken stone fingers squeezed my hand in their vice-like grip. "You should steer clear of the Light Gods' territories," the Angel warned me.

Then the darkness dissipated.

I came round on the slab of granite drenched in my own blood.

What was that now? Did that mean that everything I'd just seen was only a feverish delusion?

I touched my left eye socket. My fingers

Kingdom of the Dead

traced an ugly scar. The bleeding had stopped; the wound had healed.

And the flamberge! Its undulating blade was now covered in fine patterns of frost, its hilt burning my fingers with icy cold. My crystalline eye glittered where the steel pommel used to be.

I looked up at the vandalized statue. It glanced back at me without even trying to conceal its smirk.

You have received a new quest: The Two Shards of the Sphere of Souls for the Spawn of Darkness.

Dammit! I cussed but decided not to open it just yet. The entrance to the cave glittered with flashes of white light. It could only mean one thing: the white witch was back and she was looking for me.

Steer clear of the Light Gods' territories, I remembered the Angel's advice. I shook uncontrollably. Easier said than done!

Suppressing a bout of panic, I hurried to utter the return portal activation formula. The light was burning even brighter, its sharp white rays dispelling the gloom and blinding my single

✝ An NPC's Path: Book Two ✝

eye as I feverishly rattled off the unintelligible words not even bothering to pronounce them right. I just needed to make it!

The portal popped open. I dove into its ragged shadow. A moment later I was already rolling over the cobblestones of a dark inner court.

I made it!

The moment I thought so, I bumped into someone's steel greaves. My body reacted on its own accord, squirming, as I shot aside in a convoluted backflip combo.

Flamberge at the ready, I froze about ten feet away from my opponent.

Oh wow. How's that for Dodge?

Chapter Four
The Dead Burglar

1.

A SOMERSAULT, A BACKFLIP, a swing with my flamberge! An unnatural cold burned my fingers. The world had grown brighter, coming into focus. My blindness was gone. What's more, I seemed to be able to somehow control the situation around me. It was as if I'd been snapped out of virtual reality and transported back to the good old world of isometric graphics.

Thanks a bunch for your gift, mister Angel!

✝ An NPC's Path: Book Two ✝

I laughed, lowering the sword. I had no one to fight: the person I'd stumbled into as I'd rocketed out of the portal was none other than Goar the green-skinned orc paladin.

He chewed on his meaty lip. "What happened to your eye?"

I winced but chose not to explain anything now, just took out my mithril mask and put it on.

The orc shrugged, balanced his sword on his shoulder and headed for the arch. "Let's go. Isabella's waiting for us."

I shuddered. I tried not to even think how she'd react to my promise of surrendering the fragment of the Sphere of Souls to the Spawn of Darkness.

Having said that, did she really need to know? The most important thing now was to get the other fragment. If we did, then we'd come up trumps. But in that case, we had to do something about the vampires.

"You coming?" Goar asked impatiently.

"Yes! One moment!" I hurried to open the stats window a I walked.

Oh wow. The Angel didn't do things in half-measures, did he? He'd promoted me to Apprentice straight away, thus unblocking my

🗡 Kingdom of the Dead 🗡

ability to improve Dodge until level 35. I promptly invested all the available points into the skill and paused, admiring the result.

Dodge: 30

Not bad at all!

And then a realization struck me. Intellect! I'd exchanged Perception to Intellect, hadn't I? That had to have affected my magic skills!

Indeed, the Lich had received an additional spell levels 1 to 3. It wasn't much but could come in handy, I suppose.

"John!" the orc barked, losing his patience. "Move your ass!"

Ignoring the interface windows, I hurried after him. Immediately I discovered a considerable drawback in my current condition. If holding the flamberge in my hands had endowed me with some sort of universal knowledge, then for the rest of the time I virtually couldn't control the area to my left.

That wretched eye!

I had no idea how to adjust myself to this situation. Still, there was nothing I could do about it. I had to carry on living with one eye.

✝ An NPC's Path: Book Two ✝

Living? What kind of bullshit was that? I was beginning to confuse real life with virtual reality! I didn't have to *live* with one eye. This was only a game. A game!

But how could this have happened at all? Having scars was one thing, but all the lost limbs and body parts were supposed to restore every time you resurrected, weren't they? I used to be taken apart before and everything had been fine! What had changed this time?

The white witch, who was she? She definitely wasn't a player. More like a supernatural being, seeing as the Angel of Darkness himself hadn't dared to challenge her. But why had she picked on me? That hadn't been a chance encounter. She'd tracked me down, then immobilized me, intending to-

Intending to do what?

I had no answer to this. Not even a theory.

I shrugged. To hell with her! She wouldn't find it easy on the Dark side. And there was no force in hell capable of luring me back onto the Light territories.

I followed Goar into the back yard of the alchemist's shop and froze in disbelief. Neo sat on a bench under an ancient oak tree and was

Kingdom of the Dead

throwing acorns in the air for Scarecrow who deftly caught them with his powerful beak.

On seeing me, the dead phoenix ruffled his feathers and emitted a hoarse croak. Neo turned round and jumped off the bench.

"Uncle John!" he screamed rushing toward me, his arms open for a hug. "Thanks for saving me! Without you I'd have already been dead! Thank you so much!"

I tousled his hair. "How did you get here before me?"

"That was the phoenix's portal! Would you like me to show you?"

"No, thanks," I hurried to add, having no desire of experiencing the holy power of Light again.

Neo sniffed, embarrassed. "Did I hurt you bad, Uncle John?"

I laughed. "Not at all. It was bad but not too bad. Otherwise I'd have never made it out of there."

Goar climbed the porch and cleared his throat meaningfully. I had to follow him into the shop where Isabella and the shop assistant were busy studying some dusty tome, apparently following the auction results for the Crown of

✟ An NPC's Path: Book Two ✟

Chaos.

The orc emitted an annoyed cough. Isabella turned round.

"Here he is, in one piece as promised," Goar said. He then scratched his head and added, "Sort of."

"Why, what's wrong?" Isabella demanded, anxious.

"He'll show you. I must be off," Goar left and closed the door behind him.

Isabella stared at me. "And?"

I gasped a curse, activated Almost Alive and removed the mask.

Isabella gave an amazed whistle. "Has Kitten picked a fight with some bad dogs?" Gingerly she reached out, touched my face with her fingertips and winced. "I can sense both Light and Dark. What on earth happened to you?"

I chuckled. "I followed in Odin's tracks," I tapped a finger on my left temple. "Got myself some wisdom."

Isabella wiped her hand on her skirt and shook her head. "You should've followed Scarecrow. Not this one, the one from the Oz book. At least he didn't have to swap an eye for a brain."

✟ Kingdom of the Dead ✟

"Sorry. It just happened."

"Great answer, Kitten. Fits every situation."

"Please," I said, suppressing a sudden bout of insecurity. "Did you manage to find out who'd scorched us by the monastery?"

Insecurity! Dammit! I'd all but sold my soul to the Angel of Darkness! At the very least, I'd definitely flogged the key to my own resurrection. And what if we never found the lost fragment?

Did it make me scared? You bet! I could be dead, but the sheer thought made me shake in my shoes.

Instead of replying, Isabella lobbed a heavy money bag to me.

"What's that?" I asked in surprise.

"Your cut of the loot proceeds."

"Shit! What's with the attackers?!" my voice broke. "Did you find them?"

"Keep your voice down," Isabella said. "Yes, we've tracked them down. The vampires are out now probing around. Once they're back, we'll decide what to do next."

"We need to teach them a lesson!"

She nodded. "We will if we can," she gave me a meaningful wink. "Trust me."

I got the hint and didn't mention the

✝ An NPC's Path: Book Two ✝

Sphere of Souls.

Isabella turned away to the shop assistant, "So how's it going, Ulrich?"

"They just outbid us."

"Dammit!"

"They've put another lot up."

"Start bidding!"

I slumped into an easy armchair for customers and untied the money bag. It contained seven thousand gold.

Was it a lot? Yeah, sort of. Still not enough to add to my Deadman's Set. Talking about which...

I pulled out the Soul Killer broken by the white witch and cussed in disappointment. Its bone blade had snapped off by the hilt. There was no way you could use it now.

What the hell? It was supposed to be indestructible! Could I fix it? Was it even possible?

"Ulrich," I turned to the assistant. "Is Mr. Lloyd in?"

He grew pensive for a while as if unable to switch over to a new task.

"Come on through, John," he finally said.

When I pushed the door into the demonic

☦ Kingdom of the Dead ☦

alchemist's workshop, Mr. Lloyd was sitting at the table studying a bone rune through a huge magnifying glass, The rune looked plain and fire-damaged. Fine gray dust hung in the air which stank of chemicals.

The old man grinned at me. "Talk about the devil!" He sat up, anxious, and gestured at his own face. "What's this, some kind of new fashion?"

I winced and took a chair in front of him. "It just happened." The expression was quickly becoming my catchphrase.

Not even trying to conceal his disgust, Lloyd chucked the rune into the far corner. "Lucky you," he said. "I wish things would start happening for me," he pulled out a handkerchief and wiped the tips of his horns. "No idea what kind of bone I could use! Even dragon's bones don't work!"

I laid the broken bone hook on the table. "And what would you say to that?"

The alchemist leaned forward. His inhuman eyes glinted with disbelief at seeing the remains of the supposedly indestructible weapon. "Talk about heavy-handed..." he cut himself short and stared at me. "But how? How did you do it,

✝ An NPC's Path: Book Two ✝

Holmes?"

"It just happened."

The old man drew the pieces of the bone hook toward himself and shook his head. "To break an indestructible item! That's a first! Not even many higher beings are capable of doing that!" he snapped his fingers and brought the broken blade up to his magnifying glass. "Yes! This is perfect! I can use it to make a rune which would fit your Deadman's Set!"

I can't say I was impressed by this proposition. "Can't you repair the hook?"

"Sorry. As the song goes, *Once you pull out your hair you can't put it back in*[1]," Mr. Lloyd replied.

I cussed. "I need the hook."

He lobbed the broken blade on the table and shrugged. "Anything can be repaired. It's just a question of materials. I think you could procure a bone of a higher being?"

"Would a bone from a demon do?"

"Is that a joke?" the half-demon cringed, apparently taking my words personally.

I didn't bother to explain. Instead, I

---

[1] A line from the song *Tutankhamun* by the cult Russian rock band Nautilus Pompilius.

☦ Kingdom of the Dead ☦

produced the bone of Nest Hunter.

The alchemist recoiled. The aura of phantom fire surrounding the demonic bone burned my hand — but the infernal curse couldn't harm a deadman.

But the old man was another matter. He turned blue and began gulping some potions.

"Where did you get this?" he asked once he felt a bit better.

"I killed him."

"Didn't you perform a cleansing ritual?"

"Should I have done so?"

Lloyd slapped his forehead and pointed at the door. "Get the hell out of here! Leave the bone! I can work with it. I'll see what I can do."

He seemed to be feverish with excitement. Still, the moment I rose from my seat, he got a grip. "Wait a sec! Who's gonna pay for it?"

I heaved a sigh and reached for the money bag. "How much?"

"A lot. It's gonna cost you... gonna cost you... a lot!"

I was desperate to get the hook back so I didn't even try to haggle but threw the heavy money bag on the table. "That's all I have."

The alchemist sized up the clinking gold.

✝ An NPC's Path: Book Two ✝

Still, he seemed to be so excited about the upcoming job he didn't even count it. "Go! And tell them not to disturb me!"

I walked out and quietly shut the door behind me. Isabella was still whispering with Ulrich who kept casting suspicious glances my way while Isabella kept giggling.

"What now?" I demanded.

The priestess brushed away a tear from the corner of her eye and shook her head. "Kitten is a TV star! You're back topping the weekly ratings!"

Ulrich doubled up and added, laughing, "As the best supporting actor to the real star! The horse!"

"Which horse?"

As it turned out, they were talking about a video featuring the amazing eight-legged stallion that Barth Firefist rode as he'd chased me. Filmed in the streets of the Marble Fortress, it partially included the combat which had followed — but the comments were almost exclusively about the unique beast and its owner. Everybody agreed that this was an alpha creature which meant that the Paladin too was on the game's Top 100 list. No one seemed to be interested in the player he'd been chasing.

⚔ Kingdom of the Dead ⚔

The best supporting actor indeed!

"Barth Firefist!" Isabella shook her head. "Why would he have it in for you?"

I tensed. "Why, what do you know about him?"

"It's been a while since he last logged in. Too many people are pissed with him, both Light and Dark. But you, how did you manage to get on the wrong side of him?"

I glanced at Ulrich and replied vaguely, "I didn't. It's his brother Garth I had problems with. One is *Garth*, the other is *Barth*. Do you get it?"

Isabella opened her eyes wide. "You don't mean it!"

"I do."

"Aren't you the lucky one," she said slowly.

At that moment, the auction resumed. Immediately she forgot all about me and the two-faced Barth/Garth. I dreaded to even think how much she was prepared to bid for the Crown of Chaos.

I spent some time pondering over the news, then forced myself to put all the bad premonitions out of my head and opened the Lich Magic tab. It didn't take me long to sort out the spells. I selected the Sphere of Dead Flame, the

✝ An NPC's Path: Book Two ✝

Arrow of Death and the Mantle of Death. The first one exploded, blinding your victim, while the two others were advanced versions of the Touch of Death. The Arrow was a distance weapon affecting an individual target while the Mantle enveloped the caster, striking his or her attackers. All of them required industrial quantities of internal energy but they just might come in handy one day to actually kill someone.

I leaned back in my chair, cracking my fingers. "How's Mark?"

By then, Isabella had already been outbid which explained her less than cheerful mood. "Don't ask," she growled.

I chuckled and immediately choked on my merriment. The shop's door swung open, letting in a dark-blue figure in a suit of armor covered in golden swirls of protection runes, its pauldrons shaped as lions' heads baring their teeth.

Prince Julien. This time he carried his tiger's head helmet in the crook of his arm.

My hand closed around the hilt of the flamberge leaning against the wall.

"Stay cool, Kitten," Isabella hurried to say.

Prince Julien cast me a contemptuous look. "Your time is up! I need the shard now!"

🗡 Kingdom of the Dead 🗡

Isabella laughed. "Are you sure, boy?"

He took a decisive step, towering over the priestess who was head and shoulders below him.

"Would you two be so kind as to go to our conference room?" Ulrich hurried to interfere, apparently worried about the safety of the goods on the shelves.

Isabella picked up her staff and sashayed toward the door he was pointing at. The Prince heaved a labored sigh but followed.

"I need the fragment!" he repeated as soon as we entered. "Now!"

"Can't see how I can help you," Isabella replied calmly. "I have a deal with your clan, not with you, my *bello*."

The Prince turned crimson — either in anger or embarrassment, I couldn't tell. At least this time he didn't put his helmet on to hide his face.

"Listen, you," he wheezed. "This is important."

Isabella shook her head. "If I come across another fragment, we might talk about it, baby. But now... I'm sorry."

She blew him a kiss while I laid my hand

✝ An NPC's Path: Book Two ✝

on the sword.

Immediately my nervousness was gone. The world had come back into focus, once again becoming clear and predictable. Now I knew exactly where to point it in order to pierce his snazzy armor. Having said that, I wasn't even sure I'd be able to deal him a second blow.

Still, the Prince was full of surprises. He licked his lips, swung round and headed for the exit with all the grace of a steel-clad rhino. I'd barely managed to get out of the way.

"Why a Prince and not a King?" I asked him as he walked past. "King Julien! Sounds great, doesn't it? You even look like him."

Ignoring my quip, he swung the front door open. Seeing his retinue waiting for him outside, I just couldn't help myself. "Oh. Don't adults let you out on your own yet?"

He turned round, pointed his fingers to his own eyes, then to myself. "I'm watching you!"

Strangely enough, the clichéd phrase sounded ominous. I might end up on another black list if I wasn't careful.

The Prince disappeared outside. Isabella giggled,

"He's watching you! Did you hear that,

Kingdom of the Dead

Kitten?"

Pensively I turned my head from side to side, stretching my numb neck.

Isabella walked over to the window, watching the cavalcade disappear. "I'd love to know what the hell brought him here. Can you tell me?"

I didn't miss the chance to take a jibe at her. "He's fallen for you, can't you see?"

"You should be thankful he hasn't fallen for *you*," she paused and heaved a sigh. "Finally a cool guy but a total wuss."

"He may be a wuss but he's made of money."

"Money doesn't buy happiness, Kitten."

"Maybe not but it goes a hell of a long way."

Deciding to have the last word, I walked out into the backyard. Isabella followed. She took one look at Neo playing with the phoenix and asked, "Kitten, are you sure you're all right?"

"How do you mean?"

"Before, you used to be wary of the Prince. And the way you looked at him now, it was as if you were about to rip his armor apart with a can opener."

"I'm getting better."

☦ An NPC's Path: Book Two ☦

"It's not just about the Prince, Kitten," she shook her head and added sneakily, "You're not afraid of the Spawn of Darkness anymore, are you? I wonder why?"

A cold shiver ran down my spine. She was shrewd, wasn't she? I must have thought that the deal with the clan was as good as done which was why I must have behaved so cockily. And Isabella had immediately picked up on it. What an idiot!

I decided not to tell her about my agreement with the Angel of Darkness. "Too many things happening just lately," I said with a smirk. "I'm sick and tired of being scared."

I meant it too. I was tired. Too tired and had already gotten used to it. I'd been in the game for too long. Doubtful that many had been in the game longer than myself.

Isabella gave me an intense look but had no time to ask any more questions. A little gray cloud whizzed into the back yard and promptly materialized into the Count.

The vampires' leader staggered, adjusting to new sensations. He glanced at me and smiled. "You back already? Good. We've got things to discuss."

† Kingdom of the Dead †

Isabella gave Neo a long look and opened the shop's door. "Let's talk inside."

The three of us returned to the conference room. The Count slumped into a deep armchair, crossed his legs and crunched his fingers.

"We've found them!" he announced, looking utterly pleased with himself.

Isabella took a seat opposite him and smoothed out her skirt. "Carry on."

"It's a Dark clan," he told us. "The Three Wizzies. Three Elemental mages levels 90 and above. Air, Earth and Fire. They must have tried to get into the dungeon but couldn't get to the sanctuary so they left a warning system."

I nodded, remembering the strange pressure I'd felt the moment Neo had entered the monastery basement. The Count's theory seemed to be quite close to the truth.

"So where are we supposed to look for them?" Isabella asked. "If they manage to sell the fragment before we get it back... And what if they've already sold it?"

"No, they haven't," the Count said. "They've put it up for auction for two hundred grand, can you imagine? They want to coin it in. The market is in turmoil. The prices keep growing but so far they're nowhere near the two hundred thousand they want."

"Why is the market in turmoil?" I asked.

The vampire laughed, baring his long needle-like fangs. "Apparently, there're way fewer fragments than previously thought. None of the clans have managed to collect the necessary number. If we fleece the Three Wizzies, we'll be rich."

"Fleece?" Isabella frowned. "You have any idea where to look for them? Or where they keep the fragment?"

"They always log in together, all three of them," the Count muttered instead of an answer.

"Where. Is. Their den?" Isabella enunciated, impatient.

The Count faltered, then admitted, "They're got a fortress in the Southern Mountains."

"What kind of fortress?" Isabella demanded.

"A level-7 Aery," the Count replied half-heartedly. Then he added even more reluctantly, "Its power field source has been modified using the mosaic intellect scheme."

The priestess cussed in disappointment.

To me, his words had sounded like total gobbledygook. "What kind of scheme is that?" I

Kingdom of the Dead

asked.

The Count rolled his eyes and slumped back in his chair. "Who have I got myself involved with!"

Isabella decided not to vent her fury. Instead, she drew a square with her finger on the dusty table and divided it into smaller cells like the grid for tic-tac-toe. "If the outside attack is too strong, the energy gets redistributed to reinforce the relevant sector. Because attacking from several directions at once is only viable during a full-blown siege. In an emergency, the source of power switches off all the lower-priority inner fields and sends the released energy to the dome."

"What type of energy source is it?" a voice sounded from the front door.

I turned round and saw Mr. Lloyd who'd joined our discussion.

"It's not a dome, it's a sphere," the Count replied with a sigh. "You can't dig under it."

"What type is it?" the shopkeeper repeated.

"A Fiery Diamond."

The alchemist pushed his green glasses onto his forehead, hooking them over his little horns. For a while, he appeared to be deep in thought. Then he shook his head. "You can't break into it. Only if you ask the Goddess directly..."

"I'm not a High Priestess yet!" Isabella snapped, giving me the evil eye as if I was entirely responsible for her stalled career.

Having said that... she was probably right.

I walked over to the table and drew a circle inside one of the little squares. 'Does that mean that any external attack will cause the fortress' internal defenses to be switched off?" I asked, drawing a cross in the cell next to it.

"It might, if the attack is strong enough," the alchemist agreed. "But in any case, as long as the defense is active, we can't get inside. Portals won't work."

"Does that mean that the external defense doesn't let anything through at all?"

"The shield burns all living things. Same goes for the undead," Isabella cast me a meaningful look. "It destroys all organic matter and disables all active spells."

I chuckled. Organic matter, she said? How interesting. "How about arrows and stone projectiles?"

"They might penetrate it if they're not

magic," Lloyd said. "If you're thinking about depleting the energy by showering the fortress with arrows, it's not gonna work."

"How about the treasury? It's the most sacred place in any fortress. Would it be possible to strike so hard that its defenses would switch off?"

"What difference does that make?" the vampire groaned. "We still can't penetrate the outer shield!"

I waved a dismissive hand. "Let's presume I can get inside. But I won't be able to disable the treasury's defense. Would it switch off during the storming or not?"

"If the alarm doesn't go off before that, it would," Lloyd reached for a pencil and a notepad. "The question is, how much energy it might take," he added, engrossed in some complex calculations.

The Count gave me an interested look. "Johnny, do you really think you can get inside or are you talking out of your ass?"

Isabella sniffed. "He can slip in anywhere," she said, apparently latching on to my idea.

"I can slip in," I said, "but I can't break into the treasury. I'm just not up to it."

✝ An NPC's Path: Book Two ✝

"You don't have to," the alchemist announced. "You have a good chance of diverting all of the fortress' energy to the outer shield. Once that done, all you need do is blow the doors. It might take some preparation but it's quite doable."

"That's bullshit!" the Count shouted, jumping to his feet. "We're talking three Elemental mages! Levels 90-plus! The moment the alarm goes off, they'll log in and drown us in our own blood!"

"And what if they don't log in?" Isabella's voice rang with a sinister promise. "Would you agree then? Having said that, we don't really need you…"

The vampire gave her a studying look. "Can you guarantee the mages won't be there?" he said, visibly doubtful.

"This I can promise," she gave him an innocent little smile.

The Count turned to me. "Can you guarantee you can get inside?"

"Easy."

He winced. "Very well," he said with a dismissive shrug. "Count us in."

"Don't be so quick, my friends," Mr. Lloyd

☦ Kingdom of the Dead ☦

unhooked his glasses from his little horns and returned them to his eyes. "In order to overload the dome, you'll need some quality tools. Which don't come cheap."

"Like what?"

"Like class-9 power pins. You'll need at least twenty of those."

Isabella cussed in disappointment. "At today's exchange rate, each pin will cost us at least ten grand! That's virtually impossible!"

The Count nodded, frowning.

Still, dear old Mr. Lloyd didn't seem to think so. "There's nothing virtually impossible in virtual reality," he offered a clumsy pun. "The prices of power pins have been artificially hiked because someone was buying them in bulk. And just by accident, I happen to know where one of their shipments is."

Isabella squinted at him. "What is it you want? A cut?"

"Not at all," the old man said with a soft smile. "The shipment is stored in a warehouse which also contains some chemicals used in alchemy. You get them for me, and we'll call it quits."

The priestess bit her lip, mulling over his

✝ An NPC's Path: Book Two ✝

proposition. The Count's train of thought, however, seemed to be going in a different direction.

"A shipment of twenty pins? Can't we just sell them? That's one hell of a lot of money!"

"Not so easy," Mr. Lloyd said. "They'll only give you a quarter of their real price because they're hot," he waved a warning finger. "And sooner or later the current pins' owners will find out — and then they'll make an example of the thieves to teach everybody a lesson. So we need to do it without violence and we need to make sure we don't leave any calling cards. No one should see you. And I mean no one!"

The Count grinned. "Don't teach your granny to suck eggs. Who do we need to upset?"

The alchemist pulled the corner of his lip down with his finger, exposing his pearly-white teeth. "I'm talking about our toothy friends. The orcs."

2.

WE SPENT a few more hours discussing all the details. Once the alchemist gave us the warehouse's coordinates, we had to pore over the

Kingdom of the Dead

maps, working out a detailed plan of operation based on less than sketchy information about the place's security.

"We should send Goar to investigate," Isabella finally suggested. "This way we might lose a day but at least it'll be done nicely. Am I right, Kitten?"

I nodded. "*You* are going to do it nicely. Without me."

"Why, what is it?" the Count tensed up. "What's up? Are you gonna pull out?"

"Without me," I repeated calmly. "I can't show up near the border. There'll be problems."

Apparently, the orcs had been planning a raid against the Lights which was why they'd set up a secret warehouse in the disputed area just next to the border. And what if that white bitch showed up there looking for me? It wouldn't be funny!

Isabella paused, then said emotionlessly, "We can do it without you, Kitten. You'd better have some rest and conserve your energy. And put your eye back in, please."

The Count laughed. I had difficulty not to whack him across the head with something sufficiently heavy.

✝ An NPC's Path: Book Two ✝

"Well, seeing as we're done," the alchemist rose from the armchair and motioned me to follow him, "John, let's go and see about your bone hook."

We bade farewell to the other two and returned to his workshop. Almost immediately we smelled smoke.

"What's that?" the old man ran to the door, pushed it open and cussed, "You bastard!"

The room was filled with billowing smoke but we couldn't' see any fire. The tabletop was smoldering. My Soul Killer was still in the vice, oozing black demonic flames which poured down its hilt and dripped onto the table, leaving ugly burn marks on the stained wood surface. The once-white blade was now black; the only thing that remained unchanged was its predatory crescent shape.

What could have happened here? How could it have changed so radically?

The old man reached for the restored weapon but promptly jerked his hand back. "Take it!" he demanded.

I stepped toward the table, doubtful. The memory of my flesh being burnt by the Nest Hunter's black flame was still fresh.

🗡 Kingdom of the Dead 🗡

"Hurry!" the alchemist screamed as he began to unscrew the vice. "Grab it, quick!"

I took a deep breath and lay my hand on the hilt.

It didn't burn my fingers; in fact, it was only slightly warmer than usual. The black flames quivered and withdrew back into the bone blade. But the clots of darkness didn't go anywhere; they leaked onto my arm, licking it with the poisoned infernal fire.

The Cursed Hook: Black Soul Killer (The Deadman's Set: 9 our of 13)

Damage: 5 to 9

Properties: the widening of a wound increases damage exponentially and is considered equal to soul magic or infernal fire damage.

Curse: poisons its owner with Darkness.

What a toy! Thank you, Mr. Lloyd! It was better than it used to be! I was immune to both poisons and curses, wasn't I?

When the smoke began to gradually dissipate, Isabella peeked into the wide open door. She sniffed the air and cringed, "You all right, boys?"

✟ An NPC's Path: Book Two ✟

"Can't you see?" Mr. Lloyd grumbled. "Everything's just fine!"

"Kitten, tonight you're staying with this old misery guts," she said. "You room's on the second floor. I must be off, then. See ya!"

She left. I slung the cursed hook behind my belt, "What's with the mask?"

The alchemist stopped wiping the charred tabletop and growled, "Get lost!"

His eyes behind the green glasses burned with an angry fire. I stepped back to the door just in case but lingered, unwilling to flee his shop like a coward. "Can you give me a more positive answer?"

He heaved a sigh and flung the cloth on the table. "Okay, okay! I'll see what I can do! Don't worry! But first I need to give it a good think. You don't want to get another cursed item, do you?"

"Would you like me to take it back for the time being?"

He shook his head. "Not worth it. And please do me a favor and get lost! I still need to choose the right chemicals."

Unwilling to try his patience any further, I left and went upstairs to my room. I leaned the flamberge against the wall and slumped onto the

☦ Kingdom of the Dead ☦

couch.

I wasn't tired at all. The dead don't get tired. Still, my heart was weighed down by some inexplicable apathy and yearning. My left temple began to ache; my left eye socket throbbed. It was as if the Darkness was trying to make its home in my head.

I really didn't like it.

Another thing I didn't like was insecurity. Would I manage to fool fate or would I end up kicking myself? Would I ever get into the Kingdom of the Dead or had all this been for nothing?

And most importantly, how was I supposed to get the Scroll of Rebirth, dammit?

I didn't even want to think what would happen if it didn't work. I'd have loved to get some sleep but a deadman's brain doesn't need it, so I was obliged to lie on my back staring at the ceiling.

The door slammed. Neo walked into the room. "Good evening, Uncle John!"

"Have you already eaten?"

"Yes, they fed me," the kid faltered, insecure. "I'm gonna sleep in the attic. Can I take Scarecrow with me? It's not nice there alone."

✝ An NPC's Path: Book Two ✝

"Sure," I said. "Or you can take the bed here if you want. I'm not going to sleep, anyway."

"Oh no! It's really nice in the attic!" Neo said happily. Behind the window, the dead phoenix crowed his approval.

The boy swung the door open. But before he could dash out of the room, I sat up on the couch and called him, "Neo, wait!"

"Yes, Uncle John?"

"Do you remember anything that happened after the fiery tornado?"

He shook his head. "No, Uncle John. I can't remember anything. When I came round, I was already in the destroyed temple. Thanks a lot for not abandoning me!"

I chuckled. "Don't mention it."

My empty eye socket began to throb again. What a shame I'd allowed the alchemist to talk me into leaving the mask behind. That way at least no one would have seen me grimace.

Neo tapped his forehead. "I completely forgot! Here, take it," he handed me the tarnished silver chalice which had turned black in places.

The Moon Grail
Properties: permanent residual traces of holiness

✟ Kingdom of the Dead ✟

I took the chalice from him and weighed it in my hand. Should I sell it for scrap? Or might I still need it? These "permanent residual traces of holiness", what the hell was that? Did it make it some kind of holy relic? Like the bones of saints? A holy relic — and a Light one, at that.

Strangely enough, the silver felt pleasantly cool to the touch. It didn't burn my fingers at all. The sparks which occasionally jumped between the Grail and myself tickled my skin.

"Uncle John!" Neo called. "Do you remember the Order's Grand Master? Does he come to see you?"

I forced my gaze away from the chalice. "The ghost, you mean?"

He nodded.

"He came once to tell me how to rescue you. Why?"

Neo sighed. "He comes to me often and tells me lots of things. He tells me about the Order's glory. He talks about how we'll bring it back. He says it's the load I have to carry but adds that he'll always be with me," he sniffed. "He's angry with Scarecrow too. He calls him a carrion crow and the spawn of the Infernal abyss…"

I suppressed a bout of laughter. "Just

forget it. The guy's stuck in the past, that's all. But he's sort of right about Scarecrow: he is indeed a bit of an undead and a bit of a demon to boot. You can't be angry with those who tell you the truth."

"But the ghost tells me to get rid of Scarecrow!" Neo announced. "He threatens to scorch him once he's back in power!"

I shrugged. "Then let him get back in power first. You think he won't have more important things to worry about rather than hunt our Scarecrow? Don't let it worry you. That canny bastard can take care of himself!"

With a flapping of wings, the dead phoenix landed on the windowsill and began boring a hole in me with his deathly stare, his white unseeing eyes glowing a barely noticeable red.

"You see," I smiled. "You shouldn't worry about him too much!"

Neo wiped his tearful face with the back of his hand and stretched his arm out toward the bird. Scarecrow sprang onto his forearm. The boy didn't even twitch.

Of course. He was now a Knight of the Order, wasn't he?

When the two friends had disappeared

Kingdom of the Dead

behind the door, I picked up the Grail again. It seemed to draw me to itself. Was it the residual holiness? Or could it be some Moon effect, maybe?

A strange serenity was coming over me. I overcame it and took the chalice down to the shop's first floor. Mr. Lloyd had already logged out but Ulrich agreed to take a look at the artifact.

"A holy blessing," he promptly pronounced his verdict, set the chalice aside and began wiping his fingers with a handkerchief. "Although it's very weak, there's no doubt it's holy. You can use it as a shield against dark ghosts."

"And against demons?"

"Nah. It wouldn't even scratch a demon. But actually, the chalice can in fact break a warlock's spell. On two conditions: one is immateriality and the other is the presence of Darkness. Remember that."

I shrugged. I would rather have preferred a weapon against material beings of Light.

Then an idea struck me. I asked him if they had a length of thin steel chain a dozen feet long. The thing was, I'd just remembered the efficiency with which Barth had brandished his chain mace. Maybe it would suit me too?

He actually found a length of chain just like I wanted and didn't even charge me for it. I went back upstairs to my room, tied the Grail to the chain and began practicing. My very first swing broke the mirror and the second smashed the wardrobe door.

Never mind. You have to start somewhere! I kept practicing. In any case, it was Isabella who'd have to pay for the trashed room. I didn't have a dime.

3.

THE RAID ON the orc's warehouse went like clockwork. No idea how the conniving alchemist had found out about the secret stash but its owners must have been absolutely sure their hidey hole was safe. At least the security there was a joke — apparently because the orcs didn't want to arouse the Lighties' curiosity.

In total, we'd procured twenty-five power pins one of which we'd used to break into the treasury. And still the Count remained grim and miserable.

Kingdom of the Dead

"Why did they have to mark us as the enemies of the Swords of Chaos?" he fumed. "Just like that!" he cast a suspicious look at me. "Is that why you didn't come with us? You knew already, didn't you?"

"Relax," I grinned. "I've been on their black list for ages and I'm still in one piece."

"What difference does it make to you? You're a Lich, aren't you?" he cringed. "Never mind. When are we going to get down to business?"

"Tomorrow evening," Isabella said. "We still need to get everything ready for it."

"You sure the Three Wizzies won't be there?"

"They won't."

"I hope you're right," he said menacingly. Then he left.

"*I hope you're right!*" Isabella mocked and headed for the back yard. There, she began building a portal to a secluded place in the vicinity of the three mages' fortress, using the coordinates procured by the vampires.

Talking about the mages...

"How are you going to rid of the fortress' unfriendly owners?" I asked her. "Just don't tell

✝ An NPC's Path: Book Two ✝

me you were bluffing!"

"I wasn't," she assured me, drawing a complex figure on the rocks. "I'm gonna play on their vanity."

"How's that?"

"I'm gonna make sure that one of the gaming channels invites our three inseparable wizzy friends for a live interview. That's exactly when we're going to attack," Isabella met my astonished stare and giggled. "Watch out or your other eye will pop out!"

"Are they going to invite them to speak on air just so that we can burgle them?"

"Oh please. Don't be so naïve. No one's safe from Internet pranksters. Not even Presidents, let alone three lazy overage bums."

I shook my head. "That's low."

"You've gotta hustle if you wanna make it," she crumbled a power crystal, activating the portal which opened with a soft popping sound. "That's it! We're all set!"

"Wait a sec," I reached out with my left hand and used my Lich's skill to summon Scarecrow.

Obediently he landed on my arm and gave me the evil eye, his talons screeching on the steel

Kingdom of the Dead

bracer, then emitted an ear-splitting squawk. He'd grown a lot recently, to the point where I struggled to hold him on my outstretched arm.

"If you peck me, I'll wring your neck," I promised, then turned to the portal. "Let's go!"

Without replying, Isabella stepped into the portal. I followed.

Immediately I found myself in a dark narrow crevice which went straight up. Scarecrow jumped off my forearm and flapped his wings in panic, trying to fly up, but lost his balance and fell back down.

"Calm down," I growled as I pushed him under my armpit, then began scrambling up the crumbling slope after the priestess.

The place picked by the vampires was guaranteed to remain unnoticed by the guards. But as for me, this crevice looked a bit too much like an open grave. They could have found an ordinary cave or something.

As soon as we'd climbed out of it, the phoenix began to struggle, trying to free himself from my grip so I had to strangle him just a little. Still pressing him to my side, I climbed over to one of the boulders and began studying the fortress towering on the opposite side of the

✝ An NPC's Path: Book Two ✝

creek.

It rose on a steep cliff surrounded by powerful walls, its towers grinning their dark arrow slits. A drawbridge led toward the gate. Still, it looked as if it was only lowered once a year and even then just to check its mechanism. Tricolor pennants fluttered on the spires, looking slightly faded due to the power shield which surrounded the fortress.

I weighed up the distance to it. "Isn't it a bit too far?"

Isabella shielded her eyes with her hand, then pointed at something on the side, "That's where we're gonna take up our positions. The pins can reach from there. It's not as if we need to storm the fortress."

I nodded and shook the stirring Scarecrow. "Listen, birdie," I growled. "All I need from you is one tiny little favor. Then you can fly where the hell you want."

The phoenix hissed by way of reply.

Considering it as a yes, I produced the charmed skull, then promptly snatched it out of the way of his greedy talons. "I don't think so! Say, '*Aaaaah*'!"

The phoenix emitted a hoarse squawk. I

Kingdom of the Dead

shoved the skull down his throat, pushing it deeper and deeper. Scarecrow struggled himself free, leapt away and perched himself on a nearby boulder, ruffling his black feathers. He looked utterly pissed and very offended.

"I want you to fly up," I told him, "then dive onto the fortress. When you resurrect, don't go anywhere, I'll still need you."

The phoenix crowed malevolently and took to the air until he turned into a black dot in the clear blue sky. He didn't head for the fortress straight away but began gaining altitude flying in wide circles.

I didn't take my eyes off him. Isabella slumped on a flat rock and stretched her legs barely covered by the tassets of her armor. It didn't look as if her ashen-gray Drow skin could tan but she wasn't at all fazed by the fact. She began rearranging her elaborate hairdo, rolling strands of her hair on dagger-like hair pins.

"What kind of creature is he?" she asked.

"A deadman needs a dead pet," I joked although I had a funny feeling it wasn't as simple as that.

Had an ordinary player received the lighthouse quest, then once he'd defeated the

✝ An NPC's Path: Book Two ✝

Nest Hunters, he'd have resurrected the perished Order's symbol: the Silver Phoenix. But as a deadman couldn't have become the Order's Disciple, he'd hatched a dead monster in place of a sacred bird. That had caused the entire Order restoration story line to go awry, and I doubted very much whether Neo's involvement could help me bring it back on track.

For a brief moment, the black dot hovered in the air above the fortress. Then Scarecrow folded his wings and dropped like a stone.

Brilliant flashes of light traced toward him but he successfully dodged every attack and hit the protection dome with a blinding flash.

I strained my remaining eye until it hurt but couldn't make out where the skull had dropped. Never mind. I was bound to find out soon.

Isabella set a small wooden box in front of herself, raised the lid and showed me a baton made of some silvery metal. "This is a power pin. I just hope one will be enough to get to the treasury and break into it. You can't take two, anyway, because of the risk of self-detonation."

I shut the box. Self-detonation! Wonder where she'd learned words like that?

⚔ Kingdom of the Dead ⚔

Isabella rose gracefully to her feet, "Are you sure it's gonna work? What if the dome won't let you through?"

I shrugged. "The attack is going to weaken the dome, anyway. You have more pins so that might buy me some extra time. I'm more worried about how I'm going to get back out."

"Leaving is not a problem. This type of shield only works one way. And yes, Lloyd is going to cover you."

"Why would he bother?"

Isabella laughed. "He still can't get over all the treasures that have come his way. The chemicals we stole from the orcs are enough to blow up half the capital."

I whistled in surprise. "You don't mean it!"

"Oh yes I do. The orcs were planning a big bada boom and we upset their applecart."

I shook my head. "I just hope that was their only stash."

With a pensive nod, Isabella finished my thought, "Provided it was their own initiative. The Swords of Chaos-"

A silvery light flashed among the cliffs. We grabbed our weapons. I hurried to stealth up. The chainmail hugged my body like fish scales;

✝ An NPC's Path: Book Two ✝

my breastplate lost the last of its visibility. With the exception of the steel sleeve protecting my arm, my armor didn't hinder my movements at all.

The moment I'd equipped my sword, the world had come into focus, gaining color. A wave of universal knowledge flooded over me. Still, there was no need to use the flamberge: it was Neo who'd climbed out onto the cliff.

"What do you think you're doing here?" Isabella gasped.

"I'm looking for Scarecrow," the boy explained as he did up his jacket which had been blown open by the wind. "And where's Uncle John?"

I unstealthed and sheathed the sword behind my back. "What you're doing here is pretty clear. The question is, how on earth you managed to get here from the opposite end of the continent!"

Neo shrugged. "Easy. I can transport anywhere I want."

Isabella squinted in disbelief. "Anywhere? Are you sure?"

The boy thought about it, then sniffed and shook his head. "Not really. I can only port to the

Kingdom of the Dead

Temple of the Silver Phoenix and to Uncle John. And to you too, Auntie Bella. We seem to be connected somehow."

I heaved a sigh and tousled his hair. "And how are you going to go back to the capital?"

Neo fluttered his eyelashes but quickly came up with an answer, "You're going back there, aren't you? I'll come with you, that's all. And where's Scarecrow, Uncle John?"

"I still need him," I said, then turned to Isabella. "As soon as I'm ready, I'll send the phoenix back to you."

"Okay," she nodded and took the boy by the hand. "Let's go now. We have to go back to town."

They climbed down the cliff toward the portal, leaving me alone. I sat in the shadow of a big boulder to make sure I didn't get noticed by any potential observers and pulled out the generic plan of this type of fortress. The treasury was supposed to be located in the basement and I still had a very vague idea how I was going to get to it.

Finally, the resurrected phoenix arrived. He landed nearby and began sharpening his beak on a jagged piece of granite, casting unfriendly

✝ An NPC's Path: Book Two ✝

glances at me.

"Hey, cool it," I said.

He ruffled his feathers, then leapt off the cliff and spread his wings, soaring toward the sea surf which crashed against the foothills. A flock of seagulls scattered on seeing him but judging by his spinning XP counter, Scarecrow had smoked quite a few of them. Bloodthirsty bastard.

I moved over to the very edge of the cliff and heaved a sigh. It was so good here! Too good. On one side, all you could see was the mirror-like surface of the sea reaching out to the horizon. On the other, white mountain peaks pierced the clouds, The fortress, the cliffs, the white-crested surf... the three mages had chosen an excellent place for their castle. Very picturesque.

It started to get dark. Bright sparkling stars glittered in the sky; the wind had changed direction and was now blowing toward the sea. The seagulls cried; the shadows of the clouds flitted below. The moon shone bright. Beautiful, just beautiful.

But who was this beauty for? What difference did it make to players who never had a spare moment to stop and enjoy it? They were

† Kingdom of the Dead †

constantly on the run, completing quests, fighting or searching for new stuff. Or was it meant for those few weirdos who only logged in to take a break from reality? Eight hours of peace after the purgatory of polluted cities didn't sound so bad.

Don't know. I wasn't sure. I got the impression that all of them headed directly to the taverns.

4.

WHEN THE SUN had finally begun to rise, I stepped off the edge of the cliff, tumbling down like some suicidal parody of a bungee jumper. The wind whistled in my ears; my only eye filled with tears. The surf foaming over the reefs came up to meet me with astonishing speed.

And then a splash, followed by darkness. No light at the end of the tunnel. No tunnel, either. Only oblivion.

HEAT. FIRE. Smoke.

I came round in hell. Fire raged around me, confined by blackened brickwork. A turnspit

✝ An NPC's Path: Book Two ✝

hung over my head. A heavy cast-iron fire guard blocked the exit.

A fireplace! The wretched phoenix had managed to drop my skull down the chimney!

I climbed over the fire guard and rolled over the floor, trying to extinguish my burning clothes. I finally put the flames out but in doing so, I hit a table and knocked down the pots and pans which had been piled up on it. The saucepans scattered on the floor with a deafening clatter.

I head the sound of heavy steps approaching the door. I shoved my charmed skull into the inventory, darted into the darkest corner and stealthed up, crouching in the shadows.

The door swung open. An incredibly tall knight in red-hot armor stepped in. Orange flames escaped his visor and all of the joints in his armor.

I was more than sure that the *Ifrit* — an Arabic spirit of fire imprisoned in this suit of armor — possessed magic vision. Luckily, my ability to become invisible to sorcerous charms must have kicked in because he didn't notice me.

When his heavy steps died away in the corridor, I warily stole over to the window and looked out. Unfortunately, it opened out into an

✝ Kingdom of the Dead ✝

inner courtyard meaning I couldn't contact Scarecrow.

I had a stupid urge to spit on the heads of the guards marching over the cobblestones below. Suppressing it, I walked over to the door and gingerly prized it open. At first I peeked out through the crack, then slid out and froze, taking in my surroundings.

The wall-mounted torches weren't burning. The thick shadows were luring me to step into them, merging with the darkness, and walk through the fortress as an incorporeal spirit, sneering at the clueless patrols.

I might have done so — but my meeting with the Ifrit had clearly shown that any drop in my vigilance could cost me my head. Had I met another one of the fiery guards, there was simply nowhere to hide in the corridor. And it wasn't even my death that scared me but the fact that they might raise the alarm. If we alerted the garrison prematurely, our plan would go straight down the drain. As it was, it already had quite a few drawbacks.

Which was why the first thing I did was to drop down on all fours and bring my ear to the floor.

✝ An NPC's Path: Book Two ✝

At first I couldn't hear anything. Still, soon the stone tile began to shake, echoing with heavy regular footsteps. I hurried to go back into the kitchen. And once the Ifrit went past the door, I slid out behind his back and darted in the opposite direction.

Finally, the staircase. I ran like crazy up to the top floor and hid in a niche to let another magic guard go past. Once the fiery knight had disappeared around the corner, I too continued on my way.

I climbed up into the attic, took a look around and scrambled toward the skylight. Immediately I noticed the air moving in a circular motion outside against the backdrop of the shimmering protection dome.

I froze. What the hell was that now? Was this some kind of magic trap?

The whirling had stopped. For a moment, I even thought that it had been the play of sunrays on the dusty window pane. But then the roof began to shake the tiles off overhead. The whirlwind reappeared and froze, allowing me to take a good look at it.

An Air Elemental! Of course! The three fortress owners were Elemental mages, weren't

Kingdom of the Dead

they? The fiery Ifrits, the Air Elementals and... stone golems? Probably.

I cussed under my breath. I couldn't climb out onto the roof, then. I could barely see the air spirits but they would notice me easily.

What was I supposed to do?

I laid my hand on the window pane and mentally reached out to Scarecrow, investing all of my powers into a desperate call.

At first, nothing happened. A wave of disappointment flooded over me. Then suddenly I sensed him and sent him to circle over the place we'd previously agreed upon.

That was it. I'd sent the signal.

Exhausted, I slumped to the floor and pressed my hands to my face, waiting for the silver amulet to restore at least some of my depleted mana. Unfortunately, I had no time to waste. I had to get up and scramble back to the staircase.

I looked down and glimpsed the glinting of fire escaping red-hot armor. I froze, counting seconds until the Ifrit returned.

This proved to be a very good idea. The top floor was patrolled by three fiery knights so I even had to hide in the niche before I had the

✝ An NPC's Path: Book Two ✝

possibility to run over to the stairs. I didn't even think about hiding in any of the rooms: even though they weren't locked, in my haste I couldn't tell whether there were any magic alarms installed there or not.

Only when I'd finally reached the first floor, I started coming across people. The numerous guards ceremoniously paced the corridors; kitchen boys, messengers and other servants kept scurrying around like crazy. The fortress lived its own life which meant that some absent-minded idiot could easily bump into a stealthed-up intruder and raise the alarm. So I had to keep my head down lurking in niches, hiding behind curtains and even having to climb under tables a few times.

By the time I found the staircase leading to the basement, I was completely tuckered out. At least the fiery guards had stayed upstairs so I didn't have to worry about being detected by their magic vision.

But when I'd reached the basement, I got stuck. Under normal circumstances, people couldn't notice me. But there were two torches burning by the staircase. A patrol was posted next to it, thoroughly checking everyone who

✟ Kingdom of the Dead ✟

went down or came back up and barring the armored door every time. Also, a sorcerer's apprentice was hanging around next to them so you couldn't very easily walk past him.

Now why would the three mages need this illusion of normality? Did they really want to feel like lords of the manor or had they simply bought a generic ready-made fortress?

Time went past as I stood in a dark corner waiting for the right moment to slide down into the basement. Most of the visits to the cellar were made to fetch food as kitchen boys brought out platefuls of sausages and joints of ham, then returned with the empty plates. But every time the guards unlocked the doors, it resulted in a kerfuffle as everybody was in a hurry to get inside. And I wasn't looking forward to become unstealthed because of an accidental poke in the ribs.

Suddenly the light in all the windows dimmed. I looked out and saw a flying ship mooring by one of the towers. Soon gangplanks were set up and the servants began to roll a multitude of fat barrels onto the mooring platform.

My time had come.

✝ An NPC's Path: Book Two ✝

The guards wedged the basement door open and the sorcerer's apprentice got busy counting the booze. I walked over to the nearest torch and gave it a light push from below. It came out of its mounting, dropped to the floor and went out. The corridor became very gloomy, forcing the sorcerer's apprentice to step away from the door toward the window.

I took my chance. I ran past the barrels and scampered down the stairs into the basement. There, bundles of sausages and ham hung under the ceiling; jugfuls of oil and wine were lined up in locked storerooms behind rusty bars. Every other torch along the way was unlit, making it easy for me to stay away from the light so that my flickering shadow didn't betray me.

Soon I left the food stores behind and walked along the rooms where they kept coal, bolts of canvas and sheets of tanned leather. They were followed by barrelfuls of arrows and crossbow bolts. Missiles for scorpio ballistas were stacked up against the walls.

Soon the corridor forked. I stopped and tried to remember the generic plan of this type of fortress' dungeon. It looked like I had to go straight on, especially because I could hear

Kingdom of the Dead

strange banging sounds from the side corridor and smell something burning. They must have had some kind of workshop over there.

I walked straight on and very soon came across some bars blocking the way. The lock struck me with its fanciful complexity. To top it all, the thick bars surged with charges of defense magic.

Behind it, I could see a dark staircase leading to the lower level. It was almost within reach.

Bummer! There was no way I could open such a complex lock. I might have to spend some of the power pin's energy to open it. But what if I came across them at every turn? This way, I might not even make it to the treasury. No, I had to look for some alternative ways first.

I returned to the fork in the tunnel and waited for some grimy characters to fill their handbarrows with coal. Once they were gone, I turned round a corner and sniffed the air. It smelled of burnt leather. Could it be some wizard bladesmiths branding runes into the armor?

I wasn't at all looking forward to meeting them. Still, I pressed on a bit further. To my surprise, fate had brought me to some of my own

✝ An NPC's Path: Book Two ✝

colleagues.

Not Liches, no. Executioners.

Burly guys clad in pants and high boots had put some unfortunate bastard on the rack. A fat important-looking dude in a velvet justicoat was pressing a red-hot rod to his chest to determine whether he was dead or just unconscious.

The prisoner groaned and struggled in his fetters. The fat man stepped closer to him, grinning,

"That'll teach you not to steal from the master!"

Still, he didn't torture the thief anymore. He flung the rod which went hissing into a pail of water. "Take him back to his cell! We'll carry on tomorrow."

The burly guys began to unshackle the prisoner. I ran down the tunnel, trying to clear out of the way of the local big wig. I secreted myself behind a corner, took a cautious peek out and froze in disbelief.

A heavy bunch of keys swung around the fat man's neck. Who was he — a quartermaster?

You're exactly what I need, mister!

The fat guy walked unhurriedly, then

☦ Kingdom of the Dead ☦

stepped next to one of the closets, unlocked the door and began filling a clay jug with wine.

Immediately a plan formed in my head. I channeled the energy of the Touch of Death into my left hand, used my right one to draw the bone hook from my belt and stepped into the closet.

The black infernal flames singed my fingers. Never mind. The most important thing was, the quartermaster hadn't noticed anything.

In a flash, I stepped behind his back, grabbed him by the neck, paralyzing him, and sank the bone blade into his throat, then moved my hand sideways to open the wound up.

Blood gushed everywhere. The fat man began to shake. He turned black, burned from inside out like a piece of charred wood.

I dragged his dead body behind some barrels, wiped the crimson splashes with some rags and locked the closet — but not before relieving him of his keys. That had been the whole purpose of my exercise.

The bars blocking the descent to the lower levels were still surging with flashes of protective magic. I didn't try to find the right key to open them; instead, I stood against the wall waiting for our storming to begin. Time went by but nothing

✝ An NPC's Path: Book Two ✝

happened, except that the guards started running around the basement in alarm.

I was beginning to seriously start worrying that they might discover the quartermaster's body any minute when the rock finally shuddered. The surges of defensive magic flared up, then expired.

I promptly shoved the fanciest key into the lock. It turned with remarkable ease.

Yes! It worked!

I didn't lock the bars behind me. I ran down to the lower level and froze with my back to the wall.

A giant creature stomped toward me, the sounds of its gait echoing through the passage. A golem, cut out of a solid chunk of granite. His head almost reached the ceiling, his eyes glowed with menace. I really didn't look forward to crossing paths with him.

Luckily, this particular level served as the arsenal. Its walls were hung with weapons; more of them were stacked along my way. The corridor was lined with full-height mannequins clad in chainmail and suits of armor.

I promptly dove behind one of them.

The golem didn't notice anything and

Kingdom of the Dead

continued on his way. I headed deeper into the dungeon until I came across some locked doors on my way. Every time I had to waste time trying different keys. If I used the power pin to break in, that was bound to attract the golem guards' attention. Any way you looked at it, I'd been incredibly lucky with the quartermaster.

The further down the arsenal I moved, the more intricate the engravings on the sword blades became and the more gold decorated the armor. Here, the swords glittered with combat magic, their runes glowing with molten silver. A common thief wouldn't have resisted the temptation to pilfer something as a memento of being here.

Still, I was only interested in the lowest level. The treasury had to be somewhere close by.

Another stone guard loomed out of the darkness. I ducked behind some halberds hanging on a spear rack. Their fancy blades glinted with the noble dark hue of mithril. My hands seemed to be drawn to them on their own accord but I resisted the temptation and ran on.

The stairway to the lowest level was barred too. One of the keys fitted the lock. I darted down the stairs, taking the footworn stone steps two

✝ An NPC's Path: Book Two ✝

and three at a time.

Once I'd reached the lower tunnel, I stopped and breathed a sigh of relief. The castle owners had never gotten around to posting guards here. The magic lamps under the ceiling weren't burning — but still the corridor wasn't completely dark, illuminated by the weak glow of the trophies lining the walls.

The things they had there! The kinds of rarities they'd amassed!

There was the fiery Sword of the Archangel; the Pride of the Astrologer sash laden with gemstones; the glittering Breastplate of the Nine Kings glowing with amber; the silver Poleaxe of the Gods Under the Mountain; and even the Wall of the Titans full-length shield.

The Seraphim's Necklace, the Whip of Hell, the Claw of the Chasm, the Greaves of Darkness, the Pipes of Pan...

I didn't know where to look first. Each one of these articles cost a fortune, and they were just hanging there! How could I not help myself?

The force shield blocking the entrance to the treasury kept blinking but it hadn't yet deactivated. In theory, I could have indulged in a bit of freebooting but I forced myself away and

☦ Kingdom of the Dead ☦

headed for the treasury. All these toys were nothing but decoys. The moment the alarm went off, I could forget ever entering the treasury.

The magic shield blinked stronger. I stood opposite the entrance and produced the power pin. Cast of some silvery metal, the baton felt unpleasantly cold to the touch. I changed my grip on it, holding it with both hands, and pointed it directly at the center of the armored door. I didn't dare approach it too closely for fear of activating some secret traps or setting the alarm off.

Come on now! Quick!

Two statues of winged angels towered on both sides of the passage. Their reproachful marble eyes watched my every preparation. Both giant figures were equipped from head to toe, wearing charmed cuirasses and magic swords. And their crowns-

Crowns?

I froze in disbelief. One of them was wearing the Crown of Chaos! The bone golems' captain had been wearing it too, hadn't he? I'd managed to get a good look at it then.

I was itching to jump up and grab it for Isabella — but just then the floor quaked underfoot. Immediately the protection shield

✝ An NPC's Path: Book Two ✝

expired. The light in the statues' eyes died and the angels themselves stopped looking like works of art, turning back into chunks of carved rock. Not that I cared.

I activated the artifact. A beam of blinding light escaped the baton and pierced the thick sheet of metal. The pin shook in my hands so hard that I struggled to control it as I drew an uneven circle on the treasury door.

The smoking chunk of metal rattled to the floor. I dove into the hole. Smoke billowed from the storeroom heaped with glittering treasures; the glass showcases had been sliced in two by the beam, their contents scattered all over the floor. Diamonds crunched underfoot like broken glass.

I darted for the shelf on the far wall and grabbed a clot of pallid light, then dashed back to the exit, scooping up everything within my reach into my bag.

Come on, quick! Faster!

The dungeon shuddered. The moment I shot out of the treasury, the power shield popped back on behind my back. I'd made it!

The Find a Shard of the Sphere of Souls

Kingdom of the Dead

interim quest is complete!
Experience: +2500 [45 029/49 500]; +2500 [45 073/49 500]
Undead, the level is raised! Rogue, the level is increased!

I very nearly screamed with joy. Overwhelmed by emotion, I jumped up and tugged the Crown of Chaos off the left-hand statue's head.

Bad idea.

The crackle of electricity spread through the corridor. All the weapons and armor hanging on the walls dissipated, leaving only their hooks. All these riches had been only an illusion, a bait for reckless idiots.

The Crown of Chaos? I clenched its metal rim in my hand until it hurt. The crown was real all right.

Unfortunately, so were the angels.

The stone statues jerked to life. They jumped off their pedestals and went for me, revealing themselves to be camouflaged golems.

At the very last moment I managed to dodge an icy blade lunged at my head and immediately recoiled, avoiding a swing from a

✝ An NPC's Path: Book Two ✝

fiery sword. I wasn't even thinking; my body was controlled by instincts and reflexes alone.

With a series of twists, vaults and somersaults, I leapt and rolled out of their reach. As it turned out, a Disciple of the Dance of the Darkness school of combat wasn't that easy to catch! Still, as far as golems went, the two angels had proven remarkably quick. If they cornered me, that would be the end of me. No matter how hard I tried, I just couldn't shake them off.

I tried to counterattack but the flamberge rebounded off the marble, only leaving a tiny chip on the angel's chest.

Dammit! With these two, you might need a pick or a sledgehammer!

The fiery sword flashed before my face; the icy blade clanged against my steel pauldron, scratching my phantom armor. I leapt out of their reach and swung round, raising the power pin. Almost discharged, the artifact emitted a short flash, throwing one of the angels to the floor with a hole in his stony chest. He collapsed right at the other golem's feet, tripping him. I seized the moment, turned round and ran like hell.

I had to get out of here! Time was slipping through my fingers!

Kingdom of the Dead

5.

IT PROVED QUITE EASY for me to fool the clumsy golems guarding the arsenal's next level. The problems started on the level above. Unfortunately for me, by the time I'd ripped the golem's crown off, the magic alarm system had already kicked back in, prompting all the guards to scurry around searching for the intruder.

We'd clashed in the food stores. It would have been okay but the sorcerer's apprentice was there too, supporting the ten guards who'd attacked me. This time, his search magic had proved stronger than my Stealth level.

The shadows concealing me quivered, dissipating. The guards raised their swords and lunged at me in unison, trying to immobilize the intruder and expose him to the magic attack.

As if! I threw my left hand in front of me, lassoing the wretched sorcerer and pulling him from behind their backs. There! The cursed hook sank into his neck, breaking his spine and practically beheading him.

Take that, you bastard!

The guards went for me all at once but I'd

✝ An NPC's Path: Book Two ✝

already drawn the flamberge from behind my back and met them with a powerful swing of its frosty blade. The Scythe of Death scattered them, leaving only their commander standing albeit immobilized. I skewered him with my sword, then dashed along the corridor toward a second wave of sentries. As I ran, I wrapped myself in the Mantle of Death and rammed their ranks like a cannonball.

Their movements slowed down. Some of them froze; a few collapsed to the floor. All I had to do was dodge their halberds, dishing out short well-calculated blows.

You would have never been able to pull this trick off with players. But the garrison's NPC warriors had proven to be a pushover for my undead Executioner. They hadn't even scratched me, just made me lose time.

And time was what I didn't have in the end. As I exited the basement, I got caught in another scuffle with more guards. As soon as I was done with them, I hurried into the inner court, planning to climb one of the watchtowers.

That's when I heard the sound of a breaking window.

I barely managed to jump out of the way of

☨ Kingdom of the Dead ☨

a fiery Ifrit who'd dropped onto the cobblestones. He was armed with two scimitars which he brandished with a terrifying speed.

I stood my ground: at first, with the help of my lightning reflexes and then thanks to Dodge. Ducking out of his way, I delivered a powerful blow to his shoulder. My blade sliced through his steel armor, releasing a long tongue of flame from the gap.

Oblivious to his injury, the Ifrit attacked again. I parried his left scimitar with my steel sleeve but the right one pierced my hip, charring the flesh and very nearly breaking the bone.

I recoiled. Damn you!

Immediately another Ifrit jumped out into the courtyard. This fight threatened to become a protracted struggle and I had no time for such luxuries.

I didn't even try to stealth up from these infernal creatures clad in armor from head to toe; I just turned round and ran toward the watchtower. Their steel boots clattered along the cobblestones behind me with a terrifying speed. Still, I managed to win just a little bit of leeway. I rushed over to the stairs and slammed the door shut behind me. The next moment it exploded in

✝ An NPC's Path: Book Two ✝

a cascade of smoking splinters.

I ducked and darted up the footworn stone steps. The flamberge was still clutched in my hand, supplying me with universal knowledge, so I had no need to turn round to know that the Ifrits were a mere few paces behind me.

That's when a third fiery knight stepped in my way.

His scimitars whistled through the air. But just before they came down on me, I activated the Leap, miniporting behind his back. I then kicked hard, hitting him in the small of his back.

The Ifrit lost his balance and tumbled down the stairs. As he fell, his head hit the wall, ripping the helmet off and releasing the imprisoned spirit. Like a tongue of fire, it darted after me, licking my back and singeing my cloak. The liberated Ifrit had almost frazzled me — but then the flame roared up, setting everything on fire.

I ran for all I was worth until I came to the firing platform. With a swipe of my arm, I bundled a crossbowman off the parapet, looked down and cussed. The chasm was on the other side of the fortress!

I jumped onto the parapet and leapt onto

🗡 Kingdom of the Dead 🗡

the roof. Immediately a spear released from a scorpio ballista breezed past me a hair's breadth away. The ballista crew on the neighboring tower hurried to crank up the mechanism again.

A wisp of murky air tried to block my way. I took a swing with my flamberge but it went right through the Air Elemental without harming it. The Elemental knocked me off my feet and swept me up into its vortex, drawing me toward the roof's edge. The courtyard below meant certain death.

I wriggled out of its grip and whipped out the Soul Killer, slashing out at the Elemental with its bone blade. The air exploded in a black flame, with little effect: all it did was repulse my attacker.

In the blink of an eye, I'd jumped to my feet, run to the edge of the roof and dived down into the chasm.

ONCE AGAIN the surf foaming over the reefs came up to meet me. I glimpsed the outline of a flying carpet banking into a steep turn as it caught up with me.

Mr. Lloyd's demonic lips opened in a silent scream, "Catch!"

✝ An NPC's Path: Book Two ✝

A bundle of rope uncoiled toward me.

The reefs approached with threatening speed. I really didn't want to die. Respawning on the sea bottom was the last thing I wanted.

I grabbed at the rope and desperately began hoisting myself up. The alchemist moved at the same speed as myself, so this temporary absence of gravity had served me well.

Yes! The flying carpet was almost within my reach. But the cliffs were a mere thirty feet away now!

Straining every sinew, I hauled myself up onto the carpet. Immediately Lloyd started to come out of his dive, jerking the front of the carpet up. The pressure of G-forces caused the carpet to dip until it almost collided with the crest of a wave but it immediately leveled up and began gaining height.

We'd made it!

A beam of fire sliced through the air a mere few feet from us. The carpet banked into another sharp turn, missing it by a hair's breadth. The beam hit the water below, raising a cloud of steam. We flew right though it, getting soaked to the skin, but it didn't prevent Lloyd from banking again, escaping a new attack. The carpet shook

Kingdom of the Dead

and nearly capsized due to the shock wave. Another beam of fire flashed behind out backs as we disappeared around a nearby cliff.

The flying carpet soared upwards, its speed dropping. Still, the alchemist's calculations proved correct: the power of the carpet's magic motor was just enough to see us over the cliff and toward a portal glittering with an abundance of energy.

Yes! In the blink of an eye, it had transported us far far away.

"We did it!" Lloyd yelled at the top of his voice as he ripped off his large colored goggles. "We did it!"

Almost touching the roofs, the carpet flew over the capital city. Finally, it turned and floated softly down into the back yard of the alchemist's shop.

I lay sprawled on my back and stared up at the blue sky still swimming before my eyes — or my eye, rather. "Won't they track us to here?"

"No, they won't," Lloyd replied confidently.

The Count appeared as if out of nowhere. "Have you got it?"

I was tempted to lie to him but in the end, I chose not to. "I have."

✝ An NPC's Path: Book Two ✝

The vampires started hugging and catcalling. Isabella breathed a sigh of relief but immediately gave them a sharp, penetrating stare. Goar was the only one who didn't show any emotion at the news because he wasn't gaining anything from the sale of the fragment of the Sphere of Souls, anyway.

The alchemist, however, proved quite insightful. "Was it only the fragment you took?" he asked, wiping his little demonic horns with a piece of velvet. "Nothing else?"

Instead of an answer, I reached into my bag and began scooping out the treasures I'd stuffed into it as I'd run away. A dozen large pearls, a few uncut diamonds, a ruby ring, another one with an emerald, a handful of gold pieces, a bunch of necklaces and pendants...

The vampires greeted every new trophy with shrieks of joy. But once Lloyd had studied the treasures and appraised them, their jubilation subsided. He'd valued the whole lot at ten grand which, when divided by seven, didn't amount to a lot.

"Never mind," the Count said with a dismissive wave. "Give us the fragment!"

Isabella who stood behind his back, took a

☥ Kingdom of the Dead ☥

better grip on her staff and cast me a meaningful look. I shrugged and produced my main trophy.

The opalescent blob of light began to glow. But the moment the Count reached out to take it, its deathly white surface became veined with darkness.

"Damn!" the Count recoiled. "What kind of shit is this?"

"Really, Kitten," Isabella hissed. "What kind of shit is this?"

Taking in the situation, Goar stepped behind my back and laid his hand on his sword. I was his employer, after all.

Still, I was going to at least try to settle the matter peacefully. "Calm down," I hurried to say. "Please. I can explain."

"Be my guest," the Count growled, tense as a taut spring. "What the hell is the mark of darkness doing on my item?"

Both the Marquis and the Baron stepped away and bared their weapons.

"You sort it out," Lloyd said as he disappeared into the shop taking the trophies with him.

"Calm down, all of you," I demanded, showing them my open hands. "You'll get your

✟ An NPC's Path: Book Two ✟

money. All it means is that there's a buyer for the fragment, that's all."

"The Spawn of Darkness?" Isabella's voice shook with fury. "Did you seal a deal with them behind my back?"

The Count eased her aside. "How much? How much are they prepared to shell out?"

"Fifty grand."

"What?" the vampire gasped. "That's a pittance! Its market value is twice that!"

"Very well," I hurried to add. "You'll get a hundred grand. Our fragment was valued at fifty thousand and this money is all yours. Plus a tiny bonus."

The Count gave me a grim look, apparently not believing a single word. "What kind of bonus?"

"The raid on the Kingdom of the Dead. They'll give us the right of free passage."

"Wow!" the Baron said, unable to help himself. "Cool!"

The Marquis promptly hurried over to him and gave him a slap on the back of the head. "Shut up!"

The Count shook his head. "A hundred grand is too little."

Kingdom of the Dead

"But at least it's upfront. Plus the raid. Aren't you interested?"

The vampire winced and admitted grudgingly, "I am, John. I'm very much interested. When is the money coming?"

I pointed at Isabella, "As soon as she speaks to them and sets up a meeting."

The vampires stared at the priestess who flashed them a nonchalant smile, "I will, Kitten, don't you worry. That's not a problem."

She may have appeared composed but I could see she was still seething inside.

"If you're planning on ripping us off, you're gonna regret it!" the Count warned.

The vampire trio turned round and went into the alchemist's shop to claim their cut of the trophies. I put the fragment of the Sphere of Souls back into my bag.

Isabella turned to Goar. "Are you up for it?"

"You mean the raid on the Kingdom of the Dead?"

"Yeah."

"Sure," he replied unhesitantly.

"In this case, we'll meet up here tonight," she told him. "You can go now."

Goar gave me a quizzical look. I nodded.

✝ An NPC's Path: Book Two ✝

The moment he left the yard, Isabella walked over to me and said in a soft, calm voice,

"So you decided to go behind my back, Kitten?"

"The second fragment guarantees us passage to the Kingdom of the Dead," I replied. "Wasn't that what we'd been trying to achieve all along?"

"Behind my back!" she shouted. "Without even asking my opinion!"

"The clan's representative was very convincing. He didn't leave me a choice!"

"That doesn't excuse you!"

"In this case, how about this?" I reached into my inventory and produced the Crown of Chaos which I hadn't shown to anyone yet.

Isabella's breathing seized; her eyes became the size of saucers.

Having said that, there was nothing unusual about the artifact. It was just a circular strip of rusty steel with the broken tips of dagger blades soldered slapdashedly onto it. It had neither gemstones nor any intricate engravings.

And still Isabella's hands were shaking as she reached out to take it.

"Is this for me?" she whispered.

Kingdom of the Dead

"Sure."

She must have come to her senses because she asked, "How much do you want for it?"

"It's a gift," I said magnanimously.

She promptly snatched the crown and placed it on her head. Her skimpy armor began to lengthen and merge together, forming a full-body suit. This time her head too was protected as the Crown of Chaos had turned into a knight's helm.

"This is crazy!" she jumped with joy.

As soon as her armor had returned to its normal insignificant state, she gave me a big hug and a kiss. Immediately she shrank back and spat with disgust. "Dead meat, yuck!"

"What did you expect?" I laughed, pleased that I'd managed to defuse the situation with my well-timed gift.

"You know very well what I expect!" she gave me a meaningful look. "People are supposed to give me these kinds of gifts in order to bed me. But with you, it's the other way round!"

"Soon it's all gonna change!"

She heaved a sigh. "Soon..."

Then she logged out without as much as a by-your-leave. For a while, her translucent silhouette stayed shimmering in the air; then it

✝ An NPC's Path: Book Two ✝

too disappeared.

I shrugged, sat down on the porch and opened the game stats. I improved both my Strength and Stamina, added two points to Dodge and invested the professional skill point into Execution.

Execution IV

Sometimes executioners simply don't have the time to properly prepare their victim for torture, being forced to literally prize the warriors out of their suits of armor.

The knowledge of the armor's vulnerable spots gives +25% to your chances of penetrating it.

+8% to your chances of dealing a critical hit

+4% to your chances of dealing a crippling blow

Apart from that, I'd also received a higher chance to one-shot an immobilized target. Still, what interested me much more were the level-5 spells I could now access.

Choosing just one of them proved to be not so easy! For a while, I hesitated between Plague, Deadly Withering and Ashes. What would I prefer — to infect an enemy with a deadly disease, to

Kingdom of the Dead

syphon off some of their Life or to crumble to ashes in order to avoid their blow only to be restored to my normal self a moment later?

Unfortunately, my Intellect level didn't allow me to completely kill my opponents using Plague; all it could do was weaken them. I also didn't like the idea of swapping mana for Heath as the second spell required. And as for Ashes, it had to be activated in advance but once that done, it took very little energy to keep it active.

Which was the thing that sold it to me.

Ashes!

I rose from the porch, activated the spell and walked into the shop, intending to retire to my room. Still, Mr. Lloyd waylaid me. He'd already paid the vampires and was pensively clinking some coins in his clenched hand.

"John? Come with me," he said.

"Are you going to pay my share?"

"Your share?" he snorted. "You still owe me!"

He swung the workshop door open. I walked into the cramped room and stared in disbelief at the mithril mask lying on the table.

✝ An NPC's Path: Book Two ✝

It wasn't completely black anymore. Its right half was now ashen gray, with a complex pattern of one of the Soulkiller's bone runes spreading over the temple. The opposite eye hole had been blanked off; the temple on that side was seething with the grim flames of darkness itself. Droplets of thick fire trickled onto the cheekbone but before they could fall onto the tabletop, they burned out and dissipated into the air.

"What the hell have you made?" I asked, reluctant to pick the mask up.

He laughed, looking utterly pleased with himself. "On the left is the rune I made from the demon's bone. On the right, the one I fashioned from your bone hook. The effect is funny, don't you think?"

I sniffed. "Get away with you!"

Still, I picked up the mask, then very nearly dropped it when new system messages began flashing before my eyes,

Deadman's Set: Altered
Deadman's Set: Saved

What was that?
"This is one hell of a surprise," I muttered,

🗡 Kingdom of the Dead 🗡

unsure what to make of the fact that the mask had apparently become part of the Deadman's Set.

"It's the fragment of the bone hook," Lloyd explained. "It preserved its identity as part of the set. That's how it must have happened..."

I stared intently at him with my one eye. "How about warning me first?"

He sniffed. 'And what if you'd refused? So much work for nothing? Oh no. Do me a favor and try it on!"

I cussed and brought the mask to my face.

A Fire-Damaged Mask of Darkness and Ashes (The Deadman's Set: 10 out of 13)
Armor: 10
Protection from Fire, the magic of Light and the magic of Darkness: 20%
Status: Unique

With a chuckle, I stood in front of the mirror. What I saw was a grim individual in a crumbling cloak woven from shadows and a sinister mask which exuded a dark fire on one side and revealed deathly gray bones on the other. The flamberge's frosted hilt showed above

† An NPC's Path: Book Two †

my shoulder.

This was a perfect look for the kind of talks we were about to enter into.

They weren't going to be easy, that's for sure.

Chapter Five
The Kingdom of the Dead

1.

SPAWN OF DARKNESS had sent a flying ship to pick us up: a small and nimble corvette, its hull lined with magic beam pulsers. It came to a stop hovering directly above the alchemist's shop. We didn't have to climb any rope ladders though as the captain had a landing cage lowered for us.

I thought at first that the clan's top brass were afraid of an attack from their competition. But when I saw the giant knight in dark blue armor standing among the guards, I began to

✝ An NPC's Path: Book Two ✝

doubt my first conjecture. It was almost certainly Prince Julien who'd decided to put on a show for us. Not really for us, but for Isabella who this time hadn't even bothered to cover her skimpy armor up with as little as a translucent pareo.

Ignoring me, the prince gave her a warm welcome. "I can see you've got yourself some new gear," he said, noticing the crown on her head.

"It's a gift," she said pointedly.

The prince frowned and cast me a jealous look. Still, he didn't say anything, only chuckled and walked off. This time I wasn't wearing a chain and collar nor did I look like a rightless slave. That could become a problem but we had to expect problems, anyway.

I rolled my eyes theatrically, then grinned to Isabella, "It looks like he's seriously fallen for you!"

She laughed. "Finally someone who doesn't have problems with blood circulation! A gal could develop an inferiority complex around such a useless bunch as you guys!"

"'Blood circulation is the least of his problems," I said. "He'd better start worrying about his armored codpiece. Every time he sees you he has to walk around on tiptoe!"

🗡 Kingdom of the Dead 🗡

She snickered and turned away, gazing at the city floating below.

The view was admittedly awesome but I didn't care too much about the scenery. I felt ill at ease. You'd think that everything had been decided; all we had to do was close the deal. And still I was ridden by doubt.

Dammit! Getting into the Kingdom of the Dead was only half of the job. Then I still had to find that wretched Scroll of Rebirth before the Spawn of Darkness scouts could get to it.

If only I had the most basic of maps with nothing but a tiny marker on it! Unfortunately, this was a luxury I wouldn't have even after I'd ported there.

The Mist of War, yeah right...

WITH THE CREAKING OF MASTS, the ship steered confidently toward the residence of the Spawn of Darkness. The island's airspace was patrolled by archers and wizards astride gryphons and pegases. But besides those swift creatures, the clan must have also had much more powerful mobs in store waiting for their time to come. Using dragons for mundane patrolling must have been too expensive even for the Spawn of

✝ An NPC's Path: Book Two ✝

Darkness.

Our ship crossed over the canal. I sensed the light pressure of the magic shield. Isabella grabbed at a handrail and winced.

"What's this, protection?" I asked.

She nodded.

Accompanied by two gryphons, we sailed over the outer wall. The ship dropped speed but didn't land in the residence's yard; instead, it moored on the grim tower. The sea breeze rocked the ship from side to side, making it very uncomfortable to walk down the gangway toward the landing platform. Prince Julien offered his hand to Isabella. I had to manage on my own.

This time they didn't let us stew in the reception room. The moment we'd entered the spacious hall with an impossibly high vaulted ceiling and matching windows, our hosts arrived: the knight in black armor and the lady clad in ice, her face concealed by a snowy veil. Or should I say, the mysterious Lord High Steward and Lady Blizzard?

The Lord High Steward stepped forward. The darkness which played on his armor had lagged behind, creating the illusion that he kept disintegrating only to rematerialize in another

Kingdom of the Dead

place. Just one look at him made the left side of my face ache. As for Lady Blizzard, the sight of her icy armor hurt my eyes so much that I averted my gaze to the statue of my good old acquaintance, the Angel of Darkness.

He didn't even wink at me, the bastard.

"We all know why we've gathered here so let's get straight down to business," the Lord High Steward snapped his fingers. "Your money."

A servant appeared out of nowhere and handed Isabella a carved box filled with gold.

Isabella shook her head. "Fifty grand is the price of one shard. We have two. That makes a hundred."

"Didn't you say that the second shard was smaller?" Lady Blizzard reminded her.

You couldn't fluster Isabella so easily. "In any case, you're going to get a 30% market premium!"

"Market premium?" the black knight repeated, indignant. "You call this a market? Those bastard profiteers hike up the prices and wait. They're never in a hurry to close deals! This isn't a market, this is doggy doo!"

Most likely, he wasn't lying. Somehow I didn't think that a couple of million could make a

✝ An NPC's Path: Book Two ✝

big hole in the clan's treasury.

Ignoring his attack entirely, Isabella produced the shard glowing a soft crimson. "So are you interested in closing this deal or not?"

The Lord nodded to the servant who brought out another carved box.

"Where's the second fragment?" the Lord asked. "And please put that wretched thing away! It doesn't belong to your Goddess anymore! It's the clan's property now!"

Isabella ran her hand over the fragment, cleansing it and turning its color to a deathly white.

The Lord High Steward reached out for it but the priestess handed it to me as agreed. I clenched it in my left hand and produced the other fragment I'd procured from the Elemental mages. Then I brought my hands together, crumpling the glow and uniting the two shards into a single piece.

"There's a slight complication here," I smiled, watching their eyes widen. The metastases of darkness began to spread over the glowing piece which now resembled a sinister-looking flower.

"What the hell?" Prince Julien thundered,

Kingdom of the Dead

grabbing his sword.

The Lord High Steward raised his hand, stopping him.

Silence hung in the room. All I could hear was the wind roaring outside.

Finally, the Lord asked Isabella,

"What kind of complication are you talking about, Priestess?"

He must have considered talking to zombies below his status. Still, I didn't feel offended.

"You receive the fragments and in return, you grant us access to the Kingdom of the Dead," I replied. "That was our agreement."

He stared at me like he'd seen a piece of wood talking. Then he tilted his head to one side, "Who did you make this agreement with, may I ask?"

I pointed behind his back. Mechanically he turned round and looked at the statue of the Angel of Darkness. I watched him startle as the clan's patron bestowed his knowledge upon him. How I understood him! It felt like having a nail driven in your brain.

The Lord High Steward shook his head, then reached out his hand. "We confirm this

✟ An NPC's Path: Book Two ✟

agreement."

Both Lady Blizzard and Prince Julien stared at him in amazement but knew better than to ask questions. I stepped forward and laid the merged piece into his steel gauntlet.

The remaining white glow was immediately swallowed by gloom. The blob of light had just become a concentration of darkness.

The Two Shards of the Sphere of Souls for the Spawn of Darkness quest is complete!
Experience: +5000 [51 019/56 900]; +5000 [51 063/56 900]
Undead, the level is raised! Rogue, the level is increased!

A shiver ran down my spine. A wave of euphoria swept over me even though I was quite a bit worried about what I'd become once I'd reached the next undead level.

I just had no idea! Maybe it would be better not to raise my level at all? Surely Liches, even young ones, must be respected in the Kingdom of the Dead?

The Lord High Steward promptly brought me back down to earth. "We can only allow

✝ Kingdom of the Dead ✝

access to the deadman. That was the agreement."

I froze open-mouthed, desperately trying to remember my conversation with the Angel of Darkness and my exact words. Had I been so sloppy when I'd discussed such an important deal with him? Without my friends' support, I might find it infinitely harder to succeed!

At least being a deadman I wouldn't have to fight. The thought soothed me somewhat.

But Isabella seemed to be completely thrown by his decision. "Wait a sec!" she exclaimed. "We can be useful too! We could go on recon missions or..."

The Lord High Steward waved her arguments away. "The clan doesn't need your services!"

"What's the point in you going there blindly? We won't even charge you anything!"

"The audience is over! You can go!"

Isabella cussed under her breath in impotent fury, then swung round and strode back to the terrace toward the moored flying ship still hovering by the tower.

Me, I didn't even move. "When?"

The short word seemed to have nailed the High Steward to the spot. He turned to me. The

✝ An NPC's Path: Book Two ✝

darkness behind the eyeslit of his visor scorched me, more powerful than any demonic flame.

That didn't scare me, though. I was past that.

"We'll let you know, deadman," he announced, then dissolved into thin air. Lady Blizzard followed suit.

Escorted by the guards, I too headed for the gangway. Isabella stood on the terrace in the company of Prince Julien. I looked at her askance.

"Piss off!" the priestess growled. "I'll talk to you later!"

Oh well. Dream on.

The Prince puffed his chest out and even seemed to stand taller.

I took the unstable gangway over to the ship. A few minutes later, Isabella joined me. I thought it wise to hang on to the guard rail just in case but Isabella seemed to have forgotten everything about me.

Once the ship had slipped its cable for the return voyage, I just couldn't help myself any longer. "Won't you even try to throw me overboard?"

She laughed out loud. I didn't expect this

✟ Kingdom of the Dead ✟

kind of reaction at all.

"Kitten, do you really think those pompous turkeys can stop me? I'll get to the Kingdom of the Dead by hook or by crook!"

"Actually," I faltered, "there's no need for that. As long as I get there, everything will turn out right."

She chuckled. "That's a matter of principle. Especially because I already know how to arrange it."

I breathed a sigh of relief. I could use all the combat support I could get. "But that's great, isn't it?"

Isabella gave me a nasty smile. "It certainly is, Kitten. But I'm afraid you might not like the details."

?.

I SPENT THE REST of the flight trying to draw some details out of Isabella who only smiled mysteriously and cast me condescending looks, just like a spider who had bitten his victim and was now patiently awaiting its death.

I even suspected that she didn't have any

✝ An NPC's Path: Book Two ✝

plan and that she was simply trying to frazzle my nerves. Still, by now I knew her well enough not to even consider this scenario. Oh no. I could bet anything that she was up to something much bigger than just asking me to smuggle in a portal scroll. The Spawn wouldn't allow me to bring in anything of the sort.

What a cow! I would have spat in disgust had it not been for the mask covering my face. I had to force myself to calm down.

In the end, I stood next to Isabella and grabbed the railing with both my hands. "What did Julien want from you?"

She sniffed. "And what do you think?"

"Did he try to get it on with you?"

"He did," she said, frowning. "But that's irrelevant. You'd better tell me what got into our Lord High Steward? Why would he decline our services and potential cooperation? You'd have made a perfect scout!"

I kept asking myself the same question but didn't have the time to admit it to her. The corvette was already hovering over the alchemist's backyard.

The moment we were lowered to the ground, the Count popped up next to us.

Kingdom of the Dead

"And?" he asked without ceremony.

"It's all done," Isabella reassured him, pouring out the gold pieces onto a small table set up under the oak tree. "Take it!"

At the sight of the pile of gold, both the Marquis and the Baron momentarily became speechless, then started whooping in joy. The Count, however, didn't lose his cool.

"What about the Kingdom of the Dead? Are they going to let us in?" he asked, scooping the glittering coins into his bag.

I looked curiously at Isabella.

"Everything's still on," she confirmed without batting an eyelid. "We'll keep you posted."

"So you see!" the Baron shouted. "Didn't I tell you the map would come in handy? And you told me it was too pricey! Come on, get your money out!"

Isabella and I stared at him in incomprehension.

"What map are you talking about?" I asked.

Laughing haughtily, he spread a sheet of time-worn parchment on the table. "Yesterday the Champions' raid group cleansed yet another dungeon and smoked the Chief Disciple of

✝ An NPC's Path: Book Two ✝

Death," he began to explain. "Apart from two fragments of the Sphere of Souls, he dropped a map of the Kingdom of the Dead. Those guys weren't born yesterday. They know better than to auction it. They simply sell copies of the map to all and sundry for five hundred apiece."

I tried to draw the parchment toward me but I couldn't. The item turned out to be non-transferrable.

The Baron gave me a wink and snapped his fingers. "Do you understand where the catch is? Any clan who organizes a raid will be obliged to buy maps for all their scouts and advance party commanders. The guys will make a whole heap of gold!"

Isabella and I exchanged irritated looks. The High Steward's strange behavior now made sense. He'd been simply too stingy to pay some crafty salesmen for the map but he knew that no scout was capable of creating anything so detailed. So he'd simply taken it out on us.

I leaned over the table and began studying the parchment riddled with markers and symbols. The drawing contained no references to the entire game world map. The territory of the Kingdom of the Dead wasn't too large, almost a

Kingdom of the Dead

quarter of it occupied by a walled city.

The moment I traced the map with my finger, the symbols began turning into 3D pictures of buildings complete with their legends.

The South Gates. Old Castle. The Town Hall. The Mint. The Tower of Decay. The Guild Hall. The Arsenal. The Magic Academy. The Royal Library.

I moved my finger further but immediately brought it back as something in one of the descriptions had caught my eye. Something important.

Yes! There it was!

The Royal Library housed a collection of magic scrolls, with the Scroll of Rebirth being the jewel in its crown.

"That's what we need," I said, tapping the library symbol.

The Baron sniffed. "What the hell would we want there? We should either burgle the Royal castle or rob the Mint!"

Immediately the vampires started arguing with him. Their priorities seemed to differ a lot.

"There's a whole lot of magic weapons in the Arsenal!" the Marquis reminded.

"And plenty of artifacts in the Academy,"

✝ An NPC's Path: Book Two ✝

the Count objected. "What's the point in wasting our time on trifles?"

Isabella gave me a curious look and asked smarmily, "Really, Kitten, why would we need the library?"

Never before had I told the fickle Elfa anything about how exactly I was going to come alive again — and I had no intention of doing so now. "Haven't you forgotten something?" I gave the vampires a long look. "In the best-case scenario, you're gonna enter the Kingdom of the Dead in the second wave!"

"So what?" the Count shrugged dismissively, then pointed at the town center. "The Spawn of Darkness will go directly for the Tower of Decay!"

"But not before they send a looting team to the Mint, I assure you," I replied. "Both the Royal castle and the Arsenal are bound to be well-fortified, and as for the Academy, it's probably chock full of magic traps and Death Disciples. Doesn't sound too good, does it?"

The Count pursed his lips, "What are we supposed to do with old books?"

"Really, Kitten, tell us," Isabella added, pouring oil on the flames.

Kingdom of the Dead

"The scroll repository," I said. "I need one of them for myself. The rest we can sell."

"Which scroll are you talking about exactly?" she asked quickly.

Everybody stared at me. I ground my teeth in annoyance but decided to put my cards on the table. "The Scroll of Rebirth."

"You don't want much, do you?" the Baron said slowly. "And what if there's nothing else of any worth there?"

Isabella seemed amused with his suggestion. "Nothing of any worth in a scroll repository?" she laughed. "There'll be plenty of good loot for all of us there, trust me!"

"The scroll repository..." the Count said pensively as he took a closer look at the map. "It's not that far from the city gates, either... What do you think?"

The Baron sniffed his indignation. The Marquis shrugged. He didn't look too sure. None of them seemed too excited by my suggestion. Their eyes couldn't see past all the heaps of treasures. Still, they wanted to bite off more than they could chew and the Count must have understood this only too well.

Isabella sensed their hesitation. "Are you

✝ An NPC's Path: Book Two ✝

with us?" she asked bluntly.

The Count offered her his hand. "Deal."

We spent some more time discussing all the details. Once the vampires had left, Isabella popped into the shop and bought two copies of the map of the Kingdom of the Dead. One she took for herself and gave the other one to me.

"I'm not sure we can count on our vampire friends," she winced. "Now look: there's a wide avenue going from the South Gates to the Tower of Decay. The library is a short way off but not too far, either. Which means we might get some visitors."

I stared at the spread-out parchment, nodded and cracked my knuckles. "Do you think our support team might become a problem?"

Isabella smiled. "You know someone more reliable? Personally, I wouldn't let any of my own ilk anywhere near the library."

I paused, thinking, then grinned. "I could think of one."

3.

WE MADE AN APPOINTMENT to meet Grakh in the bar on a nearby island. The burly Barbarian

✟ Kingdom of the Dead ✟

whom I'd met during the defending of the Stone Harbor had already risen through the clan's ranks, becoming co-chairman of the Black Trackers. Still, he remained true to his attire of short leather boots, a kilt and the bandoliers which crossed his powerful chest. Accompanying him was another old acquaintance of mine, Victor the half-elf.

We didn't hold back anything from them but started off by offering to organize a raid on the Kingdom of the Dead.

"You pay me a grand for every warrior ported," Isabella announced her terms. "But if you agree to fight under the flag of the Mistress of the Crimson Moon, it'll only be five hundred. Plus three free resurrections in situ."

Grakh winced and rose from the table. "John, this has to be a rip-off. I don't know you well enough to risk the clan's money."

"You don't need to pay upfront," the priestess said. "You can simply arrange a letter of credit."

The Barbarian slumped back onto the bench. "Can this letter be arranged after we've been ported?"

She nodded.

✝ An NPC's Path: Book Two ✝

The barbarian sniffed. "Guys, I just don't understand you! We can't pay a fraction of what top clans could offer you!"

"There's one more thing," I smiled. "We can only open a portal after somebody else reaches the Kingdom of the Dead. So you'll have to be second, I'm afraid."

Grakh and Victor looked at each other. The tattoo on the top of Victor's head had become even more intricate since I'd last seen him.

"What do you think?" the Barbarian asked Victor.

The ranger shrugged. "If we're not risking anything, why not? But the contract should include resurrection."

Grakh nodded and turned to Isabella, "How many people can your raid altar handle?"

"There're no limits," she said. "I'm going to set up a camp sanctuary."

"Really?" Grakh chuckled, not even trying to conceal his surprise. "Very well. Where can you port us?"

She laid the map out on the table and pointed at a small park by the entrance to the Royal library. "Here."

Grakh and Victor spent some time studying

Kingdom of the Dead

the map, then rose from the table in unison.

"We'll need to discuss it with the others," without saying goodbye, Grakh made his way to the door.

Victor proffered me his hand, then hurried after his friend.

Frowning, Isabella watched them leave. "You think they're gonna bite?"

I sighed. "I don't even doubt it. I'm sure they will."

'Bite' was the right word. If the Spawn of Darkness sent one of their advance parties to take the library, the Black Trackers might find themselves between a rock and a hard place. They wouldn't find it easy, that's for sure.

Isabella must have heard the sour note in my voice. "Is Kitten tormented by pangs of conscience? Forget it! This is just a game!"

A game, yes. For everybody except me. That's just the way I was: a unique sonovabitch.

Having said that, there's no bigger stupidity than suffering from pangs of conscience over some dirty deed. You should do them with an easy heart or not at all. Unfortunately, not everything depended solely on me.

I had to console myself with the fact that

✝ An NPC's Path: Book Two ✝

for everybody else it was indeed just a game. The problem was, one day I too might join the ranks of the NPC pieces on this chessboard.

Dammit! I'd already joined them! For somebody like Garth, I was nothing but digital junk.

I RETURNED TO THE ALCHEMIST'S SHOP feeling a bit down: not because of all the spiritual strife but because of all my doubts and reservations. The waiting was becoming unbearable; I was desperate to start straight away. I wanted to live, not hang around.

"How are you going to open the portal?" I asked Isabella. "They aren't going to let me smuggle a scroll in."

"Everything in its own time," Isabella replied evasively, then returned to the shop.

I went upstairs, slammed the door shut, flung the flamberge on the bed, took a seat by the window and looked outside.

So what was I supposed to do now? I mean, really?

A new system message popped up, reminding me to raise my level.

That got me thinking. Was it worth the

Kingdom of the Dead

risk? Now I was a Lich albeit a Junior one. And what would I be next? One shouldn't change horses in midstream. I might become a Senior Lich; by the same token, I might turn into a bone dragon or an ethereal spirit. And then what? No one would let me anywhere near the portal then!

But in order to win and be the first to recover the Scroll of Rebirth, I might have to squeeze my char for all it was worth and then some. I wasn't in a position to pass up on the possibility of becoming stronger and quicker.

I ground my teeth. In a single sharp wave of my hand — so that I didn't get the chance to change my mind — I started the process of raising my stats.

Strength. Agility. A couple of points into Dodge. Training with two-handed swords. *Accept, quick! Move it!*

Yes!

John Doe, Executioner, Hangman
Undead. Junior Lich. Level: 30/ Human, Rogue. Level: 30
Experience: [51 019/56 900]; [51 063/56 900]
Strength: 32.

✝ An NPC's Path: Book Two ✝

Agility: 32.
Constitution: 24.
Intelligence: 10.
Perception: 10.
Life: 1440.
Endurance: 1680.
Internal energy: 660.
Damage: 440—572.
Covert movement: +25.
Dodge: +34.

Critical damage when attacking a target unable to see the attack.

Professional skills: "Incognito" (4), "Execution" (4), "Hangman".

Fencer: two-handed weapons (4), weapons in one hand, "Sweeping Strike", "Powerful blow", "Power lunge", "Sudden blow", "Accurate Blow", "Crippling Blow", "Blind Strike", "Rapid Strike", "Lightning Reflexes".

Creature of the Dark: night sight, penalty for being in sunlight, Lord of the Dead, Almost Alive, Skin of Stone +10, resistance to magic: 5%; +10% to internal energy.

Neutrality: the undead; subjects of the Lord of the Tower of Decay

Enemies: Order of the Fiery Hand, the

Kingdom of the Dead

Swords of Chaos clan.

Immunity: death magic, poisons, curses, bleeding, sickness, cures and blessings.

Achievements: "Dog Slayer" Grade 2, "Tenacious", "Man of Habit", "Destroyer", "Slayer of Circle-5 Demons", "Defender of Stone Harbor" Grade 1.

A Lich! I was still a Lich!

A wave of unbridled joy flooded over me. Overtaken by the feeling, I grabbed a stool that stood nearby and smashed it against the wall. The wood splintered into a thousand pieces, showering everything around.

Immediately I began to convulse. My body started to transform; my flesh withered; the skin pulled taut over the joints.

I didn't care. Soon it would be over. I'd be alive again!

When the convulsing had subsided, I removed the mask and stood in front of the mirror.

My new appearance was sinister to say the least. My cheeks had hollowed completely, my remaining eye had sunken; my lips had turned into two colorless strips. The black strips of

✝ An NPC's Path: Book Two ✝

tattoos had become more refined, forming intricate writings and strange symbols that covered my body head to toe.

I looked a sight, I tell you!

Very well. What about magic?

Unfortunately, my low Intellect numbers still hampered the development of magic skills. Now, too, I only had one level-6 spell available and that was it.

The choice of listed spells was impressive. After some deliberation, I finally selected the Cloud of Death. On top of dealing magic damage, it also restricted visibility within its range which suited my rogue just fine.

What a shame I couldn't activate it beforehand and leave it on standby the way I did with the Ashes!

There was a knock at the door. I hurried to cover my face with the mask. "Who's there?"

The hinges creaked. Neo peeked into the room. "Everything's all right, Uncle John? I heard a noise…"

The remains of the stool lay all around the room. I grinned, "I was just training."

The lad stepped inside. "Are you getting ready to go to the Kingdom of the Dead?" he

🗡 Kingdom of the Dead 🗡

asked curiously.

I frowned. "Why do you think that?"

He shrugged and perched himself on the windowsill. Scarecrow landed next to him. "I'm coming with you, Uncle John."

I didn't believe my ears. "You what?"

"I'm coming with you to the Kingdom of the Dead," the boy repeated matter-of-factly.

"Nonsense!" I snapped.

Neo shook his head. "I'm afraid I have to, Uncle John. That's what the Grand Master said. I need to unlock these desolate lands for the Order."

"Bullshit!" I sniffed. "Your Grand Master is long dead!"

"So are you, Uncle John. So are you."

I have nothing to say to that so I tried a different approach. "That's too dangerous!"

He shrugged. "I've died before. Even if I die again, I'll resurrect. I'm the chosen one, Uncle John. This is the load I have to bear."

What the hell, I thought. He's only part of the program code!

"All right," I said. "It's up to you."

"Oh!" he perked up. "So are you taking me with you?"

✝ An NPC's Path: Book Two ✝

"Do I look as if I have a choice? Seeing as this is a request from the Grand Master himself..."

"Yes! Yippee!"

Scarecrow's dead eyes, however, stared at the scene with unconcealed disapproval. This wretched piece of carrion could see right through me.

He was right. Even if I could, I would have never taken the boy with me.

The door swung open again. Isabella waltzed in.

"Hi, Auntie Bella!" the boy shouted.

The priestess set up a wrought-iron brazier at the center of the room, then produced a packet wrapped in leather and flung it onto the table. Something metallic clanked inside.

"Could you leave us just for one moment, Neo?" she asked. "I'm afraid it's gonna start to stink here."

"Of course, Auntie Bella," Neo jumped down from the windowsill and walked out into the corridor.

Isabella gave him a long look. "Don't you think he's grown?" she asked me.

"Other people's kids grow quickly," I replied

Kingdom of the Dead

with a Russian saying. "What's that you've got here?"

She threw a bunch of herbs onto the brazier. They began to smolder, spreading thick smoke around the room.

For some reason, my head began to spin. How strange. I wasn't capable of breathing, was I? The smoke couldn't do anything to me.

Izabella sneezed heartily, then unfolded the packet. A set of ritual daggers lay inside. She laid all but one onto the brazier to heat up and used the remaining one to slit her wrist, then drew a protective circle around the brazier with the dripping blood.

Then she brought a wine glass to the wound. A scarlet trickle snaked down its crystal-cut side.

"Take your clothes off," she demanded as she continued to fill the glass.

I thought I'd heard wrong. "Are you joking?"

"No, I'm not."

"I always thought that necrophilia was my prerogative."

"Take your clothes off!" her voice rang with metal. "Quick! We're wasting time!"

✝ An NPC's Path: Book Two ✝

I stopped teasing her and dumped my cloak on the floor. I then removed my cuirass, the chainmail, the padded jacket and the shirt. But just as I reached for my pants belt, Isabella stopped me,

"Enough! Turn your back to me!"

"Are we playing doctors and nurses? Where's your stethoscope? I wish every nurse wore clothes like yours!"

I didn't feel the pain. I felt nothing at all. I only heard the hissing of scorched flesh. The stench of burned meat spread around the room. My Health bar had shrunk somewhat.

"Hey!" I said indignantly.

"Don't move!" Isabella growled as she moved the red-hot dagger downward. "Think about nurses in skimpy lab coats! Think about my chainmail bikini and whatever's below it. Think what the hell you want as long as you don't move!"

"Don't forget I don't heal!" I yelped as I obeyed her. "I'll have to walk around all cut up until I respawn!"

"My lady is the mistress of birth and death. You really think she won't take care of it?"

She took another dagger from the brazier

✟ Kingdom of the Dead ✟

and sliced through my back sideways, from my left shoulder to my right hip. I twisted my head to look in the mirror on the wall. The sight was revolting. I cussed.

"Don't move! Whatever you do, just don't move!" Isabella kept repeating, mesmerized, as she kept slicing through my back methodically, carving out some complex symbol that looked vaguely familiar.

"What's this?" I asked. "What kind of witchery are you cutting into me?"

"This is the base for the raid altar," she replied calmly. "Your body is no different from rock or clay. It'll be fine, don't worry."

Don't worry? Was she serious? I was in freakin' shock! First some bastard takes my eye out, and then I'm being carved up with a red-hot knife, apparently for my own good! What next? Were they going to do a Viking blood eagle on me? Was this supposed to be a game or a torture chamber?

Still, I decided not to get hysterical about it. Instead, I tried to chill out. This wasn't a torture chamber. This was a game. Just a game.

Once Isabella had used up all her daggers, she poured the blood she'd collected over my back. Then she took a needle and started stitching up all the wounds with a coarse thread, inserting a silvery cord inside them and humming a prayer under her breath.

I was an altar! Holy crap!

Having finished her handiwork, Isabella poured the remaining blood into a crystal vial, put a stopper in it and handed it to me. "Drink it once you're within the city walls. I'm gonna bind the vampires, Goar and myself to you. And as for the Black Trackers, I'll build them a camp sanctuary."

"Got it," I grumbled as I put my shirt back on and gingerly tried to spread my shoulders.

Nothing hindered my movements. Still, my health that she'd just burned up refused to restore. It looked like this part of me had been sacrificed to her insatiable Mistress of the Crimson Moon.

"Is Kitten unhappy?" Isabella squinted at me. "Has Kitten forgotten that he's the one who started all this crap and we're only dancing to his tune?"

I pointed at the door. She sniffed and left the room with her head held high. She left the red-hot brazier to me to take back downstairs.

† Kingdom of the Dead †

4.

THEY CAME FOR ME at dawn. Almost as soon as I'd received Isabella's warning message, I heard someone hammering at the door.

I looked out into the corridor and saw Ulrich in his long nightshirt and nightcap walking downstairs with an oil lamp in his hand. Picking up the flamberge, I hurried down the stairs after him and lay in wait on one side of the door.

Still, it had been a false alarm. Behind the door stood several Spawn of Darkness guards in their plate armor, armed to the teeth.

"Your carriage awaits you," one of them announced, watching me closely as if comparing me to my description. "Are you alone?"

"No," I said, reaching out my left arm. The dead phoenix leapt onto it.

Impassively the guard pointed at the carriage, "Get in, Sir."

I climbed in and made myself comfortable on the soft cushions. This was a far cry from the flying ship but I didn't give a damn.

I was going! To the Kingdom! Of the Dead!

✝ An NPC's Path: Book Two ✝

My cards had come up trumps. I'd swept the board. This nightmare might even be over today. I'd be back in the real world! One day I might even miss the game's impunity but not quite yet. Definitely not quite yet.

The mustachioed guard slammed the door shut. With a jolt, the carriage moved off and rolled along the uneven cobblestones. My escort's hooves clattered behind.

Like a cold draft that came out of nowhere, a shiver of bad premonition ran down my spine. Still, I disregarded it. The deal had been cemented by the Angel of Darkness. The clan would never go against the will of its patron. There was absolutely nothing to be afraid of.

Still, it made me feel ill at ease.

THE CLAN'S WIZARDS had set up a portal at the center of the residence's inner courtyard. A giant dark globe slowly rotated above the ground. It seemed to reshape reality, distorting and crumpling it.

The numerous guards froze on the roofs. The shadows of dragons flitted across the sky. The best clan warriors lined the walls in even ranks, ready to step into the portal at the first

✟ Kingdom of the Dead ✟

word of the Lord High Steward.

And all of them — all those elite swordsmen, powerful mages, expert snipers and elusive assassins — they were all just waiting for me. In fact, all the top of the clan was here. No wonder they didn't seem to appear too friendly, their stares filled with animosity, impatience and disgust.

We're desperate, aren't we? Whether they liked it or not, I had to be the first to go to the Kingdom of the Dead. Without me, the portal wouldn't work. At least I'd been smart enough to discuss this detail with the Angel of Darkness.

"Hurry up, deadman!" Prince Julien shouted.

His aura was bursting with the power of all the blessings he'd been pumped up with. His two-handed sword was slung behind his back. He held a short spear with a black elongated leaf-shaped head which surged with an occasional charge of darkness.

Ignoring him, I headed for the portal when the Duke of Inferno stepped in my way, clad in his armor woven of liquid flames.

"Stop!" he demanded.

I froze. Scarecrow on my shoulder spread

✝ An NPC's Path: Book Two ✝

his wings and squawked.

Paying no attention to him, the Duke waved his hands as if casting a spell. His face contorted unhappily. "What's that artifact you've got on you?" he demanded. "I can sense light magic! Are you planning on opening a portal?"

A cold shiver ran down my spine. Thanks a bunch, Isabella! The clan may have needed me, but they didn't need any competition down in the Kingdom of he Dead! They would skin me alive now. For sure!

"You're toast," Prince Julien growled as he moved behind my back.

I waved a nonchalant hand at him. By then, I'd already gotten a grip. The light magic? The power of the Mistress of the Crimson Moon was anything but light!

"I think you're mistaken," I said.

"You've got an artifact on you-"

"I've got quite a few!"

"-which can be used to open a portal."

"That's bullshit!"

The Duke of Inferno stepped closer. "You'd better show it to us yourself," his voice rang with threat.

It was pointless trying to argue with him. I

🗡 Kingdom of the Dead 🗡

opened my inventory and immediately saw the silver Grail. Could it have caused all this commotion?

I grabbed at the chain attached to it and pulled it out of the bag.

The Duke gave it a studying look. "Leave it."

"We were just talking about a portal…"

"This thing can be used as a beacon," the Duke snapped, turning to the prince. "Take it!"

Without trying to resist, I handed the chalice to Julien. With a curved grin, he swung it on its chain and hurled it into the carriage.

"Take it back to my place," I said, spreading my arms wide. "Is it all?"

The Duke ran another check, then stepped back. "You can go now, deadman."

As I moved toward the shimmering dark globe hovering over the ground, reality began to curve: that was the Sphere of Souls altering space and myself with it. It felt quite unpleasant. I even slowed down.

Immediately Prince Julien approached me from behind and pointed to a group of players that stood separately from the rest.

"Can you see them?" he whispered.

✝ An NPC's Path: Book Two ✝

An assassin, a dark paladin, a couple of sorcerers and a few scouts.

I chuckled. "And?"

"Once you cross to the other side, we won't need you anymore. They'll catch up with you and kill you. *Bon voyage!*"

I turned toward him. "Thanks for warning me, idiot."

Still, you couldn't screw around with him that easily. His face dissolved in a nasty smile as he tapped the shaft of his spear. "This thing can one-shot any deadman. I hope you last long enough for me to find you and send you directly to hell!"

He really seemed to believe I was only an NPC who would die once and for all. I didn't want to disappoint him. I just shrugged and continued toward the portal.

My every step was faster than the one before: the shimmering globe seemed to draw me toward it.

Quicker! Quicker! Quick! Into the Kingdom of the Dead, now!

The dark shimmer thickened, hardening. It spun me around and hurled me in a direction unknown.

† Kingdom of the Dead †

With a splash, I landed in a large puddle of dirt and withered dead grass. Further on rose equally dead black trees and bushes. Not a single green leaf in sight, not even a bud.

Achievement received: Pioneer!

To hell with it!

I dashed across the puddle toward the nearest bushes. Scarecrow took off from my shoulder, heading for the skies. I actually saw double: I could make out the grass underfoot, the entire surrounding area and even myself.

A deep ravine stretched before me, with a murky stream tracing its bottom. I turned away from it, unwilling to take a shortcut toward the Tower of Decay which rose above the horizon.

Seeing as Incognito was no longer of any use to me, I disabled it, then ducked under a dead black pine branch. My shoulder brushed against a nearby fir tree which crumbled away in a pile of ashes.

I sensed an echo of the force behind me. I focused, forcing Scarecrow to turn round just in time to see the assassins unstealth.

There was no way I could shake them off

✝ An NPC's Path: Book Two ✝

my trail. The only thing I could do was run.

At first, my pursuers were careful which allowed me to gain a lead of a few hundred feet. Still, very soon the scouts must have realized they had no one to fear and surged ahead at full speed. The distance between us began to shrink; the one thing that still maintained my lead was the phoenix. He helped me find my way amid all the thickets without getting lost or bogged down in a swamp. Still, my Stamina wasn't going to last long like this; very soon I might have to fight them face to face and die.

For a while, I continued to run like hell but gradually, my speed began to drop. That's when I heard a triumphant crowing coming from above.

No, I hadn't reached the city walls yet — but I glimpsed a paved road far in front of us, with a dozen riders upon it. The eyes of the dead horses glowed with ghostly flames; the dead riders clad in rusty armor were clenching swords and spears in their hands.

I began to sidle off, hurrying to catch up with them. Finally, I got to the roadside and darted toward the patrol.

An arrow whistled through the air overhead and ricocheted off a flagstone. One of my

Kingdom of the Dead

pursuers must have aimed badly at me in his haste. Still, I couldn't count on such good luck in the future.

How about Ashes? Unfortunately, the protection spell could only save me from one blow. I simply wouldn't have the time to reactivate it.

At this point, the dead horsemen started galloping.

"Live ones!" I shouted, pointing behind my back.

My neutrality worked. The riders galloped past and ran down the assassins who were just emerging from the forest.

A raging fight broke out. The problem was, I had no doubts that the assassins were going to make mincemeat out of the dead patrol. All I'd gain from it was a couple of minutes' grace.

I decided to interfere, even if just to redress the balance of power a bit. I didn't join in the hand-to-hand, though. Instead, I invested my magic energy into creating a Cloud of Death. I had to put a lot of effort into controlling the complex spell but in the end, I managed. I was a Lich, after all! Not some plague-ridden corpse but a Lich!

✝ An NPC's Path: Book Two ✝

Unfortunately, by then half the dead riders were already lying on the ground. My help couldn't possibly change anything.

Never mind. I stretched my arms out in front of me, filling the battlefield with impenetrable gray haze. There!

I swung round, about to run for my life, when a dead riderless horse escaped the sorcerous cloud. The decision came instantly. I released my control over Scarecrow, freeing him up, and focused on the horse instead, lassoing him and forcing him to slow down.

I vaulted into the saddle and yelled, "Giddy up!"

The horse dashed off and cantered down the road. His skin may have been stretched over his ribs and his mane may have been a bit mangy but any thoroughbred would have envied his turn of speed. The sparks began to fly from his rusty horseshoes.

Something flashed behind. A fireball shot past us, brushed some bushes and exploded, sending a cascade of burning flames over the ground. I clung to the horse's neck; the road took a sharp turn alongside a small wood, its dead trees concealing me from my killers.

✝ Kingdom of the Dead ✝

I opened the local map in my mental view and breathed a sigh of relief. The road did lead to the city but not directly, arching around it. I wouldn't have to force my horse over sodden fields, marshes and thickets.

Let's do it!

Gradually the outlines of impossibly high walls began to rise in front. I could see the dead warriors bustling about on them. The garrison was preparing for battle — and what was worse of all, the tall city gates were creaking shut.

Dammit! Wait for me!

The grim shadows of bone dragons flashed through the air, heading toward the open portal. Still, they didn't get the chance to investigate.

Then the sun rose. Or so I thought.

A wave of blinding light assaulted me, sweeping away the blackened wood and hitting the city walls. The dead city defenders were reduced to ashes; my horse exploded in a cloud of dust at full speed. I collapsed on the roadside, rolled backwards onto my feet and dashed toward the gap in the lopsided gates which by then was a mere five feet wide.

A flight of dragons soared past me toward the city. These ones were perfectly alive and

✝ An NPC's Path: Book Two ✝

breathing fire. Luckily for me, they were taking paratroopers to the town center; burning the dead was a job for the second wave.

I managed to take cover by ducking into the blocked gates moments before flames poured out of the sky onto the house roofs. Fires erupted everywhere, billowing thick gray smoke which immediately filled with swift stealthed shadows.

The clan's magic attack had failed to kill all of the garrison. The surviving defenders took to the walls which resounded with the popping of the ballistas. With a desperate roar, a wounded dragon lost height, collided with a house and exploded, burning all and sundry.

A vertical line sliced through the sky, then parted as if someone had grabbed at its edges and pulled them asunder.

The resulting portal was grandiose. The Light players hadn't arrived in the Kingdom of the Dead on their own: they had their gods to support them.

To spend all this time collecting shards of the Sphere of Souls only to end up with such a miserable advantage? I couldn't believe such a coincidence. Either the Sons of Light had somehow got wind of the Spawn's raid and

† Kingdom of the Dead †

swallowed their pride by making an alliance with other clans, or it had been the mods' plan from the start: to collide the forces of Light and Darkness in one tremendous battle.

I'd put my money on the second scenario — even though if the truth were known, I didn't give a shit.

By then, the dragons had scorched most of the gate defenders and had begun clearing a path directly to the Tower of Decay. Fearsome flames rained from the sky; everything was enveloped in acrid smoke; the burning figures of the dead rushed around in their ultimate death throes.

My own luck couldn't last forever, so I took the first available chance to escape the fiery inferno by turning off into a side street. The imposing building of the Royal library towered at its far end, complete with a colonnaded entrance and marble statues on the roof of the main building.

The tower housing the scroll repository was right there, almost within my reach. All I had to do was run a couple of blocks and cross a small park filled with dead blackened trees.

Let's go!

I ran like hell along the deserted street:

✟ An NPC's Path: Book Two ✟

first one block and then another. The park's low fence was already to my right when the air thickened around me as time began to fly by. I ran but I didn't make any progress.

Dammit! They'd slowed me up!

The realization sliced through my bare nerves like a razor. I swung round and saw the assassins approach incredibly fast. Two wizards and three scouts were all covered in soot and very pissed.

They wouldn't lose me a second time. And if I died now, I'd lose both time and the opportunity to procure the Scroll of Rebirth.

I produced Isabella's vial, pulled the stopper out and poured the thick briny blood down my throat. It hit my larynx like a drop of molten lead, seething inside me. Its power overflowed me and hit me in the back from inside, ripping open my fresh stiches and breaking my ribs.

A Blood Eagle? Oh yes!

I momentarily fainted from the unbearable pain. Then the divine will hoisted me in the air, turning me into something more than a deadman or even a player. A fireball hurled at me by one of my pursuers expired; a crossbow bolt ricocheted

✟ Kingdom of the Dead ✟

off my skin, unable to pierce it.

Hah! Those mortals and their miserable efforts!

Achievement received: Carrier of Divine Will! Resistance to Divine magic: +25%.

The relationship with the subjects of the Tower of Decay has been changed. Current status: enemy.

Immediately, like the messengers of the looming retribution, blurred shadows appeared behind the dumbfounded assassins' backs. The vampires who'd already ported to the Kingdom of the Dead had attacked the scouts while Goar had carved up the nearest wizard and Isabella had turned the other one into a pile of ashes with one sweep of her staff.

My support group was glowing with the ruby light courtesy of the blessing of the Mistress of the Crimson Moon. It took them mere seconds to polish off the unsuspecting assassins.

"Not a moment too soon!" I croaked as I collapsed onto the bloodied cobblestones. The divine presence had left me; I had stopped being

✝ An NPC's Path: Book Two ✝

a vessel of force and turned back into a simple human. I wasn't exactly alive yet but I wasn't completely dead, either.

In a silvery flash, Neo appeared in the middle of the road. "Uncle John!" he shouted with a tearful voice, "You promised to take me with you!"

Talk about bad timing.

"You're here, aren't you?" I gasped, trying to scramble to my feet, then turned to Isabella. "Are we gonna open a portal or are we going to the library?"

The Baron guffawed. "Stick your library up your ass!" he said. "We have more important things to do!"

Isabella frowned. "Count?"

With a sarcastic wave of his hand, the vampire leader and his two blood-sucking buddies scurried off toward the Tower of Decay.

"Scumbags!" Isabella cussed.

In the clouds of smoke enveloping the nearby crossroads, I could make out the shadows of the Spawn's advance parties.

"Open the portal!" I told Isabella. "Goar, cover her! We'll meet up in the library!"

Goar helped the priestess to climb over the

✟ Kingdom of the Dead ✟

park fence, then turned back to me. "Are you sure, John?"

"Yes, I'm sure! Go now!" I said, relieving him from his bodyguard duty.

In any case, my neutrality status didn't apply to him. Pointless dragging him along.

Then there was Neo.

"I'm coming with you, Uncle John," he hurried to say, meeting my stare.

"No, you're not," I snapped. "Help them!"

"But-"

"Quick! It's important!"

The boy complied. He put one foot in my cupped hands and rolled over the park fence.

I stepped toward the library, then gave myself a slap on the forehead. Neutrality! I didn't have it now, either! Having become a vehicle for the Dark Goddess' will, I'd turned into a mortal foe for the local inhabitants.

I very nearly called Goar for help. Still, I suppressed a bout of panic and ran along the road. Was I a rogue or just a pretty face? I was bound to come up with something.

With the portal it was different: we couldn't do without it. The Black Trackers were the trumps up our sleeves. For the Spawn, the taking

✝ An NPC's Path: Book Two ✝

of the Tower of Decay may have been a priority — as was their vendetta with the Lights — but what if they decided to check out the library and stumbled into Isabella on their way? I couldn't leave it completely unprotected while she was casting the ritual.

The pain in my ripped and burned back was easing much too slowly. Still, I gritted my teeth and got on with it.

I was a mere hundred and fifty feet away from the library's porch when I heard the sound of hooves on the cobblestones behind me. I looked back and cussed. Prince Julien had caught up with me!

I had no time to take cover behind the columns — but when the Prince tried to lance me with his magic spear at full gallop, I easily dodged his attack and slashed his horse with my undulating flamberge. The blade hit the animal between its blinkers, dealing a crippling blow.

The horse rolled to the ground. Prince Julien, however, landed on his feet and immediately went for me, holding his deadly spear in front of him.

Haste!

Kingdom of the Dead

I took off like greased lightning — but the Prince had second-guessed my maneuver and managed to parry my attack with a flourish of his spearhead.

Leap!

I miniported behind his back and swung round, intending to immobilize him by slicing through his poleyn and run away. The next moment I found myself impaled on his spear which went easily through both my cuirass and chainmail, exiting between my shoulder blades.

Julien hadn't bothered to swing round, he'd just pierced me with an underarm lunge.

He'd hit me all right, only I hadn't received any damage. My flesh had crumbled to dust under the touch of his deadly cold steel but that hadn't been the magic of his weapon: it had been my own defense spell!

Ashes!

The Prince was let down by his desire to dramatize everything. Before turning to his slain opponent, he took a theatrical pause. And this brief moment was enough for me to take a swing and lash out at him with my flamberge.

Powerful Blow! Accurate blow!

My undulating blade pierced his armor just below the knee. Julien lost his footing and waved his arms. As he did so, he forced the spearhead out of my chest.

Not bothering to finish off my crippled opponent, I turned round and legged it. I heard heavy footsteps behind my back, the sounds of swearing and the squeaking of his limping armored leg.

On impulse, I ducked aside. The spear Julien had thrown clattered harmlessly on the cobblestones.

Hah! He should've known better!

I reached the porch and darted up the marble staircase.

Immediately I rolled back down when the paladin in reddish orange armor stepped toward me from behind the nearest column.

Unhurriedly Barth Firefist began walking down the footworn stairs. The fiery mace swung casually in his hands. My sworn enemy had

Kingdom of the Dead

somehow managed to enter the city with the first wave of the Light army.

He laughed. "I thought I'd find you here!"

"What about the scroll?" I asked mechanically.

The scorched remains of the library guards lay amid the columns. He may have killed them but he hadn't had the time to break the tall powerful metallic doors. Battered and deformed, they completely blocked the entrance to the library.

Prince Julien came limping.

"Your Highness," I said matter-of-factly, "allow me to introduce to you my good old friend Barth. He's been in the game since the alpha tests. He's in the Top 100!"

The prince drew his two-handed sword from behind his back. Barth — or should I say Garth? — tramped down the stairs, swinging his mace.

My opponents were too strong. I put my faith into my high Agility, well-developed Dodge and the universal knowledge which my charmed flamberge had bestowed on me.

Haste!

✝ An NPC's Path: Book Two ✝

I invested the last drops of my magic energy into Acceleration. Then I darted toward Barth and ducked under a torrent of fire pretending I was about to pierce his head with the flamberge. I stopped in mid-swing and jerked the sword back before he could entangle the blade in the chain of his mace and rip it out of my hand.

I spun round, parrying his swing. His powerful blow had very nearly wrenched the hilt out of my hands, throwing the flamberge behind my back. I was forced to dodge the next attack. His dark sword brushed my pauldron and slid off it without piercing it.

The momentum span me around. I dropped to my knees, dodging a fireball over my head. Barth had missed too, his fiery mace hitting the hesitant Prince in the chest.

The blow threw Julien back a couple of steps. Before he could restore his equilibrium and rejoin the fight, I'd already rolled to the side, leaving my opponents to face each other.

The Prince didn't disappoint. He rushed to attack and gave Barth an almighty whack on the helmet. Barth replied with his mace.

Then all hell broke loose.

Kingdom of the Dead

The paladin was more than twenty levels above the knight. Still, their combat skills gave both fighters a considerable advantage in hand-to-hand. The fight was more or less even, so neither of them could afford to chase after me. Barth was too busy beating the Prince off with his fiery mace while Julien replied with powerful swings of his two-handed sword.

Fire! Sparks! Blood!

Should I interfere and take one of their sides? Yeah right. A squad of the Spawn of Darkness was already hurrying from the avenue toward the library. I had no time to lose.

The library's central entrance looked blocked, so I decided not to waste my time looking for a back door. I heard the sound of an explosion, followed by cheers and catcalls as Black Trackers started pouring over the park's fence to pick a fight with the Spawn's looters.

I shrank my head into my shoulders and hurried on along the gloomy library building. Just as I turned a corner, I heard Neo's voice,

"Uncle John, wait! I'm coming with you!"

The boy scampered over the fence and darted after me. I hadn't even slowed down. As I ran, I swung the back door open, then promptly

✝ An NPC's Path: Book Two ✝

rolled over the floor to avoid a blow from a black longsword.

Half a dozen bone golems in mithril armor were guarding a round hall with a spiral staircase. They all came for me like a pack of wolves. There was no way I could make it to the staircase.

I parried a blow aimed at my head, stepped into a corner and began blocking the guards' attacks in short well-calculated blows. They could only attack me in twos, with all the others just milling around, but fending off even two mechanical swordsmen was a struggle. They simply didn't notice their wounds nor did they retreat.

With a lucky blow, I lopped one's arm off and kicked another one in the chest, brushing him off, but another one immediately took his place. I didn't panic; I knew it was quite possible to give them a good hammering but time was literally slipping through my fingers. There was precious little of it left.

From the doorway, a silvery flash suddenly blinded me, its Light magic sending the golems flying. Their bones crumbled to dust; their metallic sinews snapped; the guards froze on the

☦ Kingdom of the Dead ☦

floor littered with loose cogs and springs.

I too had been thrown against the wall. My ears rang but at least this time I'd received no burns. Either Neo had mastered his power or it was the effect of the resistance to divine magic I'd received.

"Uncle John!" the boy shouted. "I'll clear a way for you!"

"Get back!" I snapped as I leapt toward him and yanked him off the staircase.

"I can help you!" he protested.

"After me!" I growled and led the way.

Crossbows snapped. I dodged two of the bolts quite easily and parried the third one with my sword, then ran up to the landing and cleft the head of the nearest crossbowman in two with my frosted sword. I swung round, releasing the blade, slashed the one next to him, then knocked the last one down with my pauldron and finished him off, pinning him to the floor.

Once again Neo tried to get in front of me, and again I shouted at him, "Get back!"

Swordsmen were already rushing toward us from the top floor. I met them with a well-practiced combo. My flamberge sliced through the air, performing a Scythe of Death and

✝ An NPC's Path: Book Two ✝

knocking down the undead guards. With a powerful swing I hacked through the remaining survivor's helmeted head. I only lost concentration for one moment as I pulled the sword out — but Neo had already lost his patience and darted up the stairs without waiting for me.

He didn't even stop at the next two floors which were lined with rows of bookcases. I wasn't so lucky: two Disciples of Death had emerged from behind the bookcases. I threw one of them down, hauling him over the banister, and hacked the other one with my Soul Killer. The bone hook left a long scorch wound in his flesh, putting the dead sorcerer to rest for good.

Their spells couldn't harm me due to my immunity to death magic. You can say what you want but immunity is much more reliable than neutrality!

Taking several steps at a time, I bounded after Neo who'd already reached the end of the stairs and popped into the scroll repository.

A pedestal towered at its center, holding a precious box of blackened silver. A figure wrapped in darkness blocked the way to it.

Unhesitantly Neo hurled a wave of silver

🗡 Kingdom of the Dead 🗡

light at the enemy. The flash ripped through the darkness, tearing it apart and dissipating it.

The darkness was gone — but the demonic golem wasn't. Spooky and impossibly tall, he was clad in black steel from head to toe so you couldn't even tell his armor from his flesh.

His shoulders and back were studded with long metallic spikes; his steel tendons creaked as he moved; his alchemic heart was beating steadily within its wrought-iron casing. There wasn't a single opening in his closed helmet which traced the outlines of the infernal creature's gruesome head.

Still, he wasn't blind, either: his two-handed saber moved quickly and meticulously. Only at the very last moment did I manage to raise my flamberge to block his attempt at beheading the flabbergasted boy.

"Step aside!" I shoved Neo out of the way and lashed out at the mechanical demon's hip. He shrank back with unexpected agility, then went on the attack, furiously whirling his saber.

My lightning reflexes allowed me to parry the blows aimed at my head; then I slid aside, took cover behind a column and stealthed up. I had no intention of leaving the boy for the golem

✝ An NPC's Path: Book Two ✝

to rip apart, so I promptly stepped into the fray and showered the enemy with a series of powerful blows.

Take that! And again!

A couple of seconds of invisibility allowed me to rain blows down on him completely unchallenged, but even though I'd managed to pierce his armor, it had also absorbed the lion's share of the incoming damage. On top of it, the demon began swinging his terrible saber, shielding himself from me with its steel whirlwind.

I was forced to try different approaches, thus losing myself precious time.

I kept hacking at the knight's armor, striking sparks off it, but I still couldn't strip him of more than 25% Health. He wasn't even staggering.

Finally, the shadows concealing me from the enemy had dispersed. I invested all my strength in a last decisive blow. I took a furious swing, intending to strike at his steel poleyn but lowered the sword at the last moment and whacked him on his foot instead.

Accurate Blow!

✟ Kingdom of the Dead ✟

My Executioner's skills allowed me to drive the blade into a joint in his armor, right between his greaves and his steel boot — in fact, so hard that I couldn't even pull the flamberge out straight away.

Which could have been my undoing. I'd given the demonic golem enough time to turn round and bring down his terrible saber on me. Throwing my elbow up to parry the blade with my steel sleeve proved to be in vain as the blow was way too strong. I couldn't keep my balance and the blow threw me against the wall.

The depositary's guardian flew at me and would have undoubtedly made mincemeat out of me had his foot not given way under him. My lucky strike had almost cut his steel foot off, so now the monster was limping, his severed stump screeching along the floor.

Greatly encouraged, I darted toward him, then promptly changed direction and slid behind him, swinging a backhander at his knee. The undulating blade sliced through his armor with ease, severing the steel cables of his sinews.

In combination with Gaze of Frost, such a wound was bound to decide the outcome of our exchange. The problem was, he proved to be

✝ An NPC's Path: Book Two ✝

immune to the cold. I'd completely forgotten all about it, so when the demon began to fall backwards, I stupidly approached him, planning to decapitate him.

His saber whirled in his hands with unexpected agility, striking me in the chest and piercing my cuirass. It stuck in my ribs so firmly there was no way even the devil himself could pull it out. Devil being the operative word.

As he fell, the demon grabbed at the spike of my pauldron, pulling me toward him. We collapsed to the floor. Immediately he buried his armored fist in my mask. My head jerked; I heard the crunching of my broken nose. The monster took a second swing and, despite all my efforts to force his arm aside, struck me again.

He was so incredibly strong I didn't even try to wrestle him. Instead, I whipped out the bone hook and buried it in the chainmail insert under his armpit.

He might have been immune to both frost and soul magic, but how about hellfire?

I heard a click followed by a cascade of sparks. With a metallic twang, something had snapped inside him. Smoke billowed out of him. His outstretched right arm stopped moving, so he

✟ Kingdom of the Dead ✟

tried to strangle me with his left. My larynx crunched as he crumpled it in his hand but failed to do much damage.

Feeling for the gap between his bracer and his elbow piece, I stuck the tip of the bone hook in it. In another cascade of sparks, his grip on my neck slackened with a metallic click.

I wriggled myself from his grasp and fell on his back, pinning him down, then unhurriedly drove the bone hook into the gap between his steel collar and the lower edge of his helmet.

With an ear-shattering pinging sound, some strings inside him must have snapped, releasing still-spinning springs into the air. An invisible cloud of magic spread around us. The demon had run his course.

I struggled to pull out the sword still stuck in his chest, then clambered to my feet and shook my head. The blow from his armored fist had deformed the mask which now seemed to sneer at you. At least the eyeslit hadn't moved and I could still see out with my remaining eye.

One of the stained-glass windows smashed, letting in Scarecrow. He emitted a loud croak, leapt onto the defeated monster and pecked his helmet. The sound of ringing steel echoed

☦ An NPC's Path: Book Two ☦

through the room. The dead phoenix gave him another peck, this time at the gap between his helmet and cuirass, striking up even more sparks.

"We don't need your kind around here!" I grumbled and stepped toward the precious box. Still, Neo had already beaten me to it and had thrown the massive lid open.

The unbearable glow of white-hot silver filled the room — but it wasn't emitted by the Scroll of Rebirth. The ghost of the Grand Master of the Order of the Silver Phoenix materialized behind Neo's back in a flash of blinding light.

"My young brother in arms!" he announced gravely. "You have discovered the Scroll of Rebirth! Fulfill your destiny and bring me back to life!"

My jaw dropped. "Don't!" I shouted.

I was about fifteen feet away from them and I didn't even have enough magic energy left to lasso the precious artifact out of Neo's hands.

"Hurry!" the ghost told the boy. "Do it now!"

"But how about Uncle John..." the boy mumbled uncertainly.

"The greatness of our Order is the only thing that matters," the ghost announced

🗡 Kingdom of the Dead 🗡

mercilessly. "You alone can't bring it back to its former glory. But together... together we can make this world take notice of us!"

Neo gave me a desperate look.

Carefully choosing my words, I began,

"Listen, this scroll is my only hope of ever resurrecting. This is a question of life and death, do you understand?"

Yeah right. As if he'd understand me! He had nothing but program scripts in his head. He simply couldn't deviate from the story line.

Would I manage to get to him before he broke the seal? As if! There was no chance of that!

"Knight of the Order!" the ghost raised his voice. "Your doubt is outrageous! Fulfil your duty at once!"

Neo's hands shook. As if against his own will, he reached out to take the scroll when Scarecrow chipped in. He gave the dead golem an almighty peck, spread his wings wide and gave an ear-piercing squawk.

The ghost was thrown into the air. "Begone, you nasty bag of bones!" he screamed, choking on his own hatred.

On hearing these words, Neo seemed to

✟ An NPC's Path: Book Two ✟

have been transformed. He stopped stooping, spread his shoulders and suddenly shut the lid of the box.

"My apologies, Grand Master," the boy said, lowering his head. Still, I heard no remorse in his voice.

"Be damned, renegade!" the ghost wailed, then disappeared as if he'd never been there.

The power of the Silver Phoenix which used to fill the boy disappeared with him. The lad seemed to have faded; his status changed from Knight to Renegade.

"Did I do the right thing, Uncle John?" the kid asked, misty-eyed.

I didn't know what to say to him. Silently I opened the box and produced the precious scroll.

Scarecrow jumped on my shoulder, then pecked Neo's temple. Blood began trickling down the scared boy's face, mixing with the darkness exuded by the dead phoenix.

The darkness entered the boy and lifted him off the floor up to the ceiling.

I heard the sound of crunching bones and stretching tendons. Neo's shoulders grew wide as if he'd grown several years in one moment. He was strong again, only this time instead of the old

Kingdom of the Dead

silvery glow he was enveloped by pitch blackness which surrounded him and seemed to be entering him.

When he finally came back down, he seemed to be slightly different. He'd become older, tougher and more sure of himself.

His description had changed, too:

The Commander of the Order of the Black Phoenix

I saluted the boy. "Farewell, Neo!" I shouted as I broke the magic seal on the Scroll of Rebirth.
Time to wake up, John Doe!
Time to go home!

Epilogue

I LAY IN MY VR capsule, emaciated and deathly pale. My skin was entwined with transparent IV tubes. My chest barely rose and fell, assisted by an artificial respirator. Lines of statistics ran along the screens of the many medical machines surrounding me, showing graphs of both my heartbeat and cerebral activity.

I lay in the capsule looking at myself from above as if through a video surveillance camera under the ceiling. Was it yet another glitch of my exhausted mind worn out by the long period of unconsciousness?

I could think of nothing better than to raise my hand. It obeyed with unexpected ease. For a

✟ Kingdom of the Dead ✟

while, I kept studying the tanned leather of my steel sleeve. Then I lowered my stare and suddenly realized I was still in my character's body.

What the hell?

I stepped toward the mirror on the wall of the hospital room and stared at my own reflection in disbelief.

I was looking at the undead Sorcerer Executioner.

The massive boots, the leather greaves, the threadbare cape disintegrating into shadows; the chainmail; the cuirass and the flamberge's hilt behind my back, topped with my frozen eye.

My one-eyed mask curved in a cruel smirk. One of its halves dripped dark flames which fell to the floor, burning holes in the lino.

I removed the mask with unbending fingers, discovering the dead face of John Doe behind it, bloodless and covered with magic writings which had long merged with the skin. My left eye was gone, replaced by an uneven scar.

No. It can't be.

Impossible!

I flung the mask aside and dashed out of the room. A spike on my pauldron had caught on

✝ An NPC's Path: Book Two ✝

the door frame and ripped it straight out of the concrete.

The hospital corridor was dark and deserted. There were no patients or staff; all I could see was the light through the rectangular outline of the open door of the duty doctor's office. That's where I headed, drawing the flamberge from behind my back as I walked. The tip of the sword drew a long scratch on the floor, its screeching sound calming me down somewhat.

This was surreal. It couldn't be! Was it a dream? A hallucination? Or was I still in the game? But what about the hospital?

I shook my head and stepped into the well-lit office.

The Angel of Darkness was sitting at an ordinary office desk. He greeted me with two slow theatrical handclaps. All my cool which I'd so laboriously regained disappeared in an instant.

"What the hell?" I shouted from the doorway. "Who are you? And where are we?"

The Angel of Darkness leaned back in his chair which creaked its protest. "Where do you think we are? There aren't many options. You're still in the game, John. It's just that in this tiny

Kingdom of the Dead

cranny of virtual reality we can speak at ease without having to worry about the walls having ears."

"That's not right!" I barked. "I should have resurrected! I should have become myself again and logged out!"

He arched a sarcastic eyebrow. "Should you have? Why, because of the scroll? I can see you didn't even bother to read its description."

I threw the sword aside, pulled out the scroll and unraveled it. As I read, I gnashed my teeth in despair.

Scroll of Rebirth
Property: non-transferrable
Restriction: only for players level 99+

"What the hell?" I croaked. "Who in God's name are you, the admin? You owe me! You should write me out of the game!"

The Angel shook his head. "I don't owe anything to anyone. All I can do is erase your identity but that's not part of my plans at the moment."

I glanced at the flamberge lying on the floor. "Erase my identity?"

✝ An NPC's Path: Book Two ✝

He nodded. "I'm obliged to do so. Officially, your identity was erased as the result of an equipment malfunction and the company accepts no responsibility for this sort of thing."

"Bullshit!"

"Not at all. Just a precaution."

I slumped onto a visitor's chair. "So what's the problem then?"

"A conflict of interests," the Angel smiled. "There are two opposing game development strategies. The first one envisages lowering the age limit to fourteen years of age; the other suggests a gradual increase in the officially permitted online time. I represent the group of shareholders who are interested in the second scenario."

"Are you serious?"

The Angel pretended he didn't hear me. "Teenagers are easy to control," he continued. " The monetization mechanisms are up and running. The creation of entertainment content has been automated. The game developers aren't prepared to make allowances for those who'd rather live in VR than just play there. We consider this to be wrong."

"Are you intending to profit from offering

✝ Kingdom of the Dead ✝

your equipment on a long-term lease?" I realized. "Bringing a capsule to every household?"

"We'll offer an alternative to euthanasia! We'll relieve the terminally ill from their sufferings, allowing them to spend their last days fully interacting with their families and loved ones. And what about old-age pensioners? The elderly usually find it hard to get used to the virtual world — but given enough time, they might be able to start new lives here! We'll give them a second chance!"

Give them a second chance? Yeah right. But only to those who could afford the long-term VR capsule rent. Or would they be able to do it through their medical insurance? In which case he was right: there was one hell of a lot of money at stake. Still, how did I fit into all this?

I shook my head and demanded more details. "Why are you telling me all this? What's the point of our meeting?"

He smiled. "Consider it an interim examination. This is a check of your mental state: its adaptivity, flexibility and stability. Also, you could use some extra motivation, couldn't you?"

I cussed. "What do you want from me?" I

✝ An NPC's Path: Book Two ✝

asked point blank. "Why me?"

The Angel crossed his muscular arms on his chest. His chiseled face grew pensive. "A group of shareholders has obtained a judgment prohibiting all long-term immersion experiments. They fear being sued in case of the test subjects' suffering brain damage. And you have nothing to do with our labs. You're a victim of circumstance and the company bears no responsibility for you. We might use your case to tip the scales in our favor."

"Let me resurrect, then! At least let me log out!"

He shook his head. "The time isn't right yet. Three months of full immersion isn't enough. With some reservations, you still show a considerably higher character development rate. You're quite capable of reaching level 99 within, say, the next six months to a year. Twice fifty levels, there's nothing impossible about it. And this could have become a considerable plus point for our upcoming publicity campaign."

"I'm not a guinea pig! Let me out, now!"

He shook his head. "Sorry. I can't."

I bent down and grabbed the hilt of the flamberge. "I'm afraid you might have to."

Kingdom of the Dead

"Would you like to see the Lady of White Silence again?" the Angel asked. "She did try to set you free. She wanted to separate you from your dead character and to right the wrong that the hacker had done to you. Seeking out rule breakers and stripping them of their wrongfully acquired advantages is her job. But here's the thing," he paused and gave me a long look. "There's a 99%-plus probability of your identity being destroyed in the process with no hope of it ever being recovered."

I picked up the flamberge, lay it across my knees and drummed my fingers on its frosted blade. «At least lower the requirements for the scroll's use. If you want to keep me here for a while, go ahead! But can't you set the level restriction at 70? Okay, 80! But 99?"

"I'm not authorized to interfere with the game mechanics," he snapped, then added with an encouraging smile, "Once it's all over, we're gonna pay you compensation for every day spent in the game. The amount will be mind-blowing, trust me. You're gonna regret it was over so quickly."

Having magnanimously offered me this proverbial carrot, the Angel snapped his fingers.

✝ An NPC's Path: Book Two ✝

Darkness fell.

I WAS STANDING at the center of the scroll repository clenching the crumpled Scroll of Rebirth. Which I could neither access nor transfer to another player. Dammit!

I suppressed a miserable moan, relaxed my hand and started back down the spiral staircase. Neo stood silently by the broken window. He appeared to be still in shock over his new status.

Never mind. He'd get used to it. What doesn't kill us makes us stronger. I knew the old adage was bullshit but it did seem to work.

Insolent bastards!

I FOUND ISABELLA on the first floor. She finished off the Death Disciple I'd thrown from the staircase and called out anxiously, "And?"

Without saying a word, I raised the scroll.

At first, she couldn't understand the reason for my despondence. But once she checked out the scroll's description, she cussed. "Does that mean you'll have to level up all the way to 99? That's real bad timing, Kitten!"

"As if I don't understand!" I snapped as I removed the mask. My broken nose crunched as I

Kingdom of the Dead

reset it with a sharp jerk.

"No, you don't!" Isabella said, suddenly appearing next to me and giving me a slap in the face. "Kogan's court hearing is in a month's time. Without your testimony, the case will fall apart!"

For a moment, I froze in amazement. "*Comrade Major?*"

"I'm a lieutenant!" she snapped, grabbing me by my lapels. "You've got to resurrect, Kitten! You've got to log out!"

"So all this was a setup, then?" I asked. "Both our meeting and your fake quest?"

"Don't be stupid, Kitten!" Isabella growled. "Without my help you'd have never gotten this far! Of course it was a setup!"

A wave of blind fury swept over me. I wanted to grab her by the hair and smash her against the wall. The desire was so strong my hands shook. I was strong enough now to have done it — but I refrained. I needed answers more than revenge.

"Do the others all know?" I asked, clenching and unclenching my fists.

"Nobody knows," Isabella replied. "And I advise you not to start blabbing about it!"

"You can shove your advice where the sun

✝ An NPC's Path: Book Two ✝

don't shine!"

"If you don't log out within a month, you're toast."

"Are you worried about not getting another star on your epaulettes?" I growled, unable to completely suppress my rage. My head was spinning with it all.

"They're gonna unhook you from life support the moment they don't need you! Can't you understand that? You've got s month to log out! Only a month!"

My blood ran cold. You'd think I was dead already but now an otherworldly chill spread through my chest as if someone had poured liquid nitrogen over my soul.

I paused, struggling to collect my thoughts, then poked her in the chest with my finger. "Have the admins fix my player's profile."

She shook her head. "Officially you're not even here. Also, the game's servers are located out of our jurisdiction. My support is the only thing you can count on."

I cussed. By then, my head wasn't just booming — it was exploding with all the doubt and speculation. I'd been loaded with too much information for one day, all of it less than

✠ Kingdom of the Dead ✠

pleasant.

And all of this had been done unofficially, bypassing all existing laws and regulations. It was the clandestine behind-the-scenes games played by cannibals each of whom had their own interest in this. And as soon as you tried to delve into it, you realized that they only differed in the cooking method.

Shit!

"Get a grip, Kitten," Isabella snapped at me again. "XP doesn't earn itself! There's a battle raging in the city and we need to take what's ours while the possibility still exists!"

Indeed, a constant clamor seemed to be coming from outside. The window panes reflected the flashes of explosions which made the walls quiver and the floor shake underfoot.

She's been right. I had to think about the future. I had to move my ass.

I pulled myself together. "Haven't the Lighties forced the Spawn out of the city already?"

She sniffed. "The Light coalition has broken up! The Orcs have renounced Darkness and made the teaching of Chaos their official religion. They've already taken about a dozen Towers of

✝ An NPC's Path: Book Two ✝

Power on the border, primarily on the Light side. Everybody else rushed to defend their properties. Only some squads of the Sons of Light are still left in the Kingdom of the Dead."

"Was it the Swords of Chaos who'd instigated the orcish mutiny?"

"Exactly. They were fed up with constantly being second-class citizens."

Very well. "Where's Goar?"

"He's still helping himself in the scroll repository," Isabella replied, listening intently, then barked, "Come here, goofy!"

Just as she spoke, the front door shattered. The knight in reddish orange armor stepped inside.

He looked awful. His dented armor was covered in blood, his pauldrons deformed, his helmet buckled.

"There you are!" Barth Firefist laughed hoarsely as he raised his hands over his head.

A soft glow enveloped his body. His bleeding wounds healed; his armor restored. All of a sudden he stood there healthy and vigorous.

"You're done for, Johnny boy!" he growled, swinging his infernal mace.

Isabella held her staff out in front of her.

† Kingdom of the Dead †

Goar dropped his scrolls and drew his black sword from behind his back. Neo who was just coming down the stairs froze, then pursed his lips and kept going. I had a feeling that darkness itself feared the newly-minted Commander of the Order of the Black Phoenix.

Unhurriedly my hand closed around the hilt of my frosty flamberge. I smirked,

"I'm done for? Well, that remains to be seen."

End of Book Two

Want to be the first to know about our latest LitRPG, sci fi and fantasy titles from your favorite authors?

Subscribe to our **New Releases** newsletter:
http://eepurl.com/b7niIL

Thank you for reading *Kingdom of the Dead!*
If you like what you've read, check out other LitRPG
novels published by Magic Dome Books.

Reality Benders LitRPG series by Michael Atamanov:

Countdown
External Threat
Game Changer
Web of Worlds
A Jump into the Unknown
Aces High
Cause for War

The Dark Herbalist LitRPG series by Michael Atamanov:

Video Game Plotline Tester
Stay on the Wing
A Trap for the Potentate
Finding a Body

Perimeter Defense LitRPG series by Michael Atamanov:

Sector Eight
Beyond Death
New Contract
A Game with No Rules

League of Losers LitRPG Series by Michael Atamanov:

A Cat and his Human
In Service of the Pharaoh

The Way of the Shaman LitRPG series by Vasily Mahanenko:

Survival Quest
The Kartoss Gambit
The Secret of the Dark Forest
The Phantom Castle
The Karmadont Chess Set
The Hour of Pain (a bonus short story)
Shaman's Revenge
Clans War

***The Alchemist* LitRPG series by Vasily Mahanenko:**
City of the Dead
Forest of Desire
Tears of Alron
Isr Kale's Journal

***Dark Paladin* LitRPG series by Vasily Mahanenko:**
The Beginning
The Quest
Restart

***Galactogon* LitRPG series by Vasily Mahanenko:**
Start the Game!
In Search of the Uldans
A Check for a Billion

***Invasion* LitRPG Series by Vasily Mahanenko:**
A Second Chance
An Equation with one Unknown

***World of the Changed* LitRPG Series by Vasily Mahanenko:**
No Mistakes
Pearl of the South
Noa in the Flesh

***The Bard from Barliona* LitRPG series
by Eugenia Dmitrieva and Vasily Mahanenko:**
The Renegades
A Song of Shadow

***Level Up* LitRPG series by Dan Sugralinov:**
Re-Start
Hero
The Final Trial
Level Up: The Knockout (with Max Lagno)
Level Up. The Knockout: Update (with Max Lagno)

***Disgardium* LitRPG series by Dan Sugralinov:**
Class-A Threat
Apostle of the Sleeping Gods
The Destroying Plague
Resistance
Holy War
Path of Spirit
The Demonic Games

***World 99* LitRPG Series by Dan Sugralinov:**
Blood of Fate

***Adam Online* LitRPG Leries by Max Lagno:**
Absolute Zero
City of Freedom

***Interworld Network* LitRPG Series by Dmitry Bilik:**
The Time Master
Avatar of Light
The Dark Champion

***Rogue Merchant* LitRPG Series by Roman Prokofiev:**
The Starlight Sword
The Gene of the Ancients
Shadow Seer
Battle for the North
The Devil Archetype

***Project Stellar* LitRPG Series by Roman Prokofiev:**
The Incarnator
The Enchanter
The Tribute
The Rebel
The Archon

***Clan Dominance* LitRPG Series by Dem Mikhailov:**
The Sleepless Ones Book One
The Sleepless Ones Book Two
The Sleepless Ones Book Three
The Sleepless Ones Book Four
The Sleepless Ones Book Five
The Sleepless Ones Book Six

***Nullform* RealRPG Series by Dem Mikhailov:**
Nullform Book One
Nullform Book Two

***The Neuro* LitRPG series by Andrei Livadny:**
The Crystal Sphere
The Curse of Rion Castle
The Reapers

***Phantom Server* LitRPG series by Andrei Livadny:**
Edge of Reality
The Outlaw
Black Sun

***Respawn Trials* LitRPG Series by Andrei Livadny:**
Edge of the Abyss

***The Expansion (The History of the Galaxy)* series by A. Livadny:**
Blind Punch
The Shadow of Earth
Servobattalion

***The Range* LitRPG Series by Yuri Ulengov:**
The Keepers of Limbo
Lords of the Ruins

Point Apocalypse *(a near-future action thriller)* **by Alex Bobl**

***Moskau* by G. Zotov**
(a dystopian thriller)

***El Diablo* by G. Zotov**
(a supernatural thriller)

***Mirror World* LitRPG series by Alexey Osadchuk:**
Project Daily Grind
The Citadel
The Way of the Outcast
The Twilight Obelisk

***Underdog* LitRPG series by Alexey Osadchuk:**
Dungeons of the Crooked Mountains
The Wastes
The Dark Continent
The Otherworld
Labyrinth of Fright
Showdown

***The Crow Cycle LitRPG Series* by Dem Mikhailov:**
The Crow Cycle Book One

Alpha Rome LitRPG Series by Ros Per:
Volper
Skurfaifer

***An NPC's Path* LitRPG series by Pavel Kornev:**
The Dead Rogue
Kingdom of the Dead
Deadman's Retinue
The Guardian of the Dead
The Nemesis of the Living

***The Sublime Electricity* series by Pavel Kornev:**
The Illustrious
The Heartless
The Fallen
The Dormant

***Small Unit Tactics* LitRPG series by Alexander Romanov:**
Volume 1
Volume 2

***In the System* LitRPG series by Petr Zhgulyov:**
City of Goblins
City of the Undead

***Citadel World* series by Kir Lukovkin:**
The URANUS Code
The Secret of Atlantis

You're in Game!
(LitRPG Stories from Bestselling Authors)

You're in Game-2!
(More LitRPG stories set in your favorite worlds)

***The Fairy Code* by Kaitlyn Weiss:**
Captive of the Shadows
Chosen of the Shadows

More books and series are coming out soon!

In order to have new books of the series translated faster, we need your help and support! Please consider leaving a review or spread the word by recommending *Kingdom of the Dead* to your friends and posting the link on social media. The more people buy the book, the sooner we'll be able to make new translations available.

Thank you!

Till next time!

Printed in the USA
CPSIA information can be obtained
at www.ICGtesting.com
LVHW010217121223
766264LV00048B/1537